# DEFUNCT

# DEFUNCT

## THE LAST PSION BOOK 1

Maxwell Farmer

Podium

# DEFUNCT

# CHAPTER ONE

# Last Defiance

King Ruken tossed and turned, plagued by a terrible nightmare. With a gasp, he shot up out of bed, cold sweat on his face.

His sudden movement awakened the red-haired elf lying beside him. "What's wrong, my love?" she asked, sleepily.

"I'm not sure. Something . . . doesn't feel right." He glanced out the window. It was unusually cold in the Kingdom of Blades, despite it being early spring. A terrible, unexpected storm had hit the capital that night with violent gusts of wind and a mix of rain and ice. Lightning struck repeatedly in an endless cacophony, making near-constant noise all night. The precipitation peppered the window relentlessly.

Something else was wrong. When the sun had set, there hadn't been any storm clouds on the horizon. The ferocity of the weather wasn't normal. It seemed to have a will of its own. As he focused his gaze beyond the hissing rain, he blinked in sudden surprise. Despite the midnight hour, his sprawling castle was well-illuminated by . . .

The king's heart began to race. He couldn't tear his gaze from the catastrophe and horror visible through the window. His castle, his home, was ablaze! Vast, roaring fires spread across the towering stone building and its surrounding structures. Ruken instinctively reached out with his mind, using his abundant mana pool as fuel, scanning for the presence of other minds over the gargantuan structure in a matter of seconds. The fire clearly wasn't the result of some mere chance lightning strike. There was a coup afoot!

"Put on your robes," he said to his beloved, his grim tone brooking no argument.

Surturia swiftly complied, equipping her enchanted gear, blood-red robes, and magic staff of spiraling wood that emanated a subtle heat. "Pretty audacious, an attack in the heart of your kingdom, don't you think?"

"Only one person I know of would dare attempt something like this," he replied through gritted teeth.

"Van Blaine," the elf spat. "That dog! I will melt his wretched bones for this treason!" She slammed the butt of her staff against the floor, momentarily causing a ring of fire to ripple around her.

"No, my love, you mustn't," Ruken said, oddly calm. As he stepped toward the fiery woman, he extended the mana from his core and drew his equipment onto his body. In a matter of seconds, the king was fully adorned in a legendary suit of armor adorned with jewels and made from a lightweight, flexible metal. He reached out his right hand, drawing the last piece of equipment to him: a small, strange ceramic jug that looked like it would hold wine.

Ruken placed his other gauntleted hand on Surturia's belly. "You must leave. Only you can ensure that our son will survive."

The elf's eyes widened in surprise, and tears began to form, her anger quickly turning into despair. "It's a boy? You know?"

The king gave her a gentle smile. "I'm a psion. It's easy."

"Come with me," she pleaded, the tears beginning to flow now. Her lower lip quivered. "Let's leave this place. We can rebuild, reorganize those loyal to you, then we can reclaim your kingdom." As she spoke, she gently brought her hand to his head and ran her fingers through his hair, still mostly black though now mixed with some grays.

Ruken shook his head. "If Van Blaine has amassed an army large enough to take the castle, then most of my allies are either subdued or dead. There is no way my subordinates would abide such destruction to my home. Besides, it's my kingdom. If I don't fight for its survival, who will?"

"We can, together, later. Help me raise our child. Together–"

"No." He cut her off. "I am a target. They will never stop hunting me. However, they do not know of our child. We must ensure his survival. Please, Surturia, do this not only for me, but for our boy. If he's anything like either of us, he's going to need your strong will to keep him in line!"

Ruken drew in a deep breath to calm his mind, then quickly took the magic circlet he'd summoned off his head. He closed his eyes and wrapped his hand around its single jewel, transferring a part of himself into it. His entire body momentarily glowed and he groaned. The process was more taxing than it looked. A trickle of blood dripped from his right nostril. Despite that, however, the king was an expert cultivator and managed to complete the process in a matter of seconds.

The king looked slightly exhausted, but aside from that, he was still prepared. He placed the circlet in her free hand, "When he's ready, give him this. Let him know it's from me," he said, glancing at the wide fireplace. Flexing his will, he twisted one of the stone lion statues beside it and triggered the secret exit to open.

The man pulled in his beloved for one final kiss, only to be interrupted by a loud banging on the doors to their room. "Go now, and hurry," he whispered, turning his back to her to face the door.

Surturia pursed her lips but did as requested. She pulled the hood of her thick robe over her head and disappeared into the dark exit.

Ruken didn't look back. He didn't need to. As a psion and an Onyx-rank cultivator of mental mana, he could sense the presence of her mind with his own. Once she began descending the stairs to the hidden exit, he flexed his will once more to close the secret passage.

The king uncorked the jug in his hand and telekinetically drew out a stream of liquid metal from within it. With a flex of his will, the metal hardened and took shape, forming King Ruken's fabled blade. It curved slightly into a katana, an ancient sword used by the humans of Midgard before the realms merged. With a powerful swing of his arm, the blade bisected the statue to the secret passage, ensuring no one could follow them. No one would hurt his woman or his boy, not while he lived. *Not sure how much longer I have, but I'll make it count,* he thought.

As soon as he flicked the dust of the statue off his blade, the doors burst open. In rushed a group of twenty cultivators, all of them young, Sapphire-rank at most. They were much too weak to pose a real threat. With no allies nearby to consider, the king unleashed his full aura. A surge of mental mana rushed out of him, engulfing the sizable chamber with his intent and will. The twenty grunts all stopped in their tracks, their bodies collapsing to the ground as the king's mana effectively broke each of their minds at once.

Another wave charged in behind the now-dead cultivators. This time, it was a contingent of Emeralds. A row of ten dwarves adorned from head to toe in heavy plate mail formed up in front of the king. Many dwarven were some sort of metal mana cultivators, and these seemed to be no exception. They interlocked their shields and activated the same technique. The ten tower shields fused and expanded together to form a wall. Each end dwarf's shield embedded into the stone of the room's walls, preventing the king from flanking the soldiers.

Right after the wall formed, a dozen human and elf archers appeared behind the dwarves, trying to catch the king by surprise. They failed. The archers fired a volley of arrows, empowering their velocity with a mix of air and nature mana. Using his Telekinesis, however, the king redirected all the shots to make a ninety-degree turn out the window, shattering the ornate painted glass. The archers nocked their bows for another volley, and the dwarves raised their maces in preparation for a unified technique attack. Ruken gave a slight smile as the arrows he'd directed out the window . . . returned!

From one of the windows behind the dwarves and archers, the dozen projectiles broke through the glass. They flew in and killed most of the flabbergasted archers plus a few of the dwarven foot soldiers. Just as Ruken had hoped, the sudden attack delayed the soldiers' next move. With some of the dwarves now dead, too, their unified shield wall technique broke down, making them vulnerable.

In a flash, Ruken had closed the distance. His sword carved a bloody path through the fighters. They fought back, but it was an act of futility. His weapon sliced straight through the enhanced bodies of the cultivators like butter. Despite the archers' lean bodies and formidable speed, they weren't enough to evade the psion's retribution. He easily dodged their attempts to fight back, even with arrows empowered by air mana. The king also ignored their pleas for mercy, as some dropped their weapons upon realizing how outmatched they were. The cowards dared attack him and his beloved. He would eliminate them, draw out their leader, and kill them too.

By the time Ruken was done, there was just one archer left, the rest of invaders now carved up into fleshy chunks and spread across the room. The archer stood there with his arrow nocked. His face was pale, and his arms trembled in fear. "This . . . this wasn't supposed to happen," he managed shakily.

"What did you think would happen?" Ruken asked, casually moving his head to dodge the archer's arrow. "That you would kill me?" He slid to the left to avoid another shot. "That I would be murdered by some whelp?"

The archer backed up and shouted in fear as he dropped his bow. In sheer desperation, he stuck his palm out and let loose a nature mana technique. A beam of purple flame shot out toward Ruken.

Instead of dodging this time, the king stood still. His pupils constricted as he glared at the beam of fire. It shattered before it could touch him, as if it had struck a solid wall of stone.

The archer just stood there, dumbstruck.

"Let me teach you your final lesson." Ruken said, and the strength of the king's aura slammed the elven archer to his back. Slowly, the psion walked toward the encumbered archer. "If you have great goals in life, you will have great opponents. If you have great opponents, you will need even greater strength to defeat them. To acquire that strength, you must do what is necessary, and you haven't. Done. Enough." He punctuated his last words by pointing the tip of his blade at the archer's throat.

Prone on the floor, the cultivator sputtered idle threats to the king in desperation, going on about how he "came from a great house" and his "family would seek retribution."

Ruken ignored his words. He stood over his opponent, and in one quick motion, drew his blade across the bleeding archer's neck. Just as he finished, he sensed the sudden presence of two more people now in the entrance thirty feet in front of him. They were different, their forms shrouded by darkness, only now revealing their power. The king was an Onyx, a rank second only to the most powerful and the very ancient. Both of these two new people were now exuding a force comparable to his.

Without warning, one of them fired out a beam of ice and frost at the king. Ruken gasped in surprise. If he didn't dodge or intercept, the technique could seriously harm him. Despite being caught off-guard, the man was resolute and had been trained for moments like this.

Sensing the imminent attack, Ruken quickly activated the enchantment on his chest piece, empowering it with his mental mana. A semi-translucent shield emerged around him, rebuffing the attack completely. Instead of the ice striking him, it spread out in all directions, encasing most of the room in a thick layer. The soldier, whose neck Ruken had nearly bisected, was struck from the recoil and frozen in a solid shell of ice. He was still alive but wouldn't be for long once Ruken was done with him.

When the beam of ice stopped, a dry, hoarse laugh came from the entrance. The two figures came into the light, revealing Lord van Blaine and his bride. He was ugly, thin, and wiry but a savage ice cultivator from a noble family in the northern part of the kingdom. Ruken let out a low growl of anger. *Of course Van Blaine would be the leader,* he thought. Van Baine's most distinctive factors were the trademark wings that sprouted from his back and seemed to be made from feathers of pure ice. No other cultivator within the kingdom possessed such an enhancement.

Meanwhile, his wife was tall and beautiful, with rich olive-toned skin. The king did not know much about her, aside from her being a rumored death culti-vator from some supposedly rich merchant family. He had never actually learned where she was from or even her name, though the marriage clearly had to have been arranged. Both husband and wife were wearing strange, conical, pointed hel-mets made from a maroon-colored metal.

"Good lesson there, Chromebane. Too bad for you, *you* are the one who hasn't done enough, *tyrant.*" Van Blaine spat.

"You are a misguided fool, Van Blaine, and you have gone too far."

"No, I haven't gone far enough. Your reign of terror is at an end, tyrant!" Van Blaine retorted. "You and your entire accursed line have been using your foul mana to manipulate the minds of our entire country! You abominations have been no better than slave drivers with your mind control! Not that we have to worry about them anymore." He gave a malicious grin as his wife threw two heads onto the icy ground.

The king's jaw tensed as he looked at the heads. They once belonged to his Royal Guards—his friends and fellow psions. Tears welled up in his eyes as he shook his head. Van Blaine had coveted his throne ever since Ruken inherited it and had threatened civil war on more than one occasion. It seemed he finally mustered enough courage—or enough benefactors, more likely—to finally go through with it.

Ruken's nostrils flared in anger, but he forced himself to stay calm and aware of his surroundings. He did not want to get baited into some sort of trap. "Your greed has blinded you to the truth and led you to kill innocents," he said, pointing an accusatory finger at the man responsible for his comrades' deaths. "My family has not only been protecting the Kingdom of Blades but all of the Great Alliance from certain doom."

"Cease your lies, tyrant!" Van Blaine's wife spat. Her accent was unfamiliar to Ruken, which was impressive, since he was well-traveled throughout Alterra.

"She's right, Ruken," Van Blaine continued. "Your mad ramblings will not sway us." He pointed to the strange helmets on their heads. "These helmets are made from Drotrium."

Ruken reached out his senses to try and touch the couple's minds. Sure enough, his reach was stopped. Drotrium was rare, exceedingly so, and the amount to make both of the helmets was likely the entire supply of the material in all of the world. That's why he hadn't known the effect it would have against his mental powers.

*How did Van Blaine know it would be resistant to me? He must have some serious backers, indeed,* the king thought. He exhaled deeply through his nostrils and readied himself. Ruken knew he couldn't talk sense into these two and he didn't want to anymore. It was time to make them pay.

Throughout the night, the trio lost themselves amid heated combat. They unleashed the full force of high-level cultivators, all of them nearing the zenith of cultivation ranking. Over the course of the fight, large swaths of the castle were obliterated, many of those engaged around them dying due to the destructive power of their formidable techniques.

Unlike his opponents, however, Ruken did not fight recklessly. Being outnumbered wouldn't normally force him to be on the defensive, but these two were different. Their strength was comparable to his. He also had the secondary goal of directing their focus away from where his beloved was escaping. That forced him to take some blows that he could have dodged under normal circumstances. Despite his gear and high level of strength, each strike dealt significant damage to his body.

The rising sun of the new dawn shone its first rays on the only structure still standing inside the royal courtyard—a tall, thin tower of spiraling obsidian. Incredibly, it had survived the three cultivators' combined ferocity and wrath, when all else had succumbed. The magic spire was extremely durable, near indestructible, and it showed as it stood alone amidst the surrounding devastation.

The three Onyx-rank cultivators were the only ones still alive from the night's fighting. Corpses of soldiers loyal to both sides of the conflict were strewn around the rubble-filled courtyard, their bodies either frozen, rotten and desiccated, or sliced to ribbons. Ruken was sure he could've taken Van Blaine on his own, but his wife fought with a battle lust that seemed to rival that of a berserker. She alone had given him pause.

All three were exhausted, and Ruken was on his last leg. He was breathing heavily. His body was covered in various patches of rotten sores and frostbite. His legendary blade was held lower, the strength needed to keep his form up now lacking.

Ruken hadn't fought many Onyxes before. There weren't many in the world to begin with, but this pair were truly some of the fiercest he'd ever gone up against. Ruken couldn't afford for the battle to go much further, but he could still end this coup. The king was sure that he wouldn't live, but if Van Blaine died also, his beloved and his son should be safe. He focused most of his remaining mana into propelling his body forward for one final strike. If he could decapitate the ice cultivator, he would hopefully cut the head off the snake.

As the king surged forward, the usurper's eyes widened in horror. Van Blaine had thought King Ruken incapable of such speed anymore. Caught off-guard, he raised his hands in a useless defensive gesture and closed his eyes, bracing for death. It did not come, however. Before the king could finish his swing, he was himself struck in the jaw by a fist covered in crackling green necrotic energy. The blow knocked him off-course, and he crashed into the obsidian spire.

Despite the speed of the impact, the spire refused to move. Instead, the king's scapula fractured into shards, his left shoulder hanging uselessly by his side. The pain forced him to drop his blade. Ruken groaned and slowly turned back to face the couple, pressing his spine against the spire for support as he breathed heavily. Not only was his shoulder in ruins, so was his face. The necrotic energy from Van Blaine's wife's attack had sent death mana into his flesh and bones. His face and neck were slowly beset with stabbing pain followed by numbness, and his jaw began to rot.

Seeing the sudden reversal of his fortunes, Van Blaine smirked, "At last your reign is at an end, Ruken. Now, I will lead the Kingdom of Blades."

The king furrowed his brow. He hadn't been able to use his mental mana directly against them all night, and he desperately sought one last way to evade defeat. While the traitor was busy gloating in his all-but-assured victory, he tried one last attack. With a flex of his will, using the remainder of his mental mana, the king telekinetically flung his sword at the weasel of a man. The blade stabbed through Van Blaine's left eye. It wasn't deep enough to kill, but still adequately rearranged his ugly visage.

The wiry noble screamed in surprise and agony. He ripped out the blade, then clutched at his ruined face. He shouted as more pain lanced through him from removing the weapon. Blood gushed freely from between his fingers. After a few seconds of the king's cries of distress, his anger helped him compose himself, and he froze over the wound to stop the bleeding. Van Blaine turned to the king and scowled. "I sense no more mana coming from your body anymore, Ruken."

With malicious glee creeping over his face, he used an especially cruel technique against his defenseless foe. "Let me give you a parting gift." He reached out slowly toward Ruken, his hand encrusted with ice, and activated Icy Veins. It was a tortuous technique that Van Blaine could only use now that he could finally get a hold of his opponent for more than a second.

At the look on Van Blaine's face, the thin noble's hand extending inexorably toward him, King Ruken's shoulders sank. He had nothing left to give. Van Blaine grabbed his wrist, and the king groaned in pain as his blood slowly cooled, crystallizing inside his body. His enhanced body was the only thing that extended his life long enough to listen to this imposter's rant as the ice grew and solidified within his veins.

"You really believe your lies, don't you, Ruken? You truly are mad," he said. His wife confidently strode over to join him, the woman standing a good foot taller than the noble.

The king shook as the technique slowly took hold of his body, his blood vessels rupturing from the cold, and his organs ceasing all function. Frost formed on his skin. Still, his mind put together the pieces of the puzzle. In a flash, his eyes widened in realization as to true motives behind this coup. "Your plan . . . will fail," the king struggled to say. "The . . . dragons will fail be . . . cause . . ." He took one last desperate inhale but didn't speak. He kept the last part to himself. *I'm not the last . . . psion*, he thought and smiled as the encroaching ice and frost overtook his whole body, and the king was no more. As soon as he passed, his enchanted items took on a life of their own, leaving his body and battlefield to fly off far and wide.

Though his lips twisted in confusion, the one-eyed ice cultivator laughed evilly. He had overcome Ruken and won the throne. Van Blaine used some of his remaining mana to refreeze his bleeding eye socket as it started hemorrhaging again. He looked down at the pathetic frozen corpse in front of him and tightened his right hand into a fist, shattering the dead king into countless pieces. "Dragons? Preposterous," he laughed at the dead king's words. "You may not be the last, mad tyrant, but I will ensure that any of the wretches who followed you in life will meet the same terrible end."

# CHAPTER TWO

# Kiru

All right, class, settle down. It's time for our lesson to begin," Elder Wong said, trying to get the teens to pay attention.

Kiru, a half-elf who sat at the back of the room, was more interested in not being noticed than in the elder's lesson. Because of his heritage, it was hard to stay incognito in his village. Bristleton was a small mining town in the eastern outskirts of the Kingdom of Blades, not exactly a major hub of trade and activity. They were practically in the middle of nowhere.

The Kingdom of Blades, a smaller country in Alterra, was renowned for its great warrior cultivators. The country was also unique in that it hosted a wide variety of races, compared to others, and truly served as a beacon for peace on Alterra. That being said, out in Bristleton, there were mostly humans and dwarves. Kiru and his mother were the only ones with elven lineage for miles. That made him stand out in the crowd. It didn't help that his lineage had wound up giving him spiky black hair with bright red tips.

"Now, today we will begin our course in world history. Does anyone know what event incited Alterra's creation, hmm?" the elder man asked, stroking his long, white beard.

A hand raised.

"Ah, yes, Ms. Albright. Go on," he said.

The girl cleared her throat before speaking. "The formation of Alterra is due to Ragnarok. The great apocalypse brought an end to many realms, but in doing so, created our newer one," she recited.

"Correct, but do you know *how* exactly our realm was formed in the midst of such calamity?"

The girl appeared caught off-guard, and she shook her head sheepishly.

"Anyone else?" He looked around the room for a minute to see if anyone else would venture to answer. Kiru didn't sink into his seat like most of his classmates, but he avoided eye contact so as to not draw attention. Plus, he was more focused on what he would be doing after this lesson.

"The answer lies in what caused Ragnarok," Elder Wong answered. "Scientists and diviners discovered that the main inciting cause of Ragnarok was the World Tree's collapse. Somehow, it had been damaged, and it collapsed partially under its own massive weight. It stirred the great beasts and brought the destruction of Midgard, or Earth, as it was known." A number of students laughed at the silly notion of someone naming their realm "Earth."

The elder chuckled too before continuing, "Even though Midgard and many other realms ceased to be, it did not bring complete annihilation to many of their inhabitants." The elder's face took on an excited look. "Instead, many of the World Tree's realms collapsed on top of each other, fusing many of them into one new, massive world, like a patchwork quilt. That world is what we live in today: Alterra."

The eager student raised her hand.

"Yes, Ms. Albright?"

"If Yggdrasil collapsed on itself, how come one of our books said that there are still other realms aside from Alterra?"

"Excellent question! I see *someone* hasn't neglected their summer reading!" Elder Wong beamed.

Kiru had to fight an eyeroll.

The elder made a motion to demonstrate. "That is because, while many realms collapsed completely in on each other, not all of the realms did. For example, Nilfheim—realm of ice, snow, and mist—still remains a separate realm along the World Tree, in addition to multiple others. Though some of the earliest scholars from the Pre-Ragnarok Age spread the doctrine of Nine Realms for millennia, Meriadoc's Theorem of the Third Age—write that down, it will be on the test— proved that there are more, but not how many more. Perhaps one of you lot will make that discovery one day, hmm?"

Most of the students just stared at him blankly.

The elder sighed, then bunched his lips in firm resolve. He raised his head and slammed his staff to the ground. "Let me guess, you lot want to learn about cultivation, hmm?"

At the mention of "cultivation," Kiru snapped his head up in excitement. The other mostly bored students perked up too, confirming the elder's suspicion. He slammed his staff angrily on the floor. "Well, then I expect a ten-minute presentation by each of you about a unique realm attached to Yggdrasil and the types of mana associated with it, due by the end of the week."

A few of the students groaned quietly, but everyone accepted the impromptu assignment. Cultivation was the means to grow, to ascend in any part of life, no matter how large or menial. Farmers cultivated mana to help crops grow, miners cultivated mana to allow them unnatural strength, and warriors cultivated mana to make them quicker and more deadly.

"Can you teach us about our cores?" Emma Albright asked, clearly too eager to wait for the elder to even call on her this time.

The elder smiled and shook his head, enjoying the bookworm's curiosity. "I suppose," he said. He slammed his staff once more on the ground. "Pay attention, class, this information is vital to your paths of cultivation. Now, cores are spherical organs that retain deposits of energy called 'mana.' Mana brings both vitality and life to the body. They are located in our chests by our hearts." He pointed at his own chest to demonstrate. "Aside from those somehow blessed by the gods, all cultivators possess one core. Everyone is born at Base-rank.

"Base-rank cores are weak and mostly inert. They cannot provide mana to the body. Until they are filled completely, they only take in mana and do not provide us any benefit. Once our cores are completely full, they ascend to Bronze-rank. Most call it 'awakening' one's core. After one reaches Bronze, they can begin removing impurities built up in their system. So, it is important to cultivate in order to help the cores become full. Everyone's core also has an affinity to a unique type of mana."

"How can we find out what type of mana we can use?" a teenage dwarf with an already extremely thick mustache asked.

"Familial relations play a major factor, young man, but that's not always the case. Some have such a strong affinity, they know it intuitively once their cores have awakened. Still, for most people, there are tools and diviners that help determine their mana types," the elder answered. "As for when someone ascends to Bronze, that varies from person to person. Typically, when one reaches maturity, their cores awaken. Though the rate someone matures is unique to the individual, most commonly, eighteen is the age cultivators discover their mana type."

"Ha!" A rather rude laugh came from the student behind the dwarf, a laugh that grated on Kiru's nerves. "Yeah, short stuff, why don't you grow a few more inches, then maybe you'll be man enough to be able to use your core like me. Haha!" The mouthy student was Ambrose Constantine, only son and heir to Vincent Constantine, a duke and the local lord, and reportedly distant relatives to King van Blaine. His new brutish lackeys sitting beside him chuckled at his cruel joke.

The dwarf visibly shook in anger.

Kiru had enough. Even if it wasn't directed at him, he couldn't stand bullies, and Ambrose Constantine was the textbook definition of one. "Well, I know some people have to rely on pills to awaken their cores, but that's only for the rich kids who are too weak to do it on their own. Of course, you wouldn't know anything about that, would you, Ambrose? I mean, someone like you who awakened their core at fourteen *must* be some sort of prodigy. There's no way you could have just cheated to get ahead, right?"

The noble boy's face went slack and turned pale white at Kiru's words. Everyone knew Ambrose's father had given him pills. The boy had been drunk on some wine he'd taken from his family's cellar one night and all but declared it to the entire village. No one ever dared bring it up, though, since the boy was known for his cruelty, and his father was known for his unapologetic nepotism.

There was a pregnant pause in the room, until one by one, the other students began to laugh. First, they chuckled. Then it snowballed into an uproar.

Ambrose's face turned red. "What are you laughing at? Of course I didn't do that! And you, mongrel," he said, glaring directly at Kiru, "how *dare* you suggest otherwise? My father will hear of this!" He spat, then stormed out of the classroom, his two goons following close behind.

Elder Wong tsked and shook his head. "I'm really worried about that one," he muttered before looking back at Kiru. "I sure do hope you know what you're doing, Mister Kiru," he said pointedly at the half-elf.

Kiru winced, suddenly realizing *who* exactly he'd just provoked. He really needed to get a better grip on his anger. It made him too impulsive. Now, instead of keeping out of the limelight, he'd just made a public scene and insulted the lord's son, along with losing face!

He averted his eyes, clenching his fist and gritting his teeth in disappointment. "Crap," he uttered in self-recrimination. He had to find a better way of keeping himself under control. After a few seconds, he realized that everyone was looking at him. "Oh! Sorry, Elder Wong. You're right. I shall endeavor to be more careful with my words from now on. Thank you for your concern," Kiru said.

The old man shook his head before readdressing his class. "Well, then, let's go on to cultivation, shall we?"

Despite the little drama that had just played out, the rest of the students seemed excited at the announcement. For many of them, this was their first guided cultivation session. They all sat in a group on the floor, mirroring the elder, and closed their eyes. They began to follow his instructions, bringing in the ambient mana present within the environment and filtering it through their pores. It was a method available to any cultivator, no matter what type or rank. Many students shook and struggled as they tried to follow the elder's instructions. For those who were able to cultivate successfully, they could only filter small trickles of mana into their cores.

The reason for such a small amount was twofold. First, while this method of cultivation was widely available, it was by far the worst way to draw in mana. By this method, the students weren't trying to cultivate a specific type of mana nor direct it through their body in a certain way. Their cores would just lazily purify any mana that happened to come into contact with them. It was literally the most basic method anyone could learn. The second reason was the students' lack of understanding and training, as evidenced by their bodies shaking with the effort. While natural ability played a factor, cultivating required practice to improve.

Kiru blocked out the elder's interaction and started his more enhanced cultivation method. Unlike Ambrose, Kiru had awakened his core without any cheats. His mother, despite many looking down on her for being a simple tavern cook and barmaid, was a very gifted cultivator. She taught him how to awaken his core via an elven method she knew, bringing him from the Base-rank to Bronze much more quickly.

He had a high affinity with his mana type, which led him to intuitively know the type he could cultivate after his awakening. His mother was delighted to see that he was a fire cultivator like she was. He wasn't about to share it with the class, but she had also informed Kiru that the generic theory that Elder Wong taught was very outdated. It had come from the fact that most cultivators, who were either self-taught or without a path, often stumbled their way to the second lowest rank if they just used the basic cultivation method.

Unfortunately, those people were often stuck at that rank from then on. Those defects in knowledge even led many commoners to abandon attempting to cultivate altogether. Children would have no one immediately above them to learn about cultivation from. That led to more gaps in knowledge and resulted in people having to learn basics later in life versus early childhood. The class Kiru was in was a prime example of that.

After his awakening, Kiru's mom also taught him a better way to cultivate fire mana. The elf informed her son that cultivating beside a source that exuded the mana you were connected to increased the potency and amount of mana absorbed. She had given him the example of an ice mana cultivator being more effective when cultivating at the top of a mountain during winter.

So, while the majority of the class started to cultivate via the standard method for the first time, Kiru sat right next to one of the open windows and started to draw in fire mana. Though the sun's heat was not a "nearby" source of flame, it still exuded more concentrated fire mana than anything else Kiru could find at the moment. The young half-elf smiled as he let the sun's rays wash over him from the window and cycled the fire mana into his core.

After the morning class, Kiru began his walk to the local smithy. The dwarf who ran the forge there was a huge fan of the boy's mother's cooking. So, Kiru had negotiated to learn his craft in exchange for a daily cooked meal from her. The gruff smith wasn't much for conversation, almost completely keeping the topic focused on his craft. Still, he had a respect for the teenager's skill and wit. Honestly, the old dwarf was the closest thing Kiru would consider a friend, and that wasn't saying much. Kiru was admittedly a loner, and his "smart mouth" had caused more than a few fights and a not-so-flattering reputation among the other youths.

So, instead of trying to make friends, he focused on self-improvement with cultivating and smithing. While Kiru found the craft of blacksmithing interesting, he wasn't planning to make a career out of it. He would use the ability to diversify his skill set, and knew it would help with his ultimate goals. Kiru's dream was to be a soldier, one of the famed royal soldiers of the Kingdom of Blades. He needed to be strong, so he could travel the world and fight injustice.

Nevertheless, his mother insisted on him taking up a non-combat trade, so blacksmithing it was. It let him build muscle and heat resistance, plus cultivating near the fires was an excellent way to help him advance. The final bonus was that Kiru got to handle weaponry. He was already learning the feel of a sword, weight, balance, and counterbalance.

Kiru decided to take the long route through the central market district that day. The kingdom's Royal Academy recruiters had stopped by their remote village, as they did every year, and the teen wanted a glimpse at their power and to see if any of the village's contestants would make it. The academy was Kiru's best shot at eventually becoming a royal soldier, but they only accepted Gold-rank contenders or higher. On top of that, you had to show what they termed "promise." Whatever that meant.

Kiru was well on his way to becoming a prime candidate for the academy. If he continued his path, with his mom's help, he'd be a tier-one Silver-rank in just a few weeks, which would put him that much closer to reaching Gold. To reach Silver, a Bronze-rank cultivator had to cultivate enough mana to force their core to condense itself.

With the condensing of his core, he would be able to control the flow of mana more easily. Bronze had no separate stages within the rank. That wasn't the case when one reached Silver. Silver-rank had six tiers, starting at zero and ending at five. Still, for Kiru to be closing in on the second tier of Silver was a feat that was exceedingly rare, especially since he was still supposed to be two years away from even awakening his core, compared to most cultivators. So, he was the highest-ranked cultivator of his age in Bristleon. Well . . . aside from Ambrose.

Kiru scowled as he thought of the noble brat. His palm began to turn red and hot as he unintentionally released some of his stored fire mana through it. The action wasn't a true spell or technique. It was the most powerful ability Kiru could do for now, though he had never manifested it intentionally, only when he was angry. He shook his hand a few times. At tier-zero Silver, he had no meridians.

Unfortunately for the teen, a well-known side effect for most fire mana cultivators was a short temper. Ever since he'd activated his core, his anger had become much more difficult to keep in check. He scowled to himself, as he gave his hand another shake. His mother had told him not to channel mana to his hand like that yet. Because he hadn't yet reached a high enough tier, it could cause permanent damage, if he wasn't careful. Feeling the burning sensation, he couldn't help but agree about the risk. He just needed to keep his head down, work hard, and not cause any trouble.

Kiru found being alone helped him cool his emotions and let frustrations go with greater ease. The noise and hustle and bustle with the academy's proctors in town was making that difficult. So, he went off into a dead-end alley for a moment of solitude. After he walked halfway in, Kiru stopped, closed his eyes, and took a deep breath. He forcibly calmed himself, and his clenched fist finally began to cool. He opened his eyes, letting a contented smile cross his face. Before he could turn back to continue his trek to the market district and the smithy, a voice reached his ears, instantly reigniting his temper.

"Mongrel!"

# CHAPTER THREE

# Duel

The half-elf gritted his teeth and turned to see Ambrose flanked by his two goons, a pair of towering, bulky human twins who looked to have traded most of their brains for brawn. The goons hadn't awakened their cores. Kiru could innately tell from the energy signature coming off their bodies—or in their specific cases, a lack thereof. Still, that didn't make them any less dangerous. The trio had cut off his only exit. He *really* regretted turning off into this dead end.

"What do you want, Ambrose?" he asked, forcing his anger back for the moment.

The boy smirked. "I didn't appreciate what you insinuated earlier. So I thought the boys and I should teach you a lesson."

"Oh yeah? And what lesson is that?"

"Don't insult your betters, peasant. How dare you, some common trash, have the audacity to insult me in front of others?"

Kiru almost attacked Ambrose right then and there, but he restrained himself. He had promised his mom several weeks ago he wouldn't start any more unnecessary fights. He'd caused her enough trouble recently, which had made her lose face in the village. It wasn't merely the fact that he awakened his core; it was that the fire mana stoked his temper much more easily which . . . led to trouble.

Kiru took in a deep breath through his nostrils as he prepared himself. It would be difficult, but he would apologize to Ambrose for his mother's sake. He sighed and bowed his head to him. "I'm sorry, noble heir to the Constantine family. Please forgive my rudeness. I am but a lowly peasant and am not worthy to be in your presence," he said, feeling disgust as the words passed his lips. He couldn't believe it had come to this, but a promise to his mother was a promise he intended to try to keep.

"Huh! Haha! I'm surprised, trash. You usually have such a mouth on you. I didn't expect for you to grovel before me, even without my men's prompting,"

Ambrose said, then sighed. "I'll forgive your offense, only this once, as long as you never repeat it again," he said, before turning his back to walk away.

Kiru kept his head bowed and sighed in relief.

But as Ambrose walked away, he said, "Guess that bitch of a mother actually did teach you something."

Kiru snapped. He could bear them taunting him. He could deal with the teasing, the bullying, the lack of friends. But what he wouldn't stand was someone insulting his mother. It was a line he drew which none could cross. A vessel throbbed in his forehead as he looked to the thugs' backs, his fire mana core now fueling him completely. For the first time ever, he let the mana stored inside flow through his arm unrestrained. "What did you say?" The words passed his lips in an angry growl. His entire arm stung as if from a bad sunburn, but he didn't care.

Ambrose stopped and turned to face the half-elf, a malicious smile on his face. "Oh, did I hurt your feelings, mongrel? I called your mother what she is, a bitch!" The two thugs beside him chuckled evilly at the insult.

If Kiru openly attacked Ambrose, there would be repercussions. Like it or not, the horse's ass was still a noble. But just because they couldn't have an open brawl like Kiru wanted didn't mean that he couldn't make the jerk pay. "I challenge you to a duel," he said, staring straight at Ambrose, keeping his face stern to show that he had no fear of him.

The cocky noble gave a noncommittal shrug, then said, "Fine. I agree." His lackadaisical attitude immediately turned hostile as he lunged at Kiru.

Kiru was caught off-guard by the sudden attack; he'd assumed there would be more formality to an official duel. He hadn't researched duels and only knew they were one-on-one fights that lasted until someone surrendered or was incapacitated.

Ambrose apparently didn't share that view, nor did he think to fight fairly, either. The young noble was a storm mana cultivator, similar to the air mana his father cultivated. It was a rare path to follow, and it made Ambrose dangerous. "Lightning Limb," he said slightly under his breath. Using his stored mana, he activated a technique to fuel his strike. Electricity crackled around Ambrose's forearm, seeming to accelerate his speed. Kiru had enough time for his eyes to widen in surprise, but not enough to fully guard himself. The noble had activated the technique Lightning Limb to help him punch Kiru square in the face.

Kiru's vision flashed white, and he heard the telltale snap of his nose breaking as he was flung backward from the momentum of the strike. As he was airborne, the pain forced him to stop the flow of mana down his arm as blood poured from his nostrils across his grimacing face. He rolled and bounced on the dirt like a rock skipping on water. Kiru barely had enough time to blink his vision clear and wipe some of the blood off his face before Ambrose's twin goons began to kick him again and again. He slowly curled into a ball to protect himself, but he was still beaten handily, bounced around by their blows and kicks.

Kiru groaned and growled as the anger still coursing through him grew, stimulating the mana in his core to rage like wildfire. Acting purely on instinct, Kiru caught a leg from each of the goons and recklessly released some of the fire mana from his core. It traveled wildly through his arms to his hands and from there to the leg of each brute. While no flames came from his hands, he'd heated them up enough to burn through their pants and char their flesh. His arms burned and sizzled.

The two brutes fell to their asses and howled in pain as Kiru retained his grip and seared their flesh, giving the twins a pair of matching handprint second-degree burns. Kiru's arms stung with the backlash from the heat, but he bared his teeth and endured it. Kiru heard the crackling of electricity once more in front of him, and he dropped their legs. He managed to roll out of the way and dodged another Lightning Limb attack.

Ambrose scowled as he turned back to face Kiru.

There was no one blocking Kiru from escaping. He could run and avoid this fight, since Ambrose had already broken the rules of the duel. But then again, Kiru wanted to win. He was holding his own, despite being tricked and outnumbered. He didn't want to miss this chance for Ambrose to truly learn who his betters were.

Kiru gestured for Ambrose to continue.

Ambrose growled at his companions, "Useless!" he spat, throwing an unempowered fist at Kiru. The half-elf raised an arm to block it, then gave the noble a shit-eating grin. The rich kid had training in combat from teachers; Kiru had learned from his previous scuffles. This duel had certifiably been turned into a brawl, and that gave Kiru the advantage.

Kiru dodged the next punch, then kicked Ambrose in the side of the knee. He followed up with a kidney punch.

Ambrose whined in pain and swung wildly in response. Kiru dodged again, using the noble's angry attack against him. Kiru reactivated his own prototechnique, making his hand extremely hot, and slapped Ambrose on the face, both insulting the boy and planting a hand-shaped burn mark on half of his face! It was a devious idea that Kiru's angered brain had devised in the heat of the moment. He smiled as the fruits of his attack bloomed on Ambrose's face.

Ambrose let out a childlike cry, clutching his burned cheek, and turned back to Kiru with his mouth agape.

Kiru took a few confident steps forward and pulled a fist back, ready to finish the fight against the uppity noble, but then he was suddenly tackled from behind. Kiru fought and kicked at whoever knocked him down. His still-unseen assailant wrapped their arms around his legs. Heart racing, Kiru bucked before quickly realizing that in all his focus and anger on Ambrose, he'd forgotten about the noble's lackeys. The brute who held Kiru's upper body slammed his skull violently against the ground.

A warm sensation trickled down his face, streaking over his right eye and partially obscuring his vision. He felt his body being manhandled, but he couldn't respond. He couldn't speak or move his limbs, like he was a prisoner within the shell his body had become. *Move!* he thought to himself, in frustration. *Come on, Kiru! Move!* His desperate internal motivation worked, and he clawed his way to consciousness. He gasped deeply as his eyes regained focus. Well, one of his eyes. The other was still covered in blood, which still flowed freely.

Kiru became keenly aware that whatever head wound he'd suffered, it was bad. Ambrose and his brutes looked down on him, all wearing the same expression of surprise. This confirmed that they hadn't expected him to be awake, but it didn't explain why they were so much taller than him. That's when the half-elf realized how dire his situation actually was. He was on his knees, his wrists bound to each other and to his ankles behind him with rope taken from some nearby wooden crates. His enemies stood over him.

Ambrose laughed. "I'm surprised you didn't die from that head wound, you trash, but it's actually better this way." A sinister, wicked smile spread on the noble's face. "Now you get to watch what I'm going to do to you." He pointed to the hand-shaped burn wound on his cheek. "No one strikes me and gets away with it, no one! Especially not some mouthy piece of filth who doesn't know his place." Ambrose shoved Kiru to the side, and he crashed helplessly to the ground. Kiru glared back up at Ambrose. Despite the position he found himself in, hatred coming off the half-elf in waves.

Ambrose scowled at Kiru's lack of fear. "You know, peasant, I bet you think you've ruined my face. Unfortunately for you, my family has access to the best potions and healers in the whole kingdom, so I'll be fine. I am a relative of the king, after all. But you, *tsk*," he said, "you're not as lucky. For damaging my perfect face, I need to pay you back in kind."

"What? You gonna hit me with another one of those weak-ass lightning punches?" Kiru spat a glob of coagulated blood onto Ambrose's shoes.

"No, I have another technique for you."

That gave Kiru pause. *Ambrose had a second technique already?*

The noble noticed Kiru's surprise. "Are you surprised? I am a prodigy among cultivators; why wouldn't I already have two techniques?" He leaned close to whisper, "I'll let you in on a little secret. It's a forbidden technique I stole from my father's library. It's called Overload."

Kiru's eyes widened. *The cultivator killer!* He'd heard of this technique before. It was outlawed in all of the countries of the Great Alliance! "You're lying," Kiru whispered. He tried to wriggle his wrists out of the rope binding them. He really wished he could reach them with his hands to melt them. A back-handed slap across his cheek halted his efforts.

"Know your place, peasant." Ambrose gritted his teeth. Then, a sinister smile grew. "No matter. I'll let my actions speak louder than my words. You tried to ruin my face. Now, I'll ruin you . . . permanently."

Kiru didn't want to test whether Ambrose was telling the truth and flailed in a desperate attempt to break free.

"Grab him," Ambrose ordered. One of his goons limped over to Kiru, picked him up by the hair, and forced him back on his knees. "Now gag him and keep him there," he said. Then he placed a palm on Kiru's chest, right where the half-elf's core was.

The goon holding him tied a scrap of fabric into Kiru's mouth, then looked askance at Ambrose, as if wondering if he, too, would be a recipient of this technique one day.

A spark shot from Ambrose's palm. Kiru shook as it made contact with his core, crackling like constant static. After ten seconds, the shock made a more permanent connection with his core, seeming to wrap around and invade it, running amok. Kiru hyperventilated, terrified of what was happening and what it might mean. He tried to move once more, but one of the goons sent a kick to his ribs, followed by a punch to his already-injured temple.

After thirty seconds, beads of sweat began to form on Ambrose's temples. Kiru could feel the increase in the amount of electricity flowing into him, almost as if it was growing from static to a true bolt of electricity. The half-elf's body went rigid.

The pain lanced through Kiru, despite him being knocked into semi-unconsciousness. If anything, it launched him back to being fully aware once more, but it was too late. Ambrose was committed, and he wasn't going to stop until Kiru was finished.

Kiru gritted his teeth and tried to yell, despite the gag. The noble flooded Kiru's core with three times the mana it could handle all at once, like a sudden tidal wave.

This time, Kiru didn't yell. He *screamed*!

His core was flooded with so much violent lightning mana, it shattered completely. The wave from the destruction was even worse than the actual technique. A flood of mana surged out of his body in all directions, tearing the ropes binding him, forcing the three humans to fly back, and obliterating a section of Kiru's spine with a sharp crack. Then, nothing. His body collapsed to the ground.

Ambrose and his brutes slowly forced themselves up. They were in a more secluded street alley, but the noise from that and Kiru's screaming had started to draw attention from others.

Kiru tried to move, to run toward the crowd, to get help, but he couldn't. His body felt extremely weak, and he could barely shift himself. *Ambrose tried to kill me! I need to get the city guard! Why can't I move?* He shifted his head to see Ambrose looking at him in surprise.

"How . . . how are you alive?" the noble asked, shock etched across his youthful features as his gaze fixed on Kiru's mangled body.

Kiru no longer felt the power or anger flowing through him like it had been earlier. It was as if he had lost some part of himself, like he was hollowed out.

"What? What are you talking about?" Kiru asked, not sure what he meant.

More people started to gather at the edge of the alley, murmuring and jostling to get a better look. Someone even let out a loud gasp.

"Shit!" Ambrose spat, then put a hood over his head. "Come on, boys! He's as good as dead, anyway," Ambrose ordered. The three ran off into the crowd, shoving a number of concerned citizens out of their way.

"Get back here," Kiru groaned as he lay on his belly. At the edges of his awareness, he could tell people were still at the alley entrance but didn't want to come any closer. He finally mustered up enough strength, and crawled toward them, every movement eliciting the grating sound of bone on bone from his body. Kiru did his best to look back at the source. The sight made his blood run cold. It forced him to push away the comfort his mind had built up as a defensive measure and address the reality he saw.

His back, his spine, was snapped in two. The two jagged ends lay spread far apart, only hanging on by a few pieces of flesh. It was at a convex angle, with one of the sections breaking through his skin. Before Kiru could do anything, his back let out another loud crack, and he lost all sensation below his neck.

The half-elf's face went white as it hit the ground. His jaw shook uncontrollably, but it wasn't from the impact. It was from the shock. Tears rolled down his cheeks and hit the dirt as he now fully understood his predicament. It wasn't his imagination; Ambrose had truly and utterly crippled him. The half-elf's eyes rolled to the back of his head, and he screamed in despair. He didn't know how long he was there, but eventually a presence stood before him, casting a shadow over the lad.

Kiru's incessant screaming stuttered to a halt as the person exuded a sort of strange calming presence. As the noise subsided, an elf with long, blonde hair and thick blue robes knelt into view. Kiru blinked in disbelief. This new pure elf didn't look either disturbed or concerned.

"My, what a tough one you are, boy. To have survived that level of trauma to your body and to your core? Quite impressive indeed," he said rather whimsically, not seeming to fully understand the gravity of Kiru's wounds.

"Help . . . me," Kiru begged weakly.

The elf looked surprised. "Oh! Of course! My apologies, I was so intrigued by your grievous wounds that I'd forgotten you're still experiencing them."

"Eh . . . what?" Kiru asked.

A bright purple powder fell from the elf's palm, "Rest," he said smoothly, as he sprinkled it over Kiru's eyes.

Instantly, the teen's eyes went heavy, and he fell into unconsciousness.

# CHAPTER FOUR

# Reality

Time was a blur for Kiru. He felt lightheaded and weak. His body was raging hot, but he was covered in cold sweat. He faded in and out of consciousness, vaguely realizing that he'd been moved, as he was now lying on his back on some sort of bedding. Kiru was pretty sure he'd seen his mother's face covered in tears at one point, her expression heartbreakingly sad.

At one point, he'd heard muffled voices and made out the words "infection," "dead," "paralyzed," "broken," and "drained." Kiru was curious what exactly those people were talking about, but the inky black took him once more before he could call out. Then, one day, Kiru fully awoke, feeling much better. He inhaled with a gasp, as if he'd been underwater. Kiru took a long look around, finally able to fully discern his surroundings.

"Oh! Thank the Archfey! You're awake!" Kiru's mother exclaimed. The elf looked at her son with heavy eyes burdened with exhaustion. Her wild, curly red hair was barely tamed into a ponytail. Different races had their own average lifespans. Being an elf, at the age of just a little over one-hundred, she was essentially middle-aged.

"Mom? Where am I? What happened? How long was I sleeping?" he asked, looking around to find that he was in a small wooden room. There was a low table with a few medical tools, a waste bin, and various gauze bandages and wraps, as well as an array of folded towels and clothing. The sun shone bright from the window by his bed. He squinted and raised his hand to cover his eyes, only he couldn't. The half-elf's eyes widened as he looked down to his heavily bandaged arm and body, staying completely motionless.

"It's okay," his mother said, trying to comfort him. She reached out and put a hand on his.

"Why can't I feel your hand?" he asked.

The red-haired elf took in a deep breath before answering. "My little flame—"
She paused to compose herself. "You've been sleeping for ten days. Now, what I'm
going to tell you is not going to be easy, but you were seriously hurt from your
fight with the Constantine boy. Both your arms were burned, and your spine . . .
was fractured. Even after you finish healing, you won't be able to walk or move
your body from the neck down."

Kiru knew deep down that her words were true, though he didn't want to
believe it. Noticing the multitude of bandages over his body, he had a flash of
memory about the gaping wound in his back. There was blood, and a lot of it.
"How am I alive?" he asked through gritted teeth, tears forming in his eyes.

"You have tough body, Mister . . . Kiru," a whimsical voice answered. His
mother snapped her head up in surprise. A blonde elf in large, loose blue robes
stood in the open doorway. "And an amazing stroke of luck, I'd say." The elf wore
a big grin as he walked into the small room. "I am Master Niajar, head librarian
of the Royal Academy. It's a pleasure to make your acquaintance," he said with a
flourishing bow.

"Um, it's nice to meet you, too," Kiru replied uncomfortably.

Niajar turned to Kiru's mom. "And you must be this boy's mother! I hadn't
gotten the chance to meet you formally with all the interviews going on at the
academy and talking with the local authorities." He stuck out a hand to shake.

Kiru's mother crossed her arms and glared with suspicion at the librarian.
"Sumiko. My name is Sumiko. What business do you have here with my son?"

"Sumiko? What an interesting name for an elf! I will certainly have to catalog that one in my library. You know, come to think of it, I've only ever heard of
one elf with a name that begins with a 'Su' sound like that. I have a book about
her in my library: 'Surtur, The Flamebringer!' It's a pretty good book, actually,"
he said, looking at Kiru as he addressed the boy's mother.

Niajar turned back to face Sumiko, who was visibly angry. "Oh, my apologies, madam. I have come to let the boy know about what happened and to com-
mend him." Before she could reply, he grabbed a chair and sat right beside the
boy. "Kiru, your injuries were far worse than a mere fractured spine. One of your
vertebrae was completely obliterated. And the blood! Oh, gods! Your spleen was
bisected from the force!"

"Enough!" Kiru's mom yelled, standing up. Her green irises turned orange,
the color of the orbs of flame she now had in each hand. Despite only reaching
Gold, Kiru's mother was a terrifying force to be reckoned with. "Tell us the real
reason why you're here now, or I will reduce you to ashes myself," she threatened.

Kiru could sense Niajar had a much higher cultivation rank than his mother,
but there was a look of true fear on the man's face. Niajar swallowed hard, and
the grin shakily returned to his face. "Very well," he said, then turned to Kiru, "I
was the one who found you after those boys ran off. Without my intervention

with my amazing set of skills, you would've died on the spot. So, I'm a *friend*." He emphasized the last word, casting an uncertain glance at Sumiko.

The woman dispelled her flames and sat back down, gesturing for him to continue.

Niajar obliged, sounding more serious than he had in the brief time Kiru had known him. "Your mother is right; you will never be able to use your body again. But I'm afraid it's much worse. One of those boys did an abominable transgression to you. Your core is . . . damaged, so much so that there's a chance you may never cultivate fire mana again. I truly am sorry."

Sumiko gasped and put her hands to her mouth. "I didn't even look at his core." She despaired. "You mean to say he's . . . he's . . ."

"A vitaldrain," Kiru finished, his heart sinking. He'd been secretly hoping, despite his paralyzed body, that the power of mana and some cultivation miracle would help revitalize him. Kiru had heard of plenty of stories like that before. Now, though, he was a vitaldrain, a cruel term given to the poor people born without a core. It was a rarity, but it wasn't unheard of. Unfortunately, it guaranteed a shortened lifespan, a likely painful death, and being the lowest of the low in terms of class and strength.

Ambrose had done what he'd promised. He'd ruined Kiru's life. The half-elf was not only unable to move, he was unable to cultivate or do anything, even. Never did he despise the term "vitaldrain" more than he did right then.

"What's the point of telling me this?" Kiru asked through gritted teeth.

Niajar just grinned, unperturbed. "Because I believe you should know the truth, Kiru," he said. "I also want you to know anyone surviving your initial wounds must possess unrivaled strength and an inner fire that cannot be quenched. That's why I said you must be commended. Despite the reality of your current circumstances, there is true potential in you." He pulled out a thick gold coin with five stars emblazoned on one side and a book on the other.

The elf placed it in Kiru's immobile palm and forced the teen's hand closed around it. "If you can somehow use your resilience to cultivate your way to Gold-rank, give this coin to any recruiters for the academy you come across. You will be accepted into the school without question."

Kiru's eyes widened. Immediately, his heart filled with hope, but he was still apprehensive. His core was broken; he was a vitaldrain. His world had been rocked. No vitaldrain had ever achieved greatness in this world. At least, none that he knew of. Then, before he had even time to fully grasp his situation, Kiru was told that he somehow showed promise and had a guaranteed spot at the academy? Why would someone say that? Niajar was certainly a unique person.

Was he a little too far off his rocker? Maybe, but he was still a staff member at the academy. He definitely knew more than Kiru or his mother did about potential. If this odd man said that he saw a path for Kiru, maybe his situation wasn't as hopeless as he'd originally thought! Kiru clung to that hope desperately. Anything was better than being stuck in Bristleton as a vitaldrain. "Thank you, sir, but . . . why me? What do you gain out of me joining the academy?"

The whimsical librarian stood up. "It's clear you're a scrappy one, a fighter through and through. Let's just say, I'm something of a gambler myself. If you enter the academy with my approval, your success will be my success. With the odds so stacked against you, if you really do succeed, it's a great payday for me," he said with a big grin. He then turned and gave a slight bow to Sumiko. "Madam," he said before walking out.

"Succeed at what?" Kiru blurted before he left.

Niajar turned his head back and gave the teen a wink. "The thing that brought you here, young man. Violence. Only the best fighters win the Warrior Games, after all."

# CHAPTER FIVE

# Noble Schemes

*Ten Days Ago*

Vincent Constantine sat in his leather chair by the fireplace, listening to his son's recounting of the day's events. He had heard rumors from the multiple shopkeepers, guards, and families in his pocket, but he certainly hoped they weren't true. His son wouldn't be so stupid as to do a blatant hit-and-run on a mere peasant boy. Even as his son spoke, Vincent was calculating what the risks were for his family, and the consequences he would have to deal with for Ambrose's rash actions.

It was only due to the comprehensive training he'd undergone with a noble tutor during his own childhood that Vincent was able to adequately control his emotions enough to conceal to the public how much he loathed his only son. Ambrose was a bastard, a mistake born out of the one time Vincent ignored his better instincts and drank too much. Ambrose almost constantly exuded the qualities that Vincent despised. The boy was arrogant, a liar, quick to anger, easily manipulated, and openly cruel. The teen served as a persistent reminder of the duke's mistake.

Nevertheless, the boy was his only child and heir. Vincent would ensure his line continued. The middle-aged man stroked his well-manicured blond and gray goatee as he processed Ambrose's story, sipping wine from a crystal goblet.

"My friends and I were lucky to get out alive after that brutish peasant attacked us unprovoked. He was like a savage beast. Only your training helped us escape with our lives," Ambrose finished.

The glass shattered in Vincent's hand, and the boy flinched away from his father's anger.

Vincent stood up and faced his son, wiping his hands clean of the glass shards and wine on them, though there was no blood. He was a tier-one Sapphire-rank cultivator. It would take more than a broken glass to draw blood. "Ambrose," he said without making eye contact with his son.

"Yes, Father?" the teen asked nervously.

"What did I say about lying to me?!" the duke yelled as he backhanded his son across the face, deliberately hitting his burn mark, and knocking the boy to the floor. With no one else present, Vincent didn't have to worry about appearances for the moment.

"That I shouldn't do it," Ambrose replied weakly as he stood up on shaky legs. Tears streaked down his cheeks as he spoke, and blood dribbled from his mouth onto the ground, making a small puddle on the floor.

"And?"

"That it disrespects you and shows I'm weak."

"Right. Do not disrespect me again, or I will send you into the mines and make sure you never return," he threatened, taking out a handkerchief and throwing it down in front of his son. "Clean up the blood."

Ambrose quickly complied, despite how much his body was shaking.

"Now, tell me the real story, or I will cut off your manhood and feed it to the dogs."

Ambrose hurriedly told his father what actually happened with the peasant boy, too scared to even omit the truth about the book containing the forbidden technique he'd stolen from his father's library.

Vincent's expression remained carefully neutral, giving no indication as to how he felt to hear this. "I see," he said. "It seems that, despite the fact you outnumbered and outclassed a peasant boy, you were still just barely able to beat him.

"That reminds me," he said. His hand shot out and grabbed his boy by the throat, lifting him up against the wall, all traces of calm replaced by wide-eyed rage. Slowly, steadily, his hand squeezed his son's neck. Ambrose started to grunt in discomfort and fear. "How stupid can you be?" Vincent growled. "Stealing not only from me but taking the Overload technique! Did you not know the king would execute you right now, without hesitation, for knowing Overload, despite his relation to us?"

Ambrose squirmed and coughed, as his father clutched at his throat even tighter, no air or words escaping the choke.

Vincent sighed and dropped his son to the ground. He fell hard. The duke turned his back to Ambrose and continued speaking. "Nevertheless, you are my son. I will ensure that you survive and my legacy endures. While you were never meant to learn the Overload technique, as it changes your path, I will travel to the capital to converse with the king. With luck, he will show us mercy and allow you to continue to cultivate, keeping that technique secret."

"What . . . about . . . my face?" Ambrose asked, rubbing his throat.

Vincent examined Ambrose's face, noting how his backhand left no visible mark; the hand-shaped burn obscured it. "You will keep your scar, boy!" Vincent spat. "It will serve as a reminder to never cross me again. No healer who values their life will work on you. I'll make sure of it."

Ambrose scowled at his father's back but didn't say a word. "And the mongrel?"

"My sources tell me that he is alive but is both paralyzed and a vitaldrain. Surprisingly, your technique worked. With all of the witnesses in my pocket, your word will bear more weight than his. However, we cannot allow this peasant to go about and slander the Constantine name. If he doesn't die from his wounds within the month, I will take care of him. Now, leave me!" With that, he dismissed his only son. Ambrose left his father's office and turned down the hall, hatred etched on his face.

Vincent shook his head in disappointment. Knowing Ambrose, the boy might do something even more idiotic if the commoner didn't die. He clenched his fist in a mix of worry and frustration. "Certainly, the boy won't be *that* stupid."

# CHAPTER SIX

# Firefight

It had been a week since Kiru had awoken and met Niajar. After seventeen days of healing, he'd been moved back to his humble home, a small hut right next to the inn where his mother worked. He'd come to one conclusion so far, having so swiftly gone from being an—for his age—advanced cultivator to a quadriplegic vitaldrain: it *sucked*. Kiru had to be fed, moved, and cared for in nearly every aspect of his life now, up to and including managing his body's waste functions.

His life ground to a miserable halt. His days primarily consisted of watching everyone going about their business in the small street outside his window, constantly wracking his brain for how in the world he could transform himself from a vitaldrain with a shattered core to a Gold-rank cultivator. To his frustration, he'd made no progress, but having something to occupy his thoughts did keep him from falling into despair. At least cheerful music often played from the tavern in the afternoon. That increased the liveliness a bit.

Not long after he'd been brought home, the local marshal had come to take his testimony. It was a poorly kept secret that the man was in the duke's pocket. Because of that, Kiru didn't say anything. He just pressed his lips together in anger and avoided eye contact. In the end, the marshal said the Constantines wouldn't be pressing charges *only* because of Kiru's "unfortunate" new circumstances, and that he should consider himself lucky after openly attacking a noble. Both Kiru and his mother were silently seething, but they kept it all in until after the marshal had left.

"What a load of horse dung!" Sumiko spat, her irises once more looking like orbs of angry flame. "These spoiled, petty noble brats in these backwater outskirts think they control everything! That fat bastard must be held accountable!" she snarled, the heat coming off her body distorting the air around her. "I will show those cowards that they can't get away with this!"

"Mother," Kiru pleaded, "Ambrose's father is tier-one Sapphire. You don't stand a chance. I'm angry, but I've already lost most of my own body. I can't face losing my mother, too." Growing up, Kiru was almost always the angrier of the two. When his mother got truly infuriated, however, she was *terrifying*. Sumiko's anger could reach cataclysmic levels, the likes of which had almost burned their home down on a couple of memorable occasions.

In times like these, the teenager's temper quickly mellowed into fear and concern. He never feared she'd hurt him in these rages. He was more afraid that she'd do to others exactly what she said she would. It was a surreal experience trying to quell his mother's fury, especially since Sumiko was usually the voice of reason, always helping Kiru control his temper, telling him to lay low and "not cause a scene."

*Was this the influence of her fire mana core?* He was also confused as to why she had gone on about their home being a "backwater outskirt" like she was more worldly than the Constantines. Kiru and his mom had never left Bristleton his entire life, no matter how many times Kiru begged to visit a neighboring village. *Does she know more of the world than she's told me?* He put those thoughts aside for now. He would attempt to redirect her ire with the same thing that had been helping him: Niajar's words about his potential.

"Now, I can't use my body, but that strange librarian indicated that there's still hope for me. I don't how exactly, but I believe there was something to his words. He believed I could be part of the Warrior Games, even."

The Warrior Games were a gladiatorial tournament between the students of the Royal Academy of the Kingdom of Blades that occurred once a year. The kingdom used it to display their power to the other countries in the alliance. The academy did its best to ensure no one ever died or was permanently injured by providing high-rank healers to supervise and intervene, but that didn't mean safety was guaranteed. Some horror stories had spread about the occasional limb amputation or evisceration that wasn't addressed quickly enough, bringing painful deaths to the fighters. Despite that, it was rare for anyone to actually die.

The Warrior Games were undoubtedly a spectacle, and Kiru had wanted to attend since he'd first heard of them as a kid. Admittedly, he wanted to go as a fan, but the librarian seemed confident that Kiru could actually be a participant. That gave the vitaldrain some hope. It was possibly foolish, but it was still better to hold onto that hope than the alternative.

"Let's focus on getting me better, yeah?" he said. "After work, will you please go see Elder Wong and see if there's any book about healing a damaged core?"

Sumiko was surprised by her son's words, the fire in her eyes quickly receding. "My boy, my sweet boy," she said, cupping her hand to his cheek. "Of course. For you, I would go to the ends of Alterra."

The midday bell rang, startling the two. "Oh, time for my shift. If you need anything, just ring the chimes," she said pointing to the metal pipes hanging by his window. It'd be a bit difficult, but Kiru could ring it with his head. He could have also just shouted to her but he didn't plan on it. Despite his current situation, he didn't want to wallow in despair. No, he needed to find ways to challenge himself, both to help stave off boredom and hopefully give him a sense of accomplishment.

"I'll crack the tavern window open," Sumiko said, then left their small home and went to work next door.

Kiru smiled. His mom's long elven ears were very effective in helping her hear. If he failed at ringing the chimes for some reason, she could have probably heard him even without cracking the window.

Unfortunately for Kiru, finding different ways to ring the chimes only kept him distracted for so long. He spent the rest of his day trying to keep himself occupied as best he could, which was rather hard as he could really only look outside, think, or sleep. He lacked the ability to visualize his core, now that he was no longer a Bronze rank, so he couldn't even evaluate the damage. If he could have at least looked at his core, he would have had a better idea of how to address the harm.

And so instead, Kiru thought again about cultivating and the looks of wonder on people's faces at seeing a person in as damaged a body as him ascend the ranks. Maybe he could make a suit of armor out of living flame and use it to move? Kiru imagined participating in the Warrior Games, skillfully besting his opponents while tossing out witty one-liners like the heroes he'd read about, as his mom cheered him on from the crowd.

Kiru thought more about his mother's strange behavior and words. It certainly seemed like she was holding information back from him. She had told him once that she was from the elven country of Anor'Voren. When he asked why she had left, she told Kiru that she fell in love with his father, a human from the Kingdom of Blades.

When pressed about his father, Sumiko was always very vague and standoffish. She only ever told Kiru snippets about the man: he was a human, a traveling bard who she fell in love with when he stopped by a tavern she was working at. They eventually settled down in the Kingdom of Blades, but he died of some illness.

That was all Kiru knew. When he tried to ask her his name, she said it was too hard for her to talk about. That didn't stop the teen from wondering. Kiru was curious if his dad was a fire cultivator like his mom, and hopefully one day he would be again, as well.

Eventually, tired from all the conjecture, Kiru fell asleep. When he woke up, the sun was much lower, at about six bells, the growing shadows making both the alley and his room much darker. Too dark. *Or perhaps dark too soon.* Kiru blinked his vision clear.

Goosebumps traveled up his neck as a pang of unease shot through his heart. Some primal instinct inside him was giving him some warning. Doing his best to stay calm, Kiru moved his head to scan the room. He looked around once, and there was nothing.

On his second scan however, he realized with shock that a small, hooded figure was leaning against his bedroom door. Its body was thick with muscle, and it raised its head to look directly at Kiru, revealing a bushy black beard and multiple crooked teeth. Under his left eye was a tattoo of a dagger with the blade pointed upward. He was a dwarf, and he didn't look friendly.

Kiru swallowed before speaking. "What . . . what do you want, friend?" he asked, jaw quivering a little. Kiru was trying his best to stay calm, and he was failing.

The dwarf gave a wicked grin. "The Constantine boy sends his regards," he said, then stood up. He drew all five of the stubby fingers of his right hand together, and a metallic sheen appeared, covering the appendage. In just a second, it grew to a sharp point, extending out from his fingers and forming a blade from his hand.

Kiru's heart raced. "Whoa, whoa, whoa, let's talk about this! I can pay you," he said, and flung his head back, ringing the chime in such a way that it seemed like an accident.

"You think you have more money than a noble brat?" The dwarf shook his head. "Though my employer wants you to die slowly, don't worry, lad. I'm not so cruel as to torture a cripple. I'll make it quick," he said as he stepped up to Kiru.

A split second later, a blazing torrent of flame shot out from the open window and struck the dwarven assassin square in the chest. The rogue let out a cry of pain as the stream of fire scorched his leather armor, launching him off his feet. He flew out of Kiru's room, crashing through the door and breaking it off its hinges.

The teen lay there in his bed, awestruck by what had just occurred. Before he could say anything, his mother launched through the window like a veteran acrobat and landed beside his bed. Her gaze never left the assassin.

"Kiru, are you okay?" she asked.

He nodded. "Yes, but how—?"

"I'll explain later," she interrupted.

The dwarf deftly rolled up and looked at Sumiko in disbelief. "You are supposed to be some tavern wench," he snarled. "No matter." With that, he spread both of his hands out wide. Each finger turned into a tiny blade. "I guess I'll just have to kill you too." The dwarf flicked both his hands downward, launching ten daggers from his fingers, all aimed at her.

Sumiko raised her hand, and a wall of flame erupted from the ground, intercepting and simultaneously melting the knives.

Kiru winced from the sudden, intense heat.

Then, without ceremony, she dispelled the flame. A section of the room was thoroughly scorched, but overall, it was still intact.

The dwarf was gone. *Had he been burned to a crisp too?*

Suddenly, the dwarf reappeared, swinging from the top of the doorway and kicking Kiru's mom right in the face. Despite his speed and weight, however, the impact did little else than force the elf a few steps back. He hadn't even drawn blood! The assassin growled, formed two blade hands, and lunged at the woman so fast, Kiru found it difficult to follow the motion with his eyes.

But Sumiko countered with ease, matching the assassin's speed. She dodged and blocked his strikes in an incredible display of martial prowess. *I knew Mom was strong, but . . . wow.*

"How are you this fast?" The dwarf grunted, then struck out with both his blade hands at her simultaneously.

Sumiko grabbed each of his wrists, stopping his momentum completely and holding him in place. "You haven't figured it out yet?"

The assassin's expression turned feral, his lips curving into a snarl. "Dodge this then, bitch!" Blades erupted from his wrists and pierced through both of Sumiko's hands. The dwarf let out a laugh, his face beaming in triumph. That lasted less than a moment before his expression turned to one of fear and confusion as to why the elf didn't seem bothered by his attack in the slightest.

In fact, she was smiling.

"Nice trick. Now it's my turn," she said. Her eyes flashed yellow, and she emitted an oppressively hot aura from her body. The assassin groaned, the sound low and muffled as that aura pressed down on him. He tried to resist, but her power forced him down to his knees, the heat causing his hair and armor to smoke.

Kiru felt the heat radiating against his face despite his mother's directed focus of her aura. The teen watched in shock as the assassin dismissed his technique, freeing Kiru's mom as he collapsed to his stomach. Kiru finally had the rogue's face in his field of vision, and from the assassin's wide-open mouth, he realized that the dwarf was screaming. He couldn't hear a thing though. The aura coming off Kiru's mother was suppressing the sounds entirely. Then the built-up heat's effect kicked in.

Kiru had to turn his face away from the wave of heat right as the rogue combusted before his eyes. The dwarf's body went up in flames and, in a matter of seconds, was nothing more than ash. Sumiko reined in her aura.

Kiru blinked his eyes clear. There was a perfectly measured circle in the floor where his mother's aura had seared completely through, revealing the stone ground underneath. A plume of smoke flew up from the assassin's ashes and escaped through the new hole in their ceiling, perfectly matching the one on the floor. Kiru had so many questions. *That guy was a real assassin. How did Mom deal with him so easily? How did she not burn the entire house down with that technique!?*

"Mother, what's going on?" Kiru asked with a mixture of admiration and fear.

Sumiko took a quick, deep breath through her nose, then turned to her son. "There's no time right now, my little flame. I promise I will explain, but please trust me. We have to go," she said in a tone that brokered no argument.

Kiru frowned, as concerned as he was frustrated. Apparently, Ambrose had tried to kill him again, and his mother was a combat badass. He didn't have a choice, though. It wasn't like he could just walk away. "Fine, where are we going?"

She walked to his closet. "Away, where no one will find us," she said, then punched straight through the hard wood of the back of his closet with ease. Sumiko pulled out a large dusty bag that had been hidden back there.

*There was a secret space behind my closet the whole time? How did I not know about that?* Kiru thought.

The woman opened the bag and pulled out a set of thick orange robes, bejeweled with a multitude of priceless gems and a few sets of runes sewn into its fabric. It radiated both heat and power. "No, not yet," Sumiko said, then stuffed the robes back into the bag.

Despite the bag's size, it seemed to be able to hold much more than it should have. *Is this a bag of spatial storage?*

Sumiko pulled out another robe, this one sleek and dark. "This will do," she said, then threw it on. Immediately, her form was shrouded in a layer of darkness. Her body was difficult to fully discern and looked slightly incorporeal. Satisfied with her choice of garb, she looked at her son. "I'm sorry we have to leave home like this, but it is time," she said. Without ceremony, she hefted Kiru up on one of her shoulders, as if his limp body weighed nothing.

Using the darkening evening and the effect of her cloak, she expertly managed to sneak across the street into the barn in the back of the inn, carefully navigating past the beasts of burden the patrons stored there. Most notable amongst them was a two-headed, solid black bipedal bird called a Tenkduo. His mother said those birds had nasty attitudes. Quickly discovering he wasn't a fan of being carried like a sack of potatoes, Kiru wanted to protest, but he thought it best not to make a scene.

Sumiko placed her son in the back of a covered wagon that the inn occasionally used as a storage space. The elf also hurriedly took ownership of a pair of large draft horses that belonged to a wealthy merchant visiting their village.

Kiru understood very little about what was going on, and that worried him. He needed to know more. "Why are we leaving, and why didn't you just, you know, knock out the dwarf? We could've used his testimony to . . ."

She cut him off, a measure of heat in her voice. "He would've said nothing. That man would have bit off his own tongue before he'd betray his employer or his guild." Sumiko let out a sigh. "I'm sorry. Any guild assassin can be bought off, but if you don't have the coin, they will not stop hunting you until either you're dead or they are. Besides, since I revealed my power, you would be in even more danger."

Before Kiru could say anything else, Sumiko hopped onto the driver's seat of the cart and snapped the horses' reins. She hissed for them to get moving, careful to keep anyone from noticing her but still conveying her sense of urgency. She quickly shot a small bolt of flame from her hand, through the barn, and into Kiru's room.

The dry wood of their home easily sparked ablaze. Sumiko carefully scanned their surroundings but managed to keep the cart going at a semi-leisurely pace. As the cart carried them further down the street, Kiru's eyes remained locked on the sight of their humble home becoming a giant pyre in half a minute.

Sumiko's reasoning for setting their home on fire soon became clear. Besides destroying any evidence, the bright flame became a beacon to all of Bristleton in the darkness of dusk. Almost every villager came out to either gawk or work to find a way to put out the house fire.

Kiru's home was one of a number of shoddy constructs built close to the multistory inn. With that close proximity, the fire threatened to spread to the entire village if not addressed. With everyone focused on the fire, few could truly give the cart or its occupants their attention. Within twenty minutes, both mother and son exited the village with their stolen cart and beasts of burden. That entire time, the image of their burning house never left Kiru's gaze. His past was literally being burned away, though he had a feeling a new stage was just beginning.

# CHAPTER SEVEN

# True History

For a few hours into the night, Kiru's mother drove the wagon deeper down the forest path. Kiru kept an eye on the path behind them, aided by the illumination of the full moon. He couldn't see all of the sky above them due to it being a covered wagon, but he was still able to catch a glimpse of some of it from the rear opening. Eventually, Sumiko took a hard right, going off the beaten path for another thirty minutes.

The route they took was much more rocky and uneven. The trees were much more densely packed here, closely surrounding the cart and obscuring the night sky. The forest was darker, but with them both possessing elven blood, they were still able to adequately see their surroundings. His mother's sight was much sharper than his. Her keen senses were the only reason he hadn't gotten into more trouble growing up.

So while he was able to see that she had brought him to a river being fed from a waterfall, he was unable to detect what was behind it. When his mom stirred the horses to continue forward through the fall, Kiru protested. Though they had a tarp, it was pretty thin. He almost couldn't process why his mom would do something so crazy as driving into a waterfall. He quickly halted his protestations, however, when the water pouring over the cart abruptly stopped as they entered the dark cave behind it.

The sloshing of horse hooves continued for the next five minutes before the cave gave way to the hollowed base of a long-dead volcano. No lava was present. There was water, however. Light from the twin moons fed into the cavernous glen, revealing an island in the center of a pond about one hundred feet in diameter that had accumulated in the base. It rose a good ten feet above water level, connected to their path via a stone bridge.

The cavern seemed almost magically illuminated by phosphorescent insects, bioluminescent amphibians, and a white cherry tree. The tree stood proudly on the island and glowed via pulsating red leaves, as if they were made of flame. Kiru had never even imagined such a wondrous spot just a few hours from his dry, mountainous homeland.

"What is this place?" Kiru asked.

"Somewhere safe, my little flame," Sumiko replied, the relief evident in her voice. She reached over to the wall beside the cart and pressed on a polished stone embedded seamlessly in the wall. "A ward stone I placed here long ago. This should help mask our mana signatures from would-be trackers." She snapped the reins and drove the wagon over the thick stone bridge to the raised island.

Once there, she made camp for the night, confirming Kiru's suspicion that it was indeed a bag of spatial storage as she pulled out a plethora of camping gear and equipment, along with food and water. Sumiko carried Kiru out of the cart with impressive strength and sat him against the lone cherry tree before she started a fire.

Kiru forced himself to wait patiently during her setup. His patience had improved with the absence of fire mana from his core, but it wasn't limitless. "Okay, I've been *very* patient with all the things that have happened, but I've waited long enough. What happened back there? How were you able to kill the assassin? And why did we leave Bristleton?" Sumiko tensed her jaw in frustration, but quickly let it go. "You're right," she said, then sat on a stone across the fire from Kiru. "Thank you for your trust, Son." She took a deep breath. "My real name is not Sumiko. It's Surturia, youngest sister of the queen of Anor'Voren."

Kiru reflexively coughed in disbelief. "You're elven royalty?!"

She nodded. "Twenty years ago, I was sent to be an ambassador to the Kingdom of Blades' monarch, Ruken Chromebane."

Where before, Kiru had coughed, this time he almost choked. Ruken Chromebane was a monster of a cultivator. Kiru was taught that the man used a wicked type of mana that had driven him insane. With it, he had manipulated much of the upper kingdom to bend to his will. "The Mad Tyrant?!" he asked in disbelief.

"Do not call him that! The rumors about him are complete lies!" Surturia spat, anger rising at that phrase.

Kiru winced at his mother's words. "Um, I'm sorry. I . . . didn't know." He stuttered out, still digesting what she had said.

"I know," she continued before he could say anything else. "I found the human to be both strong and tender, deadly yet merciful. Rare qualities in a leader. After four years, we fell in love and were to be betrothed, securing our countries' strength within the great alliance.

"That was when Van Blaine and his witch of a wife led a revolt against Ruken, using lies and fear to fuel their campaign. Ruken could indeed use mental mana, but he *never* manipulated the people like some dictator. In the end, Ruken sacrificed himself to ensure that his unborn son and I survived. I went into hiding under a false name, staying away from Anor'Voren for fear of what would happen to my family if I returned, deciding instead to hide in plain sight."

Goosebumps crawled up Kiru's neck. It took him a good minute before he could say anything, "I'm a Chromebane?"

"You are. You are Kiru Chromebane, son of Ruken Chromebane, the rightful ruler of the Kingdom of Blades."

"Why are you telling me this now?"

"Because we need your power to prevent all of Alterra from falling to ruin."

Kiru cocked his head. "Power? What power, Mother? I'm not only a vitaldrain, I can't use my body either. Is this just all some cruel joke? Because I am *not* finding this funny whatsoever!"

She shook her head and smiled slightly. "You are upset because you do not understand yet. You will." Surturia pulled out a small, simple circlet from her bag of spatial storage. It had a single, clear, diamond-shaped crystalline jewel at its center. "I was going to give this to you on your eighteenth birthday, but . . . circumstances change," she said.

Kiru rolled his eyes, thinking the gift was both oddly strange and pointless. He wasn't one for such jewelry, anyway. Despite his protests, he literally couldn't put up a fight, so she fitted it on his head. After a few seconds, Kiru cried out in pain as the circlet squeezed down tight. *Is this a gift or a torture device?* He screamed and desperately flung his head about, trying to force the circlet off, but it wouldn't budge. It felt like it was going to pop his head open like a grape!

His mother grabbed him tightly by the shoulders. He locked eyes with her, anger and fear running rampant in his heart. He was terrified that he was going to die a horrible death right there. Then, as quickly as it came, the pain suddenly and miraculously lifted. Something was different, though—a distinct weight to his head that wasn't there before.

His mother held up a small hand mirror to show him that the circlet had embedded itself completely inside his head. It left no evidence of its existence, aside from the crystal at the center of his forehead. The jewel was now bronze-colored.

Before Kiru could ask what had happened and why he now sported a strange jewel within him, something even more unexpected happened. He felt a distinct "click" inside his brain. A strange, but somewhat familiar power began to accumulate directly in his skull, fed directly from the circlet embedded in him. It was as if the circlet was a flowing spigot of water and his head was an empty bucket being filled by it.

His eyes widened in shock. The power was mana! The circlet had forced mana into him, but that meant he had a functioning core . . . in his head! *How?*

As if in response, the jewel in his head started projecting a holographic image in front of him. Kiru had only seen a few of these before. Nobles and merchants would occasionally display them to the town to show off their wealth, the latter often using it as some form of advertisement for their wares. None of them did so from jewels embedded in their skulls, though!

The hologram formed into the image of a well-muscled, middle-aged human man. His salt and pepper hair flowed down to his shoulders, and he had a finely tapered beard. The man possessed a noble bearing as well as one other distinct feature: he wore the same circlet as Kiru, although his wasn't fused to his body. Kiru also noticed the man's eyes—they were bright blue, just like his.

Despite what his mother had told him, part of Kiru still didn't want to believe her words. He didn't want to be a fugitive or possess some taboo power that would make others want to kill him. Seeing the powerful king in front of him, a king with his eyes, Kiru couldn't fully explain it. He just somehow knew that this man, Ruken Chromebane, was indeed his father. His mother was speaking the truth.

Surturia's eyes became teary as she once again gazed upon the form of the man she loved.

The king spoke, not looking directly at Kiru, indicating that it was a recording. "My son, I am glad this recording has made it to you. It is time for you to learn the truth. You are no ordinary cultivator," the man said in a booming, regal voice. "You are, like me, a psion. We possess cores inside our brains that allow us to cultivate mental mana. Unlike most cores, mental mana cores typically cannot be pushed to awaken by regular cultivation. Instead, they awaken on their own, or after being forced to intake a massive influx of mana they can't resist. Most likely, you dealt with the latter. It can be . . . unpleasant." Ruken winced slightly.

The projection quickly regained his composure. "There is a chance that you possess a second core as well. There have been a few so fortunate, and if that's the case for you, I know your mother will be delighted." He said this with a slight smirk. Kiru's mother chuckled happily at that, but then her face grew somber as realization hit her. "If you are seeing this recording, my son, it means I did not get the opportunity to meet you. For that, I am sorry," Ruken said.

His expression took on a look of resolve. "We cannot afford to dwell on what could have been. If I am truly dead, then I suspect all other psions may have passed as well. A large responsibility has fallen on your shoulders. My son, if you do not cultivate your core to reach the pinnacles of cultivation, you and all of Alterra are doomed."

Ruken snapped his fingers, and Kiru's brain was suddenly flooded with information. He gasped as he took in the overload. "The . . . dragons," he managed to force out.

"The dragons," Ruken said, almost as if he were actually there, replying to his son. "Millennia ago, the dragons and their servants, the drakonids of New Draconia, led by Nidhogg the Devourer, waged war on all of the peoples of Alterra.

"It was known as the Draconic Campaign. With a mutual enemy threatening death and enslavement to all, warring nations ceased their petty conflicts and formed a coalition known as the Great Alliance. They were led by the original psions, our ancestors. Those psions were the true reason the Great Alliance was able to overcome Nidhogg and his horde. They used their psionic powers to control the dragons and, with the aid of the gold drakonids who turned on Nidhogg, they defeated the foul creature."

He continued, "They couldn't control Nidhogg, but the psions were successful in subduing him and pushing his forces back. Information concerning the psions was kept secret so as to not cause fear among the people. Only a select few know the truth." Ruken chuckled grimly. "Even less now, given that I am dead."

The king seemed to grow concerned. "Time grows short, my son. I cannot delay. After Nidhogg and his horde were pushed back to their homeland of New Draconia at the edge of the world, the first monarch of the Kingdom of Blades ensured a method for Nidhogg to never return. There is a tower inside the royal castle. It serves as an amplifier of mental mana. As long as a psion rules the throne of the Kingdom of Blades, that tower will amplify and project their mana to keep the dragons at bay."

Kiru's eyes widened as he took in this information. He wouldn't have believed this story if he hadn't seen the dead king before his very eyes and felt the same mental mana flowing through him.

"During my rule, I've filled the tower with enough mana to continue its projection for twenty-five years after I'm gone. But once it runs out, Nidhogg will return. You must gather your strength to prevent that from happening. In each country of the Great Alliance is a piece of my equipment. Each one of them will prove vital in aiding you to retake our country. The power of my items can only be used by a true psion. I ask—no, I beg. Please, son, gather my items. Reclaim your throne. And save this world."

The hologram began to fade "You can change the world. Do not give into despair when times are tough. Remember, fate only binds you if you let it." Ruken smiled, then snapped his fingers once more, and with that, he vanished. The device, at his command, instilled Kiru's mind with the locations of his artifacts.

Kiru's eyes went distant as he processed the literal world-changing information that had just filled him.

"Kiru, are you okay?" Surturia asked after a good minute of silence from her son.

The half-elf blinked his vision clear. He felt oddly calm. Kiru had felt like a victim of fate after he was injured, but now, he knew that no matter what, his fate was his own. He wouldn't let it bind him.

Based on what he just learned, Kiru was likely the one sole surviving psion after Van Blaine's purge, leaving him the only one capable of preventing Nidhogg's horde of dragons from invading his home once more. Despite the grave conse-quences if he should fail, Kiru felt confident. He had always aspired to be some-thing more than a commoner in Bristleton. With this new power and purpose, he had a second chance to do just that.

He looked at his mother and smiled warmly. "I'm fine. Though I have my struggles, I somehow know that this can help me adapt to them." His heart began to race in excited anticipation now that he had spoken these thoughts out loud. "Mom, can you teach me what to do? Can you teach me how to har-ness this power?"

# CHAPTER EIGHT

# Familiar

Kiru's mother informed him that she indeed was not a psion like his father. Still, he figured she knew more than he did regarding mental mana. As it turned out, she didn't possess any knowledge that provided him any particular benefit, but she did pull out a scroll from her bag. Kiru smiled as she told him that it was a technique passed down from his father.

Sumiko—no, he supposed her name was Surturia—took a small dagger. With it, she made a shallow cut into Kiru's thumb, drawing a tiny trickle of blood. Then, she pressed his thumb onto the seal of the scroll, and the magic paper glowed purple and unfurled. The words on the scroll began to glow in the same purple hue, flashing once and imprinting the technique information on it into Kiru's mind. That done, the magic scroll crumbled to dust.

"Did it work?" Surturia asked.

Kiru smiled as he channeled his mental mana to activate his new technique. With a flex of will, the paralyzed teen raised his right arm and gave his mom an extremely shaky thumbs-up. He had Telekinesis! Maybe he couldn't move mountains but a body was within reason. Moments after he attempted that technique, expending the small amount of mana he'd accumulated in his core, Kiru passed out from exhaustion. Turns out that nearly getting assassinated, then realizing you're the world's only hope, can wear down someone's psyche.

The next morning, Kiru woke up in their new hidden oasis camp to the smell of cooking meat. He was lying on a box in the back of the cart and was elevated enough to see over the rim. To his surprise, an entire rabbit was skewered and cooking over an open fire, rotisserie-style. The teenager didn't know where his mother had caught it, but he was grateful nonetheless. She was an excellent cook and favored making things spicier, which he loved. She had also set up a full campsite, complete with two tents and a washbasin, and had even used her fire mana to carve out a latrine of scorched earth for their waste!

Surturia spent the morning caring for her son, re-emphasizing to Kiru the need to get his body moving on his own again. He didn't need any convincing. Though he loved and appreciated his mother, he'd rather be the one to clean his own nether regions. She set him down against the tree once more to ask him, "So, where is the nearest of your father's artifact items? Last I saw, he was wearing them. He must have found a means of dispersing them after his . . ." She trailed off, too uncomfortable to say more.

"It's okay," Kiru said. She didn't need to say anything else. He closed his eyes, searching through his memory. "There's one here in the kingdom!" he said in realization. "It's in the prize room under the Grand Academy Stadium."

The elf nodded. "I know of it. But it's going to be harder to obtain than you might think." The stadium was part of the Royal Academy's grounds, which was situated on a secluded island on a lake. The stadium itself was underwater beside the island. It only arose once a year during the Warrior Games.

On that realization, Kiru's heart fluttered in trepidation. Getting into the games was the best way to gain access to the prize room. The other way would be trying to swim deep underwater while the room was hidden or sneak into the prize room during the competition, while posing as a simple spectator. Ignoring the need to possess either superb stealth or swimming skills, he would need to steal the key to the prize room. That seemed unlikely, given Kiru had no idea where the key would be in the first place.

Being a psion gave him a lifeline to somewhat recover from his injury. It gave him the chance to one day move and appear uninjured, but how in the world would he be able to fool so many high-level cultivators to even look like a remotely passable candidate? How could he impress a recruiter? Kiru gave a slight smile as some hope kindled in his heart. That librarian had given him a free pass to get into the academy *if* he reached Gold. Still, they wouldn't take him if he looked unable to move. Now, he just needed to make himself not appear disabled. The thought of that would have been laughable just yesterday. Now, though, he wouldn't discount it. He had made his arm move with mana alone.

"Looks like I'm going to have to enroll in the Royal Academy," he said.

"Absolutely not!" his mother retorted as she stood up. "We need to be covert, not flaunt you right in front of the nobles of the kingdom!"

"Do you know of a better way?"

She opened and closed her mouth a few times, trying to think of some response. Nothing came out. Eventually, she sat down and sighed.

"It's the only way that I know of right now, Mom. You know it," Kiru said, trying to be both gentle and understanding. "No one knows I'm a Chromebane, so I'm safe in that regard. If we find a better plan, we can go with that, yeah? Oh, also, I have a guaranteed spot with that coin from the strange librarian. So, I'm good to go, as long as I reach Gold." He gasped in sudden concern. "My coin! Did you get my coin?"

She smiled and nodded.

Kiru sighed in relief.

His mother didn't say anything else for a good while. She just stared at the fire, likely contemplating their situation and her son's words. Eventually, she spoke. "I don't like it, but you're right. You need to get busy to reach Gold-rank, then. I trust your father imparted some enhanced cultivation methods for your mental mana?"

Kiru closed his eyes and searched the recesses of his mind. It was dark with the exceptions being pockets of light in the blackness. The lights were of various hues and intensities. Some were bright, while others were more muted. When he focused on the light, he was granted the specific information his father had left him.

Kiru checked each light and he focused on the information each presented him. There were the locations of the artifacts, information about mental mana in general, information about his Telekinesis technique, and the advice given by his father's hologram. Kiru also noticed that the light representing his father's advice and the one for mental mana information were more dull whereas the one that had the artifacts' locations shone the brightest.

Kiru pondered why that would be the case. Fortunately, understanding eventually came to him. *It's the depth of knowledge I'm given regarding those* things, he thought. The circlet had granted him thorough and specific knowledge regarding the artifacts' locations, but much less in regards to mental mana as a whole and the information the hologram was able to teach. While admittedly frustrating, somehow Kiru also knew that the duller shades of light could brighten one day, meaning he could get more information. He reasoned that when he acquired another artifact like his circlet, he may be granted more knowledge.

In a mixture of sadness and hopeful optimism, Kiru opened his eyes and shook his head. "Unfortunately, enhanced cultivation was not one of the things the circlet contained. Looks like I'm gonna have to just go with the standard method of cultivation for now."

His mother stood and paced back and forth, pondering while tapping a finger to her mouth. "No, that won't do. You need a teacher."

Kiru gave the woman an incredulous look. "A teacher? Where? My father implied I'm likely the only psion left."

"Indeed," the red-haired elf answered. She smiled, "That doesn't mean that we can't find someone, or something, to teach you." She then reached inside her bag of spatial storage to pull out another high-quality item. It was a smooth, round, light blue rock which was pulsating with a faint light. "This is a familiar stone. I will admit my knowledge on these things are lacking. What I've come to understand is that it has been given the power to bond with your core and become a permanent siphon. In exchange, it uses the mana the core's aligned with to summon a spirit that lives from the ether. Essentially, it creates a creature that utilizes your mana and acts as your companion. If we can find something that uses your mental mana, they may be able to teach you."

Kiru shrugged in easy acceptance. He trusted his mom. She had sacrificed so much. She had to stay in isolation, away from her family, to protect him all his life. He had no reason to doubt her. The psion also couldn't think of any better alternative. "How do I use it?"

"Simple. You place it in your hand where it can bind and resonate with your mana. After a period of time, the stone will shatter, and your familiar will appear."

"Just like that?"

"Just like that," she said, and turned Kiru's palm up. She promptly put the stone in his hand and set them both on his lap before walking away.

Not knowing of any faster way for him to advance himself in the meantime, Kiru closed his eyes and practiced the basic standard cultivation method everyone knew. The mana supply the circlet had used was now blocked off from Kiru, preventing the young psion from drawing on any more of its power. Still, that didn't mean he couldn't cultivate mana at all. Mana was everywhere, and it was the source of power that molded the world and gave everything life. It was also extremely variable, resulting in innumerable types. Despite that, however, mana was still mana.

Through the standard method, Kiru visualized the base mana being drawn into his body and directed to his core. The unabsorbed mana was then excreted out through the body's natural processes. The only notable by-product was a strange, sulfurous odor to the waste. That was why the outhouse by the school was literally the worst in all of Bristleton, as it had the highest concentration of cultivators using the standard method.

Kiru was unsure of how long he cultivated. He had even drifted off for a while once. However, eventually, he was startled by the sound of cracking. He opened his eyes in time to watch the familiar stone shatter. Despite its small size, the stone sounded like a glacier breaking, and a cloud of smoke erupted from the stone in his hand.

A deep, villainous, menacing voice came from the smoke. "Wrahahahaha! Free at last! You have chosen wisely to bond with me, mortal! Together, we shall . . ." The voice trailed off as the smoke dissipated, revealing its source.

It *really* didn't match. There, standing on Kiru's hand, was a small demon. It was thin, almost sickly, with a hunched posture. The little fiend had blood-red skin, beady yellow eyes, and a long, curved nose. And the top of its head was . . . missing. There, for all the world to see, was a bright pink brain that was clearly exposed!

This creature was an ugly little thing, and it didn't seem to realize it as the demon looked down on its body, as if for the first time. He then looked up at Kiru, who just looked back at the hideous thing, mouth agape.

"Yes, gaze upon my magnificent form, mortal. Together, we shall destroy all who oppose u—"

"Oh no, an imp? Ugh," Surturia said, interrupting the small demon's tirade.

The imp turned to the woman. He looked affronted by the insult.

"I am not just any imp, she-elf. I am a psychic imp!" he declared, then raised himself up to float in front of her in a display of his power. "Now, bow before my master and I, or I'll . . ."

"You'll *what*, imp!?" Surturia interrupted, staring daggers at the audacious creature. She exuded a fraction of her power, and the small demon fell a couple of feet to the ground, landing square on its ass.

"The . . . the Flamebringer," the demon said with distinct reverence, then quickly hopped off Kiru and bowed to the woman, both knees and exposed brain touching the ground. "I'm sorry for any offense, Flamebringer."

"Your master is my son! You would do well to remember it."

The imp nodded furiously.

"Now, explain how you're here, imp. My son cannot use fire mana any longer, so you shouldn't have been summoned."

The imp had an uncomfortable look on his face that said, "I'm about to tell my superior they're wrong, and I fear retaliation," but the imp, to his credit, answered her question. "That is not true in my master's case. We familiars are created from taking an unbound spirit floating around in the ether between the realms of the World Tree and fusing them with the mana that make up the core of our masters. My master has two cores, a fire and a mental one. Though his fire core is not functional, it is still there. The stone acted as an anchor point for my spirit, and it bonded with not only my master's fire core but with his mental core as well."

Kiru was surprised at the imp's answer, not suspecting it would know so much about Kiru's complex situation. Sumiko shared the same expression as him, making the psion think she felt the same about the little demon. Kiru would have to figure out how the imp knew who his mother was, though, at some point.

Surturia seemed to be satisfied with his response. "Very well. Since my son created you, you are loyal to him, yes?"

"Of course, Flamebringer. Together, we will destroy all enemies before us! They will cower before our power and our wrath!" the imp said, before letting out a villainous laugh.

Kiru decided to not bring that up for now. "Can you teach me to cultivate mental mana?" he asked, eager to learn.

"Of course, Master," the imp bowed. "As a creature created from mental mana, I know well how it works in concept."

"In concept?"

The imp grimaced slightly. "Yes, since I have been recently summoned from the ether, my methods of cultivation are untested. They're theories I've developed from my understanding of how mental mana works. The methods should be much more effective than any base method, however."

Kiru shrugged—or he would have if he could. This was still his best bet. He would just have to be this imp's guinea pig. "Very well, what do I call you?"

"You may name me, Master, but if I may, I'd prefer something that demonstrates my glorious form like *The Destructor!*"

Kiru fought to suppress a chuckle. "Probably not that."

"How about *The Mind-Bender? Captain-Killer? Will-Breaker?*"

"I get the point. Unfortunately, those names are rather long." Kiru didn't want to divulge the fact that, while those were great titles for some character in a story, they were terrible name options for a companion. It didn't inspire trust to have a familiar named *Will-Breaker.* "How about William?"

"William?" the imp asked, saying it slowly as if he was tasting it. "What does this name mean?"

Kiru truly didn't know. *Guess it can mean whatever I want it to.* "For you, it's short for Will-Breaker." He sold the pitch off with a wink.

The ugly imp stroked his chin. "Hmm, William. Yes, I am William. Tremble in fear before me!" he declared.

Kiru and his mom shook their heads at the ridiculous little familiar, and then she took her leave to go forage for food. Despite having rations, she wanted to make sure they had plenty of extra.

"Now, Master, let's begin your mental mana cultivation. First, put your body in the lotus position."

Kiru sighed and took the time to fill William in on all the necessary details: his royal heritage, his paralysis, and his overall plan to reclaim the throne.

The imp actually took most of it in stride. He was extremely pleased that his master planned on claiming a throne, and the thought of conquest seemed to animate him.

William did grimace in frustration at his master's paralysis, however. The little demon reminded Kiru of a child pouting. He grumbled about having such a weak foundation to build off of. Despite that, the imp helped position Kiru into the lotus position. It was almost comical to watch the little demon strain his small body to move the psion limb by limb. He was determined, however, and did manage to get Kiru in place. Once in the correct position, William took a good minute to catch his breath, then began to teach Kiru about cultivating mental mana. "First, imagine drawing mana directly from outside into your core through your head, through *only* your head. Instead of drawing mana through your pores, think of your head as one big pore."

Kiru focused. William's instructions were simple in concept but much harder in practice. Eventually, after half an hour and much grumbling from the malformed imp, Kiru could feel the flow of mana. It was all around him. Kiru could sense it being drawn into his head as if he was a drain and the mana around him was water. It was pulled inward but at a very slow pace, making Kiru feel as if there was some kind of clog obstructing the rate at which the mana was drawn. Despite that, it did seem that the mana was still being absorbed faster than the standard method.

Most of the mana was going into his core than from the standard method too. That meant that, overall, he was gaining more usable mana more quickly. He told William that, and the imp explained that it was because there was less distance for the mana to travel to be filtered out, so there was more to infuse into his core.

"Now, we are going to work on building mana meridians."

"Meridians? But I'm still a Bronze. I can't build meridians until I'm at least Silver," he protested.

"What do you know about meridians?"

Kiru frowned defensively. "What do *you* know about meridians? Technically, I summoned you to life not even an hour ago."

William growled but quickly composed himself. He replied to his master with forced calm. "That is true, but need I remind you, *Master*, that I was born from an unbound spirit fusing with two mana cores. So, it seems to be the reason that I *may* know more than you."

Kiru fought to not roll his eyes. He failed. "Fine, meridians are channels that cultivators . . . open in their bodies with mana to allow it to flow better through them. People have to open them all to ascend from Silver to Gold-rank."

The imp nodded, acting like some sort of sage, the cocky little thing. "And where does it say that cultivators cannot start to open them before Silver Rank? Also, where does it say cultivators cannot create their own extra meridians?"

Kiru was at a loss for words, "I . . . uh . . . don't know."

"Exactly," the villainous-sounding fiend said as he snapped his finger. "There is no rule that says so! So I want you to make an extra meridian that directs the flow of the mana going into your head to wrap around the inside of your skull. Once you master this, I theorize that you will ascend from Bronze to Silver much more rapidly than any fools who would dare challenge us."

Kiru grumbled to himself, skeptical of the imp's claim.

At that, William cleared his throat and amended his statement. "You should be able to do this quickly. Just close your eyes and visualize yourself extending out a new path of mana outward from your core like pulling from a spool of string. Once you understand that, it should be easy. I do suspect this will take you much longer than your previous feat, though, Master. So I will go and do what I was created to. I will conquer!" The imp set off after a squirrel who had crawled into their hidden oasis like he was the fabled Midgard emperor Iskandar.

Kiru sighed in irritation. He was going to say something, then he realized with some surprise that the familiar actually *was* summoned to conquer, just not as the imp intended. His helping Kiru would help the psion conquer and reclaim his kingdom. Plus, William hadn't been openly malicious toward him yet, and rapidly ascending to Silver did sound tempting. So he let the imp have his fun, even though he was a terrible hunter. William liked to announce his attempts to pounce and would cackle much too loudly when attempting to sneak up on his prey.

Kiru knew meridians to be paths of mana throughout the body. He knew that they gave cultivators access to use their mana more easily since it could flow through their bodies readily without risk of self-harm such as he dealt with when he used the fire mana on his palm. Still from his conversation with William he realized that he knew surprisingly little about meridians as a whole. The concept of opening meridians before Silver was mind-boggling and eye-opening. It was as if the little imp opened some metaphorical curtain to allow for Kiru's understanding.

*What else have I always believed to be true that isn't?* he thought. With that settled, the psion closed his eyes, focused inward, and began his attempt to direct the mana to form a meridian.

# CHAPTER NINE

# Silver

For the next month, Kiru practiced trying to form his first meridian by forcing his mana into a circle around his mental core. Every day, though, he became more convinced that this method was more of an exercise in futility. William became grumpier and more frustrated with the lack of progress as he wanted instant results. Patience was definitely not the strange imp's virtue.

A personal challenge for Kiru was attempting to switch positions from standing to sitting and vice versa. He was like a toddler on wobbly legs or a limp puppet being forcibly moved by a large string on his back. It either looked like he had an uncontrollable tremor or that all his limbs were limp, which in fairness, they were. Still, he worked hard to make the actions looks as smooth possible.

Kiru and William had at least one good argument every week, and on more than one occasion, the psion tried to use his Telekinesis to fling the ugly imp into the pond. Unfortunately, William's exposed brain wasn't just for show, and the imp used his own telekinetic technique to counter Kiru's, rendering it null. Kiru was often frustrated that he couldn't dish out richly deserved retribution for William's pranks.

Like a mischievous cat antagonizing their owner in the middle of the night, William occasionally farted right on Kiru's sleeping face. When Kiru would wake up in disgust, the imp would run away, shouting over his emaciated shoulder that once Kiru reached Silver, he would stop. Kiru was typically still half-asleep, so he wasn't able to focus and use his Telekinesis on William before he got away.

As if all of that wasn't bad enough, the imp was also a horrendous cook. The first bowl of rabbit stew his familiar prepared, Kiru had taken an enthusiastic mouthful. The overly spiced concoction nearly melted the psion's face off. Even thinking back on it now, he had to suppress a cough. The only consolation was that Kiru got to learn more about the truth of the world and who his mom really was.

Instead of being a mere Gold, she was actually a tier-one Sapphire. Sapphire was a good two ranks above Gold (Ruby being the level in between). At reaching Sapphire, she could form a shroud around her body and conceal her cultivation level from any prying eyes. Well, that was the case unless someone at her rank or higher was actively trying to sense her cultivation level. Apparently, she previously had some sort of enchanted amulet that boosted her concealment ability as well. Unfortunately, though, it only worked as long as Surturia didn't unleash her true power, so it had been rendered useless when she fought off the dwarf assassin and revealed her full strength.

Now knowing his mom's actual capability, Kiru truly understood that she was by far the most dangerous person he had ever met. That assassin hadn't stood a chance! He also learned more about her family and that she was the youngest of three daughters. Her eldest sister was Sorbia, the current queen of Anor'Voren, the country of the elves to the East.

Surturia explained that only a select few individuals within the various countries in the Great Alliance knew of the existence of psions. Those individuals were mainly the rulers of allied nations, the notable exceptions being the dwarven council of Stonereach and the human king of Rowe. She hadn't even known what a psion was until her beloved had shown her.

Still, those who did know the truth about psions played innocent amidst the declaration of their presence and charges against the mental mana cultivators by the Kingdom of Blades. While the kingdom was the smallest of the nations in the Great Alliance, it was without question the strongest and could easily decimate any of the other nations' forces. That was in part due to the training that the kingdom's Royal Academy provided to its citizens and the resultant years in military service required in payment afterward. The other part was due to the Blades being one of only two nations possessing an Onyx-rank cultivator, namely Van Blaine himself.

Van Blaine had interrogated, tortured, and killed nearly everyone associated with Ruken. That made him particularly effective at purging psions. There weren't many to begin with, according to Ruken, so it hadn't taken the wicked noble long to commit psionocide. After the purge, Surturia disappeared. It helped that numerous corpses were rendered unrecognizable during the coup at the royal palace. People had assumed that one of them was hers. She had capitalized on that rumor and refrained from contacting her family.

Hearing her story, Kiru was even more motivated to help. It also emphasized how strong Van Blaine was. Now, Surturia was undoubtedly strong herself. Most commoners never got past Bronze or the middle tiers of Silver-rank. Van Blaine, however, was an Onyx. Only Diamond was higher than that, and to Kiru's knowledge, aside from the gods and greater fiends, the only confirmed Diamond was Nidhogg, but Kiru had attributed it to myth until now.

Kiru also learned why William called his mom "Flamebringer" and treated her with such respect. "Once, there was a small fleet of pirates attacking the northern coast of Anor'Voren. Against my sister's advice, I went out on a small vessel disguised as a merchant to act as bait. I eventually found them attacking a tiny fishing village. Their ships were larger and outnumbered theirs three-to-one. When they saw my vessel, they halted their attack to come after me, thinking I would be a more valuable target. That was their first mistake." Surturia then made a pained face. "I . . . don't know if I should tell you this."

"No, please, keep going," Kiru said, excited to learn more about his mother.

She sighed but then continued. "Their three ships went straight toward me. They were closing distance but still a quarter mile away. Even at that range, I could smell the blood in the air. I could hear cries of despair and pain the villagers let out. Many of them were dead, injured, or taken as slaves as their homes burned. I couldn't take it. Instead of waiting for the pirates to come to me, I rushed to them."

"You rammed your smaller boat against theirs?" Kiru asked.

She chuckled and shook her head. "No, I jumped. Fueled by fury, I leapt off my ship and surged forward through the air as fire mana propelled me. Before I even landed on one of the ship's main decks, all three of the pirate vessels' masts were burning. I let my anger get the better of me then, and I burned every single one of those scum to a crisp." A tear trickled down her cheek. The sadness written on her face stood in contrast to her victorious story.

"Mom, what's wrong?" Kiru asked.

"I was so focused on vengeance that I let it consume me. I nearly used the forbidden Implosion technique during that battle too. With my rage fueling me, I forgot what was important: the villagers. By the time all my enemies were dead, it was too late. The three ships were just pyres at that point. I . . . let them die."

There was a heavy silence after those words. Kiru wanted to ask more, but he waited, letting his mother speak again when she was ready. He began to contemplate her words. *She said she nearly used Implosion? She's able to use a forbidden technique?* he thought.

Kiru had been taught that throughout the nations of the Great Alliance, there were a dozen forbidden techniques. All of them were considered verboten due to some reckless or insidious cultivators who had used them to bring about great ruin and harm. A great example was Overload. Kiru was unsure what Implosion did, but based on his mother's reaction, he knew it had to be extremely dangerous.

Before Kiru could ask her about it, however, she continued. "The villagers who hadn't been taken praised me for slaying the pirates and didn't blame me for what happened to their families. Instead, they instantly forgave me, grateful that I had brought them vengeance. It was after that I was known a 'Surtur the Flamebringer.'"

At those words, Kiru wondered if the librarian had an inkling at who his mother was after all. The revelation made him a bit concerned, but he couldn't dwell on it. Like it or not, Niajar was his ticket to getting into the academy.

She continued, "It took me a long time to process that, to trust myself to be able to control my anger. While I've tried to deal with that guilt, I'm still haunted by the memories of my mistakes." Tears readily flowed down her cheeks at this point.

Kiru's heart sank. He wanted to hug his mother, to provide her comfort, but due to his injuries, he was stuck. So he had to help in another way. "You made a mistake, Mom. That doesn't erase the good person that you are." He smiled fondly as a lesson she had taught him in the past came to mind. When he was younger, he gave a kid a black eye kid who he thought had kicked him. Only later did Kiru learn it was someone else entirely. When he apologized, however, the boy refused to forgive him, even after Kiru offered to let him punch his face in return.

Kiru had felt a lot of guilt then. At the time, his mother had said to him what he now repeated to her: "That pain won't go away. It never will. You're meant to learn from it to be a better person, to use it as a boon for the future, not to lament the past. I love you."

Surturia turned and looked at her son with affection. "My little flame," she said, wrapping her arms around him, "thank you."

Kiru smiled, glad he could help. "Of course, Mom."

That evening, though he was already tired from cultivating all day, and his mother had already retired to her tent, Kiru decided to put in some extra effort and continue practicing. It also didn't help that William was sleeping in his tent and snoring obnoxiously. Not wanting to wake either of them, Kiru decided to cultivate while lying on his cot.

To his surprise, he suddenly had a slight but noticeable increase in the mental mana flowing into his core. He thought about why that would be, and then realization slapped him in the face. *William is dreaming!* he thought.

When Kiru used to cultivate fire mana, he was able to bring in a larger quantity when in close proximity to sources of flame or in direct sunlight, as they exuded more fire mana. *Dreaming brains must produce an excess of mental mana. So if someone is going through complex problems in their head, would that also cause more mental mana? It's worth exploring.*

Using the influx of mental mana, Kiru was more easily able to control the flow of mana moving inside his head. With careful guidance, the mana encircled his brain and his mental core. When he finished, Kiru let out an exhale in amazement. *The damn demon was right!* The psion felt a more concentrated flow of mental mana enter his core than ever before with this ring around it. If he kept it up, his core would be forced to condense, leading to his ascension to Silver.

Because of the increased power flowing through his head, Kiru could also use his Telekinesis for longer and with better control than before. He mentally picked up random items in his tent: a boot, a blanket, then a hairbrush. Kiru noticed how much easier it was and how he felt less strain with the technique.

The psion was able to rotate and move the items with a bit more control too. It was as if he had been moving things with one string and now he could use two. Kiru wasn't a Silver-rank yet, but he was well on his way and much more capable than before. Feeling the high from this progress, he plotted a way to get back at his conniving little familiar for his morning pranks. The teenager stayed up and cultivated all night, keeping his eyes closed to pretend that he was sleeping. When William finally did awaken to find the "sleeping" Kiru, he giggled mischievously and crawled over to Kiru's cot.

The giggling was cut short when Kiru opened his eyes and used Telekinesis on him. Kiru invested more mana than he ever could have before on the technique, and both the amount invested and the surprise caught William off-guard.

The little imp went flying unceremoniously out of the tent and into the pond.

"Looks like your cultivation worked, asshole," Kiru said with a smile at the sound of a hard splash. It was the best morning he'd had in a good while!

Using Telekinesis on himself, Kiru slowly moved to a sitting position. It was definitely not the *most* natural-looking of motions, each leg having to be moved one at a time, followed by him raising up his back But it was still *much* better than his previous attempts. Kiru smiled. He could actually do it! Kiru still couldn't truly feel anything, but man, was it awesome to be able to move again!

William came trudging in looking like a wet bipedal cat, only much, much wetter and uglier. "I see my method worked for you," he grunted. "While normally a great creature such as myself would be offended by your display, I consider this a victory! This means we are even closer to being able to spill the blood of our enemies!" he exclaimed fervently, sounding like a waterlogged tyrant.

"Oh, the blood of our enemies?" Surturia asked as she walked up behind William. "Does that mean you've successfully helped my son reach Silver, imp?"

William's face took on a nervous expression, "Uh, not yet, Flamebringer."

She raised an eyebrow at him, and what looked to be a glove made of pure fire grew around her hand.

Before she could say anything, William hastily added, "But he is making great progress, Flamebringer. I assure you! It is clear your talents have made him a gifted student."

She huffed in amusement before looking to her son and giving him a wink.

Kiru couldn't help but release a little chuckle in return.

Surturia dismissed her flames and began to walk away from the pair. "Very well, imp. Keep up this good work, and we may get to see our enemies' blood quicker than you expect. I'm going to gather firewood and scout for any would-be intruders. Carry on, imp."

Though her back was turned to them, William bowed in deference to the elf. "Yes, Flamebringer." The imp then turned back to Kiru and gave him a savage grin. The promise of future bloodshed had clearly motivated him. "Your next task is to spin the spiral twice more. With three rings, your core should be forced to condense, and you'll make Silver-rank a week after that." He then turned to leave the tent. Before he left, though, he looked back to Kiru. "Oh, and every day you don't reach that goal, I will be cooking your food."

Kiru's eyes bulged. Kiru loved spicy food, but the demon's cooking was an assault on his taste buds. He tried to complain to his mom, but she didn't seem to mind the imp's clearly unbearable food. Kiru wondered what his mother's stomach was made of to not be in gastrointestinal stress after eating the liquid fire that William liked to cook. William may have been sadistic, but he was also effective in motivating Kiru! With this extra "encouragement,", coupled with his new knowledge and familiarity with cultivating and controlling mental mana, Kiru was able to make his second meridian spiral around his core in two weeks versus a whole month.

Summer had turned to fall, and their safe little oasis was slowly being covered in shed leaves and detritus. Kiru was growing more concerned about his stomach from repeated exposure to William's meals. The little demon waved off his concern like it was no big deal.

There was also one other thing that was bothering Kiru. His body was withering. Without constant movement, his muscles had been atrophying over time. That was hard for Kiru to experience. He had apprenticed under the local blacksmith, and he'd developed a strong body because of it in which he'd always taken special pride. Now, though, he was becoming more skin and bone. Kiru thought he might have to wear some baggy robes when he got to the academy, to cover himself.

After another week, Kiru had finally wrapped three meridians around his mental core, tightening them like a spring. Even though it really messed up his sleep schedule, he decided to pull another all-nighter cultivating the mental mana coming off the sleeping imp and his mom. After about five hours, Kiru felt an enormous amount of mana flow into his core—so much so that there was a new, distinct sense of almost heaviness to it.

He was at the threshold.

"William, William!" Kiru shouted.

The imp snapped up in surprise, looking around and snarling defensively before locking eyes with Kiru. "What is it, Master?" he asked in clear frustration at his interrupted slumber.

"I'm . . . I'm ready to ascend! Tell me how to get to Silver!"

The imp's yellow eyes went wide. "I don't know!" he said.

"What?! How do you not know? I've been trusting you with my cultivation this whole time, and you don't know how to ascend ranks?!"

"Hey, I just have a strong connection with mental mana. In terms of ascension, your knowledge is as good as mine."

Kiru grunted in irritation. "Then go to my mom's tent and get her, quick!"

The imp scurried off to do as he was bid.

Surturia came in a minute later. Though her eyes were tired, she had a smile on her face. "Is it true?"

Kiru nodded.

Still, she extended her awareness to sense his power level. When she confirmed it, she gave him a warm smile. "Incredible, Son! Your father would be so proud of you, Kiru. To reach the threshold to Silver just two months." She smiled. "Would you like my help?"

"Yes, please," Kiru answered.

Compared to how his mother had helped his fire mana core condense and ascend to Silver when they were back in Bristleton, getting his mental mana core to that rank was very different. Fortunately for Kiru, the way to ascend to Silver-rank was pretty similar to his previous work in developing meridians around his core, only this didn't require as much fine-tuned control.

Kiru had to just force the mana churning wildly inside his core to spin in a guided pattern that matched the spinning of his meridians around it. It took some effort. The psion found it like stirring molasses versus a watery soup. It required a lot more concentrated effort. What helped most was the advice from his mom that he had to keep the mana rotating inside his core consistently.

After about ten minutes, he was able to get it moving as desired. Once that was done, his mother told him to spin it faster until his core vibrated. That part took about half the night to achieve as getting the thicker concentration of mana to move even faster to get it to vibrate without also causing it to leak was a delicate balance. Simply put, it required some trial-and-error.

Kiru clenched his jaw as his head shook from the vibrating core inside him. "What now?" he asked through gritted teeth.

"Now I want you to exert your will on the core, using the meridians you've made, to squeeze down and condense it until it's no longer vibrating."

The paralyzed teen nodded, even as he shook from the exertion. Sweat and impurities were being forced out from the pores all over his body. Kiru drew his senses inward once more and exerted his will on the core. He imagined a hand wrapped around the orb and squeezing down in a slow, firm motion as if it were made of clay. The core resisted, pushing against Kiru's will as if it *wanted* to continue stirring self-destructively.

Kiru would not quit, though. Whether they realized it or not, the people of the world were relying on him; even more so, *he* was relying on him. He had been made weak and reliant on others, but he was now given the rare opportunity to overcome that. To never feel that fear of being unable to control his body again, of being unable to defend himself. No matter what it took, he *would* tame his core.

Kiru didn't know how much time had passed, but finally, the power inside him condensed, then blossomed. It was as if his core possessed a small storm that was now under his control. *Silver!*

Kiru focused again on his environment, and he opened his eyes. His mother was smiling, but it looked pained. William was pinching his nostrils closed with one of his clawed, bony hands while waving his other hand in front of his face and sticking his tongue out in disgust. There was a putrid odor to the air, but Kiru didn't give it much attention as his body was running on pure adrenaline. Using his mana and enhanced control from ascending, Kiru activated his Telekinesis once more, slipping it over his whole body to stand. He raised his fists up in the air, declaring, "I've done it!" before collapsing to the ground once more.

# CHAPTER TEN

# Who's the Boss?

Kiru woke up later to the sight of his mother and William looking over him, the latter patting his forehead with a towel as his mother pressed a hand to his cheek lovingly and said, "Well done."

Kiru smiled. "How long was I out?"

"Two days, Master," William answered. "And I'm glad you're up now. You . . . reek, and that's coming from a demon." He used his free hand to pinch his large nostrils closed to emphasize the point. Kiru peeked down to confirm that all of his clothes were stuck to his body from a layer of sweat.

"The Flamebringer was insistent that we don't move you, or it would interfere with your recovery. Now that you're awake, though, she can clean you up. I'm going to get some air."

"No, you're not," she retorted. "I may be his mother, but you're his servant. I think this will be a good bonding moment." At that, she gave the imp a predatory grin. "Once *you're* done, come find me. We must discuss our next steps." She quickly left the two in the tent.

Both Kiru and William just looked at each other awkwardly for a moment before exchanging sighs. The imp gave off the impression that he didn't want to clean all the waste off Kiru, and the half-elf didn't want to be taken care of.

Then Kiru smiled, recalling that he was no longer a Bronze-rank; he was Silver! Using his Telekinesis technique, Kiru stood up. It was still shaky. His movements were more like a puppet on strings rather than a person in full control of their neurological functions, but with him being able to move now, the cleaning process could be done sooner.

The pair went down to the water. Kiru saw his reflection and was surprised to discover that the bronze jewel embedded in his forehead was now silver. Apparently, the gem reflected his current rank in cultivation of mental mana. After the awkward process of having an imp clean all his . . . crevices, Kiru and

William walked back over to Surturia. Kiru was now wearing clean, simple clothes, which he was grateful for. Even though he could move a little, even able to walk on his own, it was still odd and jerky for Kiru. It was rather strange not having tactile sensation of his body as he moved across the island. The first time he tried to sit his body down on a stump by the fire, he fell straight on his back. It looked like having a proper sit-down without any back support was beyond his current fine motor skill level.

Kiru's mother was sitting across from him, writing in a small notebook. After Kiru laid his body down with his back against the tree, she snapped it shut. "You should take your time to adjust to being a Silver again before rushing to Gold," she said.

Kiru furrowed his brow. "Take my time? Time is not on my side, Mom. I need to reach Gold. Staying at Silver gets me nowhere."

"No, taking your time to get used to your new level of power will help you establish a better base to build from. If it's not done properly, you could permanently hamper your growth," she retorted.

"Well, it's a good thing that I have you here to make sure I do it *properly*," Kiru said, his resolve unchanged.

Surturia's lips twisted and her nostrils flared. She let out a deep exhale though her nose and conceded the point to her son, "Fine. What do you know about going to Gold, Little Flame?"

Kiru shook his head. "Nothing."

She looked to William. "Imp?"

William took on a sheepish appearance and scratched behind his right ear nervously. "Uh . . . my knowledge is a bit limited when it comes to Gold and above, Flamebringer. I was able to gain understanding of the concepts of mental mana but not much more during my time in the ether. I know the meridians in the body must be activated, but I do not know how or even how many there are," he admitted. Not wanting to anger Surturia, however, he bowed. "But please, Flamebringer, tell us how to get my master to Gold-rank, so that we may make our enemies tremble before our might."

Kiru's mom nodded with an amused half-smile. She tossed the notebook to Kiru, who halted it with his Telekinesis. "That has information on ascending to tier-one Sapphire, specific to my cultivation path. I wrote it down in hopes to teach it to you in the future," she said with a hint of somberness. "Still, while it's almost useless now, some of the basics in there may help."

Before Kiru could start to read, William was there at his side. "Oooh! Gimme!" he shouted and quickly stole the notebook from Kiru, opening it to the page about Gold. Then he haughtily cleared his throat and began to read aloud as if he were a wizened scholar giving a lesson. "It says there are three tiers to the Gold-rank.

They are Zeta, Beta, and Alpha. Each of those tiers is dependent on the number of techniques you know."

The imp continued, "Now, it says there are two steps ascending to Gold. The first is saturating your body in your specific type of mana to activate the meridian pathways naturally carved into your body."

"Yes," Surturia confirmed. "With each of the six main meridians opened, your power and thus your tier in Silver increases until you open the final one. Then, you just need to affirm your path.

"Affirm his path? What does that mean?" William asked.

Surturia nodded sagely, as if expecting the question. "Cores are naturally tied to one's soul and their identity. In order for one to be able to ascend to Gold-rank, one must truly have an understanding of the mana they cultivate and path they follow."

Kiru cocked his head slightly. "By path, do you mean cultivation path or a more vague sense, like why I do the things I do?"

"Your cultivation path, Kiru. Take me, for instance. Even though I cultivate fire mana, my path can be completely different from others. I am on the Path of Fiery Doom, while my eldest sister is on the Path of Phoenix Fire. Above all, what matters is *how* we use our mana. Once you open your six main meridians, you will need to accept your path and affirm it. Only then will your soul be in sync with your body and help you ascend."

Kiru grimaced. *I knew Mom was scary, but the Path of Fiery Doom?* He knew not to mess with his mother when she was angry, but that just brought it to a whole new level. *She must've struck fear into those who saw her in the battlefield!*

Kiru's focus then turned from his mother to thinking about how he himself was going to grow. It certainly was not going to be easy. *First, how am I going to saturate my body with mental mana?* If he could still cultivate fire mana, going to a volcano would be the easiest way to find an abundance of that specific mana type, but for him, that was going to be harder.

Second was his path. Almost every cultivator who aspired to reach at least Zeta—the first tier within the Gold-rank—had an experienced teacher in their particular type of mana who would guide them in the same cultivation path. Sure, one could argue that it suppressed individuality, but teaching others an established path was undeniably effective. Kiru had no such luck. While William had been instrumental to Kiru's base understanding of mental mana, it was clear that the imp was no wise instructor. That meant Kiru was going to have to trailblaze a path on his own.

He expressed his concerns to the others.

His mother nodded in agreement. "That is difficult. Your father would have known the best way to help, but I am uncertain. As for your path, even though you have no typical teacher, you don't need one. You just need to think about how you currently use your mana and how you plan to use it in the future. Inspiration will come to you then."

Kiru understandably had difficulty with both of the necessary steps to ascend to Gold. It required him to truly affirm who he was and who he wanted to be, syncing himself with the mana in his core in addition to finding a place that was abundant in his unique type of mana. He could tell why going for Gold-rank was challenging for many people and why so many never made it there. A lot of people could spend their entire lives having never fully grasped who they were. Also, if you were in some sort of area that didn't match your type, say a desert for a water mana cultivator, it could take you a lifetime to accumulate enough mana to activate your meridians.

Six months were left until the next wave of recruiters made their rounds throughout the kingdom to seek out new students. Kiru believed that he could make it this year. He spent the next couple of months cultivating, pondering his options on where to find enough mental mana to saturate his body, and getting aggravated at his apparent lack of them. Sure, more mental mana was available from his dreaming familiar and even his mother, but it wasn't nearly enough to flood his entire body. Meanwhile, Surturia grew frustrated at her inability to help her son and frequently left the hidden cove they made camp in. She kept herself occupied by hunting and scouting the surrounding area for possible threats. The elf would also gather firewood for them as well.

Eventually, after those months, an answer to one of his issues came to him by pure accident.

Kiru and William were fighting once more. The bloodthirsty imp was angry at Kiru's lack of progress as well as his lack of "conquering foes," so he stole a section of Kiru's squirrel kabob. He greedily scarfed it down before the half-elf could stop him. Kiru chased him around, moving around limply like a living puppet, occasionally falling over due to his exasperation ruining his control.

William laughed in pure glee, having a blast as he easily avoided Kiru's repeated dodges at him. Eventually, the little demon ran up the one tree on the island, now devoid of its leaves as winter was in full swing. As Kiru ran up to the tree, the imp decided to turn the tables on this cat and mouse game. The familiar jumped down off the tree, yelling some strange phrase: "Cowabunga!"

Kiru's body, though mobile, was moved purely by mana. To emphasize the latter, his muscles had continued to atrophy as time passed, making him look more and more skeletal. So, when William came crashing down, he was easily able to tackle Kiru to the ground, forcing the psion on his back.

Kiru groaned and reflexively moved his head up. "Get off of me!" he shouted.

"Hahaha! No, I'm bored, and this is fun!" William declared. "We haven't gotten to crush any of our enemies yet, and though you're my master, you've been acting like a weakling. So, I'll be the master now!" The imp pressed his hand on Kiru's forehead and shoved him down.

"Hey!" Kiru shouted. He began to raise his head once more, but William was there to immediately push him back, laughing . . . well, impishly.

"Look at you! You don't even have the strength to raise your head. I've decided. I should be the master now."

Kiru scowled and tried to raise his head once more.

This time, William just kept Kiru's head pressed firmly against the ground. He quickly scanned around for Surturia. After he confirmed that she wasn't there, he gave a bloodthirsty grin. His ugly face was just inches away from Kiru's nose. "Say it. Say I'm the master, weakling!"

Kiru scowled. The bloodthirsty little bastard was staging a coup! "I'm the master. I will be king!" he spat.

"Ha! I thought so, too, but you can barely stand, and even though you've ascended, you're still so weak! I am clearly the stronger of us, so I should be the master. You can't even raise your big head against me! If you could, maybe I'd consider you up to the task, but you're clearly not. Just say it! I'm the master!"

Kiru scowled. William was right. He was still too weak to achieve his goals. His neck wasn't even able to push against the imp's strength. No, he was no longer a vitaldrain; he was a psion. If his body wasn't up to the task, his mind was. Kiru had never used Telekinesis on his head before. Still, having sensation from the neck up, he never needed to.

"No, you're not!" Kiru shouted, his voice echoing through the hidden glen. With his mental mana surging through the meridians in his head, and the target of his ire touching his head, the strength of his Telekinesis was magnified. Like a catapult, Kiru's head shot up and launched William off of him with violent force.

The imp's body crashed into the tree, cracking some of its bark and dazing the familiar. By the time William's eyes regained their focus, Kiru was on him. The psion wrapped a hand around his body, squeezing down. For extra measure, he also used Telekinesis to bind and squeeze the imp tightly. It was time for them to truly understand their relationship.

There was a rather large koi fish in the pond surrounding the island. Kiru was pretty sure it was one of the rare, highly evolved creatures known as sacred beasts. They were usually stronger and smarter than their counterparts, and this fish was no exception. Instead of dumbly biting any bait from a lure, it only went after certain prey. Like William. On more than one occasion, the imp had nearly been swallowed whole from the fish jumping out of the water in attempts to eat him.

So it was not shocking that, when Kiru went down to water level and held William just above the edge of the lake, the imp began to panic. "Say it," Kiru growled.

William continued to flail about in his grasp, repeatedly grunting the word "No." His attempt to move himself via Telekinesis was failing, so he started to claw and bite at Kiru's hand. But Kiru couldn't feel a damn thing. Still, he needed the imp to focus. He dunked his familiar in the ice-cold water and raised him back up to stare directly into his beady yellow eyes. "Say it. Say, I'm the master."

William started to shiver, his eyes racing back and forth, scanning for a way out and for the koi of his nightmares. Sure enough, there was a loud splash, and the small demon turned his head just in time to see the shimmering scales of the koi's tail sinking back underwater. "Grah! Lemme go! I'm the master, me!"

Kiru didn't like that answer. He dunked the small imp into the water for a few intentionally dragged-out seconds before pulling him up. The fish was swimming straight for the meaty morsel that was William.

William let out a large gasp. "Gah! You're the master. You're the master! Please let me go! I promise I'll never challenge you again, just please don't let it eat me!" he pleaded.

"Swear it," Kiru growled.

"I swear! I swear!"

"On your soul," Kiru said seriously. In Alterra, swearing on one's soul wasn't just mere words. It was literal and came with grave consequences to those who broke the promise. Usually, it was an inescapable, painful death as one's soul was ripped to shreds from the broken vow.

The imp swallowed hard and looked the psion in the eye. "I swear, on my soul, that you're my master, and I will never betray that, ever again."

Though Kiru's body was devoid of most sensation, Kiru did feel the vow, somehow. The koi made a dash for William, but Kiru raised his familiar out of reach even as the fish leaped out of the water to try to grab him.

William let out a sigh of relief, but that was short-lived.

While he now trusted that the imp would no longer act like a childish bully, Kiru was still pissed off. Utilizing his Telekinesis, he pitched the imp with serious force at the tree. William let out a scream of panic, crashing hard into the plant. At the thump of impact, Kiru began to worry. He hoped he hadn't squashed his familiar's exposed brain with that throw.

Fortunately, William's fleshy pink brain was still undamaged. The imp was standing in some sort of humble position by the tree, expectantly waiting for Kiru like a dutiful servant, but there was a comical, imp-shaped indentation in the tree's bark above him. Despite that trauma, the familiar's disposition had made a complete one-eighty, and he seemed eager to aid his master.

"Thank you for sparing me, Master. I promise, I will no longer doubt your power and nature."

"My nature?" Kiru asked.

"Yes, Master. The way you asserted your dominance was positively blood-thirsty! You were a true conqueror, and I look forward to seeing you use your wrath to destroy your enemies!" William exclaimed.

*He enjoyed that? Of course he would make it all about wrath and violence,* Kiru thought.

Kiru rolled his eyes. At least he and his familiar weren't going to have any issues with who was in charge from now on.

"By the way, Master, how did you get so strong there? You couldn't raise your head against me, then you flung me with great force."

Kiru pondered his familiar's words as he walked over to the fire, remembering that conflict. Even though he couldn't feel his body, he had to keep his extremities warm and dry so as to not lose them to hypothermia. "It must be because of the meridians I created in my head," he said. "The channels of mental mana enhanced my Telekinesis technique when I directed it from the area of the meridians."

"Too bad you didn't extend your channels to forcefully open your meridians on the rest of your body. With the enhancement and control it would provide, you wouldn't look like a silly human puppet anymore." The imp's eyes bulged as he realized what he'd said. "I'm sorry, Master," he apologized, bowing on both knees to the half-elf. "I meant no disrespect."

Kiru liked this new, more respectful William. He wasn't even mad at the comment about being a human puppet. "You're okay, William. You don't need to bow to me."

"Thank you, Master," the imp said and began scraping off the dirt stuck to his brain.

"You know, I think you're right, William."

"I am? I mean, of course, I am. The familiar of the great Kiru the Conqueror is always right!"

Kiru pointedly ignored this new title. He looked at the clothesline his mother had set up and chuckled. He shook his head, not believing that he hadn't realized it before. When a breeze hit any point of the line, the whole line moved. It was all connected. Kiru should be able to do the same, but with his mana inside him! "Believe it or not, I think you've helped me find my path to Gold-rank."

That evening, when Surturia came back from hunting and collecting firewood, Kiru laid out his idea to her. The chance of his finding a location to saturate his meridians enough to open naturally was very low, but that didn't mean he couldn't use a work-around. "Okay. So, if I can't saturate my meridians from mana *outside* my body, why can't I just force them open manually with the mana *inside* my body instead? Now that I have an understanding of how to direct and guide my mana, I should be able to direct it across my body so as to forcefully open each of my meridians, one at a time. It would be slow and arduous, but it should work," he explained.

His mother agreed. "Have you discovered what your path is?" she asked.

He nodded. He opened his mouth to tell her, but she raised a hand to stop him. "Do not say it. Only affirm your path *after* you've opened all your meridians."

Kiru promptly shut his mouth, grateful for his mother's insights.

# CHAPTER ELEVEN

# Going for Gold

Surturia drew out the locations of the paths of the six main meridians throughout the body. They were all connected to the core in his chest, though. Kiru would have to do it differently. Fortunately, meridian paths weren't set in stone, but Surturia's diagram showed what was most commonly formed by those who had their bodies saturated by external mana, so he could use her drawings to guide and help him literally carve out a path for his mana to flow through.

That night, while his mother and William were sleeping, Kiru started forming a new tendril of mana, this time directly from his core. Pulling from his core was substantially easier than from the environment, as it was a much more potent source of his mental mana. Kiru groaned as the mana forced its way across his body. He didn't physically feel it, but having the tendril of mana directly connected to his core gave him a whole new level of sensation: a literal sixth sense.

He forced the mana toward his right arm, which began to shake as he flooded the appendage with the accumulated mana from the core and forced open the meridians inside. Inch by inch, he slowly advanced his mana down the path along his arm his mother had shown him.

It took Kiru the whole night to accurately control the mana flow in his body. Since he'd now been working for hours, his whole body shook from the magical exertion. The length of his arm was much longer and farther away from his core than his head. To continue forcing the mana along the set path, Kiru was required to invest so much more mana than he ever had before. Unlike physical exhaustion, running low on mana was draining to the mind. The closer he came to empty, the stronger the headache that would accumulate. Based off that sensation, Kiru felt like he was going to run out of magical energy before he finished this endeavor.

Eventually, though, after many hours, Kiru succeeded in manually creating his first main meridian in his body. There was a strange snapping sensation as Kiru stopped the mana from going any further, making the palm of his hand the end of the meridian. Breathing heavily, Kiru opened his eyes. He looked down at his arm first, then registered how bright it was inside the tent. The front flaps were open, revealing that it was at least midday.

His mother and William were standing above him, looking concerned. "Did you do it, Master?" William's deep voice asked.

Kiru was weak, too weak to even use Telekinesis at this point. So, he just nodded before passing out from exhaustion. He slept through to the next day. That next morning, while feeling much better, he also noted how much less mana he had cycling through his core. It had taken him months to get to the point where he could attempt to open the meridian through his arm. Accumulating enough to open the others was clearly going to take a significant amount of time.

Surturia's diagram taught him that he had at least five more main meridians to open. He needed to activate his left arm, each leg, his intestinal meridian, and his heart meridian. They were called the main meridians, because all cultivators wishing to reach Gold always had to have at least those six open. Once they were, a cultivator could no longer create any more. That was one of the reasons she also suggested forming an additional meridian to encircle his shattered fire mana core as best he could. It would help prevent some accidental release of fire mana that could harm him, in case someone were to ever strike him where his core was. Also, having more meridians in strategic locations could help improve his cultivation base and aid him in ascending to future ranks.

When during one of his lessons, Kiru asked why most cultivators don't form a lot of extra meridians aside from the main ones, Surturia smiled. She was expecting the question and had a ready answer. "I myself asked the same question during my studies. There are two parts to the answer. The first is knowledge. It is a closely kept secret that one can form additional meridians, and even if you know about them, the knowledge as to *how* to form additional ones is guarded as well."

"So they can hoard more power?" he asked.

She nodded begrudgingly. "Precisely. It isn't a perfect world, and you well know there are many unkind individuals in it." She then refocused on his original query. "Now, the second reason everyone doesn't just go and load their bodies with meridians is how they ascend. If one puts themselves in a place with such strong and overabundant mana of a specific type that they can't control it very well, the mana can forcefully open their main meridians before they even have a chance to make additional ones. That is quite common and happens to many cultivators."

It was an important lesson that he thought about as he dreamed.

When Kiru awoke, though he felt better, he also realized he'd soiled himself thoroughly in his cot. *Guess that's a fun side effect of forcing my meridian open. Let's hope that doesn't happen again.* Apparently, Surturia had expected or smelled her son's condition. When he walked out of the tent, there was soap, a towel, and a set of clean clothes folded right outside. Kiru graciously accepted the items and went to the pond to bathe. William was clearly disgusted by his master's state but forced himself to offer to help.

Kiru waved him off. Despite most of his body still moving around oddly, that was no longer the case with his right arm. That appendage moved smoothly and seemingly with more strength. It was as if he could almost actually *feel* his limb; he was just using his mana as a conduit instead of electrical stimulation through his nerves. He wriggled his fingers and smiled as he walked back to his tent.

After he had cleaned himself off in the wintry water, he put on the set of clean clothes and walked back up the island in the hidden glen. His mother told him to throw his clothes into the fire, because they were no longer salvageable. Kiru complied, and they both wrinkled their faces in revulsion as the scent of the burning, ruined clothing hit their nostrils. Quickly though, it subsided. Kiru noticed that his mother was adorned in a new blood-red robe with embroidered runes. Her thick and wild curly red hair was now forced into a tight bun. Her green eyes were more focused and had flickers of orange light flashing inside them. She had a firm expression on her face and wielded a staff in her hand. Kiru was a little taken aback at the sight of her. She was fierce. She was powerful. He could tell that this was a more "real" version of Surturia. She was serious, yes, but she exuded a degree of confidence and comfort in her adorned equipment that Kiru had never witnessed before. It made him smile slightly.

"It is good to see you are now on the path to Gold, my son. It has been difficult being unable to help you more," she said, with an obvious pang of regret.

"You've helped plenty, Mom. There's nothing to feel bad about," he protested.

She shook her head, "No, I have not helped enough, Kiru." She stood up and looked at him directly in the eyes. "That is going to change now. Since you healed and are now on the path that should bring you to Gold, I will not neglect the rest of your training anymore."

"Training?" he asked, unsure of what she could teach him, due to their different types of mana. But it wasn't cultivation she was talking about. It was combat.

"You know well that the kingdom is a militaristic one. The Royal Academy will require you to not only train in base knowledge but fighting as well. They will teach you combat, warfare, how to fight, and group tactics. Plus, the Warrior Games are not without risk, either."

Kiru nodded. "Okay, so where do we start?"

"You will need to pick a weapon to specialize in," she said, then began pulling items from her bag of spatial storage and setting them on the ground. There was a mace, a pair of knuckles, a bō staff, a dagger, a greatsword, and a pair of short swords. None of them were of any great quality, like his mother's. All were made of iron and had some imperfections—a dent, a chip broken off, flecks of rust. They were adequate for training but paled in comparison to his mother's grand equipment and attire.

Kiru scanned the items. If he were being honest with himself, they were all appealing. Before his injury, he dreamed of becoming a great cultivator warrior, destroying foes with his strength of cultivation and weapon mastery. Maybe he was more like William than he realized.

The little bloodthirsty imp came scurrying up to Kiru. "Master, this is so great! I've been so looking forward to seeing you fight! With Flamebringer's training, you'll be able to spill the blood of anyone who crosses us! Oooh! I should go get a snack!" He scurried off, unable to contain his excitement.

Kiru shook his head. He felt a desire to use all the weapons, but after a minute or so, one stood out above the others. He picked up the pair of shortswords. It was easy for Kiru and his mother to see how much more fluidly his arm with the opened meridian moved compared to his other. The former seemed to function fully normally, while the latter still seemed to just be held up by strings.

His mother smiled. "Good. Now, first lesson," she said. Then in the blink of an eye, she slapped Kiru across the cheek with her staff, knocking the psion to the ground. Kiru groaned and looked up at the elf. "Always fight dirty. Fighting fair won't gain you any points. The only thing that matters is who wins. Ambrose knew that. You must, too."

Being reminded of the noble jerk who nearly killed him hit Kiru hard, cementing his mother's words into his psyche. This was not a game; this was life and death. If he showed weakness, there would be countless others who would take advantage of that and end him. The half-elf let out a shot of anger and swung his swords at his mother.

She easily deflected his blow, then kneed him in his gut.

Kiru gave a cough as some of the air was forced out of his lungs, then grinned. If he wasn't a quadriplegic, that probably would've been painful. Kiru headbutted Surturia square in her nose, the enchanted jewel in his forehead being the only thing hard enough to draw blood. It was just a small trickle, but it was a wound nonetheless.

William sat on the tree, cheering on his master for that attack, excited by the visible signs of damage. "Yeah!"

The fire cultivator growled, but she didn't move.

Despite the effectiveness of Kiru's attack, Surturia's nose was not broken. In fact, the bleeding was from a cut that was barely a scratch. In reality, Kiru was an insect compared to her strength, his drawing blood from his opponent clearly more due to surprise than skill. Surturia could kill him and not even break a sweat. "Good," she said, then tripped Kiru to the ground and whacked him straight in the temple.

Kiru groaned in pain. If his mother hadn't been going easy on him and he didn't have coiled meridians shielding his mental core, that attack would've given him brain damage.

"Second lesson, keep your strengths hidden and try to gauge your opponent's. In war, information, not the sword, is the most valuable weapon. If your opponent doesn't know what you possess, they'll be the ones on the defensive. Then, when they expose a weakness, you strike. Your lack of feeling in your body is both a weakness and a strength, my little flame. Keep that knowledge hidden," she said, then offered a hand to help Kiru up.

Kiru took her hand. She raised him up slightly before punching him square in the nose and dropping him once again. "The third lesson is not to forget the first two!" she shouted.

"Shit," Kiru muttered as he clutched his nose, blood flowing readily from it.

Thus Surturia continued his lessons every day, and he would cultivate at night. Kiru was getting less sleep than ever, averaging around six hours, but his energy level in the morning made him feel like he was getting eight to ten every night. Both his elven heritage and cultivation work were paying off. As anyone continued to climb higher among the ranks, they will need even less sleep, even if it was only a few minutes each time.

The attacks he made with his right arm were stronger and more accurate than his left, reinforcing the benefits of opening his meridians. It was as if he was moving the right arm from the inside out whereas the left required more mana to make less fluid movements. Kiru also realized he had to take fewer breaks to regain his mana when training with his mom. Since he had to use his mana to force his body to move all the time, the psion had to deal with mental fatigue versus something draining his stamina. Adding on having to pay attention to the nuances of combat training—what his opponent was doing, strategy, stances, etcetera—it really hit home how much mental strain Kiru was under. So the psion was forced to take some time every hour or two in order to accumulate enough to use his Telekinesis technique again. He could go on longer, but he was also working to keep enough mana inside his core to open another meridian in the future.

Using the more concentrated method William had taught him had helped with regathering more mana quicker, especially now that he was a Silver with his three additional meridians around his mental mana core. Kiru's mother even noted that, by condensing his core in the manner he'd done, he could absorb mana much faster than most Gold-rank cultivators. She had remarked that the controlled spinning of the mana inside his core made it naturally stronger in drawing more into itself even without Kiru's direct guidance.

After a few months, Kiru had amassed enough mana in his spiraling mental core to create two new meridians. As his mother suggested, he formed an extra meridian in a ring shape around the broken fragments of his fire mana core, creating a protective barrier in his chest. Both the extra meridian in his head and chest seemed to be less taxing on his body compared to when he'd opened his right arm meridian.

*Was it because the extra ones I formed were next to mana cores?* he thought to himself as he watched William nearly getting eaten by a fish again. Funnily enough, William's bane had also grown stronger like Kiru. It was now as big as a shark, according to his mother.

Still musing, Kiru went on to form his left arm meridian. While the task was still difficult, he seemed to cut a few hours off his time, compared to the first attempt on his other arm. Now that he had the meridians fully opened in both of his arms, his prowess with the dual swords immediately improved.

Surturia began teaching him proper elven sword forms, as well. In particular, he had learned at least six dual sword forms within her style, Monarch's Razors. He couldn't say he'd mastered those forms exactly, as his legs were still not the most stable, but he understood the basics enough. It had helped that she had intentionally taught him forms that didn't require much fancy footwork. Both the easiest and possibly most risky form he'd learned so far was a full-frontal lunge attack aptly called Stag's Desperate Charge. It was a simple and straightforward form that was to be used more as a last resort. She promised to teach him more of the complexities once he progressed with his meridians.

To his chagrin, when he was ready to open another meridian, his mother advised that he open his heart and intestinal meridians *before* opening his leg meridians. She said that it would make him more stable throughout his body, increasing the oxygen content his blood carried as well as helping his system better remove impurities. It would also aid in opening his leg meridians, help him become healthier overall, and would be fundamental for living a long life.

Kiru felt a wave of anger at the advice his mother gave him. He wanted to move better, to be able to use the sword forms she was teaching him more fluidly. He couldn't control fire mana like his mother, but he had a chance to be an effective combatant once again. After the nearly-two years of hiding out, recovering, and discovering how to cultivate a new type of mana, his patience at his situation was wearing thin. To know that he could have the ability to move capably again but *not* act on it—that felt like too big of an ask to Kiru.

He wanted to shout. *What does she know about what it's like?!* He wanted to defy his mother's advice. And he was about to do just that, when he felt her hand on his shoulder.

"I know it's been hard. I cannot imagine how difficult the challenges you have been facing, my little flame. Know that I only have your best interest at heart. Trust me, and one day, you'll do even greater deeds than Surtur the Flamebringer ever could," she said with a gentle smile.

Kiru instantly deflated at his mother's loving words. At once, he realized she was right. She had protected, raised, and loved him his entire life. She had earned his trust. So Kiru followed her instructions.

He first manually flooded his heart meridian. Doing so forced Kiru to cough out more than a small amount of blood, but afterward, he felt powerful! It was as if he had strong espresso coursing through his veins instead of blood. The blood pumping from his heart also reinvigorated his lungs, helping him to take deeper and fuller breaths. He felt like he could take on the world! Even though his muscles had continued to atrophy, Kiru's body was stronger than it had ever been.

# CHAPTER TWELVE

# Puppet Master

I t had been two years since Kiru and his mother went into hiding. Two years since he'd started training as a psion. Kiru now measured six feet tall, a few inches higher than his mother. And just as he had grown physically, his relationships with Surturia and William had grown as well. The imp, while undoubtedly mischievous, was now unquestioningly loyal to Kiru. No more half-baked coup attempts occurred, and in addition to their shared violence and bloodshed, William and Kiru also formed a bond over food. Hiding in the wilderness, the available ingredients remained very limited, but Surturia did very well for the trio, particularly when it came to spiced meats.

The imp liked his food way hotter than Kiru would prefer, but they both had an appreciation for the dishes Surturia cooked up, And Kiru hoped that one day William would be able to taste her food when she had the whole spectrum of flavors to work with one day. When he told his familiar that, the small demon was nearly as excited as he was at the sight of bloodshed.

With Surturia no longer having to conceal the truth of her identity, she was able to be more open and honest with her son during their secluded training. At night, if he had finished his sword forms, she would regale him with stories of her youth and teach him about her family—*his* family. William would also listen and cackle gleefully any time there was talk of violence.

Kiru learned of his aunt, Queen Armenia Emberbrand, how she and his mother were close growing up. They were also some of the top cultivators in the queendom. They were nicknamed "The Twin Torches." He also learned that, despite their fondness for one another, his aunt had grown more distant and cold as she began being groomed to rule. In the end, they hadn't spoken for years as Surturia's fiery and emotional nature put them at odds more than once. They undoubtedly loved each other, but a rift had grown that hadn't yet been bridged.

"I hope to rectify that one day," Surturia said.

It was now late summer, and the academy's scouts would be traveling around the kingdom once more to recruit promising new cultivators. Kiru was close to Gold. At his pace, to go from Bronze to Zeta Gold in that short amount of time was incredible. Kiru was aware he needed to keep up that exceptional pace in order to achieve his goals. He knew what he would declare his path to be and had opened every meridian except the ones in his legs.

The intestinal meridian name was a misnomer, as it encompassed every other organ within his abdomen as well. With the meridian open, all of their functions went into overdrive, filtering out waste buildup and impurities in Kiru's system. He had never had to use the bathroom so much within a twenty-four hour period in his life! His mother had said that was normal, though.

As Kiru continued to manually open his meridians, he became more skilled in doing so, better understanding how to control mana flow and its intricacies. That didn't mean there weren't some mistakes along the way. The first time he tried to open his intestinal meridian, he invested too much mana too quickly. The rapid accumulation of mana nearly forced the blood vessels to burst from the increased pressure, so he had to let go of the technique and the months of work he had built up.

Now, though, he was going to open his right leg meridian, and he felt confident that he could do so in about an hour. If he did this right, he would almost have enough to open his other leg immediately. Doing it "right," though, meant he couldn't make a single mistake—not one bit of rushed opening. Still, Kiru felt sure about it.

About halfway through the process, however, something went very wrong. Kiru's core felt the pressure of hostile mana. Someone had found their tunnel and broken the protective ward. Before Kiru could shout a warning, there was a loud *whoosh,* and a sudden wave of heat shot through the tent. Voices clamored outside, including his mother's, and she sounded like she was in danger.

Strong waves of heat and mana shot out from outside the tent. Whoever was fighting Surturia was on another level, almost sending Kiru rocketing from his meditative state.

"Master, Flamebringer is fighting some intruders! We should go and rend their bodies to shreds!" William cried.

Kiru felt panic and fear rush through him. He knew that whoever his mother was fighting was above his ability to combat. He then noticed that there were others much lower in cultivation ranks present as well. He couldn't help his mother with higher-ranked opponents, but he could fight off the others. "My thoughts exactly," he agreed. It sucked, but he had to rush the job of opening his meridians and ascend to Gold. He would not have as much mana to use for fighting, but being at a higher rank could make all the difference. Using his acquired control, he brute-forced the meridian, expending about half of his reserve for opening the other leg.

Kiru stood, feeling much stronger on his "new" leg. He now looked like someone with a leg injury instead of a living puppet, as William had once called him. After Kiru put on his belt with his sword sheaths, William hopped up on his master's shoulder and cackled.

"Now, let the legacy of Kiru the Conqueror be known!" the imp declared as Kiru rushed out of the tent.

He quickly realized that he should have stayed in.

His mother was out on the island. In the entrance and spread around the canyon walls like spiders were at least twenty hooded figures, all brandishing various daggers and blades. It took Kiru only a second to put together who they were: assassins, like the dwarf who'd come to kill him in his bed! All at once, they turned to look at Kiru, malicious grins plastered on their faces. Since his core was Silver, he could now sense, at least to a degree, the ranks of other cores. The rogues they faced ranged from Gold to Ruby, with one Sapphire.

"Give the boy to us, woman, and we'll let you live," a tall, bulky assassin ordered. He stood about a good six feet tall and gave off the same sense of power that Surturia did. Kiru realized that he must be at the same rank. It was evident that this man, brandishing a pair of hooked daggers glowing the sickly green of poison mana, was the leader. Kiru's mother had taught him that this was possibly the most deadly type of mana out there, often just as likely to kill its users as their opponents. Even never having encountered it before, he could tell the mana had a poisonous aspect—even just looking at it made him feel a little sick.

Despite that, Surturia showed no fear. "Even if I were to give up my one and only son, which I won't, we both know you're lying."

The man gave a cracked-toothed grin. "Clever girl," he said with a smirk. That's when the assassins attacked. The ones at the entrance charged while the ones on the wall leaped or flung their knives.

Surturia was ready. Instantly, just as when the dwarf assassin attacked Kiru back at their home, she erected a wall of flames, only this time, it encircled the island they were on completely, forming a protective barrier. The flames incinerated the airborne rogues and the flying projectiles to ashes in an instant, taking out five opponents at once. Feeling the power coming off his mother, Kiru knew his help wasn't needed. He might as well have been a flea offering aid to a dragon.

As soon as the wall of flame disappeared, a fiery cloak engulfed Surturia, completely enshrouding her form in a bright red blaze. Two curled horns jutted out from her forehead. She looked like a fire demon about to inflict doom upon her foes.

The assassins hesitated at the unexpected display.

"If any one of you so much as *thinks* of running, I'll kill you myself," the bulky assassin barked.

At their leader's threat, they came at Surturia once more. Kiru watched in awe as the woman moved faster than his eyes could fully track, outpacing the agile killers around them. She launched a bolt of fire, burning a hole straight through the chest of a dwarf to her right. Then she backhanded a pair of humans with cutlasses to her left. She partially melted one of them. The one who took the brunt of the impact from the cutlass was functionally incinerated by the heat, and their body was knocked into their ally. They both fell into the cold water below with a splash.

Surturia killed about half of the rogues in less than a minute, and the air was now tainted with the scent of burning flesh and sulfur. *This is the true power of a Sapphire-ranked cultivator? How can there be anyone stronger than her?* Even the bloodthirsty William just watched her with a slack-jawed expression. The fire mana cultivator shot out a wave of spikes made from her flames, spreading out in all directions, narrowly missing her son.

"Maybe we should sit this out, just this once? You know, we wouldn't want to steal the Flamebringer's glory," William suggested, trying to save face.

"Agreed," Kiru swiftly replied. When he turned around to hide, though, he discovered that they were not alone. The lead assassin stood a mere twenty feet away, a wicked smile on his face. The half-elf's blood ran cold.

Drunk with his own power, the assassin licked his poisoned blade. His devilish smile never wavered, as he was completely unaffected by his own toxin. In a flash of movement too quick for Kiru to process, he was shoved straight back on his ass.

But the assassin had not struck the boy.

No, when Kiru looked up, his mother was the one standing in front of him. Only her fist, feet, and horns of flame were still present, the rogue's green blade piercing through the side of her abdomen. She coughed out some flecks of blood and gritted her teeth.

"No," Kiru cried. Because the assassin was the same rank, Kiru instinctively knew that if his mother didn't remove the toxins from her system, and fast, she would surely die.

Surturia tried to headbutt the assassin with her fiery horns, but the man jumped back, leaving his weapon embedded in the elf. She fell to her knees from both the disorienting toxins and pain.

He cackled evilly and pointed to her belly, as two of his allies appeared out of the darkness beside him. "Stupid woman. I knew you'd throw yourself in to protect him."

He turned to face Kiru. "The weak die in this world, boy, and because of your weakness, your mother will die, too."

Kiru's heart raced. Before he could respond, Surturia let out a menacing growl. "No, my son is strong. My son will live. He will ascend, and he will watch *you* die instead," she said, spitting out a glob of coagulated blood, extending her palm to Kiru. Immediately, a shield of lava formed around Kiru and William, protecting them from a pair of knives thrown at him by the other two assassins. The killers' eyes went wide as the woman stood up, ripped the sword from her belly, and let out a monstrous roar. Flames spat out of her mouth. "If I die, I'll take you with me!" she screamed, then lunged at the assassins in bestial fury.

The psion watched in dismay as his mother recklessly attacked the three rogues. One of the two lackeys was caught off-guard, and she ripped his throat from his body, Surturia's heated claws carving through his flesh with extreme ease.

William slapped him across the face, shaking him from his shock. "Master, you need to get to Gold-rank, now!" the imp begged with pleading eyes.

"Wha? Why?"

"The Flamebringer, she's imploding her core, and it's only getting worse!" William said in unnerving fear.

"Implosion? But that's . . ." Kiru swallowed the word "forbidden," his mouth suddenly dry.

His mind flashed back to a conversation he had with his mother after one of their sparring sessions. He had finally asked her directly about the Implosion technique and what made it forbidden. She had told him that, unlike Overload, which forced too much external mana into a core, Implosion compressed the whirling internal mana within the core and supercharged whoever dared it. The core—and the cultivator—would soon explode into a violent burst of mana.

It was considered forbidden due to multiple reasons. The first was because of the suicidal nature of the technique. Secondly, it would either morph or incinerate, most often the latter, everything else not at least Gold-rank within a nearby radius. Kiru's heart raced as he now knew that his mother had three minutes before she'd self-destruct in a violent end that could literally change the landscape.

Feeling the heat and power emanating from her, Kiru could see the danger it posed. At Silver-rank, Kiru himself would also burst into flames when Implosion finished!

*How could she put my life at risk like that?* he thought as he furrowed his brow. He shook off his initial reaction, however. His mother wouldn't have saved his life and put him through all this training in isolation just to kill her only child at the eleventh hour. No, she went on this suicidal charge to save him.

*She must believe that I can ascend.*

Despite the whirlwind of emotions running through him, Kiru forced his mind to be the calm in the center of the storm. If he didn't find a way to open his last meridian and affirm his path, he would die. The psion closed his eyes and began draining his mental core as much as possible, hastily opening his meridian. Kiru quickly made progress, but he soon found out he didn't have enough to fully do so.

The psion ground his teeth and groaned from the exertion. Sweat rolled readily down his forehead both from his effort and the heat. He wasn't sure how much time had passed, but he knew it was running out. He was only halfway through, and it felt like he was pushing and failing to go against a downhill current. If he didn't continue the process soon, the backlash from failing to open his meridian so recklessly might cause damage to his new core. He didn't want to experience core damage again. He needed more mental mana. In desperation, he opened his eyes. There was nothing else inside this tiny cage of molten rock except . . .

"William," Kiru forced out.

The ugly little demon looked down at his master.

"Give me . . . your mana," he said through gritted teeth. The psion was mad at himself for not realizing it before. William was made using a blend of both fire *and* mental mana. Of course, the imp had some mana to spare! Kiru had no environment to provide a flood of external mental mana to his limb, but he didn't need an environment. William was a perfectly adequate external source for his current needs.

The familiar seemed to fully understand what Kiru meant, too. He frantically nodded, pressed his squishy brain to Kiru's leg, forcefully flooding the appendage with his mental mana. In a rapid rush of power, Kiru's final meridian opened with a *click*. The psion inhaled, and his body began to once again vibrate. This time was different, though. Unlike his shaking from strain, his body was overloaded with power.

Kiru's vision went white as he approached the threshold into Gold-rank.

Then, William's deep voice hit his ears. The imp sounded exhausted but still tenacious, "Master, Kiru the Conqueror, will you allow anyone to stop you from becoming the king you are?"

"No."

"Will you allow these insignificant cowards to deny you your destiny?"

"No," he answered, practically feeling the drive and anger emanating from his familiar.

"Who. Are. You?"

"I am Kiru the Conqueror!"

"What is your path?"

"I am on the Path of the Puppet Master!" Kiru declared.

His eyes opened as the raging mana coursing through his body instantly yielded to his control, completely bound to his will and path. The mental mana, accepting Kiru's chosen path, molded his broken body to match. His already meager and atrophied muscles were compressed, thinning throughout most of his body, making him look almost skeletal in appearance, at least from the neck down.

His spine had previously been "healed" with Niajar's magic. The elf had Kiru's body form scar tissue to replace his shattered vertebrae and serve as a bridge to reattach the psion's spine, but it still hadn't been able to restore any nerve sensation. The affirmation of his path didn't provide any further healing to his spine either, but it did remold the scar tissue to allow his back to be stronger, more erect, and more stable in the midst of mobility. Lastly, the gem in the middle of his forehead went from Silver to Gold.

It was a good thing, too, because it would assure his safety from the implosion. Kiru immediately turned his head to see his mother outside the cage. She had a dagger in her neck and some kind of sickle running completely through her chest. She had the head assassin's neck in her hands. He was writhing in pain, and he was stabbing at her gut repeatedly. She wasn't fazed. The fire cultivator just scowled and squeezed. The assassin's screams were suddenly cut short as his neck gave way with a pop and his entire head became engulfed in flames. Surturia dropped the corpse to the ground.

The elf, now free of opponents, fell to her knees, the fire inside her burning out. She wheezed and turned to face her son. Her eyes were now just orbs of flames, and her skin was ashen gray with orange cracks running through it.

Her gaze flicked to the gold jewel on his forehead, and she smiled. "I knew you could do it," she said in a raspy voice. "My armor is now yours. I know you'll do me proud. Your father and I love you, my little flame." Then the fire in her eyes went out.

# CHAPTER THIRTEEN

# No Going Back

Eyes brimming with tears, Kiru screamed and reached out for his mother, desperate to stop her fate. It didn't matter. In a flash, an orb of red light shone brightly through Surturia's body. The next instant, it completely disappeared. What followed was a sudden explosion of flame that erupted in all directions.

Normally, a release of unrestrained fire mana would burn everything in reach, but somehow, even as it killed Surturia, it still followed her dying will to protect her son.

Instead of being burned alive, the psion and his familiar were simply struck by the force of the blast. It knocked them back, destroying the cage they were in.

The same couldn't be said of their hidden oasis.

The ground was completely scorched, all grass charred to ash. The large tree was ablaze. Kiru's mother had explained in the past that they indeed had been living in a dead volcano this whole time, and now she had revived the inferno! The water in the pond had been replaced with active molten magma, the typically cool air now stifling hot. Every single bit of their camping equipment was destroyed, including Surturia's amazing bag of spatial storage. William ran up and hid behind Kiru, hanging off his shirt in a desperate attempt to avoid getting scorched.

Kiru was distraught. His mother had died right before his eyes.

All that was left of her was her armor and a small, enchanted storage ring. Despite a few scorch marks, the pieces of gear were, remarkably, still intact. His eyes welled up with tears as he stared at where his mother last stood. It felt as if someone had torn a hole in his chest. His mom, the woman who'd raised him, kept him safe, and put her life on the line for him because she loved him more than she loved herself, was dead. Kiru's heart beat strong and fast. It was the only sound he could hear as the rest of the world around him tuned out. He was truly alone.

His descent into despair was abruptly interrupted, however, when a small red hand slapped him across the cheek, breaking him out of his downward spiral. "Master, we cannot linger. If we want to honor the Flamebringer's wishes, we have to leave!" the imp pleaded.

Kiru just shook his head, still in shock. He put on the ring and clutched his mother's armor, desperate to cling onto the last remnant of his family. Adrenaline pumping through his body, he began to sprint across the stone bridge to the exit, not thinking about the ease with which he now used Telekinesis to move.

Something struck the back of his left calf, the force of the blow tripping him and making him drop his mother's armor. A dagger hilt was sticking out of his leg. He spun around to see another rogue, this one an elf. The power of a fellow Gold-rank cultivator radiated from the assassin.

"Guess it's my lucky day," the elf said maliciously. She brandished a dagger in one hand and a cutlass in the other. Both were made out of pure darkness. A shadow cultivator, then. "With everyone else dead, I don't have to share the spoils. Also, with that asshat of a boss dead, I'll be promoted. Good thing you're not a vitaldrain like our informant had said. That would've taken the fun out of killing you," she said and drew her cutlass back to swing.

Before she could bring it down, though, William struck. The imp surprised the assassin, jumping up from her flank and scratching furiously at her face.

The elf screamed in pain. She grabbed the imp and threw him off, flinging his body hard against the blackened tree. The elf turned back toward Kiru, but the psion was ready now.

Kiru had used the William's distraction to stand back up and draw his short swords. Acting on pure survival instinct, he swung his blades at the woman. The dexterous assassin was clearly used to sneak attacks, though, as she managed to block Kiru—mostly, that is. His new rank gave him a fresh reserve of power, so he managed to push her dagger back to slightly cut her bicep.

The elf gritted her teeth, then kicked him in the chest, forcing him back a couple of feet. She then took a brief moment to gauge his power. "You're already a Gold?! Impossible!" She spat.

The psion glared right back. "It's a good thing you're a Gold. That would've taken away the fun of killing you," he mocked angrily.

"Bastard!" she growled as she readily accepted the bait and charged. The assassin attacked with sharp, quick motions, no large or wild swings. She was going for vital points repeatedly, attacking with increased speed to stay on the offensive.

Kiru, however, was now at Gold-rank. Though his outward appearance was frail and gaunt, he had both power and speed greater than he'd ever possessed before. Plus, he hadn't spent the past two years *just* cultivating. His mother had been teaching him war tactics and a rare elven sword form, the Monarch's Razors. That training was finally paying off.

Kiru managed to block and dodge the repeated thrusts at his body. Though he wouldn't be able to feel it regardless, he still wasn't keen on getting stabbed, if he could help it. He still had a dagger in his leg. No need to add any more injuries. Kiru was able to get in a few surprise attacks, using one sword to block her cutlass and the other's increased range over her dagger, but the injuries were still superficial.

Then, as if a switch had been flipped, Kiru started breathing heavily too. He was struck by exhaustion not from overuse of his body's stamina, but from his core's mana depletion. Though he'd received a fresh reserve of power from ascending, his hasty method of getting to Gold had made that reserve too small for a prolonged fight now. He'd used up almost all he had in having rapidly opened both his leg meridians. He was now almost immediately using up the rest of what he had to move his body in this fight. He was very close to empty. His head ached, and it was getting harder to concentrate. If he didn't find a way to end this, and fast, he would be dead.

The assassin marked his weakening strikes and deflections, too. She finally managed to score a cut across his cheek, then cackled in sadistic glee. "Guess you've hit your limit, boy."

Kiru stared her down. She was right; his body was close to becoming a limp noodle. He needed a plan and fast. He was momentarily distracted by the emergence of what looked to be a shark fin emerging from the pool of lava. He gasped just slightly in realization as he figured out what it was. *The koi fish!* he thought in excitement. That damn sacred beast had survived Surturia's implosion!

As inspiration struck, Kiru consolidated the majority of his remaining mana, allowing himself to fall to his knees. His arm dangled over the edge of the small island above the lava flowing thirty feet below, and his skin started to peel back and burn from the heat. Kiru ignored it, which was rather easy since he couldn't feel the limb. Still, the smell wasn't pleasant. The large fin immediately turned and started toward his direction. *Come on*, he pleaded silently. *Come and try to get this meal.*

The assassin dispelled her dagger and increased the length of her cutlass into a curved longsword.

"Wait!" Kiru pleaded, trying to buy more time.

The assassin shook her head and clicked her tongue. "No, boy. This place is getting too hot for me to handle." She raised her longsword to stab Kiru. "Time to die."

Kiru's eyes widened as the mutated koi fish jumped out of the lava toward him. The thing was bright orange and its scales flickered as if it were made of iridescent flames. Using what mental mana he had left, the psion stopped using Telekinesis on his body and instead focused it all on the large fish. His body went limp as his mind took full control of it, like a puppet master.

As the assassin slammed her sword downward, Kiru flung the airborne fish at her. The sudden appearance of a shark-sized koi completely caught her off-guard, and before she could move to block or even finish her strike, the massive, fiery fish swallowed her whole. Kiru completed the fish's arc, propelling it with his Telekinesis technique until the koi splashed back into the lava on the other side of the island. "Guess she was right. This place *was* too hot to handle," Kiru said in between heavy breaths.

He collapsed with his back to the rocky island, now covered in ash. After a few minutes of the oppressive heat steadily rising inside this re-ignited volcano, he called for William. Despite his fire mana core being shattered, his mother had told him over a meal that he still should have some latent resistance to heat. Even with that boon, Kiru wasn't going to last much longer.

The imp limped over to Kiru, looking just slightly better than the psion felt. "Good job, Master. Guess that damn fish was actually good for something. That woman was the first in a long list of your felled enemies. In time, all will fear the name—"

"William, that's great and all, but could you help get us out of here?" Kiru interrupted.

William's lips made a perfect O, then he looked around the volcano. "I don't know, Master, I mean an imp could get used to a place like this." His musings were cut short when the massive koi fish surged out of the lava to swallow the charred husk of a large bat whole beside him. "After reconsideration, I concur with your assessment, Master," he promptly amended. For the next twenty minutes, the tiny imp slowly pulled Kiru and his mother's armor out of the cave exit from the side of the hidden volcano.

Fortunately, outside the cave, a normal waterfall tumbled from the hillside, seemingly unaffected by the nearby volcano. As the duo exited, the ground began to shake. Apparently, a volcano reignited by a Sapphire-rank cultivator could affect tectonic activity, too. William pressed Kiru's back against the stone outside the hidden entrance the imp had pulled him through. After a couple of minutes, the shaking stopped.

"Thank you," Kiru said.

"Master, from now on, you can do the carrying," the imp replied, then pressed his exhausted body against the stone and sank down beside the psion.

Feeling at least a small modicum of safety, Kiru allowed himself to process what had happened. Tears streamed down his eyes once again as he allowed himself to mourn fully. His mother had died right in front of his eyes. She sacrificed herself for him. If only he hadn't been so weak, she wouldn't have had to take the assassin's poisoned blade. If he hadn't been a liability, she would've handled them all with ease.

The psion wept. William grumbled something in annoyance, but Kiru didn't listen. He was overcome by what had just happened. *It's my fault. I was too reliant, too weak. Because of that, I got my mom killed.*

Abruptly, Kiru's eyes snapped open with fierce determination.

William subconsciously gave a grin as a metaphorical fire was lit within the psion.

Kiru ground his teeth in a mix of anger and resolve. He would never be so helpless again. He would be this conqueror, so that he may never lose anyone dear to him again. Kiru was on his Path of the Puppet Master now. There was no going back. He would either succeed or die trying, and he wasn't planning on the latter.

Now that he was at Gold-rank, he just needed to find the nearest recruiter and show them . . . Kiru gasped. *The coin!* He'd forgotten to grab the damn coin he'd received from Niajar! "Shiiit!" he groaned.

"What is it, Master?" William asked.

"The coin I needed to ensure my entrance! I left it back in the volcano. It's probably destroyed now. Fuck!"

The imp cocked his head like a bemused dog. Then, his beady eyes widened in realization. The imp stuck a couple of clawed fingers into his head, wedging them between his brain and bowl-shaped skull. After a couple seconds, there was a wet sucking noise and *voila*, Niajar's gold coin!

Kiru grinned widely. He didn't even care that it was covered in imp brain goo. "William, you beautiful bastard!" He laughed as tears of relief and joy flowed down his face.

"You're welcome, Master," William managed. The bony imp, seemingly wanting to not get all emotional, coughed, then wiped the dirt from his exposed brain. "Yes, well, we'd better get out of here soon. The sudden resurgence of an active volcano is bound to draw unwanted attention. Not like it matters, though. We'll crush the bones of anyone who defies us to dust," he said, clenching a fist, a manic glint in his eyes. Was he conveniently forgetting that they just had their asses handed to them and were only saved by a giant koi fish?

Kiru rolled his eyes. "Yeah, yeah, sure. Put this armor on me while I cultivate, okay?"

"But, Master, this armor is for females," William protested.

"I don't care, William. Look at me. Any armor is an improvement over a hooded tunic and heavy cloth pants." Kiru noticed he still had the assassin's dagger lodged in his calf, blood still trickling out from it. "Shit," he spat. If he didn't get this wound dressed, he'd eventually die from infection or blood loss. Kiru had William rip a piece of his tunic off, then wrap it tight to form a tourniquet. Before he could give William any more instructions, the imp ripped the dagger out of his leg with a wet *thwack*. Kiru's eyes bulged at his familiar as even more blood flowed from the wound.

He was about to yell at the imp when William raised a hand to wave off his concerns. "Not to worry, Master. I got this," he said. Then his clawed red hand began to glow. With a forceful slap, he pressed it deep into Kiru's wound. The skin began to sizzle, and Kiru winced reflexively, but then realized he still couldn't feel anything. He opened his eyes to see the imp using Kiru's Hot Hand technique to cauterize the injury!

The imp cackled. "You should've seen the look on your face! Haha!"

Despite the gross smell of burning flesh, Kiru couldn't help but give a small chuckle. He was once again reminded that his familiar was created by two types of mana. This creepy, bloodthirsty companion of his could also use the Hot Hand technique that Kiru had used back in Bristleon, only it didn't burn the imp's palm in the process. *Good to know.*

After the familiar finished cauterizing Kiru's wound, he dressed the young psion in Surturia's armor. Kiru took that time to close his eyes and cultivate, giving his severely depleted core some much-needed mana. When cultivating not near a source of readily available mental mana such as someone sleeping, Kiru estimated that it took a good eight hours to refill his entire core, if he was ever at the point where he was completely empty. If he didn't overdo it too much, that eight hours could last him the entire day in terms of needing to move.

Intellectually, Kiru knew that to be an incredible feat. To be able to constantly or near-constantly use mana for ten to twelve hours and not be completely drained or overwhelmed was an accomplishment that many Golds would brag about until they died. Too much had happened recently for the psion to revel in that, however. He needed to reach much higher than Gold in order to make sure his parents' deaths weren't in vain. In order to keep the sense of loss from overwhelming him, Kiru focused on his current goals as he cultivated: getting into the academy and getting his father's item. Those were the short-term goals that he put his thoughts towards, not his recent trauma. After about thirty minutes, the imp was almost done, and Kiru had accumulated enough mana to safely use his Telekinesis on himself once more . . . as long as he didn't push himself.

His mother's armor was made of some sort of flexible metal plus leather. The armor was a bright red color his mother called cinnabar. It definitely wasn't built for stealth. It covered his torso and shoulders, and had sleeves that covered the entirety of his arms except his bony hands. The last bit of armor were the boots. They were definitely tight, as William had to cram the psion's feet into them to get them to fit even to a degree. But after he jammed the final boot on, something unexpected happened. To both his and William's surprise, the armor *changed*.

The snug gear began to morph, expanding in some places while shrinking in others.. Instead of being too bulky and feminine appearing for Kiru's tastes, it grew to form-fit most of Kiru. The boots spread out so Kiru's feet were no longer cramped. The sleeves still covered him but no longer hugged his rail-thin arms tight enough to expose his atrophied body to everyone. The sleeves spread out and expanded. They formed some kind of muscle suit around his arms, making Kiru look kind of beefy.

By the time it had finished, the armor now seemed tailor-made for the psion, completely hiding his atrophied form! The armor covered his torso, arms, and feet, and his baggy pants hid his skinny legs. Both master and familiar stared at the armor in awe. "You're right, Master. This is much improved." William said.

Kiru nodded in agreement and stood up, feeling strong. Tears nearly welled up in his eyes again, as thoughts of his mother resurfaced. The psion suppressed them, though. He needed to focus and move. Kiru had William hop up on his shoulder and stuck Niajar's coin in his pocket. Then, they started trekking down the river. Kiru's knowledge of the world outside of Bristleton was lacking, but his mother taught him that rivers led to towns, and towns led to people. If he could find people, he could find the recruiters.

Kiru and his companion trod down the path. At first, he thought about just floating along as it would be less intensive for his mana use, but he knew he needed to continue to practice a "normal"-looking gait for when he interacted with others. He continued on for about ten minutes, when the ground began to quake once more, then BOOM! Through the trees, the volcano rose in the sky, and a gout of lava flowed out of it!

It wasn't a true eruption, but Kiru didn't want to be near when the molten rock reached ground level. So he picked up the pace. It was a good thing, too, because he felt an overwhelming presence soaring above him. The strength of . . . whatever it was . . . literally applied pressure on Kiru even though it was high up in the sky. The psion fell to the ground, flattening his body up against a tree in pure survival instinct. Whatever or whoever it was struck fear into Kiru's heart.

Various woodland creatures had the same idea as the half-elf and sprinted past him, fleeing in terror. The psion dared to try to peek up and as a result actually saw the figure with such an imposing aura. Up in the sky was a man. He was thin but adorned in glistening gold and black armor. An iron crown fused with an odd, conical helmet, graced his head. The most notable things were his wings. The man had a pair of huge, light blue wings flapping and keeping him in the air.

Kiru's heart sank. In the whole Kingdom of Blades, there was only one man known to possess wings. "Van Blaine," he muttered. The man who killed his father! Sure, he was hundreds of feet away, but he was right there!

"Master, we have the element of surprise. Let's kill him!" William growled.

Kiru shook his head, "We have no chance. We have to get stronger first."

The imp snarled in frustration but conceded Kiru's point.

Suddenly, the winged man snapped his attention down to the forest. Kiru's blood went cold. Van Blaine turned toward Kiru's hiding place when another flying man came up to him. This was another human, adorned in fine leathers and wearing a thick cape. He had a large nose and a receding hairline. Unlike Van Blaine, this man didn't have wings. He had both palms facing downward, and constant pulses of air were keeping him afloat.

This man was an air cultivator. His nose was also very distinct. It was the same as Ambrose's. This was Vincent Constantine, Duke of Bristleton and distant cousin of the king. The only reason Kiru was sure of the man's identity was his years of growing up with Ambrose around. It had to be the Duke. Vincent's sudden arrival fortunately distracted the king. Van Blaine began to shout at the noble, but Kiru couldn't make out the words. It was easy enough to gather that the king wasn't happy about this new volcano near a key mining settlement.

Kiru decided to use this new distraction to slip away unnoticed. He quickly and carefully continued along the river, now deeper in the forest to avoid any eyes from up top, but still following the river. Eventually, he garnered enough distance to no longer feel the pressure of Van Blaine. It didn't take long before he was bluntly reminded that he had no food or much of anything at all, for that matter. Fleeing for his life thankfully made breakfast of less import, as his appetite had all but evaporated. At least he had access to fresh water.

He could find food. That wasn't the priority in Kiru's mind. What *was* the priority, was finding an academy recruiter.

# CHAPTER FOURTEEN

# Fox Hollow Recruitment

I t took Kiru a few days to reach civilization. Granted, he could've made it to a town much sooner if he took one of the official roads, but he wasn't taking any chances. Trailblazing through the wilds was definitely more dangerous than going on a set path, but wanting to avoid one of the most dangerous cultivators alive took precedence. Still, whenever he felt relatively safe and had a good amount of foliage to hide him, he cultivated. Once when he was hiding in a tree, it helped him avoid a rather nasty-looking boar, besides the usual bonus to his available mana.

The psion also took some time to examine the ring his mother had left him. It was a jade band flecked with gold and adorned with a single small ruby. It certainly seemed like a well-crafted item to him. Kiru wondered if he could sell it, since he had no money, but part of his heart clung to the memento from his mother, unwilling to let go of something that connected him to her. Then while he sat staring at the ring, the jewel suddenly flashed, and a translucent screen appeared in Kiru's vision.

It was a ten-by-ten square grid. This was a storage ring. Each square indicated a slot where he could store up to one hundred items. All were empty, except for three squares. They were all dark, not revealing what was inside. Kiru tapped on one of the squares, but all he got in return was a pulse of hot energy from the ring. His mother had put those items in there, and Kiru could instinctively tell that only she or someone stronger could claim them. If he wanted to discover what she left, Kiru would need to reach at least Tier-One Sapphire. It was a lofty goal, but it was a good thing he was already planning to become that strong.

The river Kiru followed had continued to widen and increase in intensity until it had become full-on rapids now. When the fast-flowing water eventually slowed and met a stone dam, a settlement lay nestled in the clearing. Kiru had heard of this place. It was ten miles from Bristleton if you took the main road and about three times the size of the village where he'd grown up. This place was a river town known as Fox Hollow. Just like Bristleton, there was a large wall surrounding the place, only this was constructed of mostly wood rather than stone, which made sense given the abundance of trees nearby.

A number of people were outside the fortifications looking past the trees where Kiru was hiding. They were talking quietly amongst themselves while moving very expressively. More than one of them made an explosive gesture with their hands. *Probably discussing the new volcano*, he thought. Some of them were adorned in fine robes, jewels, armor, and garments. One of them was a rather large man wearing a black cloth sash that William was eyeing greedily. While Fox Hollow was a thriving river town, such opulent wealth was not common-place here. They were still near the outer edge of the kingdom's territory. Most wealthier people and merchants only came for special occasions, like when academy recruiters were in town.

Recruiters came by once a year, not long before the new semester started for the academy's yearly calendar. Kiru smiled as he realized he was just in time. The psion backtracked, tracing the main dirt path that led to the front gate. While Kiru took some time for a restroom break, William made an *ugh* noise and hopped off him. Afterward, Kiru followed the path until it bent around a corner, away from sight. Then, he finally hopped out of the woods. Kiru had William brush off any dirt or debris on him so that he looked presentable. He didn't want them to suspect he'd been trodding through the woods, fleeing their monarch. He couldn't feel if anything was poking him or see if there was a smudge on his back, so the imp proved valuable in his aid. There was even half a small tree branch wedged in his boot that William managed to pull out.

He was about to start walking down when the imp cleared his throat.

"Yes, William?"

The small demon just looked at Kiru and tapped the center of his forehead.

Kiru copied the gesture, and there was a *tink* as his finger tapped the gold jewel embedded in his head. "Crap." Walking around in this bright red statement piece was already going to draw unwanted attention. Having some random piece of jewelry embedded in his forehead wouldn't be helpful in trying to keep a low profile, either.

"Not to worry, Master. I, William, the breaker of wills, have the solution."

"You do?"

"Yes," he said confidently. Once more, he reached into the crevice between his brain and skull. "Now where did I put it? Oh! Yes, here it is." He pulled out a long sash the color of blood. It only had a mild amount of his brain slime on it, compared to the coin.

It was the psion's turn to make the *ugh* noise. "Wait, did you . . . ?"

"Yes, I stole it from the fat man talking with the others about the volcano. The fool never even saw me. He's going to be so mad! Haha!"

Kiru sighed. He wasn't a fan of stealing, but he couldn't just go up to the man and say "Sorry, my imp stole your sash so I can hide this gaudy jewel in my head." Resigned, he wiped the slime off the sash as best he could and tied it around his head, resolving to find a way to pay the man for the item one day.

Once he'd made himself as presentable as he possibly could, Kiru began walking down the main path toward Fox Hollow. Soon enough, he was nearing the entrance.

The group of concerned citizens noticed and ran up to him. "Good sir, you came from the direction of the volcano. The king ordered the guard captain to keep anyone from going any closer to it. Did you see what happened?" "What's going on?" "Is the kingdom under attack?" "Nice headband."

Kiru raised his hands. "Whoa, easy, everyone. I was just on my way to see the academy recruiters. As to what that thing is, I have no idea. It just suddenly emerged from the ground, but I was already past it, so I don't know. It looks like just a volcano to me. I wouldn't fear, though. Our illustrious king surely has everything under control," he lied. In his head, Kiru chided himself for not approaching Fox Hollow from a different direction to help avoid suspicion.

"Pfft! You can't be serious," the rather bulbous and noticeably sashless man accused. "You came from east of here. The only thing that's out there is a small outskirt town full of miners and peasants. No one aside from those of noble blood or a prodigy could even think of attempting to enter the academy at such a young age. What are you, twelve?"

"Eighteen," Kiru growled.

William had stayed hidden but appeared to tolerate the man no longer. "How dare you insult my master!" the imp bellowed, crawling up to stand on Kiru's shoulder.

The large man recoiled at the sight. "Ugh! What is that?!"

William cocked his head and gave a cracked-toothed grin. He hopped down to the ground and pointed a clawed finger at the man. "I am William, Breaker of Wills, and familiar to my master Kiru the—"

"Just Kiru's fine," the psion interrupted. "And yes, this is my familiar."

The crowd fell silent. The man looked at William, then back to Kiru, then back to William, then to Kiru again. He finally composed himself. In a rehearsed manner, he said, "My apologies, sir. Anyone who could afford a familiar must certainly be from noble stock. I, the humble merchant Ramuz, beg that you please take a fifteen percent discount at my shop when next you peruse my wares. I trade in fine clothing, and my trading caravan travels all over this kingdom."

Kiru didn't realize that the familiar stones were so expensive. *Good to know.* He could use that to his advantage. Now that he thought Kiru was a noble, the rude merchant was sucking up to him, and the psion figured he might as well act on it. He took in a deep breath as he summoned up memories of Ambrose from years ago. Despite the gap of time since they'd last interacted, Kiru was easily able to conjure up memories of him and his manner. Taking a page from Ambrose's book, he lifted his chin indignantly at the man. "Hmph, I will take no less than a permanent twenty-five percent discount *if* I ever deign to patronize your shop."

He turned his back to the portly merchant and set off toward the city. "If you ever insult me or my familiar again, my father will hear about it, Ramuz," he threatened over his shoulder. A few people laughed at the flustered merchant as he called out his agreement to Kiru's terms.

The guards heard Kiru's words too. They nervously allowed him entry without question.

William cackled like the little imp he was after they made it through. "Hahahaha! Did you see that? The fat fool almost fell on his ass! He was so enamored of my glorious presence, he didn't even notice his stolen garment right in front of him!"

"Yeah . . . enamored," Kiru said, unconvinced. He had a hard time believing that *anyone* would ever be enamored with the tiny demon.

Not long after they entered the town, paper signs plastered on buildings advertised that the recruiters were indeed here. They were testing recruits in the market district, wherever that was. There were also a few quests from various merchants and guilds posted on the local board. The most recent ones inquired about the new volcano, asking for materials or creatures that may be there. These people didn't let an opportunity go to waste!

After getting directions from one of the locals, Kiru and William began their trek to the market district. Many people gave the pair wide berths and stared wide-eyed at their passing. Half-elves were a rarity. Half-elves in cinnabar-colored armor with an imp on their shoulders were another matter entirely. Kiru couldn't blame them. Though the kingdom was diverse, out here near the border, it was primarily dwarves, humans, and gnomes.

They smelled the market district before they saw it. Their nostrils were greeted with the aroma of cooked meats and fresh pastries. Both master and familiar's stomachs gave audible growls, William's sounding monstrous, like it belonged to a massive ogre. "I wish I'd had the foresight to take some money when we left home all those years ago."

"Not to worry, Master, the fat man provided for us once again," William said, pulling out a handful of coins from his head cavity. *How much room did he have in there?*

"William!" Kiru admonished.

"What?" he asked defensively. "He had it coming, and I didn't take *all* of his coins, just the shiniest ones."

Noticing more than one bewildered expression at the small imp talking loudly on his shoulder, Kiru quickly moved into a small alley away from curious eyes. "Shh! Keep it down," he whispered.

William rolled his eyes exaggeratedly, "Ugh, fine. So, as I was saying, when you were putting him in his place, I thought he might as well pay a fine for insulting the future ruler of the Kingdom of Blades. Here," he said, handing the slimy coins to Kiru.

The psion sighed. He'd just add it to the tab he owed the man. Kiru wiped the slime off the coins onto his pants and began counting. His eyes bulged; William wasn't wrong. He'd definitely swiped the shiniest coins from the man. In his hand, Kiru counted one silver, ten gold, and even a platinum! The average peasant back in Bristleton made five silver every two weeks! When you factored in that the conversion factor for each coin was one hundred, you could understand how impressive of a thief William really was.

He quickly stashed the coins and accelerated his pace into the market district. The area had vendors hawking their wares and goods. Many people were selling pastries, hides from forest animals that local hunters had killed, lots of different meats either in pies or kebabs, silks, and even a variety of exotic spices. The district in general was buzzing with activity, and everyone seemed happy to be milling around. There was a large crowd of people moving throughout the stone courtyard, a large portion of them gathered in a circle on the other side. The place was lively, and most of that excitement seemed to be directed toward where the crowd had been gathering.

Kiru went over to a lovely smelling food cart and bought a pair of lamb kebabs for one copper each. William's pupils grew wide as Kiru handed him one of the kebabs. The imp looked uncharacteristically subdued and humble. "You promised me you would get me new food to try," he said before giving it a large sniff. "You're such a good master." Then, before Kiru could reply, William began devouring the kebab as if he were a rabid dog. Kiru recoiled a little at the gross display before sighing and starting on his own kebab. The lamb was tender and delicious, seasoned with an aromatic combination of spices. William clearly thought so, too. The imp's messy eating had caused chunks of meat and juice to spill on Kiru. To avoid his armor getting any more stains on it, he found a place to sit.

Both master and familiar ate every bite of the kebab, and in William's case, that included the sharp stick it was on. Kiru didn't worry, though. He'd seen the imp eat worse. After the meat, Kiru decided to order a flagon of ale. It was the first time he'd drunk it openly, other than a few sips he'd sometimes sneak when he'd visited his mother at work and she wasn't looking. This had a slightly citrusy taste to it and an orange wedge on the edge of the mug. "Not bad," he mused.

Kiru had always been a sucker for sweets, so when he smelled the alluring aroma of chocolate, he *had* to check it out. After not having proper food for two years and with money to spend, Kiru was tempted to spend the entire day just buying food and eating. If he had missed this year's recruiting cycle, he very well might have. Luckily, however, the recruiters weren't gone yet. So, he would have to get just one or two sweets for now. After procuring it, he returned to the spot where he'd left William with a couple of pastries in hand.

To the half-elf's surprise, he found the imp lifting a mug larger than himself and chugging it like a competitive drinker. The little demon slammed the drink down and let out an impressive belch that startled a few pedestrians walking by. William gave a self-satisfied smirk and scratched his now-protruding belly.

"Really?" Kiru asked.

"What? I was thirsty," William replied defensively.

"You drank almost all of it."

"So?"

Kiru sighed and after noticing people staring at them, he put the pastries away in his storage ring for later. "Come on, we should probably get to the recruiters now. No telling how much longer they're going to stay in town."

He set the notably heavier imp on his shoulder once more and walked to the area where the crowd had gathered. Between the distinct armor and cat-sized demon on his shoulder, they gave way for Kiru in what might have been either admiration, fear, or a mixture of both.

At the center of the circle was a decent-sized table at which three academy recruiters in matching blue robes just like Niajar sat with quills and papers resting in front of them. A short line of people stood waiting to be tested for the academy, including a handful who had reached Gold.

Most of the applicants appeared to be strong in body, with impressively muscular frames. Almost all of them also had a worn and gritty look. They were likely peasants, just like he thought he was once. Only the one at the end of the line seemed to be anywhere near the psion's age, which reinforced how difficult it was to attain Gold.

The one who did look younger gave Kiru a disapproving sneer when he glanced in his direction. *What did I do to him?* Kiru thought. He was an orc with a prominently square jawline, well-groomed, thick sideburns, and a hulking body, He was wearing some kind of blackened leather—was it armor or a jacket? He carried a massive great axe on his back. Kiru joined the line at the end, promptly making sure to not provoke the orc, despite William's pleas to beat the brute into submission in a display of power.

The half-elf's hearing wasn't as good as his mother's, but his pointed ears twitched slightly as he picked up pieces of conversations around him. It was mostly people talking about the applicants and placing bets on who would make it. Kiru noted a fair amount of discussion concerning the new half-elf in ornate armor. Apparently, he cut a bold-enough figure that most thought he'd make it.

After about twenty minutes, all the applicants ahead of Kiru had been evaluated by the proctors. From what he could tell amidst the cacophony of the surrounding citizens, they were asking fairly basic questions. But this was apparently just the first part of the test, which made Kiru even happier that he had Niajar's coin. It would be one less challenge to go through! Almost all of the cultivators applying from this area were water mana users. From his limited understanding, that made sense to Kiru. They were in a river town where there was a higher influx of water mana. Of course, more water cultivators would ascend in rank here.

Other noteworthy mana types were stone and nature. From Kiru's experiences, it was usually dwarves who were almost always either stone or metal cultivators in particular. After several minutes, Kiru finally made it to the proctors at the end of the table. So far, out of a dozen or so cultivators that had applied, only two had made it through the first round. The first was a human water cultivator who looked to be in his seventies. He was a healer and displayed a mana technique he used to heal a cut on his arm.

The snobbish, leather-clad orc in front of Kiru was also accepted. The psion heard him proudly declaring that he was a rarity in this part of the kingdom, because he used blood mana. His technique caused his already large muscles to swell and grow to a monstrous degree, partially tearing his prized jacket. The recruiters nodded in appreciation and told the orc to stand over by the human healer.

Now that Kiru had made it to the table, he was able to get a better look at the trio of proctors all in matching blue robes. They were two elves—one a female with bright blonde hair, the other a male with tanned skin, dark brown eyes, and hair that matched. In the middle was a bald, middle-aged human, who was clearly very tired, his eyes dark with heavy bags under them.

"Name?" the human asked.

"Kiru."

"Kiru what?"

Kiru opened his mouth to say "Chromebane," but quickly closed it before he could let it out. Growing up as a peasant, he'd never had a last name. So, he'd roll with that. "Just Kiru's fine."

The tired man looked up at the psion, unamused. He let out a loud exhalation through his nostrils, and the tan elf spoke up. "You know this round of testing is for citizens of the *kingdom*, right? Those who wish to join the academy from another country must have an approved voucher from their land's governing body."

Kiru looked at him with a confused expression. "Uh, yes," he answered, unsure of what the elf was getting at.

"Do you expect us to believe you're some kind of peasant cultivator with no house name looking like that?" the tired human asked, his eyebrows raised, indicating clear disbelief.

Kiru's heart began to race. *Are they onto me? Do they know of my heritage?*

"The way I see it, you're one of two things," the male elf said. "You're either some noble's bastard son, denied from using the house name, or you're a runaway from Anor'Voren. No one out here in the sticks just walks around in such finely crafted, elven-made armor. Not to mention you've been afforded a familiar. So . . . which is it?"

Kiru had to think fast. He knew his armor was high quality but didn't realize it was so above average that it even topped other enchanted gear. He chided himself for not continuing to act like a noble as he had with the merchant. The psion thought that maybe if he had approached the recruiters with that attitude, they wouldn't have been so forward with their questions.

Realizing it was too late to go back now, Kiru decided to use a tactic that had worked for him when he got in trouble with his mom: he deflected and changed the subject. "My familial history doesn't matter. I believe this will suffice as proof that I am qualified to join the academy," he said, placing the gold coin from Niajar onto the table.

All three of the recruiters' eyes went wide at seeing the coin, and the human let out a pained sigh. "You're one of Niajar's recruits."

"Yes," Kiru said confidently.

"That damn librarian," the man muttered. "Okay, *Kiru the peasant*," he said with heavy sarcasm. "What type of mana do you cultivate?"

"Fire."

"Path?"

"Fiery Doom," he answered. Kiru had thought this question might come up, and his mother's path was his best option. William's presence would help reinforce that, too.

"Fiery Doom?" the female elf asked, speaking for the first time. "That's a rare path. It's said to be reserved for . . . elven royalty."

Kiru's jaw tensed. *Shit!* he thought. Well, he couldn't rescind what he'd said now. Back to deflection. "Well, are there any other things you need to know for my application?" he asked, looking back to the haggard man.

The recruiter sighed, then raised his head to look at the psion. The bald human's eyes seemed to flash for a moment, and he squinted, looking directly at Kiru's chest. "Well, you're giving off the energy signature of a Gold. So, you must've opened all of your meridians."

Kiru's body reflexively tensed, then relaxed. He knew he was a Gold, but part of him was still nervous that someone was going to be able to detect his mana type by scanning him.

His moment of relief was interrupted when the bald man spoke up again, "Techniques?"

"Excuse me?"

"Techniques! What techniques do you know?" he asked bluntly, not hiding his displeasure in the slightest.

"You didn't ask the other applicants what their techniques were," the psion retorted.

"That's not your concern," the man said with a passive aggressive grin.

Kiru pressed his lips together. "I . . . don't know any," he reluctantly lied.

"Don't know, or can't learn?"

Kiru let out a deep exhale through his nostrils. "Can't learn."

The man began to chuckle. "Wait, so that means, you're a Defunct?"

"A what?"

"A 'Defunct' is a term for a cultivator whose core has a defect, or their connection between their souls and core is so poor, they cannot use any techniques. Oh, this is rich! The enigmatic elf goes and uses his one recruitment slot on a damn Defunct."

"That makes sense to me now," the blonde elf affirmed. "He's clearly of some noble stock but was disowned once he displayed his lack of talent or potential," she said, as if Kiru wasn't even there.

Before Kiru could protest, William beat him to the punch. The bony imp crawled out of Kiru's pocket and glared at the three recruiters. Kiru hadn't even realized he was there. "How dare you utter such lies about my master!" he spat, pointing a gaunt, clawed finger at the dark elf. "He is a great conqueror! You should consider yourself lucky to have him!"

"Is that so?" the male elf asked, clearly amused.

The imp puffed out his chest in pride. "Yes, and he is clearly far superior to those two halfwits that have made it past your questions," he said, pointing to the man and orc.

Kiru snatched the imp. "Excuse us for a moment." He then turned his back to the recruiters and glared at William. "What are you doing, trying to get us killed? We can't afford to anger the recruiters. Those three could crush us into paste!" he whispered harshly, then noticed a slew of crumbs around the imp's mouth.

William's eyes were manic. He grinned, revealing chunks of pastry crumbs embedded between his crooked teeth. "Don't worry, Master, I have a plan!"

# CHAPTER FIFTEEN

# Examination

E r, hem." The elf cleared his throat rather loudly.

Kiru turned back to face the three cultivators and smiled nervously. "Sorry about him," he apologized.

The bald man sighed. "So, you think our candidates, two Beta Gold-rank cultivators with impressive techniques, are halfwits?" In Gold, there were three tiers. The lowest was Zeta, which meant you had no techniques. Next was Beta, which meant you had at least one technique. The final was Alpha. It meant you had at least three under your belt. While every Gold-rank cultivator gave off the same amount of power when scanned, the general rule of thumb was the more techniques equaled a more skilled cultivator, and thus more valuable.

Now, Kiru learned from his mother that while you could learn techniques at Silver, the more you learned at that rank increased the risk of destabilizing your core and meridians. That was because your body hadn't established a firm enough foundation to handle the demand that creating a technique required. That was why Kiru was so surprised when Ambrose had displayed the ability to use two those years ago.

"No," Kiru said to the man, then William redoubled his stance.

"Of course!" the small demon declared. "Those two can't hold a candle to my master's strength."

Kiru scowled and knocked William off his shoulder, angry at the fires the imp was stoking.

The tired human plastered a wide grin on his face. "Well, if you're so insistent on this Defunct's greatness, then he can help with the second part of the examination," he said, leaning over the table to look at the imp on the ground.

"Excuse me?" Kiru asked.

"People of Fox Hollow, we have found two new recruits who have shown enough potential to enter the academy!" the tired man bellowed with a tenacity and volume that caused Kiru to wince.

The crowd cheered.

"However, just because they've shown potential doesn't mean they will automatically enter." The applause quickly changed to murmuring.

The bald man gestured at Kiru. "This cultivator here has already been accepted into the academy by one of our colleagues and has kindly offered to help test the recruits for the second round of the examination."

Kiru raised his eyebrows. His mother had told him what the second round of tests typically consisted of. It was a mock fight where a recruit would demonstrate their mettle against an instructor. No one ever got hurt because the instructors were so far beyond any recruit's capabilities, it was like child's play for them. This, however, was different.

The bald man gave a predatory grin. "This cultivator, Kiru, has agreed to fight our two recruits in our stead. That is, if he isn't afraid. Not to worry everyone, though injuries are likely to occur, we will ensure that no death or serious harm will result from this."

Kiru was afraid. He hadn't been at Gold-rank for that long. He didn't feel confident enough to face two opponents at the same level at once.

"My master is no coward! He accepts!" William blurted.

The crowd began to cheer loudly in anticipation. This appeared to be out of the norm for them. While Kiru knew that, while seeing a potential recruit fight an expert might be fun enough for them, seeing cultivators at the same level fight could potentially be more bloody. More bloody meant more exciting to many commonfolk.

"Excellent! Fighters, take your positions," the bald man declared, then stomped his right foot hard on the ground. The cobblestone began to rise around the cleared area, rising about six inches to make a small ring for a makeshift arena. Without hesitation, the two elves took the table and chairs away, too. The crowd's excitement rose, some people cheering and others placing bets.

Kiru's anger had become much more manageable over the years since he damaged his fire mana core, but William was clearly determined to push him closer to the edge. It became increasingly apparent that William represented the psion's competitive nature, the fire in his belly. Admittedly, "frustrated" was a more accurate description for how Kiru felt. Instead of a hassle-free acceptance, he was caught having to fight a two-on-one battle. But he couldn't back out now. Everyone was watching, and his familiar had already agreed for him. The psion walked toward the end of the arena he had been directed to, scowling at William. "Was this part of your plan?" he growled.

William smiled enthusiastically.

Kiru was caught off-guard. "Really?"

"Yes, Master!" the imp declared. William then reached into his exposed brain and pulled out a piece of pastry. He crawled up to Kiru's shoulder and grinned.

"Eat this." William shoved the slimy pastry into Kiru's mouth before the psion could respond.

Kiru reflexively coughed and gagged, nearly vomiting it up right then and there.

"It's good, right?! It gives me power! It'll give you power too, Master!"

Everything made sense. The bloodthirsty little demon was on a damn sugar rush! "Uggh, we're going to have a serious talk about this later," Kiru said after he swallowed the pastry and wiped the drool and bile from his mouth. Despite the unintended situation, Kiru had no choice but to fight. He needed to find a way to overcome his circumstances, like he had so many times before.

The psion took out his twin short swords, then took a deep, calming breath, slowing his heart rate and suppressing his anger. He took a good look at his opponents. The water mana cultivator was standing behind the musclebound orc, going with a clear strategy of staying back to heal. The brute had a smug look on his face, clearly confident in their victory. Kiru understood why as they outnumbered him, but he didn't like being underestimated. So, he let the anger return. This time, however, Kiru was in control. It wasn't an unbridled rage—no, this was a cold calculation.

During their combat training, Kiru's mother had taken quite some time to teach him basic combat theory from an old pre-Ragnarok book called *The Art of War*. She quoted, "'If your opponent is of choleric temper, seek to irritate him.' In other words, let his anger bring about his doom." William particularly favored the last bit. The elderly human seemed to exude a rather calm demeanor, but the well-groomed jerk of an orc was clearly short-tempered. The axe-wielder, however, was the biggest threat. Kiru needed to take care of him quickly.

Fortunately, he was very skilled at pissing people off. It was a skill he had developed over years in Bristleton, and despite having only his mother and William to talk to over the years of isolation, he hadn't lost his touch.

He pointed one of his swords at the orc. "You're the best this place has to offer?!" he asked incredulously. "Wow. The quality of cultivators sure has gone down here. Tell me, what are you compensating for with that ridiculous-sized axe of yours?"

The crowd paused in stunned silence. Then, a round of chuckling began, followed by more murmurs, bets, and even some raucous laughter.

The orc, however, did not take kindly to those words. "Compensating?!" he shouted angrily. His eyes turned red, the dark pupils alone left unchanged. Like before, his muscles bulged, only this time much larger and more rapidly. The orc grew about a foot in size, completely ripping through all of his clothes until he only had veritable rags left.

*This . . . may be a little harder than I had thought.* Still, he had succeeded in his goal—the orc was Pissed with a capital P!

"You can do this, Master! Use the sugar power!" William said, giving the psion a thumbs-up before gripping his shoulder armor tight.

Kiru turned back to face his opponents and braced himself, positioning his body in one of his mother's elven sword forms. Now, the orc was going to be reckless, and Kiru needed to capitalize on that. Brute strength wasn't an option for him, so speed would have to do. Kiru focused his mental mana into his legs.

"Ready?" the bald man said, raising his hand. "Begin!"

The orc charged at Kiru, closing the distance halfway in a matter of moments. He raised his axe, ready to bisect the psion. That was when Kiru struck. With a flex of his will, Kiru directed his mental mana to propel him like a bolt of lightning. The psion flew at the orc, whose stance left wide openings, signaling a lack of formal training. Though Kiru felt bad, he didn't hesitate to act as needed. Using a form his mother taught him called Demon's Inciting Strike, Kiru sliced the orc's right arm at the armpit, cutting through the tendons in one quick motion. Using his forward momentum, Kiru then spun behind him and cut through the blood cultivator's ankles, severing both of his Achilles tendons. The orc groaned and fell flat on his face, dropping his axe. The crowd stood in stunned silence at how swiftly and definitively Kiru had defeated the blood cultivator.

All were quiet except for Kiru's other opponent. The man's hands began to glow blue. Behind Kiru, the fallen orc began to exude the same color, and the pooling blood returned to his body.

"Master, the man is healing the green one! Let's destroy him!" William was right, but the water cultivator was a good distance away; by the time Kiru got to him, the orc would be recovered.

Then an idea came to him.

"Yes, let's," he said and grabbed William. "You're up, bud." With that, he pitched the little demon like a ball at the man. Kiru subtly used his Telekinesis to guide and accelerate the imp's speed. To both the demon and the water cultivator's surprise, Kiru's mark was dead-on. The psion smiled excitedly when William crashed right into the man's face, knocking him to the ground.

In a fit of pure surprise and fear, William desperately clawed at the cultivator's face and began to use Hot Hand while Kiru moved up to assist. The old guy was clearly not a fighter, and his cries echoed throughout the market district. William didn't stop attacking until the elder cried out, "Ah! It burns! I surrender!"

Kiru nodded in satisfaction, thinking they had done it. That was, until a shadow loomed suddenly overhead. Kiru just had time to turn around before being kicked square in the sternum. The psion was flung backwards, his back crashing into the water cultivator, who was now curled up in a ball. William stood on top of the man. He had just enough time to look down at his master before his beady eyes bulged.

Kiru coughed and rolled to the right, just in time to miss the great axe's descent. The weapon crashed into the ground, nearly hitting William and shattering the cobblestone below. As Kiru rolled to his feet, the orc he had downed stared him in the face. Absolute rage dominated the brute's expression as his tiny pupils fixed on the psion.

Kiru's opponent had recovered enough, it seemed. He could see his legs were intact once more, but his right arm hung limp and bleeding. Still, the odds had shifted in Kiru's favor. His mother's teachings about basic combat tactics were wise, and her first lesson came to his mind: *always fight dirty*. Kiru intended to do just that. He smiled as he rapidly began to form a strategy.

To the psion's surprise, the orc was faster than anticipated. The brute left his weapon stuck in the ground and closed the distance. He grabbed Kiru by the neck and began to squeeze.

Kiru gagged and wheezed in shock as the orc raised him in the air until they were eye-to-eye with one another. The barbaric fighter's smug expression returned. Fortunately, that put Kiru in the ideal position. With all the concentration he could muster, he used his mana to kick his left boot straight into the orc's groin. The muscular fighter let out a squeak of pain, and his grip on Kiru's neck loosened.

Kiru pulled his head back, then slammed it against the orc, square in the nose. The jewel in the psion's head shattered the bone with a crack. The brute's grip went completely slack, and he dropped Kiru. The psion fell to his feet, quickly positioning himself to continue, but the blood mana cultivator took a couple of wobbly steps backwards. The orc's eyes rolled in the back of his head before the brute fell to the ground, unconscious.

As his last opponent was *finally* defeated, the crowd sat collectively silent in awe. Then, after a few long seconds, they erupted into enthusiastic cheering at the spectacle they'd just witnessed. William ran and crawled up to his master's shoulder. He stood proudly, basking in the crowd's praise and the part he'd played in it. Even the psion couldn't help but smile as the crowd began to chant: "Kiru, Kiru, Kiru!"

The female elf recruiter ran up and swiftly began channeling mana, healing the orc's wounds. Kiru was glad they were indeed keeping their word about tending to the combatants. The other two recruiters approached, a mixture of frustration and regret on their faces. "It seems Niajar knew what he was doing," the tired man conceded, albeit with obvious difficulty. "Welcome to the Academy, Defunct."

# CHAPTER SIXTEEN

# En Route

Kiru wasn't a fan of the "Defunct" title he'd been given. Technically, it wasn't even true. He could very well use a technique, just not a fire mana one. In that regard, though, he could actually be said to be worse than a Defunct. *I suppose it's better than being a vitaldrain*, he thought.

Despite the label, he agreed to his acceptance into the academy, especially when he heard the familiar voice of a rude merchant in the distance shouting about a thief who'd stolen his coin purse and sash. Once Kiru's opponents were healed, they were promptly informed that they had not passed their spontaneous "test," so they would not be welcomed into the academy this year.

The orc began to complain, but when reminded that he'd just lost a two-on-one fight, he grumpily conceded. The brute still shot Kiru a glare that managed to simultaneously convey both anger and fear. After that, Kiru was escorted to Fox Hollow's port. There was a pipe-smoking gnome sitting by a very small, almost child-sized sailboat with a black and yellow striped pattern on the sail. The boat was a water taxi, and he was her captain.

The bald man handed Kiru a scroll and Niajar's coin, not looking him in the eyes as he scowled. "Give this scroll, along with your sponsor's coin, to the guards at the academy entrance. This man will get you there within two days," he said without ceremony, then promptly turned away and left in a huff.

Kiru rolled his eyes. William looked like he was about to shout something at the man, but the psion clamped his hand over the imp's mouth.

Kiru turned back to the gnome, who had a long goatee and a straw hat.

"Howdie do?" he greeted, tipping his straw hat in acknowledgement.

"Hi." Kiru hopped in the small boat.

"Name's Albert. So, you're the academy's newest recruit, huh?"

"I'm Kiru, this is William, and that's the plan," Kiru said, ready to head off . . . but they didn't. He turned back to see the gnome's hand out expectantly.

"Payment?"

"Wait, didn't he rent you out?"

The gnome nodded. "He rented out to reserve me, but I still charge per customer per trip. He usually pays me that when he drops one of you young 'uns off. I figured he'd have given you the coin."

"He didn't." Kiru gritted his teeth.

The gnome gave a good-natured chuckle. "Hehehe! Well, I'm sorry, young 'un, but I'll do you a favor. Passage to the academy will usually cost you two gold, but since the baldy tricked you, I'll let you pay me just one, as long as we add another customer. I'll charge 'em three, and that way, I can get what I'm owed." Albert winked.

"Really? Thanks!" Kiru said. He reached in to grab a gold when he noticed the man William had robbed in front of the town now standing at the other end of the port.

The man also noticed Kiru, and his eyes widened in fury. "Guards! Thief!" he shouted, pointing at Kiru who conveniently was wearing his stolen sash.

"You know what, I'll give you three gold if you can get us out of here real fast," Kiru quickly said to the gnome.

The water taxi driver deftly took the coins and dipped his straw hat at Kiru. "One speedy exit, coming right up!" Albert said. With practiced ease, the gnome pulled up the small anchor and kicked off of the port. The boat seemed to spin of its own volition to face downriver. Albert turned out to be a water mana cultivator; he jumped over Kiru to land in the back of the boat, put both his hands in the water, and activated his technique.

Kiru had just enough time to see the fat man scowling at him before the small sailboat rocketed across the water. Both Kiru and William had to brace themselves to keep from falling over. The small imp screamed in terror while the gnome just cackled in his shrill voice. After a few minutes, their speed slowed once they were well out of sight of Fox Hollow. Albert giggled again, but Kiru noted a layer of sweat over the gnome's forehead. Apparently, that technique took a lot out of him.

The small sailor, however, didn't need to rely on it again as they traveled the calm waters. He proved himself more than adequate at his chosen profession. The gnome expertly maneuvered his small craft to take advantage of the wind and currents. They passed by a few more towns, each growing progressively larger as they moved toward the academy. Kiru had researched the school extensively when he was younger, as he had already wanted to go there. Water travel was particularly advantageous.

The academy was located on a lone island located in the middle of a lake, which was originally fed by the Tori River, the largest in all the kingdom. The Tori River was fed by numerous smaller bodies of water, including the one they were currently traversing. Eventually, after passing by the third settlement, which turned out to be a military base smaller than Kiru's hometown, they made it to the edge of the Tori. While there was still plenty of forest, Kiru had seen many well-maintained fields of farmland as well as many more rocky outcroppings as they continued to sail.

Their travel took up the better part of the day, and the gnome refused to navigate the river at night. So, they made camp on a small sandbar. Albert told Kiru that their final stop would be at Waketown, the city near the academy, which was about six hundred miles away from Fox Hollow.

Kiru had heard of it. It was a huge metropolis that provided a number of the best cultivators in the kingdom. It wasn't as prolific as the capital, but it was still a very powerful place. The psion was also unsure as to how fast they were moving on the water for the six or so hours but he knew that they couldn't have made it anywhere near six hundred miles yet.

While on the sandbar, Kiru was able to cultivate and fully take in the sight of the massive waterway that was the Tori River. On an intellectual level, he knew that the world was a much larger and grander place than where he'd grown up. The river before him was a much more palpable reminder of that.

While the water had been moving faster the more downstream they went, the river now before them was a wild and raging torrent. It was hard to hear anything else over the sound of the wind and rushing water ahead of them. Kiru didn't need long to figure out where most of the distance of the journey would come from.

After both Kiru and William awoke rested and full of energy, they quickly ate some of the food Kiru had stored inside his ring, packed their belongings, and hopped back into the water taxi. As they neared where their rivulet fed into the Tori, Albert gave Kiru and William a shit-eating grin. "Hold on to your butts!" And with that, they crested into the large river. Just as when Albert had used his technique earlier, the small craft was propelled with a wild burst of speed. While Kiru and William made almost comical cries of fear, the water taxi driver was letting out a shrill laugh of excitement.

The psion was surprised that their small craft was able to hold together as the vessel rode some high waves and went airborne multiple times. At one point, a large fish, bigger than their boat, shot up out of the water, narrowly missing its attempt to swallow it whole. It looked very much like the orange koi sacred beast back at the volcano. William seemed to notice that, too, and the usually boisterous imp huddled notably closer to his master.

Despite the danger, Kiru quickly realized that all he needed to do was use Telekinesis on his hands and feet. He was already getting tossed about, so he didn't need to worry about looking like he was sitting normally. So, with his use of his technique just on his appendages, he was able to stay safe on the vessel and minimize his mana usage. Toward the end of their journey, the river finally calmed. At that point, Kiru started to use Telekinesis throughout his body once again.

After an hour of repetitive seeming near-death experiences on the wild river, Kiru and William let out a collective "Whoa," in unison as they came upon a massive structure. A quarter mile ahead of them was an utterly gargantuan bridge. The metal construct towered over the massive timbers on each side of the river, dwarfing any other edifice that Kiru had ever set eyes on.

"That's the bridge that leads to the academy," Albert said.

Both Kiru and William gave the wily gnome an incredulous look.

Albert laughed, understanding their shock. "What, you didn't think the top cultivator academy in the kingdom *wouldn't* have some gaudy entrance?" The gnome cackled.

"How are we supposed to get up there?" Kiru asked. "It looks too high for the boat to reach."

"There's a port 'bout a half mile away in Waketown," Albert said. "From there, you'll be able to reach the bridge. With the number of recruits coming in these past few weeks, the town has been abuzz. So, it'll probably take you a few hours to reach the place."

Though Kiru hadn't seen much of the world outside his home, he still became familiar with the art of negotiation during his time working under the local black-smith. Often, people had a certain look when they were willing to make a deal but didn't want to admit it. Albert, right now, had such a look. He had a slight grin and a knowing glint in his eyes. There was information he had, information he seemed willing to share . . . for the right price.

"Any places I should visit or ways to make things go quicker?" Kiru asked, flipping a silver to Albert.

"Now that you mention it, I know just the place," the gnome said, then turned the small boat hard left. Albert expertly guided them through a series of rocks, then maneuvered them between other watercraft, all of which were larger than theirs. The sailor guided them toward a round inlet carved into the stone wall, one Kiru was suspicious of being a sewer.

These suspicions were confirmed when the stench hit their nostrils. "Um, why are we going toward a sewer pipe?"

Albert just chuckled. As they neared, the water mana cultivator quickly rolled up his sail. The sewer entrance was large enough to actually accommodate the small vessel completely as Albert guided them in. Kiru still didn't see any hints of malice in the gnome's face, so he continued to trust him, despite the sailor remaining intentionally vague. After another minute, they made it to an unas-suming port inside the sewer.

Albert hopped off and tied the boat to one of the wooden beams, then gestured for Kiru to follow. The psion and familiar obliged, though William grumbled about the stench.

"You're a demon for crying out loud," Kiru said.

"I am also a familiar. I was in the ether between realms before you summoned me. It's not like Muspelheim where the demons have to smell brimstone and sulfur all the time. Yuck," William retorted as if he was some sort of high-class demon.

Kiru smiled and shook his head at the imp's antics.

Once they joined Albert, the gnome untied a nearby rope. Immediately, they were lifted up into the air on a large version of a dumbwaiter. As they rose, he wondered if he had been moving convincingly enough for Albert to notice any-thing strange. He had been careful to not give anything away, but the gnome was clearly a sly one. Kiru couldn't ask Albert directly, either. So, based off the fact that the gnome didn't bring up any weird movements on Kiru's part, the psion took that as a good sign. As they continued to rise into a stone tunnel, the light from the sewer faded until they were in complete darkness.

Albert kindly lit a small torch for his passengers after a few seconds, the large dumbwaiter halting with a subtle *thoom*. Albert quickly tugged downward on the psion's chestpiece, forcing him to bend down. "Albert, what are you doing?" Kiru asked.

The gnome chuckled nervously, "Sorry, young 'un, the ceiling is . . . gnome-sized," he said, then pointed up.

Kiru glanced in the direction indicated. The sailor had saved him from some serious head trauma, pulling him down an instant before his skull could collide with the stone above. "Well, all's forgiven," he said, grateful to have avoided the damage.

The gnome's large grin returned, and he let go of Kiru. Then he reached up, grabbing a handle embedded in the ceiling, and cranked. It moved, and Albert opened some sort of door.

Kiru let out a sigh of relief as he stretched his back out once more to find . . . a home? Apparently, this tunnel was hidden under the floor of a humble, open-concept home, even smaller than Kiru's childhood house in width but just as high, to the psion's relief. "Is this where you live?" he asked, curiosity getting the better of him.

Albert nodded proudly.

"Why don't you just dock at the port instead of the sewer?" he asked as he collected his items and hopped out of the tunnel.

The gnome gave a wry look. "Let's just say it's good business to not have to have your vessel tracked or have to pay a quartermaster any fees. That's some advice I'll give you for free, young 'un."

Kiru thanked the gnome for his help, then headed out of the small house. With that, Kiru was able to get his first glimpses of Waketown. It was massive! He'd gotten some sense of it from the boat, but being there in person was something else entirely. The buildings towered multiple stories high, and there were people everywhere. Vendors advertised their wares, and a courier was traveling on a strange vehicle with two wheels. To see and be in a city of this scale was almost too much for Kiru to process, but he kept it together. A deep shadow loomed over the place where Kiru stood, and he turned to see that Albert's home was in a section of the city right beside the large bridge, which is what was obstructing the sun's light and was where Kiru needed to go. The sailor and likely smuggler really *had* gotten him a lot closer.

The psion began walking to the bridge's entrance, having to ask directions a couple of times along the way to get his bearings. On two different occasions during his short trek, he had to stop an act of thievery. The first was a small urchin boy, who they only caught because of William. Kiru felt bad for the scrawny kid, so he tossed him a silver. Right after he did so, the psion turned and gasped as he saw his familiar then try to swipe a warm chocolate muffin from a tray set out on someone's windowsill! Kiru quickly yanked the little demon by the tail and stared directly into his beady eyes. "No. More. Sugar," he hissed.

# CHAPTER SEVENTEEN

# Orientation

A pair of armored cultivators stood guard by the bridge entrance, their equipment, including the handles of their halberds, sporting the same royal blue color as the recruiters' robes. They also sported two different symbols emblazoned on the chests. The left was a quill crossed with a sword in an X pattern, the symbol of the academy, the right was a hand, each of its fingers a sword, the symbol of the kingdom.

The armor made sense to Kiru. The royal academy was under the purview of the royals . . . *Or usurpers*, he thought to himself. Almost all of the students ended up serving the military in some capacity. Kiru walked up to the nearest guard and handed him the scroll that the bald proctor had given him. The guard accepted it wordlessly, opening it up and reading it without even looking at Kiru.

The stoic visage of the man cracked a bit as he continued to read. He whispered the word, "Defunct?" in disbelief, as if it had slipped out without his knowledge. The guard looked at Kiru with a look of pity before snapping back to his stoic look.

The psion's jaw clenched, and he had to repress rolling his eyes in annoyance at the inaccurate label. He knew he was going to have to live with it for the entire time he was at the academy. *Might as well get used to it.*

While the one guard looked at Kiru pityingly, the other guard had the opposite reaction, scowling at Kiru upon hearing the word. "Welcome to the academy, student," the guard said, rolling up the scroll and handing it back to Kiru.

"My name is Corporal Tavish. This is Private Keaton." Keaton just glared at Kiru.

Tavish didn't acknowledge the hostility. "We are some of the guards that the king has assigned to keep the academy safe. On academy grounds, our authority answers only to two people, the headmaster and the king himself, so you best not cause us any trouble."

"Understood," Kiru replied.

"Good," Tavish said. "Your scroll states that you're one of Niajar's recruits, right?"

"I am, but I'm confused as to why that matters."

"It'll be explained in due time, First Year," Tavish replied. He then looked at his fellow guard. "Keaton, grab one of the tablets."

"You serious, Tavish?!" Keaton cried out angrily. "What's the point? It's a waste of time helping some Defunct."

"It's not our job to discern that, Keaton. Our job is to protect and serve this school, and that's what we're gonna do. This young man is a student, despite his status," Tavish answered firmly at his comrade's outburst. "Now, Private, you will watch your tongue and grab him one of the tablets and his supplies."

Keaton shook in anger, but kept in composure in front of his superior officer and complied, marching into the room nestled in one of the beams at the bridge entrance and bringing out a small tablet around the size of Kiru's forearm. Keaton shoved it hard against the psion, reinforcing Kiru's dislike for him.

Kiru stared firmly at the rude man, not backing down or showing any weakness. Even if he was labeled a Defunct, he'd been accepted into the Academy and had overcome so much in the past two years. The psion wasn't going to let one judgmental asshole make him act submissively.

Keaton noticed Kiru's glare and scowled. He looked like he wanted to say something else, but upon eyeing Tavish, bit back his words. He then handed Kiru a large duffle bag containing the psion's school supplies, three pairs of school uniforms, toiletries, and the like. After Kiru took it, he examined the tablet. It was made from well-carved light brown stone, rectangular in shape, and covered in a series of complex symbols he presumed to be runes.

"Thank you, Private," Tavish said pointedly.

"Yes, sir," Keaton replied and went back into the room.

"You received a coin from your sponsor, right?" Tavish asked.

Kiru nodded, assuming that Niajar must be his sponsor after how many times the others alluded to it.

"Good. There's a slot at the bottom of this tablet. Place your coin in there, and the tablet will activate. Follow the instructions that show up after that. There are some seats over there." He nodded toward a circle of marble stone benches arranged in a circle around a fire pit. "You should probably sit down before you activate your tablet and *before* you walk over the bridge." He winked knowingly.

"Thank you," Kiru said.

"Just doing my job," Tavish replied before turning back to his post. "Let's just say I have a soft spot for underdogs," he said as he walked away.

Kiru looked at him curiously, but the guard didn't say anything else.

"I like that guy," William said, crawling out from hiding behind Kiru. "The other guy's a jerk. We should kick his ass!"

"Not yet, bud," the psion said, quickly spinning away and walking toward the stone seats, hoping neither guard could hear William's threat. Kiru, as suggested, placed the coin he'd received from Niajar into the stone tablet. The runes glowed white, and the tablet let out a sudden, low thrum.

Words projected from it at Kiru's eye level: "Place scroll of acceptance on tablet."

Kiur unfurled the scroll and set it directly on the stone. To his surprise, the stone rapidly sucked the paper inside it until it was no more. It reminded him of someone slurping up a ramen noodle. The projected words disappeared, replaced by more: "Welcome, Kiru. You have been accepted as a student of the Royal Cultivator Academy located within the Kingdom of Blades. To begin your orientation, say, 'Continue.'"

"Continue," he said.

The glowing white words dissolved into a pile of artificial ash. Once the words completely disappeared, the ashes shook, raising up to reform into a small, faceless humanoid the size of the psion's index finger. Despite it not having eyes, it looked directly up at Kiru.

"Ugh! What is that?! It's so . . . ugly!" William said, disgusted by the thing.

Kiru smirked, wondering how the little cretin could ever claim anything else was ugly given how objectively terrible his looks were.

The small figure gave the imp a rude gesture with one of its fingers, provoking a laugh out of Kiru, before speaking to him in a cheery, distinctly feminine voice. "Welcome, Kiru. My name is Daisy Directory. I am a construct crafted to give you an in-depth orientation for your time at the Royal Cultivator Academy."

Kiru's eyes widened. He'd heard of constructs—artificial beings created using mana as an energy source and runes to stabilize them—but he'd never seen one before!

"Uh, hello," he said back, unsurely.

Daisy Directory chuckled. "I take it that I'm the first construct you've ever seen before. Trust me when I say there are many far greater than I. Now, are you ready to begin your orientation?"

"Yes!"

"Good, honey. Then let's begin," she said. A map of the continent suddenly appeared behind her. "The school was founded fifty years after our alliance's victory in the Draconic Campaign. As you know, our illustrious academy trains only the finest cultivators within the kingdom."

A small section of the map glowed, indicating the Kingdom of Blades. "What you may not know, however, is that we also take in recruits from every other country in the Great Alliance: Imakandi, home to the orcs; the Queendom of Anor'Voren, home of the elves; Stonereach, where the dwarven oligarchy resides; the human kingdom of Rowe; and lastly, the descendants of the gold drakonids that helped our great country turn the tides of war all those centuries ago."

As Daisy Directory listed all of those different countries, each lit up one by one. All were illuminated except the home of the gold drakonids, which was still a closely guarded secret of their race. Though they were public allies and part of the Great Alliance, the golden drakonid people were aloof and very private. Only rarely did they trade, and most would consider themselves lucky to see one more than once in their lifetime. The map also emphasized the size disparity between the Kingdom of Blades, compared to the others of the alliance. All of them were larger than Kiru's homeland, and most by a very significant margin.

The construct seemed to notice Kiru was following along, so she continued. "It is important to know that, while the academy helps many grow in their specific schools of study and knowledge about cultivation, its focus is on one thing above all else. Do you know what that is?"

"Combat." Kiru answered.

William gave a bloodthirsty grin and growled a low "Yes!" in excitement.

"Correct!" Daisy Directory said enthusiastically. "Though the academy trains some of the finest crafters and the like across the world, where it truly excels is at producing the finest cultivator warriors throughout all of Alterra! In return, those citizens of the Kingdom pay in either gold or service. Every year of teaching is worth ten years in service in the Kingdom's military, since the Crown sponsors the academy's continued growth. It's because of their continued contribution that our tuition is as low as it is."

Kiru almost choked on that. If he was actually planning on staying, he would owe the kingdom thirty years of his life to the military! That was a steep price. Kiru was unsure how many years each rank in cultivation provided the person. He knew that as one rose towards the higher echelons, the number of years they could achieve was impressively high. Still, he didn't know exact numbers. What he did know was that elves were the longest-lived of the races on the continent; his mother told him they lived to be about two hundred on average. So, while it may not be as big of an ask as it would be for a human, thirty years was still a sixth of an elf's lifetime. That wasn't a small ask.

"Isn't it exciting?" Daisy Directory asked, not losing any of her pep. "Not only that, but upon graduation, you'll be automatically assigned to the elite division of the military with a chance to qualify to join the Royal Guard. If military service is not desired, though, the current tuition is set at the low cost of one thousand gold per year."

Now *that* was a steep price. *That's considered low?!* Kiru finally understood why many lower-class citizens would have no choice but to serve in order to even have a chance to ascend in cultivation, if they made it into the academy in the first place. The bulk of the nation's military was composed of those who wouldn't even be able to qualify, so it made sense that those who went to the academy and still decided to enlist would be assigned to a more elite branch.

The psion had vaguely recalled hearing about an elite division separate from the Royal Guard when he was a kid. Inside that division, they were broken up into different subsets, such as the Inquisition. The psion let out a grimace when he thought of that one. He didn't know much about the Inquisition, other than that they were violent and unmerciful. Parents in Bristleton would tell their kids stories about the Inquisition to scare them into going to bed. Kiru knew the Inquisition had some strange nickname he couldn't recall at the moment, either. Still, Kiru knew without a doubt that he in no way wanted to be involved with them.

Kiru was freed from his internal musings at Daisy Directory's next words. "One other important note, honey, is that, if you become a champion in the Warrior Games, and you still don't want to serve in our glorious military, the Kingdom is willing to accept you relinquishing your claim to one of the prizes as payment for thirty years, instead of donating from your personal coffers."

Now *that* surprised Kiru. It also emphasized how valuable the items in the prize room actually were. There was no way he was going to do that, but it was still interesting.

Daisy Directory proceeded to explain a number of the rules and intricacies of the academy. Unless given specific permission, curfew was at midnight. Fighting was also encouraged but only in a sanctioned combat arena with staff supervision. One could not enter a dormitory they were not assigned to. Students couldn't leave the academy grounds except on weekends. Kiru didn't know how exactly the other cultivators *could* even leave if they wanted to, since the school was on an island. The construct informed Kiru that the school provided meals, uniforms, laundry, and lodging as part of the tuition price.

Material and adequate space to study and train was also available. Furthermore, Daisy Directory made it clear that the better students performed and/or the higher they ranked, the more opportunities they were given, which in turn, would help them perform better. This would increase a cultivator's chance at winning the tournament. Winning the yearly tournament was the goal of most students there, Kiru presumed.

"Now, I'm sure a strapping young cultivator such as yourself will have no problem impressing the staff. After all, you've qualified to make it into the academy," she said, as if trying to butter him up.

Kiru furrowed his brow at the construct. He was nearly skin and bones, but his armor concealed that fact. *Can she tell?* he thought to himself.

Ignoring his stern expression, Daisy Directory continued, "Now, let's pull up your information, shall we?" The world map behind her faded away, and an organized series of texts appeared. She read them off as they appeared.

Kiru was surprised to see the information already transferred. He wondered if the recruiters had somehow sent it to the token or if there was some other way they transferred it over such a long distance. *Do they use runes? A high-range communication technique? Spies?*

His internal questions stopped when Daisy Directory spoke again. The cheery construct was not thrown off one bit by his cultivation ranking. "Based off your initial cultivation rank and prospected growth, you will be assigned to one of three first-year dormitories. They are, as follows: the Sword House, where our best and brightest cultivator warriors are housed. Many from the Sword House go on to become top competitors in many gladiatorial tournaments, lead famous adventuring companies or mercenary guilds, or become members of the elite Royal Guard who protect our illustrious King van Blaine.

"The Shield House, where those not suited for direct combat are housed, such as cultivators who specialize in healing or crafting. Many from the Shield House go on to become high-quality clerics, alchemists, smiths, and builders."

Her chipper demeanor cracked a little as she went on to the last house. "Finally, Fist House, where . . . *er, hem,* they keep those deemed to be best suited to serve as guards for low-ranking nobles, become the head of one of local militias to keep the peace in the kingdom, or perform many of the required jobs to keep things running smoothly throughout our country."

Her cheery tone returned in full force. "It may not be the most glamorous, but without the people performing these tasks, such as crop growth, sewage safety and management, and structure maintenance, our kingdom would not thrive to the level it has today!"

"What a stupid idea," William muttered so only Kiru heard him. "We did not come here to become some glorified farmer or to waddle about in the sewers. We came here to kill and conquer. We'd better not go to that house, Master." Kiru didn't share his familiar's revulsion toward the jobs Fist House graduates would be assigned, but he shared in the imp's hopes that he wouldn't be assigned there. From the construct's tone, it was likely not as well-invested in time and resources by the academy compared to the other houses.

Kiru hoped that his high-combat ranking would supersede his Defunct status and elevate him to Sword House. He was a skilled combatant. He'd been training intensely in that field for the past two years with his mother. Since he wouldn't be able to use his technique for anything other than to help himself move, Kiru had to focus on fighting in order to give him an edge and any chance of winning the Warrior Games in the first place.

"Now, that concludes this part of your orientation. Do you have any questions before we discuss your classes, honey?"

Kiru nodded, "Yes, what's the significance of our sponsors?"

"To get a sponsor is a rare boon. All new students are brought in by recruiters, but not everyone is deemed worthy of sponsorship. Your sponsor will provide personal mentorship, and you will intern under them as one of your daily courses. Now, there's more to a sponsor than that, but that's the main gist of it. Anything else?"

Kiru thought but couldn't come up with any more questions. He was still *very* grateful that the new year hadn't started yet. It was lucky timing.

"Good, now let's see what your stats have allotted you in terms of courses for the year." Daisy Directory gestured to the psion's projected stats behind her. "Homeland: Kingdom of Blades" glowed blue, and a class called "Kingdom History" appeared beside it, in the same blue highlighting. The pattern continued. He had a Library Internship" under Niajar and "Art of the Blade" under "Dual-Wielding."

There were three classes under the "Combat Rank: S": "Basic Combat I," "Strategies I," and "Advanced Warfare." Nothing showed under the School Year. Under his "Mana Type," there was "Fire Mana Cultivation I," while under his "Fiery Doom Path," he had the class "Volatile & Lethal Paths." Kiru was happy with what he had. In total, he had eight classes, all providing opportunities for growth and education he could only dream of when he was living in Bristleton. Part of him wished that he was still just a peasant and that he still had his fire mana core intact. If that were the case and he'd been given this opportunity, he would've been over the moons in joy instead of just merely happy.

He stilled his inner jubilation, however. His trauma and the subsequent assassination attempts had disciplined him to not become *too* hopeful. He could be excited, but his enthusiasm had been tempered, and he would keep a cool head so as to not be caught off-guard. It was a good thing, too, because the other shoe dropped when they came to his Defunct tab.

It glowed blue, and the class "Basic Cultivation I" appeared. Then, after that, the "Defunct" tab flashed red and an alarm noise arose, repeating three times before staying red. Right afterward, red lines went through several of his assigned classes. Of his original eight, only five remained unmarked. They were "Kingdom History," "Library Internship," "Basic Combat I," "Strategies I," and "Fire Mana I." Though he was classified as a Defunct, he was still labeled as a fire mana cultivator who could still bring that mana into his core.

For her part, Daisy Directory actually seemed to be remorseful. "Oh my, it appears your Defunct status has disqualified you from some of your assigned classes, honey. Well, at least you'll have more free time to practice for this year's Warrior Games."

Kiru assumed almost every cultivator who went to the academy wanted to participate in the games, but he was still suspicious. After all the trauma that had happened to him in the past two years, his guard was up constantly. Because of that, he tensed, then squinted his eyes at the construct.

She seemed to understand his suspicion almost instantly. "Having a combat rank of S and wearing high-quality armor are dead giveaways, honey. It's clear you're a fighter, and any fighter coming here wants to win the Warrior Games," she explained.

Kiru nodded in respect at her perceptiveness.

"Now, one last thing, your house assignment." The list of classes disappeared, and three floating crests took their place. One was blue with a sword in its center, the other was yellow with a white shield, and the last was red with a gauntleted fist. "Based off your stats, you've been assigned . . ." The red crest grew larger while the others shrank. "Fist House. Congratulations, honey, you're now an official student of the Royal Academy."

Kiru could hear William growling in his mind. He repressed his look of frustration at the assignment as well, taking comfort in the fact that he was actually accepted into the Royal Academy at all.

From the slot where Kiru had put his coin in the stone tablet, a red badge appeared, containing the house's crest in a black outline. There was a gold diagonal line cutting straight through it that seemed out of place. Two folded scrolls came out after that, one at a time.

"Your orientation is complete. Make sure to hand your badge and this tablet to the staff member waiting for you across the bridge. One of the parchments has your list of classes and their locations. The other is a map of the campus. Enjoy your time at the academy, and good luck at the Warrior Games. Who knows? Maybe this will be the year a Fist House student wins for the first time?" she said with what sounded to be false enthusiasm. Kiru wasn't sure. He also couldn't ask because Daisy Directory had disappeared, and the glowing runes faded.

"Ergh! What a rude little insect. How dare she belittle us, putting us in that lame house. We should be at the top of the Sword House, not fraternizing with bottom feeders!" William pouted.

"Hey, quit it," Kiru whispered harshly to his familiar. "We made it in. That's what's important. We'll get our chance to fight, no matter what house we're in. I plan to win the Warrior Games no matter what."

"We'd better get a chance to fight," William grumbled, crossing his arms like a child.

# CHAPTER EIGHTEEN

# Removing the Weeds

After Kiru calmed his familiar down, the pair began their trek across the massive white bridge. It was very large, easily able to hold eight carts wide, and was so dazzlingly pristine and white, it was hard to look directly at in the sunlight. Sure enough, there was a school instructor waiting for them on the other side, just as the construct had said there would be. It was an orc, wearing the same customary blue robes the staff all seemed to have on.

There was something . . . different about this one, though. Compared to the brute Kiru had fought back in Fox Hollow, he was thinner and with a fairer complexion. He was still taller than Kiru and well-muscled but with a leaner, more defined physique. He had dark brown hair in a fine knot on his head and a well-trimmed goatee.

"Welcome, student. I am Giiyam, caretaker of the academy grounds. Your tablet and badge, please," he said rather stoically, sticking out his hand expectantly.

Kiru handed them over.

Giiyam raised an eyebrow and stuck out his lower lip in surprise, revealing his small lower tusks. Kiru also noticed that the caretaker's ears ended in a fine tip . . . like his! The orc appeared to have some mixed elven lineage. At least, Kiru hoped so. Seeing that made Kiru smile a little. He'd never encountered another half-elf in person before!

"Fist House and a defunct," the orc said, confirming to the psion that that's what the gold slash through his badge signified.

"Indeed I am," Kiru replied. He was still excited about meeting a fellow half-elf, even if Giiyam was part orc instead of human.

The groundskeeper looked puzzled. "What are your intentions in coming to the academy?"

Kiru shrugged, "The same as most everyone else, to—"

"To crush our enemies, see them driven before us, and hear the lamentation of their loved ones!" William interrupted the psion with zealous intensity.

"To become a great fighter and win the Warrior Games," Kiru finished, embarrassed by the imp's outburst.

"Hm, to win the Warrior Games? That is no small feat, even more so for a Defunct. You sure this is what you want?"

"Yes," Kiru said, without a doubt.

"Impressive resolve, First Year," Giiyam said, nodding in approval. "There are two things you need to know." He stuck one finger up. "First, keep your goals hidden. There are plenty within the school who will not look upon you favorably. Advertising your intent to win will only make life harder." Another finger went up. "Second, find reliable teammates. As you know, the Warrior Games are a group competition, not a solo tournament. He will need more than you, little demon," he said, looking directly into William's dark, beady eyes.

The imp scowled but showed atypical restraint for once, not provoking a fight with the man. Satisfied, Giiyam nodded, then gestured for Kiru to follow. "Come."

Kiru did so. They walked in silence down a small grassy hill and continued to cut through a thick grove of trees. Kiru chewed on the half-orc's words. The first bit was easy to digest. After all, he had secret intentions. Keeping a low profile would make him less of a target. He thought about the second, and that was a source of frustration. He had entirely glossed over the fact that the Warrior Games were a group competition! He knew that it was a team-based event, but all his trials and focus on recovering and reaching Gold had occupied his attention. He was so intent on getting to the point that he *could* participate in the Warrior Games that he'd not made an exact plan as to *how* he would. He realized that looking for teammates meant that maintaining a low profile would be more difficult, especially if he had to interact with others in any in depth.

Also, that certainly wasn't going to help keep his identity as a psion secret. Lastly, it was evident that being both a Defunct and a member of Fist House made him a less desirable teammate. Convincing others to join him would be a challenge in and of itself. His musings stopped after half an hour when Giiyam led him to the bottom of the hill past the tree line.

Kiru looked up to see a massive lake before them. It had once been connected to the Tori River at some point, given their proximity and with only about twenty acres of land separating the two bodies of water. There was a small port with a number of boats connected to it as well as a group of people getting onto one of the ships, talking excitedly. That, however, wasn't what mainly caught his focus. Out on the water was a large island. On that island was another thick forest and a gigantic series of stone buildings towering over the tall trees. All in all, it was impressive. The only reason Kiru could tell it was an island was because his mother had told him about it years ago.

"The academy," Kiru said aloud in awe, without meaning to. *I've done it!* He was here! A tear rolled down his left cheek as he thought of his mother and the sacrifice she had made to get him to this point. More tears started to well up as his thoughts lingered on her. The psion quickly fought to suppress those feelings. He couldn't think about Surturia too long without being overwhelmed by sadness, and he needed to focus on doing what she had died for him to accomplish.

Kiru quickly wiped away the tears before Giiyam could see them and question him. Fortunately, his momentary sadness didn't seem to affect his Telekinesis technique, so his movements still appeared normal.

They reached the port not long after the boat departed, where an elderly dwarf with a braided beard adorned in golden beads was sitting at a small table with a metal box in front of him. Giiyam led Kiru up to him and handed the man Kiru's stone tablet and badge. The dwarf, it turned out, was some retired general of the kingdom and was named Escobert III. He seemed decidedly not thrilled at the academy accepting a Defunct and even haughtily asked why the school should waste their resources on him.

Taking Giiyam's advice, Kiru kept his true motivations secret and lied to the general, laying it on thick that he wanted to become a decorated officer just like him. Kiru went on to proclaim that he did plan to win the Warriors Games but even after that wouldn't use the loophole to forego military service, as becoming a decorated officer would be more admirable.

Kiru was pretty sure he saw the stoic half-orc actually give a slight smile at the psion's words. The retired general *really* liked Kiru's answer and said that he would personally make sure he would be teaching Kiru's Basic Combat I and Strategies I classes. The psion wasn't so sure if that was a good thing or not, as the elder dwarf enthusiastically proclaimed that he would push Kiru harder than the others due to his militaristic intent.

Escobert took out a red jacket and sealed Kiru's badge to it with some very durable adhesive. The dwarf informed Kiru that Shield House wore yellow, and Sword House wore blue. He gave it to Kiru, informing him that red was the color of Fist House, and he would be required to wear the jacket at most times. A mischievous glint lit the retired general's eyes.

"Mister Giiyam, you told me that we've had an issue with abyssal weed growing not far from the docks, correct?"

The half-orc raised an eyebrow. "Yes," he answered simply.

"Well then, I think it's time you got some help with that. I found the source of the infestation not a quarter mile north of here. If you follow the shoreline, you'll find it. If you would be so kind, I would like you to escort Cadet Kiru here to handle the problem personally."

Both the psion and half-orc looked at the dwarf in surprise. He was already getting an assignment. Also, Kiru wasn't technically a cadet.

Escobert smiled. "I told you, Defunct, I will push you harder if you wish to serve in the military. Now I'm hungry, and I'm heading back to get me some food. Dismissed!"

Before Kiru could say anything, Giiyam unceremoniously tugged his shoulder. "Come."

"Wait, can he do that?" Kiru asked as he followed Giiyam.

"Do what?"

"Force me to pull weeds. Isn't that—I don't know—not what cultivators of this academy are supposed to be doing?"

"Since you are a student of the academy now, the retired general can indeed order you to do almost any task. As for your second question . . . You'll find that this is *exactly* what cultivators here should be doing."

Kiru mulled over the groundskeeper's words but didn't understand. Despite Kiru's follow-up questions, Giiyam remained silent. Eventually, they made it to the edge of a small bog next to the pond. Giiyam stuck his scarred arm out to stop Kiru. He then put a finger to his mouth, signaling for him to be quiet. Kiru was confused as to why.

"Do you see those three plants there?" Giiyam whispered, pointing into the bog.

Three strange mushroom-like plants, about four feet in height, stood arranged in a triangle. They were crooked, ugly things, colored a sickly mix of black and brown.

"Those are abyssal weeds. They are nasty plants that choke off and kill all other plant life. They are also predatory plants, so be careful. To stop them, you need to cut out their bodies and stab your weapon directly downward to get all the way to their roots. Understand?"

Kiru blanched a little at the description. He'd never heard of a predatory plant before.

"Good. Now, go," Giiyam whispered, taking the psion's jacket and duffle bag, and forcefully shoving him into the bog.

Kiru looked back, upset at being forced into the muddy water that now went halfway up his boots. Fortunately, he was able to prevent himself from making too much noise as he stepped in.

Giiyam didn't seem bothered by the psion's mood in the slightest.

Kiru groaned a little and then turned back, trying to trudge through the bog as quietly as possible.

"Hey, Master, I was thinking, why don't I go and kill those plants? I've been itching to get some more combat experience since I kicked that healer's ass back at the village."

Kiru remembered said "ass-kicking" very differently, but he didn't say anything about it. "If you want to, sure." He shrugged.

"Aw, yes! I'm so excited!" the imp shouted. Kiru could've sworn he saw one of the weeds move out of the corner of his eye, but when he looked at them directly, they were still.

Before Kiru could shush his familiar, William had already hopped off the psion's shoulder and began quickly crawling across some fallen logs. "Hahaha! Prepare to die before my might, you stupid weeds!" he declared, now only a couple feet away.

At that, the plants responded. Suddenly, all three of the abyssal weeds stalks opened wide, revealing hideous maws, which began to shriek. Each one of them then uncovered a pair of wickedly barbed vines that had previously been hiding under the water's surface. One of the weeds whipped one of those vines directly at the imp.

"Oh, shit!" William said, ducking and narrowly dodging the attack. The familiar turned tail and ran all the way back up to his master's shoulder. "I've changed my mind. I'm no longer excited to fight them. I defer to your great fighting ability, Master."

"Thanks," Kiru said, giving a slight chuckle at the imp's complete one-eighty. He unsheathed his short swords. At least the weeds were stationary, so they shouldn't be too much trouble.

Then the monstrous weeds charged toward them through the bog.

"Oh, shit!" This time, both Kiru *and* William swore in shock. As in his fight at Fox Hollow, Kiru began to focus his mental mana more into his leg meridians. As the weeds neared, he launched himself. The two weeds at the front lashed out, but their vines bounced off his armor as he went past them. In one quick motion, Kiru bisected the abyssal weed in the back. Remembering Giiyam's advice, he spun and stabbed straight down into the plant's exposed body. The stalk gave a small shriek as it wriggled for a second, then went slack. *One down, two to go.*

"Master, look out!" William said, just before a vine wrapped around the psion's right wrist and flung him into a nearby pine with a *whack*. Kiru coughed as some of the wind was knocked out of him, then quickly got to his feet a millisecond before they were on him again. The style that Surturia taught Kiru was mostly offensive, but she did teach a few defensive forms in there too. Using one of those, Kiru quickly cut off part of the vines lashing out toward him and rolled to the right. He splashed in the water and soaked William, but he managed to avoid the weeds' follow-up strikes.

The nearest abyssal weed screeched and shot out its two thorny vines directly at the psion, as if seeking to impale him through the gut. Using *just* a little bit of Telekinesis on the vines so that Giiyam wouldn't be able to notice, Kiru directed them to veer slightly to his left and miss him while he charged forward. He quickly closed the distance, cutting off the vine arms right near the base. The abyssal weed screamed and bit down on his right forearm.

Kiru grunted from surprise rather than physical pain. He was about to swipe at the weed with his left sword when the other one joined in, wrapping both of its vines around his free hand and holding it in place. Both of the predatory plants growled like dogs as they held tightly to their prey.

Kiru's heart raced. He was stuck unless he used Telekinesis. He couldn't make it obvious, though. Giiyam was likely still watching him, and he had to keep his identity as a psion a secret. What else could he do, though? By himself, he was stuck . . . but luckily he wasn't by himself! "William, use Hot Hand on the one to my right!"

The imp looked unsure, "But—"

"Now!" Kiru barked, not giving any room for hesitation from his familiar.

Startled by the harsh command, the imp complied, jumping on top of the mushroom-like head of the abyssal weed and using the Hot Hand technique on the plant. Smoke quickly started to arise from the plant, and the smell of burnt foliage permeated the air. The weed opened its mouth, freeing Kiru's arm. Then it began screaming and wildly flailing in an attempt to get rid of the pesky imp.

The psion did not let the opportunity go to waste. At once, he used his free right-hand sword to cut the vines restricting his left hand and attacked the lone weed. Kiru cut through the wriggling vines as he moved forward. When he made it to the main body, he cut the invasive plant into eight pieces before stabbing downward to kill its roots.

With the other two down and the third now without its vines and being straddled by William, the fight didn't last much longer. William's trademark confidence returned as well, bolstered by his contribution to the abyssal weeds' demise.

Using a form his mother called "Dragon Ascends the Sky," Kiru positioned both his blades pointing low then slashed his weapons upwards in a diagonal direction, bisecting the weed. The psion quickly followed up with a final stab down into the plant's base. William climbed back up to his perch on Kiru's shoulder. "Hahaha! Take that, you stupid plants! None can stand before the might of Kiru the Conqueror and William, Breaker of Wills!"

Kiru flicked the grime off his weapons and was about to sheathe them when he heard movement through the water to his right. Acting on instinct, he swung one of his blades out in a horizontal strike. To his surprise, however, his momentum was suddenly halted when something extremely strong grasped his wrist. Kiru turned to see that it was Giiyam! Kiru blinked in shock. The man was just the groundskeeper, and subconsciously, Kiru had put very little stock in what the man was capable of. To see that Giiyam was capable of stopping the full force of Kiru's telekinetic swing with just one hand made the psion instantly re-evaluate him.

The stoic half-orc nodded, seemingly unfazed by the weapon just inches from his face. "You have a good instinct for fighting. I see that you favor the elven sword forms, choosing dexterity over brute strength, but you are still sloppy. You are going to have to practice a lot more to compete against the other students." He let go of Kiru's wrist. The groundskeeper turned back and started walking out of the bog, waving for Kiru to follow. "Make sure you work to impress Escobert. You'll need his knowledge if you're going to win the Warrior Games."

Kiru sheathed his weapons and followed the groundskeeper. He had a long way to go, indeed.

# CHAPTER NINETEEN

# Lay Of The Land

Kiru followed Giiyam out of the bog.

"You must have a high pain tolerance. The barbs from an abyssal weed's vines are known to be agony-inducing to most," the half-orc said.

Not wanting to give anything away, Kiru promptly ignored the implication of the groundskeeper's words and tried to appear more injured than he actually felt.

The stoic groundskeeper gave a low sigh and handed Kiru a pill, telling him that it was restorative and would help Kiru's wounds heal more quickly. Kiru had taken pills before but only ones of middling quality. True pills, like the one he was being offered, were powerful displays of alchemy. Kiru took a look at the superficial cuts on his hand and swallowed the pill. As soon as he did, his skin began to sizzle. He didn't know if it was supposed to hurt or not, but he watched in awe as his cuts sealed up before his very eyes, his skin letting off small streaks of smoke from where it was regenerating.

Kiru thanked the half-orc for the healing. When they got back, Escobert was notably impressed to see how quickly he had finished the job, and he happily had the two join him on the final boat to the academy. It was just the three of them, as Kiru truly did appear to be the last student to cross the bridge that day, as well as the muscular human woman pulling the chains across for the boat ferry. She eyed Kiru's red jacket suspiciously but said nothing. Though she was clearly strong, Kiru could tell that it was going to take some time for the woman to get them to the academy, so he decided to be productive. He laid down, leaned his back against one side of the boat, stopped doing his Telekinesis, and instead cultivated. Kiru smiled a little to himself. He was growing more confident that people couldn't detect his "unique" way of moving. It gave the young psion a sense of progress and growth that couldn't be objectively measured. As he laid there without having to use his mana, he was able to recover some of the losses from his fight against the weeds.

As they neared the academy, the impressiveness of the buildings only grew in Kiru's eyes. Sure, there was plenty of wood around, but the sheer size and number of stones needed to construct such elaborate structures must've taken the work of thousands of people—or a few extremely powerful cultivators—to attain!

Though the stone buildings of the academy grounds were large, however, they were still dwarfed by the dense forest surrounding the grounds. The woods also seemed darker and seemed to radiate an ominous energy.

Giiyam seemed to notice Kiru's concern. "As you may have guessed, the forest surrounding the academy grounds is not safe. The island contains a large source of ambient mana. While that helps cultivators replenish their mana stores faster, it also has evolved its fair share of animals into sacred beasts, as well as attracting others from a distance."

Kiru felt William tense on his shoulder, no doubt reminded of his dreaded nemesis, the koi fish sacred beast.

"Not only that, Giiyam. You forgot the most important part. The main reason we get so many sacred beasts in the forest is because deep inside it are the ruins of an ancient dungeon," Escobert added.

That gave Kiru pause. "A dungeon? As in, an official dungeon?" he asked before he had time to think. Kiru learned from Surturia that there were two types of dungeons in the world. The first was a prison and was often referred to as such. The second was a living chamber, seemingly designed to bring danger and kill cultivators. With risk, though, came benefits. Those who could survive would be rewarded, typically with items that made the adventurer a more effective combatant or advanced them in their cultivation—and this school apparently had one!

Escobert gave a smile. "You're right, Defunct." The word seemed to take the dwarf's joy from him, because afterwards he immediately sighed. "It won't matter to you, though. The dungeon is only safe for those at least at Sapphire-rank. Best not to think about it."

Kiru suppressed a frown but also still held out hope. They only *thought* he was a Defunct, but truly, he was using a technique more frequently than anyone else at the academy would ever realize. Kiru still had a chance to make his first dungeon dive.

Once they reached the island, Escobert left them to give a report to the headmaster about the new students, leaving Giiyam to take the psion on an abbreviated tour of the grounds, though the half-orc only did so begrudgingly. First off, there was a large stone boundary wall marked with protective runes encircling the campus. This was meant to keep everyone safe inside.

Right inside the walls was a large grassy courtyard with a pair of white-barked trees with orange leaves. There were many buildings spread around the courtyard, including a large, interconnected castle with three giant, notably wide spires. That was the academy's main teaching facility, with a spire dedicated to each year of students. Off to the left was another grandiose square stone building, nowhere near the height of the castle spires, but still impressive. That was the library, where he'd have his internship with his sponsor.

Beside the library was a large tree that looked to be made of stone with a dome of glass instead of leafy foliage. It had spiraled over itself repeatedly and was just as tall as the library. Inside each layer that coiled upward were various windows indicating where rooms were. It was an apartment complex—the dormitory for the Sword House, according to Giiyam. It even had a sword insignia emblazoned on it. Faculty Housing was just fifty yards away, which indicated clear, convenient advantages for those of the Sword House.

To the right of the castle was the Shield House dormitory. It was a large, round building that was made of brick and glass with some wood accents. Much of the glass was stained, making an ornate, complex picture of a gold shield. The structure was neither as large nor as beautiful as Sword House, but it was still significantly better than any place Kiru had lived in by a long shot! There also appeared to be a small shrine beside the building. It wasn't very large, but it had the distinct architecture of the houses of worship Kiru had seen back in Bristleton. Kiru wasn't very religious, though, so he only knew the basics of the pantheon.

Not far off from those structures were a few domed structures which Giiyam explained were practice arenas that students could reserve for training. The groundskeeper also informed him that the stables, bestiary, and greenhouse were on the other side of the castle. Inside the castle itself, aside from classrooms and offices, were multiple common areas, an observatory, and a cafeteria.

The last building the psion was shown was the least impressive of them all. Unsurprisingly, that ended up being the Fist House dormitory. It was simple, small, primarily made of wood compared to the stone of the other buildings, and only had two levels. Each of the other dorms had five to six, by Kiru's estimation. The structure was also right by the border wall, about a hundred yards from the campus grounds entrance.

Kiru grimaced at its location compared to the other houses. Sure, those of Fist House were of the lowest import, but this seemed unnecessary.

William agreed with Kiru's feelings, muttering angrily under his breath.

Giiyam led the psion to his room, which was 209, and handed him the key. "Breakfast at seven bells, lunch at mid-day, and dinner at five bells. I will leave you to your room and to explore the campus grounds. Classes start in two days." With that, the half-orc left Kiru. The psion promptly unlocked the door and went into his room. As he suspected, the inside matched the outside: shabby. He had a simple cot, a desk, a slightly crooked chair, a wardrobe, and drawers that had trouble closing, a trash receptacle, a mirror, a lamp, and a large wash cauldron. All in all, it was actually a slight improvement upon where he grew up. It even had a soft red carpet to keep his feet warm. Though the flooring was dingy, Kiru would call it a win.

The wash basin had a faucet with fancy, rune-etched temperature controls, too! Taking out a sponge and washcloth, Kiru decided to make use of it. He, William, and his armor had dried mud in many crevices that needed to be addressed. The water was indeed warm and pleasant. His bag also contained soap. It was just a sponge bath, but it helped the psion feel immensely better. Besides the nice, new feeling of being clean, Kiru was so taken in by the rush of new stimuli that a large smile was plastered on his face.

The psion took the time to meticulously care for his mother's armor, having William use his sharp nails to claw out the dried mud before Kiru wiped it clean. Now that both it and he were fully clean, Kiru really could appreciate the lack of rotten plant odor to which he had previously been nose-blind. That odor quickly assaulted him again when his familiar neared his face. William just grimaced after smelling one of his armpits, then Kiru used Telekinesis to fling the dirty imp into the washbasin. The imp cried in panic before the sound was cut off by a loud splash. After his multiple near-death incidents from the koi fish sacred beast, the imp seemed to have developed a phobia of submerging himself in water.

William screamed in fear as he launched himself from the basin. His bony body landed, and he hyperventilated, looking like a wet cat. "Master, I disapprove of that! I could've sponged myself, just like you!" He scowled, pointing his finger at the psion. In Kiru's estimation of the past two years with the imp, the little demon's hygiene was . . . lacking. Ever since the koi first tried to eat William, he couldn't even recall the little imp truly ever getting a thorough cleaning.

"You could've sponged yourself," he admitted. "But this was more effective." *And more fun.*

William grumbled but conceded.

After Kiru went through all his belongings and unpacked them, he examined the simple-looking uniform that he was supposed to wear under his house colors jacket. "Master, I don't think you should wear those clothes. They look dumb. Your armor is way more intimidating. You'll make the chumps here quiver in fear at the muscles they make you look like you have!"

Kiru grimaced, reminded of how unhealthily thin his body looked from his severe muscle atrophy. "I don't have a choice in the matter. I'm going to likely stand out enough being labeled as a defunct. That doesn't mean that you're wrong, William," he said and proceeded to put on the clothing over his armor. The clothes were very large and baggy, which worked to the psion's benefit. Well, they wouldn't have been if he hadn't been so unhealthily thin. So, the clothes covered his body just enough so he could wear his enchanted armor.

William nodded and gave a thumbs-up, impressed by the half-elf's idea. That was when a knock came from the door. William growled like an overprotective dog.

Kiru motioned for the imp to back off. "Who is it?" he asked.

"This is Joseph, Third-Year and Advisor over Fist House," a jovial reply came back.

Kiru felt his familiar hop on his shoulder, then opened the door. There, standing before them, was a human man in his early twenties. He had wavy blonde hair that went down to his shoulders, dark brown eyes, and a large grin on his face. "Hey, brother, you must be . . ." He glanced down to the clipboard in his hands. "Kiru! Well, Kiru, as I said before, the name's Joseph. Welcome to Fist House. The place isn't any royal palace, but it definitely beats living out in the forest. There's a washroom downstairs and a couple of outhouses not far from the dorm. In the meantime, I suggest exploring the campus grounds so you know where all of your classes are."

The cheerful guy then seemed to notice William. "Whoa! Who's this little dude?"

The imp gave an indignant scowl. "I am William, Breaker of Wills, you little cretin," he said.

"Ooh! I get it! He's your familiar! That's awesome, brother. But wait, if you have a familiar, you must be a noble. So what're you doing in . . ." He looked at Kiru's badge, and his eyes widened in understanding. Though his smile remained, there was an underlying sadness to it. "Oh, that's rough, brother." His happier demeanor then immediately returned. "Still, it's sayin' something if you still made it to the academy, despite not being able to use a technique!" he said, slapping Kiru's left arm good-naturedly. "Believe it or not, you're not the only noble in Fist House. In fact, about half of us are!"

"Really?!" Kiru asked, surprised.

"Totally, brother! Many families put their kids through the academy's curriculum because being a graduate from here provides a level of distinction recognized throughout the world. We may not qualify for the fanciest jobs like a Royal Guard, nor inherit some duchy, since we're 'the worst house'"—at this, he made air quotes—". . . but becoming an officer in an elite division of the kingdom's army ain't a small thing. Believe me, brother, despite some of the obvious danger, the king takes good care of his troops. My uncle just finished his thirty years of service. Not only did he come out with barely a scratch for his service, the Twin Blades Mercenary Company asked him to be their head!"

"The Twin Blades?!" Kiru knew of them. They were some of the best bounty hunters and fighters in the entire kingdom! A traveling bard troop would come by Bristleton once a year and do three different performances. The last one was always of the latest exploits of the Twin Blades. Kiru always loved seeing it.

"Yeah, brother," Joseph said. "Not only does he get paid well, he gets all the finest gear, too."

"That's great! Congratulations!"

Joseph blushed, scratching the back of his head. "Thanks, man. If you don't mind me asking, are you really from a noble house?" He leaned in and whispered conspiratorially. "It's just that most of the ones I've met that are part of Fist House act like they have a stick up their ass, you know what I'm saying?"

Kiru chuckled. "No, I'm not," he said, telling a half-truth. "My familiar was a gift from my mo—teacher," he quickly corrected himself. "She gave him to me before she died."

"Whoa, that's heavy, brother. Well, I'm glad she gave you something to remember her by."

Kiru nodded in agreement.

A bell then rang out across the grounds six times, indicating the time. "Ah, I gotta go, brother. It was nice meeting you. If you have any problems, just let me know. I'm in room 101."

Kiru thanked Joseph before going back to his room. He smiled. He couldn't help himself. Aside from Giiyam, Joseph was the first person who didn't treat him with any skepticism for being a Defunct. Thinking back on growing up in Bristleton, he was pretty much an outcast there too. It made him truly appreciate those who acted with genuine kindness like Joseph. That interaction really did lift his spirits. It gave him hope that there would be others. Hopefully, he could find enough other First-Years to form a team.

# CHAPTER TWENTY

# Reunion

Kiru was exhausted from all the day's events. Now fresh and clean, he lay on the simple cot and passed out almost immediately. He woke up the next morning to the sound of obnoxious snoring. William was sprawled out on the carpet, fully asleep with a trail of drool streaming from his mouth. Realizing he'd forgotten to cultivate before he'd fallen asleep, the psion took the time to intake the mental mana coming from the imp's dreaming mind. After a few hours of that, he woke up his familiar so they could explore the campus together.

First stop, the cafeteria.

Kiru was treated to a scrumptious breakfast of eggs, potatoes, and biscuits. Well, he only had one biscuit, as the server refused to give William any food, despite the demon's protests. So, Kiru gave him some of his. The psion had to keep himself from staring at all the other students around him, each in the standard red, yellow, or blue jackets. And there were such a diverse set of people, too! He saw orcs, humans, elves, dwarves, gnomes, one that he presumed to be a goblin, and drakonids.

William forcibly shut Kiru's open mouth as he looked over at the draconic humanoids. The drakonids were tall, standing at six and a half feet at minimum. Their scales were bright, as if they'd just been polished, and every single one carried themselves with distinct purpose and drive. He immediately got the impression that they were a hardy people with intense discipline, if this is how they carried themselves just walking around a cafeteria of all places.

Kiru then noticed that above many students' jacket badges was a marker. Most had either two or three golden lines, a clear indication of what year the students were in. It looked like first-years were differentiated by having no golden lines at all. Many students didn't give him a second glance; most who did gave him a scowl or a smug look of superiority. He tried to find Joseph, but the third-year was nowhere in sight. Kiru attempted to join a table populated by other Fist House Students, a pair of second-years sitting across from a pair of third-years.

The looks of contempt they gave the psion were worse than any of the others he'd received so far. "Beat it, trash!" one of them spat. "We don't need a damn defunct here with us. We have enough issues being Fist House without someone demeaning our statuses any further!"

Kiru sighed. "So you must be ones with the sticks up your asses," he said, then immediately regretted it. While his ability to control his anger had improved, his smart mouth hadn't yet.

"What'd you say, punk?!" One of them stood up, fury etched on his face. "I may be in this damned house, but as a third-year and the number-two cultivator in Fist House, I'll happily wipe the floor with you." His friends scowled as well, more than willing to assist in a beatdown.

Kiru quickly realized that this wasn't a situation where he'd have a chance of coming out the victor. He quickly grabbed William off his shoulder before the imp could antagonize the jerks any further. "You're right. I'll leave you be," he said, in an attempt to placate the upperclassmen. They continued to glare at him, but his words mollified them enough that they didn't say or do anything else.

He eventually found an unoccupied table and ate alone. William whined that his master hadn't challenged the rude students further, but Kiru waved him off. Even though the guy had been an ass, Kiru wasn't interested in a four-on-one fight. Being an S-Ranked combatant, he liked to think he could take them, but even then, they had been at the academy for years. No need to provoke someone who was likely more knowledgeable about combat strategy. Apparently, the student drama wasn't done yet, though, as just as he was finishing his meal, he heard the pointed noise of someone clearing their throat right behind him.

He turned back to see four first-years from Sword House gazing back at him. There was a gnome wielding a wooden staff taller than herself; a rather lanky gold drakonid in black leathers; a bulky, hairy human who wore no shirt under his jacket and had a great axe strapped to his back; and a thin, pale elf with straight black hair that went halfway down his torso, a rapier attached to his hilt.

And above the elf's shoulder fluttered a green and luminescent . . . person? They wore a green tunic and two fluttering wings like a butterfly. He quickly realized it was the elf's familiar. The elf had a snooty look about him, standing in front of the others. He was clearly the leader of this assembled group.

"You're in our spot, Fist," the elf said, looking down on Kiru with an air that reminded him of a certain noble from his hometown. One look at the pompous jerk was all that Kiru needed to confirm it. This elf was a bully, and Kiru *really* didn't like bullies.

"You know, the funny thing is, *I* was here first, and I don't see your name anywhere. So, I think I'm gonna stay," he said, his voice dripping with ire. He couldn't win a fight against a Ruby, a few of which he'd sensed in the room, but he could tell this guy was a Gold. Though he kept his expression firmly in place, Kiru grimaced internally. He knew he was being antagonistic and should cut it out immediately. It drew unnecessary attention to himself. Definitely *not* low profile.

The elf's pompous cracked in anger, his pale skin taking on a tint of red. "Do you not know who I am, you failure?"

William hopped over to join his master, snarling at the rude elf. Feeling emboldened as well as a little pissed off himself, Kiru gave a toothy grin. "Well, gee, I didn't ask who you were, did I? That would require me to care, and unfortunately, I don't."

The gnome and drakonid stifled laughs at Kiru's jest, while the shade of red on the elf's face grew even darker. Even his familiar's green glow seemed to darken. The elf put a hand on the hilt of his weapon just as a heavy hand fell on Kiru's shoulder from behind. "Kiru, my boy, you must have Loki's luck on your side. When I got word that you deposited your token, I nearly didn't believe it! I'm so glad you were able to recover and make it to the academy."

The psion turned his head to see the bright, mischievous grin of his patron, Niajar J'sarko. The old elf then turned to the younger elf and his group. "Ah, Zane! So good to see you! I heard that you're on the verge of developing a second technique already. I'm so proud! Now, was I interrupting something?"

The elf—Zane, apparently—looked like he was going to say something nasty but then shut his mouth and grimaced. "Hi, Uncle Niajar. No, it was just a misunderstanding," he said pointedly, looking at Kiru. "I'm sorry I can't talk more, Uncle, but my team and I need to eat and train before classes start tomorrow."

"Completely understandable. Bye-bye now!" He waved them off as they turned and walked away, his boyish grin never leaving. "Now, as you probably know by now, you'll be interning under me at my library. Come along now, my boy. I have plenty to show you."

Kiru had a lot of questions about just what happened, so he was inclined to follow. That, and his patron had just stopped him from causing a fight before his first official day of school even began. Plus, he genuinely was curious about his internship. Kiru followed Niajar out of the castle and toward the library. "So, that guy was your nephew?"

"Well, he did call me Uncle. So, that would make sense, now, wouldn't it?" He smiled at Kiru.

"Are you his patron, too?"

Niajar actually gave a hearty laugh at that. "Goodness, no! That would be my brother, his father."

"So, his dad works here at the academy, too?"

"Yes, Niazen is the headmaster of the academy, actually. That's why Zane was all 'Do you know who I am?' Honestly, the boy is a skilled cultivator, but my brother's doting has given him a big head."

Kiru sighed. "Great," he muttered. First day here, and he'd already made enemies with the headmaster's son. He'd need to watch that mouth of his. The psion followed the elf out of the castle and into the nearby library. As soon as Kiru entered the building, his mouth dropped open once again. He'd never seen so many books in his life!

There were just two stories, but both were extremely tall. It had a considerable vaulted ceiling adorned with a complexly detailed mural of what seemed to be a settlement of elves living in a thick forest full of vibrantly colored leaves. Both levels had various doors opening into rooms and closets along the walls and the upper level also featured luxurious stained-glass windows intermixed with the regular clear ones. Everything inside the library was running in a well-organized fashion, and an almost uncomfortable quiet ran through the place.

"What do you think?" Niajar asked, his voice now in a low whisper.

"It's amazing!" Kiru said. "I've never seen such a beautiful library."

"Well, it's nothing like the one at the capital or even in Anor'Voren, but my modest place of work serves me well."

Kiru's eyes widened as he took a few steps ahead of Niajar. *This is modest?!* It only emphasized how little he'd seen of the world so far.

His silent appreciation of the place was then rudely cut off by the demon on his shoulder. "*Whatever*, this place is lame," the imp said, nonplussed while he scratched at his rear end. "There's no fighting here! Come, Master, let's go back to those jerks and beat their faces in with one of these books. That would be fun!"

Suddenly, a wave of pressure overtook Kiru from behind, making his blood run cold. Niajar's grin abandoned his face for the first time in Kiru's experience, now replaced by a look of icy fury. Kiru had just enough time to note a vein bulging from the elf's forehead before Niajar moved. Faster than the psion could process, the librarian had snatched the imp from his perch on Kiru's shoulder and pinned all of William's limbs down hard.

"Gah! Unhand me!" The imp spat and squirmed but to no avail.

"Now, Kiru, I must have misheard. It sounded like your familiar wanted to use my books—the tomes of rare accumulated knowledge I have spent *a century* gathering—as weapons. To defame and stain them. But that must be a mistake. Is that correct?" Though the question was directed at Kiru, his gaze did not leave the imp. The elf's pupils constricted as he glared, giving him a crazed expression that promised pain to the little demon.

"Oh! Of course! William would never dare harm your life's work. *Would* you, William?" Kiru asked pointedly, glaring at the demon.

The psion's words seemed to finally process in the imp's exposed brain. "Oh! Yes! I meant to . . . use the *knowledge* from the books to beat our enemies to a pulp. I wouldn't dream of using them as makeshift clubs!" the demon lied emphatically.

Just as fast as the smile had left the librarian, it returned. "Excellent," he said, then dropped William unceremoniously to the ground. "First, though, Kiru, do you know how to recall your familiar?"

The psion gave a puzzled look at his patron, "Recall, sir?"

The librarian nodded. "I expected as much. I admit, I was impressed to see you gain a familiar. Though I know not exactly how you acquired one, it's clear you weren't given proper tutelage regarding familiars. I have my own and will add training in that subject to your internship's curriculum. Now, if you two will follow me, I will show you around and explain your duties." The elf strode deeper into the library, beckoning for Kiru to follow.

"Wait, *you* have a familiar?" Kiru asked as he picked up the semiconscious demon and followed the elf.

Niajar didn't answer him but instead walked further into the library, weaving with practiced ease between the multitude of shelves that seemed to be arranged almost haphazardly. Kiru had to keep his wits about him as he almost walked straight into another shelf placed in an odd manner, just as he rounded a corner.

After a couple of minutes, the librarian stopped at a shelf. Without even looking, he reached over, pulled out a book, and handed it to Kiru. It was titled *Familiars for Dummies*. The psion tucked it in a satchel he had strapped around his shoulder. Then, from inside his chest, an orb of glowing blue light that matched the navy of his robe seemed to bubble from out his chest. The orb then contorted until it had transformed itself into the shape of a hummingbird. "This is Nicodemus, my familiar. Unlike yours, which is made from fire mana, he is formed from nature mana," he said, while patting the bird on the head. "Familiars are wonderful allies, but in terms of fighting, they are not able to contribute too much."

"Hey!" William cried out indignantly.

The librarian snapped a sharp look at the imp, which quickly shut him up.

Without missing a beat, Niajar pressed on. "But just because they don't thrive in direct combat doesn't mean they can't contribute. When you recall a familiar into your core, they provide an extra reserve of mana—very valuable, especially in a fight. And when let out, they provide excellent companions and helpers in times of need."

Nicodemus chirped happily in affirmation at the praise.

"The extra benefit they provide is that they enhance your techniques' potency. Sometimes, they can even produce unique benefits. Why, it was Nicodemus's power that helped me to stabilize your broken body when I found you in that alley."

Kiru blanched, the image of his twisted, battered spine snapping in his mind's eye.

Niajar's grin grew even wider. "I told you before, anyone who can survive such injuries to their core and recover undoubtedly deserves to be part of the academy." He whistled like a bird, and Nicodemus turned back into an orb of light then drifted easily back into his chest. "Oh! Another benefit is that you can use the recall to prevent your familiar from making provocative statements that invite unnecessary problems," he said, his eyes now focusing on the imp, promising retribution.

Kiru's eyes widened. The librarian had been extremely helpful. He quickly considered revealing his psionic secret to Niajar but thought better of it. The enigmatic elf had a mischievous air to him that made Kiru feel that even when Niajar was helping, he was up to his own mischievous plans. Still, despite whatever his motives might be, he had undoubtedly helped Kiru with this book.

The smile on the psion's face grew to mirror his sponsor's. Then he also turned to face the troublemaking imp.

William began to shake as his beady eyes went back and forth from his master to the librarian. He gulped. "Oh, shit."

# CHAPTER TWENTY-ONE

# Old Rival

After Niajar gave Kiru his book about familiars, the whimsical elf guided the psion throughout the rest of the library, informing him about his daily duties. For two hours a day, every day, Kiru had to assist his patron and the rest of the staff in various tasks, including dusting, organizing, and scribing the various tomes. The last one seemed strange, until he realized that a variety of the books collected were written by hand, and the decay of time wore down on both the ink and parchment that they were written on.

Although he was still excited about being an academy student and he was an avid reader at home, Kiru had to force himself not to groan at the tedious tasks he'd be responsible for. He did perk up, however, when he learned that whenever Niajar or one of his contacts would bring in a newly collected ancient tablet or scroll from some archaeological site, he'd be allowed to assist. He hoped that he might glean some ancient psion lore and learn some ultra-powerful hidden technique. It was a lofty wish, but at least it might bring him some enjoyment during his time in the library. Transcribing old texts could get extremely boring.

After Kiru had been shown the facility and his duties, the librarian left him to his own devices. Eager to learn how to recall his unruly familiar, Kiru found one of the private study rooms he'd been shown. All of them were specifically warded with soundproof runes to ensure they wouldn't be heard.

"C'mon, Master, I don't think this is necessary. I'll be good, I promise," William pleaded.

Kiru rolled his eyes, not convinced. "It's not like you'll be recalled *all* the time, William." He decided to approach it from a different angle. "Listen, you want me to beat up the assholes, right?"

"Of course! I love beating up pompous little bitches like that elf in the cafeteria! Grr, I wish we *had* beat him up."

Kiru nodded. "And you want me to get more powerful so I can beat *more assholes*, right?"

"Most definitely!"

"Then you're going to *want* me to be able to recall you. Niajar said that when you're recalled, I get an extra reserve of mana. With you and me teaming up, my Telekinesis will be even more powerful! Plus, we'll be beating them up together! That sounds fun, right?" Kiru asked.

"I guess," the imp acquiesced, pouting.

Kiru smiled. "Good. Now, let's see if we can figure this out." For the next hour, the psion searched through the tome to learn about the surprisingly deep process of how to recall one's familiar. Apparently, both master and familiar had to have a deep connection, realizing that they were, in fact, inseparable parts of each other. Each of them were two sides of the same coin, both different and the same.

Kiru looked at the objectively ugly imp unashamedly picking his nose and wondered how he could ever be considered the same as Kiru. The half-elf continued to read, and one thing stuck out to him. "It says that both master and familiar have strengths that the other needs. If each can lay themselves bare and admit what they lack that their soulbound companion possesses, they can achieve a greater form of unity," he read aloud.

William puffed out his chest at that. "Oh, so it says I have strength? I knew that you needed me, Master."

Kiru could tell that that section held the key, but he was puzzled. What strengths did he need from William? "Well, it says we both have strengths. So, you need me, too."

"Well, yeah, but I do all the heavy lifting."

Kiru stared at the imp, unconvinced.

"Gah! Okay, you are strong, much stronger than me, and you really know how to kick ass with those swords of yours!"

"*And?*" Kiru asked intently.

The imp sighed, "And you keep me out of trouble," he reluctantly admitted.

Kiur chuckled slightly, and to his surprise, he realized what strengths he needed from William. While he was the more calm and collected one, William represented the "fire in his belly." With the imp, Kiru felt driven to compete, to win, to . . . conquer. Maybe Kiru the Conqueror wasn't such a bad name, after all.

"And you, buddy, you are my competitive edge. Your . . . zeal for combat keeps me sharp. Your honesty and bravery in the face of something wrong is admirable. Simply put, you are my courage, William. Without you, I wouldn't have kicked nearly as much ass as I have. The assassin and those other applicants back at Fox Hollow would've had me, without the edge you've given me."

"Damn straight!" William agreed enthusiastically.

They both high-fived each other, and it was at that point of contact that Kiru felt something . . . new. He felt what could be best described as a "string" connecting from his core in his head to the imp. Acting on instinct, he closed his eyes and began slightly pulling the string back into his core.

Willliam let out a startle of surprise, but quickly let it happen. The imp rapidly turned into an orb of red light before being drawn into his mental mana core.

With a new sensation of mana inside him, Kiru opened his eyes. He looked around, but his familiar was nowhere in sight. Looking inside himself, he could see the unique construct of William's mana residing inside his core, enhancing its power.

The psion more intently focused on using Telekinesis on his forelimbs. He looked at his palms and wiggled his fingers with ease. Though he had come a long way in the past two years, he could already notice a subtle improvement in control of his fine motor functions. It was like moving his body when warm versus cold. He could still move adequately and appropriately when cold, but his body might just be a little stiffer, comparatively.

There was also one other notable benefit—the *silence*. While the ugly little demon was Kiru's best friend, he never shut up.

That bliss lasted all but ten seconds before it was interrupted once more. "*Whoa! This is weird!*" William's voice rang out inside Kiru's mind.

The psion scanned the room quickly. "Uhhh, William? You there?"

"*Yes I am, Master, but . . . I'm in your head. It's . . . weird in here. Whoa! I can see everything you can! This is great! It really will be like I'm kicking ass! Ohhhh, I was so scared that I wouldn't be conscious when you recalled me. Now, I get to talk with you all the time!*"

Kiru's jaw tensed, just barely suppressing a groan as he lost his blissful silence. At least the imp couldn't cause much trouble, not being free to unleash havoc. Now that he'd done it once, he wanted to practice again to ensure he was able to do it quickly and with ease, so he let him out again. The next time he recalled William, Kiru noticed that the imp did indeed go up to his core, but that itself was a problem. His core, unlike everyone else's, was in his head, not his chest. If someone saw him recall William, it could potentially out him as a psion.

They both pondered as to how to fix it. '*Hey, William, when I'm recalling you, can you travel through my meridians to get to my core, or do you have to go straight to the core itself?*'

"*I dunno, Master. Let's find out.*"

After a couple of attempts at recalling William, Kiru was able to successfully draw in his familiar into the meridian in his right arm through his palm. The transformed imp then easily traveled across the meridian and into his mental mana core in a flash. Kiru then attempted to summon William and did so from his chest as well. The psion grinned and recalled William one more time. Not only had he discovered something about recalling familiars that was not in the book Niajar had given him, but he had a solution to prevent people from suspecting he was a psion.

His mother had suggested forming an extra meridian around the fragments of his fire mana core. He had done so, making a protective ring. Kiru was grateful for her forethought and wisdom, as it was even more beneficial than originally intended. Now, instead of recalling William directly to his head, he would recall him through the extra meridian in his chest, where his broken core was. That way, no one would suspect anything was amiss when they would see William as an orb of red light floating into Kiru's body.

Now that the ability to recall was achieved, and the problem of bringing William directly into his mental mana core was fixed, Kiru relaxed slightly and did training of another kind before he left the library. A rather scrawny rat had peeked its head out from inside the thick wooden table, catching the psion by surprise. Seeing as he was in an enchanted room with no one looking, Kiru practiced his Telekinesis on the small creature. It resisted his pull, going back into the table. With time and an exertion of effort, however, Kiru's will superseded the rodent's own and was able to subtly increase the power of his technique.

Once that bit of training was done, he decided to tour the rest of the campus grounds. As he left, he noticed a female dwarf from Shield House, by the looks of her jacket, arguing with what looked to be a robed priest. He thought it best not to get involved in what he assumed was some sort of religious debate, especially once he heard the word "shrine" being thrown around. As Kiru walked by, he did his best to ignore the multiple looks of contempt or shock from the other students at the sight of his Defunct house badge. Instead, he kept his focus on searching for where the rest of his classes were located so he wouldn't be late on his first day.

He wasn't allowed access into the other spires, since he was just a first-year. While frustrating, it was just out of curiosity versus necessity that he wanted to check them out. In the first-year spire, he found his Kingdom History and Fire Mana Cultivation classrooms. In a large auditorium connected to the central common area was his Strategies I class. The last place he needed to find was the location of his Combat I class. It wasn't in the common area or spire, so he went outside to the main courtyard.

There were a multitude of students congregating in separate cliques, most of them consisting of members from the same houses, indicated by their matching jacket colors. Kiru decided to see if he could find some other fellow Fist House first-years. Hopefully, they would be more receptive to him. As he walked across, however, he noticed how few Fist House students were present. Those of Sword House outnumbered them five-to-one. Shield House was the same, at an estimated three-to-one ratio.

After scanning about, he fortunately did find a group of nervous-looking first-years talking quietly amongst themselves, looking apprehensively at the other cultivators about. They seemed . . . scared. William noticed it, too. He grumbled angrily that he didn't want to associate with the "cowards," but Kiru ignored him. This was his best chance to make some more allies, or at least work to make others not be openly hostile toward him.

As Kiru approached, he noticed they looked older than him, most in their mid-to-late twenties. From what he'd seen so far from the other students, that seemed to be common here. At only eighteen, that made Kiru one of the younger students.

"Um, hi there," Kiru said nervously, trying to be as jovial as possible. Admittedly, he was pretty uncomfortable. While growing up as a loner with a short temper and smart mouth made him good at getting into fights, it didn't really help his social skills much. Simply put, he wasn't very experienced at making friends. Spending two years in a dead volcano with only his mother and rude imp for company didn't help, either. "Uh, name's Kiru. First day here, too?" he asked, trying his best to keep a look of worry from growing on his face.

The four of them nodded. There were a pair of dwarf brothers—twins by the look of it—a blonde elf, and a dark-skinned human. "Genevieve," the human woman introduced herself. "This is Nel, and those two are Boris and Thoris."

It took Kiru a moment to respond. Genevieve was beautiful, with warm, hazel eyes and an exotic accent. Kiru hadn't had much experience with girls growing up, so seeing and interacting with the confident, striking person in front of him was a bit daunting. "Ah . . . nice to meet you. That accent, I've never heard it before. Are you from the kingdom?"

All four of them laughed. "You must not get out much," Genevieve said, chuckling. "I'm from Rowe. All of the citizens talk like me. Have you never met someone from Rowe before? Our countries *do* border each other, you know?"

Realizing just how sheltered he'd been all these years, Kiru's face blushed with heat like he'd been slapped. "I . . . didn't get out much before now. I'm kind of from the middle of nowhere here in this country," he admitted.

"You poor country bumpkin," Genevieve said, clicking her tongue. "While the Kingdom of Blades is known for its militant force, now you'll be able to see how we of the Kingdom of Rowe produce the finest cultivators around in the Great Alliance."

"That's where ye be wrong, lass," one of the dwarves retorted. Boris maybe? Kiru couldn't tell the difference between the two. "Everyone knows we dwarves of Stonereach produce the finest cultivators 'round!"

"Finest miners maybe, but cultivators? Pfft! Please," she jabbed.

Kiru was surprised. "I knew that the academy had a recruiting process for those outside the kingdom, but I didn't know that so many were accepted here."

Genevieve nodded. "Yeah, about a third of all students are from elsewhere, believe it or not. The academy here is one of the best in Alterra, so many of the top guilds and families send their people here. My father is one of our king's personal advisors, while Pete and Repeat here . . ." Both she and Kiru smiled at the joke. ". . . come from the Longbeard Mining Company."

Kiru nodded. Being from a mining town, he'd heard of the Longbeards. They were competitors to his town's local company, and once a year, a representative in their caravan would come into town with an offer to buy them out. It was a bit odd, but the Longbeards were voracious and wanted every minable piece of rock they could get. They never succeeded in buying Bristleton's mine, and the dwarves from the oligarchy often ended up getting in a shouting match with the miners from Bristleon. Still, they brought in good business to the inn where his mom worked.

"I'm from the Kingdom of Blades, too," the elf, Nel, said. She had a quiet voice and sharp eyes that displayed an intent focus. "My family resides in the capital. You say you lived 'in the middle of nowhere.'" May I presume you're from one of the more rural areas toward the east side of our country?"

Kiru was surprised. In all the activity of the recent days, he hadn't formed a plausible backstory. In his moment of surprise, he fumbled and told the elf the blatant truth. "Uh, yeah. I'm from Bristleton, actually. It's a mining settlement nestled right against the Blades." Although most assumed the kingdom was named for its great warriors, it was actually for the mountain range that encompassed the country's border, beside the ocean.

Nel's eyes widened. "You're from Bristleton," she said in shock. "You must've seen that volcano!"

"*Master, you fool!*" William scorned Kiru inside his mind. "*We need to keep our identity a secret as much as possible. You should kill them, kill them all now!*"

The psion fought to ignore the bloodthirsty desires of his familiar. He decided to lie. "No, actually. Well, only from a distance. I was taking my exam in another town when it . . . erupted?" he said, not sure how to describe a volcano suddenly growing and becoming active.

Nel sighed. "You missed a shitshow, then. My fiancé is from there, and he told me that the king himself came to aid in stopping the lava flow. Had to create a huge crater outside the city. Now there's a lake of the lava about a hundred yards out. It's not cooling off, either."

Kiru's eyes widened. "Really? And no one was hurt?"

Nel shook her head. "Not from what he told me."

Kiru exhaled a relieved breath. He put a hand to his chest. "Whoa, that's crazy. Glad no one was hurt." He then furrowed his brow as he thought about what she said. His heart began to race as concern built up. "Wait, did you say your *fiancé*?"

The elf pursed her lips and nodded solemnly.

"Nel comes from a family of merchants," Genevieve said. "Apparently, they arranged for her to get married to some noble from the boonies."

Something tickled at the back of Kiru's mind. She was engaged to be married to a noble from Bristleton. His heart sank when he put it all together.

"Oh shit, you're engaged to—"

"Mongrel?!" The word cut Kiru off from behind.

The psion closed his eyes. Even here, the noble asshat Ambrose Constantine had found a way to rain on Kiru's parade.

"Ambrose," Kiru said with a clenched jaw as he turned around to face his childhood rival. It had been two years, but the bastard was still unmistakable. He was slightly taller but still notably shorter than Kiru. He was still a little chubby and had some patchy peach fuzz on his face now. Oh, and there was a large, hand-shaped burn mark across his cheek. Like the last time he laid eyes on him, Ambrose had a pair of lackeys behind him. They weren't the same brutes as before, but they were brutes just the same.

They both stared each other down for a good half-minute. Kiru just scowled, forcing himself not to exact retribution for his mother right then and there. Ambrose's face kept vacillating between utter surprise and rage. The psion could tell the noble was flabbergasted at both him being alive *and* able to walk. Ambrose's face then rearranged itself to a familiar smugness. "I'm surprised to see you still standing after I beat your ass so bad that you couldn't sit straight back at home."

*"Ooooh, forget about the others, Master, let's kill him instead!"* William growled.

Kiru *really* wanted to comply. He despised the stuck-up punk. As he saw the boy who bullied him, lied, literally broke him, and had hired a guild of assassins to kill him, resulting in the death of his mother, the psion physically shook with anger.

"You shouldn't hit like a wuss next time. Nice face, by the way. Guess I was unsuccessful in slapping the ugly out of you."

The other Fist House students all stifled a laugh.

The noble scowled, but Kiru could tell in his eyes that Ambrose was scared. He clearly had no way of comprehending how Kiru could possibly be standing there before him. "How in the abyss are you alive? No one should've survived after—"

"After what?" Kiru spat. Years of anger were finally getting their release, and ooooh, it felt good. "After someone broke my spine because they were too weak to take me, a commoner, on in a fair fight? After that same person was too much of a coward to finish the job, so they hired some thug instead? Huh?" he shouted.

There was a look of true fear in Ambrose's eyes as he instinctively took a step back. He'd thrown all he had at Kiru, and it wasn't enough. His back pressed against his goons, and he suddenly remembered he wasn't alone. He snarled at Kiru and tugged on his blue jacket. "I don't know what you're talking about, cur, but it sounds like you managed to survive your ordeals like the cockroach you've always been."

Ambrose then noticed the patch on Kiru's red jacket, and after a moment, his smirk returned. "Haha! Oh my gods, you can't be serious. I knew you were worthless, but now this confirms it. You're a Defunct!" He cackled, pointing at Kiru's badge.

"So what?" Kiru cut him off, his right hand subconsciously grabbing one of the hilts of his shortswords. "I can still kick your ass, right here, right now." Though the eyes of everyone in the courtyard burned into the back of his head, he didn't care right now. Kiru was so close, so close to bringing some retribution on the smug bastard, he was hardly able to hold back tears in his barely contained rage. His nostrils flared as he began to hyperventilate slightly.

While he had been a smartass to others in the academy who had been rude to him, that had been more of an innate response. He didn't like jerks or bullies. *This*, however, was different. It was as if his entire body wanted to carve Ambrose up. The loss and pain from the past two years came surging back all at once, making Kiru's neck tense as he literally bared his teeth in anger at the noble.

William practically purred in approval at the anger.

"You must've not been paying attention to the orientation, peasant. Students can't fight each other on academy grounds, not unless it's a sanctioned duel with one of the staff monitoring. Consider yourself lucky," he said, scowling.

Kiru grunted. He couldn't afford to get kicked out of the academy. He'd barely made it in! Then, William whispered a thought to his brain. Kiru smiled. This was actually a good idea! "If you're some big shot like you claim to be, then I expect you'll be fighting in the Warrior Games, right?"

"Looks like I didn't beat the stupid out of you last time. Of course I'll be fighting in the games."

Kiru's grin then turned predatory. "Good. I'll kick your ass then."

It was just for a moment, but Ambrose's face blanched in abject terror before his sneer returned. A surge of electricity surged out of his hands, striking the ground right near Kiru's foot.

Kiru let out a startled shout and took a step back.

"Haha! We can't fight until the games, but it doesn't mean we can't practice our techniques on academy grounds in the meantime, mongrel. So, you better watch your step. Come on, Nel, let's ditch this loser," he said, then began stalking away across the brick path. The elf stepped past Kiru, mouthed the word "Sorry," then followed along.

The psion just stood there breathing heavily for a few seconds. He then noticed that everyone was looking at him. Great . . . He was really doing well in the "keeping a low profile" department. As he looked around, the other students realized they had been staring and quickly went back to whatever they had been doing.

He turned back to face the other three Fist House Students. They all looked at him with a mix of awe and shock.

"You got some big balls, bumpkin!" Genevieve said, sounding impressed. "I would've said, 'do you know who that is?' but it's clear you do. They say he's distant cousins with your king!"

Kiru sighed. "Yeah, he and I . . . weren't friends when we were younger."

"That's putting it lightly!" Genevieve laughed.

"Were ye serious 'bout bein' in the Warrior Games?" one of the dwarf twins asked.

"Yeah. I was actually wondering if you three are, too?"

"Yer mad! Ye can't do techniques! How're ye gonna beat 'em?" one of the dwarves asked in obvious incredulity.

Another of his mom's lessons from her *Art of War'* book asserted itself in his mind. *All warfare is based on deception.* Right now, he was deceiving everyone. They all thought he couldn't use a technique, that he had only ascended to the level of a Gold-rank cultivator and wielded a pair of swords, when in actuality, he did know one: Telekinesis. "People tend to underestimate me. They think I'm weak, but I'm actually S-rank in Combat. They also think I'm all alone. Then, I remind them that I'm not," he said in answer to the dwarf's question.

He closed his eyes, and a red orb emerged from the center of his chest, forming into the hunched, bare-brained, malnourished-looking imp he knew so well.

"Boom, bitches!" the little demon said, introducing himself to the trio of Fist students.

Not shockingly, they all recoiled in disgust. After Kiru explained who William was, they settled down, if only barely.

"So, are any of you going to participate in the games?" he asked again.

The three of them all shook their heads, then Genevieve spoke. "You may be a better fighter than we thought, bumpkin, but that doesn't mean we all are. Nel's just a merchant. The twins here are miners, go figure, and their guild paid for them to come here to enhance their abilities to find rare ore and protect themselves in case they find some giant mole or whatever. I, however, am a fighter," she said, and icy blue frost emanated from her hands. "Not an S-ranker, but still a respectable B."

"That's great! We can team up!" Kiru said.

At that, Genevieve looked regretful. "I'm sorry, bumpkin, but no. If the games were based on sheer bravery, you'd be the one, but they're not. Though you seem like a good guy, and being S-rank in Combat is damn rare and impressive, you can't deny that the true strength of a cultivator lies in their techniques. I have to make sure that I get the best team I can to win the games."

William was about to yell at her, but Kiru raised his hand to stop the imp. Being told you weren't good enough sucked, but he also understood where she was coming from. Techniques were supernatural abilities. It was obvious that those who could use them provided a distinct advantage over those who relied on just basic warfare. "Thank you for your honesty," he said, his disappointment clearly evident on his face. "I'll see you around."

He'd only taken a few steps when she gently grabbed him by the arm, "Hey, I really am sorry."

Kiru nodded silently.

"Listen," she whispered as she leaned in conspiratorially. "If you're looking for people to team up with, I suggest checking out the practice arenas over on the south side of campus. I heard there are some other people there doing the same thing. Now, I can't promise they'll be any good, but *someone* is better than no one."

Kiru sighed. He did appreciate the gesture. and she was right. Kiru hoped there would be a possible diamond in the rough. The Warrior Games required a team of four to participate. He thanked her and waved to the trio of fellow students, heading off toward the practice arenas.

# CHAPTER TWENTY-TWO

# Brunhilda

I*can see why you didn't like that guy, Master."* William, now recalled once more, spoke inside the psion's mind. *"That guy is a total buttface, even compared to all the jerks we just met!"*

Kiru chuckled at the childish insult. William wasn't wrong. By that point, they had reached the practice arenas. There were ten in total, half of them exposed to the elements while the other half were encased in stone, preventing outside eyes from watching what was happening inside. A few students were sparring and practicing, mostly those from Sword House, but there were a few from Shield House, mostly hanging back behind their blue-jacket counterparts to provide varying levels of support.

There were also some students simply hanging out and watching the sparring sessions. Kiru asked every first-year if they had a team or were looking to participate in the Warrior Games. Their responses ran the gamut of ways to say no, from insults and threats to polite "no thank yous" and just plain ignoring him.

Their reactions grated. Kiru understood why everyone was reluctant to have a Defunct join them. He thought that being S-ranked in Combat should have more than compensated for that, though. No one wanted to even give him a chance to show just how good he *was*. Still, Genevieve's advice to try the practice arenas was solid, if only slightly more productive than his attempt in the courtyard—and that was by accident.

One of the domed arenas was where his Combat I class was to be held. Wanting some time alone to allow his frustration to cool down, Kiru decided to finish his exploration of the campus grounds by finally seeing what was behind the central castle. Just as Giiyam had told him, there was a large greenhouse, a paddock, fenced-in stalls for animals, and a humble cottage nearby where he presumed the groundskeeper lived. Beyond that stood a set of large doors in the middle of the wall, another entrance into the academy grounds. But instead of being by the water, this entrance opened into the ominous forest.

Enjoying some solitude and quiet, aside from the ramblings of William inside his head, Kiru sat down and rested his back against the stone wall of the castle. He yawned, the beginnings of a headache threatening to emerge. Roaming about, constantly using his mana to move, was admittedly draining on his system. The exhaustion wasn't exactly like a physical tax, but it was taxing all the same.

His frustration at getting rejected by his fellow classmates still gnawed at him. Cultivating had the added benefit of helping to calm him, too, however. He leaned against the castle wall and closed his eyes. After that, he deactivated Telekinesis and took the next couple of hours to cultivate using the method he learned from William back at the volcano. Instead of drawing mana in through all his pores, then having it travel along his body unguided as with the standard method, he focused on bringing the ambient mana directly into his core.

The effect of the mana-dense environment made itself known as his rate of intake was at least three times faster than usual. For him to use the enhanced standard method that William taught him in a mana-sparse area, the psion estimated that one hour of cultivation would provide one and a half hours of simple movement. So, for now, that ratio was threefold better. This more enhanced version of pulling in base mana still wasn't as potent as cultivating from the dreaming imp, though. Using mana from dreaming minds had a ratio of one hour of cultivating to three hours of movement.

But suddenly, Kiru's meditative trance was interrupted by the loud creaking of wood bending. He opened his eyes to see the large doors—at least fifty feet tall and over two hundred yards away from the castle—begin to open wide. Two guards, wearing the same armor as bridge guards Tavish and Keaton, heaved on them with all their might. The doors opened completely, revealing a large, horse-drawn carriage coming out of the forest. Two more guards rode on the carriage-driver's seat, one of them holding the reins.

Giiyam emerged from the stables to greet them. A large figure emerged from the carriage, wearing an ornate, navy robe adorned with a lot of gold filigree. They were tall, meeting the half-orc eye-to-eye, and with ridiculously broad shoulders—enough to support three heads! The figure pulled off their hood to reveal an elf. Two more guards exited the carriage behind him.

The psion couldn't hear what they were saying, but he was more focused on the elf's face. Aside from the black hair and scar above his left eye, he was identical to Niajar. He had to be the headmaster, Niazen, Zane's father. Given the look of superiority on his face and disdain he showed the elderly half-orc, that pretty much confirmed it to Kiru.

For his part, the groundskeeper didn't bat an eye, not seeming to be bothered at all by the words or attitude of his boss. The gate doors began to close, but then there was a loud *ting* of metal breaking, and the left door stopped. The guard heaved again, but it only moved a little before going back, jammed. The headmaster snapped his attention to the gate, then pressed his fingers on the bridge of his nose. The elf barked an order to Giiyam, likely to fix the gate door, then waved to dismiss the half-orc.

Giiyam bowed, then strode straight to the horses in front of the carriage, leading them into the stables while the guards in the driver's seat hopped off to follow the headmaster.

Then, unexpectedly, a dwarven student in a yellow jacket came running out from another building, shouting and waving a book to get the headmaster's attention. *She looks familiar—where have I seen her before? Ah! She was the one arguing with the robed priest outside of the shrine!* Kiru realized.

Niazen's hand went back to his nose and let out an exaggerated sigh that heaved his entire body. He turned to face the passionate Shield House student, listened to her pleas as she showed him the thick book in her hands, then cut her off with a mana-infused yell so loud that it rang out like a thunderclap. If Kiru weren't already sitting, he would've been knocked on his ass by the headmaster's *"No!"*

After that auditory assault, Kiru activated his Telekinesis once more just to rub his wounded ears! He looked back to see the dwarf still standing, which spoke highly of her constitution. She lowered her head in defeat.

Satisfied, Niazen turned away from the dwarf without another word and stormed away, not sparing the student a second glance, his contingent of guards following close behind. Meanwhile, Giiyam waved the two door guards over to the stables. All three of them seemed unfazed by the headmaster's outburst.

Time to get up and moving. No need to accidentally run into the headmaster and cause even more of a scene. As he turned to leave, William's voice rang out in his head. *"Master, what's that?"*

Kiru turned to look, and he saw an orb of white glowing light the size of his head floating right by the dwarf. *Does she have a familiar, too?*

Slowly, she turned to look at the light and began following it, dropping her precious book to the dirt as if in a trance. She trudged along, her arms at her side, as the orb began to lead her toward the open gate. The headmaster and his guards were already walking away and had their backs to what was happening.

She was being led into the forest, where dangerous monsters were lurking and ready to eat unsuspecting students like her. Before he could fully process what he was doing, Kiru was sprinting down the hill toward the gate as fast as he could. Fortunately, the headmaster and his posse were heading in a different direction, so he didn't have to worry about any awkward run-ins.

To the psion's concern and his familiar's glee, a fight seemed inevitable. To increase his speed, he focused more of his mana in his legs. The thought of her being ripped apart by some creature made his heart race; he didn't want that on his conscience. In about twenty seconds, Kiru made it down to the gate. He grabbed her book and stuffed it in the small satchel where his *Familiars For Dummies* was tucked away. The trudging dwarf had crossed past the open door not ten seconds before. He looked back, thinking to run and grab the guards, but he realized that would be counterintuitive to his attempts to not make a scene. Besides, he didn't want her to get lost, or worse, eaten. So, he took off after her.

There wasn't much space between the academy and the forest, just a ring of grass, but the dwarf had already crossed the distance, still following the extremely suspicious orb of light into the dark forest. "Hey!" Kiru called out to her.

The dwarf didn't respond to his words, but the floating orb did. In an instant, it split in two, and one of them came rushing toward Kiru.

The psion already had a hand on one of his sword hilts, but he didn't have time to draw it before the thing came within inches of his face. Startled, he yelled and took a reactive step back. He began to draw his blade a couple inches, but . . . he stopped. Kiru cocked his head.

Looking at the light, he felt . . . safe, like he was being wrapped in a warm hug. The light was inviting him to follow, to always feel protected and warm.

"*Oh hells, no!*" William shouted inside Kiru's mind. "*Master, this thing is trying to enchant you. Kill it! Kill it now!*"

Kiru's eyes widened. Acting on instinct, Kiru drew the weapon from his sheath and cut through the orb in one swift motion.

The orb let out a bestial shriek and dissipated into nothingness.

"*Oh, yeah! Take that, stupid ball!*"

The other orb seemed to sense its counterpart's demise, and it led the dwarf deeper into the dark forest with even greater haste.

"Crap." Kiru sprinted after them. "Hey!" he shouted, hoping to get her attention.

She didn't respond.

"Hey, stop!"

Still no acknowledgement as the dwarf ran, following the light, her attention completely on the orb.

Kiru quickly thought about using Telekinesis on her, but he didn't want to risk exposing himself. He knew that he had already made waves from his interactions, but he figured most people would forget eventually. If he was ever found out as a psion, they would *never* forget. Fortunately for this chase, Kiru didn't need to use his technique on her as his longer legs were proving advantageous. While the dwarf was also running, she couldn't compete against Kiru's strides. After a minute, they went around a very large tree, and he grabbed her by the shoulder. He forced her back and tried to slash at the orb, but he missed as the light floated into a small cave just ahead of them. It went a little deeper into the entrance, but it was still visible. Then it just stayed there, suddenly halted.

Kiru turned back to look at the dwarf. Her eyes were distant, still staring in the direction of the light. She tried to keep walking, still pressing forward despite Kiru blocking her way. "Hey, snap out of it!" He waved his hands in front of her face. No response.

*"Her mind's enchanted, Master. She can't hear you."* William said.

Kiru thought on his familiar's words for a moment; then, an idea came. He was a psion, a cultivator of mental mana. In matters of the mind, he was supposed to be the expert. If her mind was enchanted, he should be able to fix it. Kiru decided to follow his gut intuition. Though he wasn't completely sure how this would go, he pressed his palm against the dwarf's forehead, both to keep her held back and to attempt to reach into her mind. Then, Kiru forced mental mana out of the meridian in his arm, through his palm, and flooded her mind.

It seemed to do the trick, because her eyes regained their focus, and she recoiled with a gasp. She stood there, panting heavily. Despite the obvious danger they were in, the psion gave a relieved smile. He had done it! It wasn't exactly a technique, but he had discovered a new use of his mana and employed it effectively.

"Who . . . who are you? Where are we?" she asked, and as her shoulders heaved, her yellow jacket shifted to reveal a set of heavy chainmail beneath it. Her sleeves were rolled up past her elbows, and the psion couldn't help but wonder why.

"Well, I'm Kiru, and we're in the forest surrounding the academy. I noticed some strange orb of light leading you here, and I came to save you. Oh, also, you dropped this," he said and handed her the large book.

She looked at it in a mixture of shock and confusion. After a few seconds, she seemed to process his words. "By Hlin's mercy! Thank you! My goddess must've sent ye here to protect me."

Kiru was caught off-guard by that. *Probably best to not let her know that I have a little demon in my head.* "Oh, no problem! You just looked like you needed help."

She shook her head. "Nay, no need to downplay it, lad. I be Brunhilda Lightsworn, paladin of the goddess Hlin. Ye, Kiru, have done our order a great service today. If I can ever repay ye, just—"

Her words were cut off when a monstrous howl erupted behind them. They turned to see a hideous creature emerging from the cavern. It was at least seven feet tall, with sickly gray flesh stretched over corded muscle. Its limbs were too long for its torso, with gill slits on them as well as its thick neck. It had the head of a fish with milky, pupilless eyes, sharp teeth with a protruding underbite, and some strange, fleshy appendage growing out of its forehead like a fishing rod. The orb of light that had been luring Brunhilda into the forest floated up to the appendage before attaching itself to the bottom of it.

Kiru grimaced at the horrifying walking fish monster. He wondered if such a strange, grotesque creature could be a sacred beast, before steeling himself for what was to come.

The bipedal fish monster moaned, and globules of drool trailed out of its maw. Then, with a burst of speed, it came at them. It raised a clawed hand high and swiped down at Kiru.

Before the psion could respond, Brunhilda jumped in front of him. Two large, round shields almost as big as the dwarf's entire torso suddenly grew out of the armor of her gauntlets, explaining why she kept her jacket sleeves rolled back. Brunhilda's twin shields intercepted the creature's claws with a clang. The paladin didn't move, fully blocking the sacred beast's attacks and showing clear strength against the much larger foe.

Kiru took that opportunity to step around the paladin and slash at the creature's wrists. The creature's fishy flesh was remarkably thick, and his sharp weapons were barely able to cut into it. Still, the sacred beast screeched and recoiled at the attack. It jumped back and spewed some sort of green muck at the psion.

Somehow, as if their minds were in sync, Kiru spun back and Brunhilda stepped forward. The flying substance splashed against her left shield. Right after, there was a sizzling sound, and steam rose from the shield as it began to dissolve. "Acid," Brunhilda spat and flung the shield to the ground.

Kiru's eyes widened, and he was about to shout a warning, but it was too late. The sacred beast had taken advantage of the paladin's distraction and had closed the distance. The hulking creature kicked the dwarf square in the center of her remaining shield, lifting her off her feet and flinging her backward into Kiru. Both of the students went flying, the metal-clad dwarf impacting like a cannonball against the psion's body. Kiru's body cracked straight into a thick tree, taking the brunt of the force.

Despite the circlet, when the back of his head slammed into the tree from the recoil, it rattled both him and his core. The disruption forced his Telekinesis technique to falter, and he collapsed to the ground like a limp noodle.

Brunhilda groaned as she fought to stay standing, bracing her remaining shield against her body. She let out a small gasp at Kiru's prone form lying in a heap against the tree. His head was spinning. Turning back to face the monster, she placed her free hand back on the half-elf behind her and said, "*Rejuvenation.*" Life mana surged out of her hand in a warm, yellow light. The psion's superficial wounds, cuts, bruises, and abrasions instantly healed. His concussion was gone, too. Too bad for Kiru, his injury was too old and too severe for her technique to do anything for his spine. It likely wouldn't have mattered anyway as Niajar's more advanced healing couldn't reverse the damage even right after Kiru's spine was broken.

Brunhilda focused on the sacred beast charging toward them. It swiped at her, but she deftly deflected the blow, guiding it away. The creature used its other hand to jab straight at her chest, but she stepped on one of its webbed feet, breaking its bones with a crunch, then used a shield bash square in its face.

The sacred beast's head was flung back, and the dwarf smiled in victory.

Then the monster grabbed the top of her shield.

Kiru's eyes regained clear focus in time to see the beast's massive mouth open too wide, about to bite Brunhilida's head clean off. Quickly, Kiru reactivated Telekinesis and recklessly launched himself forward like a bolt. Before both the sacred beast or the dwarf could realize, the psion was there. He stabbed his right-hand sword straight into the creature's open mouth, penetrating the roof of its mouth and straight into its brain. The monster let out a pained shriek, and its body went limp and collapsed.

Both Kiru and Brunhilda stood there panting. William was cheering inside the psion's mind at conquering another foe. "Thanks," Kiru said between heavy breaths. "You really saved me there."

"That's what we of the Order of Hlin do: we protect people. Besides, I owed ye, ya know?"

Kiru smiled, then two more bestial moans hit their ears. A new pair of the sacred beasts emerged from the cave. Kiru's heart sank. "Brunhilda, get to the academy. I'll hold them off," Kiru said, bracing himself into a ready stance.

"My goddess would be ashamed if I didn't stay. You go, Kiru."

"*I agree with the paladin's plan. Time for a tactical retreat,*" William asserted.

Though a primal part of Kiru wanted to run away, he couldn't—more like he *wouldn't*. How could he become a king who would protect the innocent, who would prevent injustices like what had happened to his family, if he turned tail and ran to let someone sacrifice themselves? He had hoped the Shield student would take his advice and run. That way, he'd be free to use his Telekinesis on more than just his body, and no one would be the wiser.

Either way, however, the psion couldn't let Brunhilda die, so he clenched his jaw tight, squeezing his hands son his sword's hilt, as he prepared to reveal his technique before the paladin. Before he could do it, though, a green blur zoomed into the fray.

# CHAPTER TWENTY-THREE

# Hooked on a Feeling

Kiru and Brunhilda were both just barely able to register a green speeding blur to their right as it struck their opponents. The blur's form became more distinct as it went straight at the monstrous sacred beasts. In a flash, the rightmost creature's head was sliced clean off its body, falling to the ground in a heap. Standing before the remaining fish-faced carnivore was the groundskeeper, Giiyam. The half-orc was in a pose not too dissimilar to the elven form Kiru had learned, but instead of a pair of simple shortswords, he wielded two rare blades called hook swords.

Both students just stared in bewilderment. *The groundskeeper is not only strong but incredibly skilled too?!* The other sacred beast seemed to finally register that its ally had just been decapitated. It roared while it tried to gut the half-orc with a thrust of one of its clawed hands. Giiyam responded with an elegant move that conveyed both the elven grace and orcish strength of his heritage. Using his hook swords, Giiyam guided the monstrous creature's thrusting claw away from his body, forcing it to continue forward.

Utilizing its momentum, the half-orc closed in one fluid motion, Kiru's eye discerning that the motion was part of a deadly and brutal sword form. Giiyam had forced the fish-face to overextend to the front, which allowed him to move behind it. Using his hook swords, the groundskeeper struck at two different spots at once. One blade cut into the monster's right ankle, bisecting it, while the other blade hooked into its large gill slits on its neck. Unlike a simple fishing hook, the hook sword continued its motion, carving straight through bone, flesh, and blood vessels.

A surge of arterial blood shot out from the monster's neck. Its head flopped ninety degrees to one side, only still attached by the flesh on the left side, dead and leaving Kiru supremely impressed. The light hanging from the stalk in front of the fishface's face went dull and its body rigid as it collapsed like a felled tree.

"*Whoa!*" William said in Kiru's mind.

Kiru had to agree. That was pretty freaking awesome, and the groundskeeper did that with just his swords, no technique needed! In one deft motion, Giiyam flung the blood and gore off his blades, then placed them in special holsters on his back, crossing them like an X. Kiru distinctly remembered the groundskeeper not having those on when they first met. Then, in the first display of true anger Kiru had ever seen on the visage of the half-orc, Giiyam turned to them, scowling. His lower canines were not as large as a pure orc's, but they looked just as sharp and equally threatening.

"Why have you come here to the forest? You know it's expressly forbidden!" he scolded.

"I'm sorry. It's just—"

"It's not Kiru's fault, sir. It be mine," Brunhilda interrupted. "Ye see, those sacred beasts lured me here to eat me. Without Kiru, I'd be dead. He saved me from their trap."

Giiyam raised an eyebrow.

Brunhilda nodded in confirmation.

The half-orc turned to face Kiru. "Explain."

Kiru did, elaborating on the details but conveniently skipping over his resisting the enchantment. No need to make the half-orc suspicious. "So, you see, it wasn't actually her fault." Giiyam's nostrils flared, and he calmed down. He nodded, seemingly satisfied with his response. He then waved for the students to follow. "Come quickly. The forest is not safe for two Golds."

Both readily complied, doing their best to keep pace with the elder groundskeeper as they sprinted across. Kiru appreciated Giiyam slowing his pace for them. "What were those things?" Kiru asked.

"They were Beguiler, sacred beasts that utilize light mana to enchant their prey to come to them. They are wretched things but weak if you strike at their ankles and gill slits," the groundskeeper answered.

"And the school lets them stay so close? It was maybe only a couple of minutes before one of them lured Brunhilda, and that was just from a door being jammed."

The stoic orc cracked a slight smile at that. "Beguiler are some of the weakest sacred beasts in this forest."

That shut Kiru up. After their sprint, they made it back to the gate, which was now conveniently closed. Kiru was impressed that it was already functioning but also frustrated that they couldn't have rectified this issue *before* the Beguiler lured Brunhilda into the forest. Giiyam knocked on one of the gate doors three times. "This is Giiyam. Open the door" The guards immediately opened them without protest.

After all three entered, the guards closed them once more, and they shut with an audible boom. The guards then looked at Giiyam nervously.

"They were lured out by a Beguiler. You are lucky I found them before they could be eaten," the groundskeeper replied.

The guards swallowed hard, nodded, and thanked the half-orc. Giiyam nodded, then guided the students to the stables. Once there, he turned to Kiru. "It was very noble of you to go into the forest alone, being not only a Gold but a Defunct."

There was no sarcasm in Giiyam's words, but Kiru pursed his lips defensively. Brunhilda's eyes widened as she took in his patch for the first time.

The half-orc continued, "I mean it. You took an enormous risk. It was brave. Next time, though, get help. No need for you to risk your life rashly."

Kiru's unease melted away, and he smiled at the genuine compliment. It was the first time he had been validated as the type of person, the type of leader he wanted to be.

Giiyam then leaned closer, now speaking in a hushed whisper while still managing to maintain a fairly neutral tone. "I ask that we keep this incident a secret. Not only will you likely be expelled if the headmaster knew what happened, but the guards would likely be punished as well. Will you do this?"

Kiru agreed readily as he really did not want to get kicked out after just getting into the academy.

Brunhilda, on the other hand, looked uncomfortable.

Giiyam read her feelings immediately. "I do not ask that you lie, Paladin. I ask that you simply not mention this to others."

"I think my goddess will be fine with that," she said, a note of relief evident in her voice.

Giiyam nodded. "Good." He grabbed a bucket of water hanging by one of the horse stalls with a couple of wet rags laid on its edge and set it down before the students. "Now, clean your equipment before you leave. No need to scare the other students."

Kiru and the dwarf looked down. Their gear was covered in sticky Beguiler blood.

When they looked back up, Giiyam had already turned his back to them and was walking away. "Remember, don't look into the lights."

Kiru and Brunhilda each took a rag in the clean water and began wiping the blood off their jackets and gear. "I didn't know you were unable to use techniques. You fight with such bravery and deadly skill, despite your handicap," the dwarf said.

She meant well, but the words still stung as much as they soothed. It was another reminder that everyone thought he was beneath them. That no one wanted to join up with him to compete in the games. *Was this how everyone in the world views those of a lower cultivation ability?* Going from a promising young cultivator to a quadriplegic had done a number on Kiru, not just physically, but mentally, too. He was acutely aware of the position of being completely helpless, and it made him never want to experience that again.

Kiru's eyes widened. He realized that, in the past, when he had stood up to bullies, it had been purely for himself. Because he was angry, and it felt good to lash out at those jerks. To teach them a lesson. Helping those who were being harassed was just a side benefit. In that moment, it occurred to Kiru that he was behaving far more similarly to the bullies than he'd thought. Though he hadn't teased or harassed other kids, he had looked down on them as well, for their lack of skill in cultivation. He silently vowed to himself that he would not only be a protector to the helpless, but he would be an empathetic ruler and provider for *all* the peoples of the kingdom.

Suddenly he clocked a hand waving right in front of his face, breaking him out of his reverie. "Oh, sorry." He apologized and refocused on the dwarf. Kiru quickly remembered what she had said about his handicap.

"Ye okay there, lad?"

"Yeah. I'm fine," he said.

"Okay. Well, sorry for bringing up yer Defunct status. That was . . . indelicate of me."

Kiru's initial defensiveness at being thought of as weak melted at the kind smile that accompanied the dwarf's words. It was a genuine apology. Unlike most of the others here at the academy, she saw him for who he was: a person deserving of kindness and respect, just like any other.

He gave a slight chuckle. "You're good. There's nothing to apologize for." He waved off her concerns. "And thank you for what you said about my fighting skills. I *have* to fight like that—I'm going to win The Warrior Games, after all."

At that, she froze. "The Warrior Games?" she asked, unsure if she heard him correctly. "I take it back. I don't know if you're brave or crazy!" She chuckled, but her laughter held no malice.

Kiru smiled, too. "Probably a bit of both."

"Well, if you can carve 'em up like Giiyam and keep up that can-do attitude, any team will be lucky to have you."

Kiru blushed and scratched the back of his head. "Glad at least somebody thinks so." He changed the subject as they left the barn and walked back to the main castle. "So, why did you decide to come to the academy?"

Brunhilda took the bait. "To have my goddess venerated from a minor to a major deity and welcomed within my order's official pantheon!" she said with zealous intensity. "There be a lot of people with good connections throughout the Alliance who send their families here, and even more pay attention to the Warrior Games. If I can make a good impression, it'll help me convince other hopeful acolytes to follow her and help me in my overall quest for Hlin's glory.

Kiru nodded. "So, is Hlin your goddess's name?"

"You betcha, lad! So, I take it you've heard of Hlin, personal protector of Frigg?"

"*Ugh!*" William gagged disgust inside Kiru's mind at her words. Clearly, the imp was not a fan. The psion decided to just ignore him.

"I can't say that I have before today, actually," Kiru admitted, putting his hands up. He knew of the pantheon, but honestly didn't know much else. The cleric who ran Bristleton's temple was a well-known drunk, so Kiru hadn't made it to too many sermons. He wasn't overly interested in listening to any now, either, but Brunhilda seemed to be bursting at the seams to talk. "You want to tell me about her?"

"Ha! Is water wet? Of course I'll tell ye about her!" The paladin launched into an in-depth explanation of who her goddess was as well as a theology refresher for Kiru. The world's pantheon was divided into two major branches: the Aesir and the Vanir. Originally, they had been at war with each other, but after Ragnarok, the surviving deities formed a new faction named the Vasir. They had a Holy Council that was honored and ruled all the other gods of their new united faction. They were the major gods. Those who were of lesser stature and power were considered minor gods.

The Vasir religion was the major one within the world today, and the holy order that served them in Alterra was the Order of Valhalla. As an officially recognized paladin, Brunhilda was part of that order. This council of gods and their recognized vassals didn't live amongst the mortals in Alterra however, but inside another of the World Tree's realms, Ithalvlir. They were still powerful enough to influence other realms, though.

"You see, I be a life mana cultivator, just like my grandmother and uncle. When my uncle, who also be a paladin, learned about my mana type, he offered me a chance to join the holy order. Life mana be the main type that comes from Ithavlir, so it allows cultivators who use it to be in sync with the gods. Essentially, we undergo a ceremony where we reach out to Ithavlir and see if anyone responds. If any of the deities reach back out and infuse our mana with their holy power, they also give us their path," she explained.

"So, what's your path?" Kiru asked.

"The great goddess of protection, Hlin, blessed me with her path, the Path of Divine Protection. That's why I fight with two shields. My goddess requires it."

"But she's not a major god, though, right?" he asked, remembering her earlier words.

The dwarf's bright smile turned to a pained grimace. "Unfortunately, she is not. Despite her being the personal bodyguard to Frigg, she has failed to be recognized by the other gods."

"Wait, so you plan to influence the gods?! And you called me crazy?" Kiru laughed. Of the all the students he'd met at the academy, the paladin had been the easiest for Kiru to talk to. It was a genuine and honest conversation. He hadn't had to put on a strong face and pitch himself like some sort of merchant. This reminded him of talking with William, or with his mom—someone who cared and he could call a friend.

She gave Kiru a somber smile. "Aye, my goddess has fought in many fierce battles but has failed to get the respect she deserves. So she has been limited in her power. She has shown me her favor, and I will strive to do her will in recompense until the day I die.

"Hlin has shown me the path to rectify her mistreatment. If I can get a shrine to her to officially be made part of the head temple in every Alliance capital city, the gods will have to recognize her. As I said before, I need to make a great impression, and there's no better place to impress the right people than this place—and the Warrior Games in particular."

"Is that what you were arguing with the priest and the headmaster about?"

She blushed. "Aye. They say that the number of worshippers of Hlin here is too low to justify a shrine to her being added."

That gave Kiru an idea and an opening. "Well then, I have a proposal for you. Join my team."

"*Master, you can't be serious!*" William pleaded. "*We don't need some happy, holier-than-thou pipsqueak on our team.*"

Kiru ignored his familiar's protests. Brunhilda was, without a doubt, supremely devout, but she was both a good person and strong. She would be a great addition to his team. Plus, given how much of a loner Kiru had been growing up, he was encouraged by how easily they were able to converse and get along.

Brunhilda looked puzzled.

"Join my team," he repeated. "Look, I don't know if you have a team or not, but you're a clearly competent and capable fighter, despite your unorthodox style. Our methods really complement each other. You're focused on defense with your two shields and thick armor, and I was trained in an offensive style with my twin blades. I know I'm a Defunct, but I meant it when I said I'm going to win the Warrior Games. Imagine how many people will be inspired to follow in the path of Hlin, how many future paladins of protection could come about, if one of your goddess's acolytes not only competes, but wins?"

"Ye be . . . sure about this? Part of my oath requires me to fight with only shields. Ye be okay with that?"

Kiru smiled. "Definitely." In truth, he was ecstatic that she hadn't turned him down immediately. The chance to get any competent fighter to willingly join him was a major step up! "So, what do you say?" he asked, sticking his hand out.

The dwarf brushed some of her light auburn hair back and cracked a grin. "Ye know, I got a good feeling about you, ever since you saved my life. Ye put yer life on the line to protect mine, just like a paladin of Hlin should." She clasped wrists with Kiru. "Ye got yerself a deal. Brunhilda Lightsworn, at yer service."

# Brotherly Feud

Niazen sat at his stained mahogany desk, his ringed fingers interlaced. The headmaster's eyes were closed, and he forced himself to take deep breaths as he waited. The elf was trying to stay calm, to keep his emotions in check. That damn first-year student had the gall to approach him, not once but twice, and insist he do something as dramatic as interfering with the shrine layout of the Order of Valhalla. As long as he had been in charge of the academy, the order had been a hornets' nest he did not want to kick. The audacity of that girl—if she ever brought up such a ridiculous request to him again, he would let the school's cleric deal with her . . .

He gave a cruel smile thinking about what would happen before his neck tensed suddenly. Niazen swore. He'd dwelled on it an instant too long, failing to keep his mind in check for those precious moments. Because of that, the voices returned.

"*Submit!*"

"*Release us!*"

The twin haunted moans screamed out inside his mind, demanding he either succumb to them or relinquish his tentative hold over them.

He furrowed his brow as he worked to fight them off, a pressure inside his head building. Niazen shook from the effort, using his mana to force the twin powers back.

"Quiet," he whispered through gritted teeth. With that command, he regained control. He opened his eyes, and he almost immediately lost control again when he saw his brother sitting across the desk with that stupid grin he always kept plastered on his face. To his credit, Niazen didn't lose his grip, but he did get a nosebleed for the effort.

"Ah, Brother. Forgive me, I needed time to cultivate" the headmaster lied, pressing a handkerchief to his nostrils as if everything was completely normal.

Niajar's smile didn't falter. "Not to worry, Brother, though I've noticed you've been prone to far more nosebleeds than ever before since you've taken the post of headmaster. Are you sure I shouldn't call upon a physician to assess you?"

"No!" Niazen shouted. He didn't mean to put so much venom into his words, but in his distraction, he'd let some of his true feelings leak out. He couldn't afford for anyone he didn't trust to fully assess him, lest they talk and word reach Van Blaine.

"I didn't take you to be the bashful type, brother," Niajar jested.

"Cease your impudent capering, Niajar. As much as you enjoy pestering others in conversation, that is not why I summoned you here."

"Pestering is such an unkind word. I prefer . . . *provoke*. Isn't that what we educators are here for? To provoke the minds of young cultivators to growth?"

Niazen just stared blankly at the librarian, forcing himself to remain calm.

"No fun, as usual, Brother. Very well. Why have you called on me, Headmaster?" Niajar finally relented.

The voices beat against their cages, but Niazen tightened his hold, forcing them to submit. "Because you seem to enjoy making a mockery of our fine institution, Niajar. It has come to my attention that you permitted a Defunct boy into our school, and he is already causing trouble with our best and brightest."

Niajar's face turned to a look of surprised realization. "Oh, you must mean when your son and his group tried to bully him earlier, four against one. You're right, such a troublemaker."

"Niajar," he warned.

The librarian sighed. "The boy is harmless. I do not think your training of my nephew is lacking enough to not be able to handle him."

"That is the point," Niazen asserted. "We are the premier academy in the world. We cannot allow such a defective cultivator to be enrolled. Besides, do you honestly think he's worth the wager?" Though not all of the betting was technically legal, gambling on the annual Warrior Games was an extremely lucrative endeavor and provided a major amount of the academy's funds. The practice had been around since the school's inception. It not only provided the chance to grow financially for people simply betting on the games, but it also provided a source of major motivation to the recruiters. Every staff member was given a certain quota of students they were allowed to enroll, from two to five, and the number was up to the headmaster. If one of the students was a participant on a winning team in the games, that recruiter would receive a considerable bonus as a "finder's fee."

It encouraged the staff to recruit only the best. It also enticed professors to each officially sponsor a student as well, requiring more resources to personally teach a pupil, but also granting them an even larger financial gain if the pupil proved victorious. Niazen only ever gave his brother a maximum of one student to be enrolled and to sponsor, but he rarely used his slot. When he did, the students always seemed to sow chaos in the school.

Niajar's recruits so far had never won the Warrior Games, but they either always got far in the tournament or had such a penchant for trouble that they became major headaches for almost all of the staff during the school year, Niazen included. The headmaster distinctly remembered one of his brother's pupils nearly destroying half the campus grounds one time, had the headmaster not interfered. Simply put, Niajar and his pupils were infamous among the academy.

The blond elf's grin returned as he looked at his dark-haired twin. "I do, in fact, think he's 'worth the wager.'"

"Enough of your games, Librarian," Niazen said, asserting his superior position over him. "You will revoke his enrollment immediately and be grateful I don't demote you to becoming the janitor," he threatened.

"You know, that gives me an idea, *Headmaster*," Niajar said pointedly. "Why don't we make a little wager ourselves, if I may talk plainly?"

Niazen raised an eyebrow. After a couple of seconds, he silently indicated for his brother to continue.

"I am intrigued by this recruit of mine. I believe he shows great promise. His eyes show determination, despite his setbacks. I can only think of two others who had such eyes. I will wager with you, personally, that my recruit will win this year's Warrior Games for the first-years."

Niazen coughed back a laugh. The mere idea of a Defunct winning the games was preposterous! "Truly?!" he asked, unable to fully contain his mirth. "You've never won before, and now you think this defective boy will be your winning pupil?"

Niajar's grin widened. "Indeed. As long as you don't interfere with Kiru's growth, I bet that he will win. And when he does, I get your job."

The headmaster's chuckle was immediately wiped away, replaced by a scowl. He opened his mouth to reprimand his brother, then realized that his brother's own imbecilic ideals in investing in the weak would finally be his undoing. It would put Niazen at some risk but not really. There was no way a Defunct could win. It was a certainty. The dark-haired elf gave a sinister grin, a malicious version of the librarian's. "Fine, as *long as the boy doesn't break the rules*, I will leave him be," he said, emphasizing the condition.

Niazen then raised a finger to add on another condition. "But if I win, you will never be allowed to recruit another troublemaking student ever again, and you will relinquish your claim as head of our family forever to me. As such, you will forfeit all items, technique manuals, and treasures that belong to our family. You, Niajar, will be my lesser . . . forever."

Both brothers stared each other down, locking eyes, each with manic grins. They clasped wrists and invested their souls in the agreement, sealing it as they said in unison, "Deal."

# CHAPTER TWENTY-FOUR

# School's in Session

After Brunhilda and he parted ways, Kiru made it back to his room. William still wasn't the biggest fan of having a paladin on their team. Apparently, demons weren't so big on the holy order. Kiru didn't care, though. She was a good person, and beggars couldn't be choosers.

*"Why don't we ask the half-orc to join our team? He was a badass! Did you see how he cut up those fish faces?"* William said.

Kiru remembered it differently. It wasn't that he didn't concur with William's assessment, but he now remembered it more vividly than any memory he'd ever had before. He could accurately recall every detail as if he were back there, living it out again: Giiyam's stance, the angle he'd swung his blades, even his grip. That was odd for Kiru. He had a good memory, but he'd never been able to evoke recollections in such explicit detail before.

*Why?* he wondered as he let his familiar out. As William roamed about the room and eventually went to sleep, Kiru idly pondered to his question as he closed his eyes and cultivated.

The next day, Kiru's first day of class began with Kingdom History. It was in a large auditorium. Kiru tried to look around for a spot to sit. Brunhilda had told Kiru that she didn't have this class with him, so he knew he didn't need to save a seat. He had seen the elf Nel sitting off and thought to join her since she had been kind to him but then thought better of it. No need to cause any more conflict with Ambrose for now.

He found a spot towards the back, as that's where he had always felt more comfortable in Bristleton. William was remarkably quiet inside Kiru's core. The psion figured that the imp was likely sleeping.

In a few minutes, the room was almost completely filled with students. The last to walk in was an elderly gnome. He had bushy gray sideburns that connected to his mustache and wore a matching tan outfit from his boots all the way up to what Kiru heard his other classmates call a "Pith Helmet." Kiru could feel that he gave off the power of a Ruby.

The elderly gnome slowly made his way to the front of the class and gave a kindly smile. "Hello, class. I am Professor Barnabus Copperknob," he said with a shaky, light tone. "I am an archaeologist and will be your instructor in Kingdom History I. Now, can any of you tell me why you must take this class when it isn't a requirement for all students, hm? What commonality do we all share?"

The students began to look around, searching for something they might have all had in common. Kiru couldn't tell. There were humans, elves, orcs, dwarves, and gnomes in the class. Aside from their jackets, they had varied sets of clothing and builds, too. There were a good ten seconds of silence before Nel tentatively raised her hand.

"Ah. Yes, miss?"

"Nel," the girl answered. "Is it because we're all citizens of the Kingdom, sir?"

"Correct! Though the Kingdom of Blades is the smallest among the Great Alliance, we are undoubtedly the most varied. It is because of this rich, diverse history that we are so strong, and why our illustrious King van Blaine had felt it so important to teach you the truth about our noble nation," Copperknob declared proudly.

Upon hearing Van Blaine's name, Kiru was instantly turned off. If the man who killed his father had any part of this class's curriculum, he couldn't trust any information to be valid. He audibly coughed in disbelief when the gnome then said that part of their curriculum would be about the life and heroics of their "noble" king. Kiru knew he would have to make sure to play along with that class but also do his absolute best to *not* stand out. With the gnome being such an obvious supporter of Van Blaine, he would need to exercise caution around him.

The next class on his schedule was Fire Mana I. This class had notably fewer participants—only about twenty by Kiru's count. He found a spot to sit in the middle of the room. It wasn't his ideal choice, but at least he wasn't in the front row. The classroom was notably humid and low-lit with a majority of light coming in from three windows. Kiru also noticed that, rather than the more general amicable nature that his classmates had in history class, all the students here seemed on edge, like a fight was about to break out at any moment. About half of them were gold drakonids, and their reptilian eyes continued to scan back and forth, sensing the tension.

One of them moved his thick tail and accidentally smacked against the leg of a man behind him. "Hey! Watch it, lizard!" he stood up and shouted. Aside from his Sword House jacket, the man was bare-chested, with a bushy brown beard and mop of hair on his head. He appeared to be a barbarian of some sort, and Kiru recognized him to be part of the crew that followed Zane.

"Who are you calling lizard, pig?" the drakonid angrily snapped back at the man. At that, he stood up and locked eyes with him. The drakonid snarled and his mouth began to glow orange.

The barbarian wasn't deterred in the slightest, and he grabbed his axe and lit it aflame, growling right back at him.

Before things could turn violent, however, a powerful voice boomed from the back: "Enough!" At that word, the dimly burning torches in the class grew in intensity, causing the heat to turn oppressive for a moment before dying down.

The students all stopped and looked back to see a human woman who looked to be in her forties, with skin as black as night. Her lips firmly pressed together were a bright red which matched the color of the flowing dress she wore. Her long dark hair was braided and tied back into a ponytail, and her dark eyes gazed angrily at the students. "Sit!" she ordered.

The two students who were about to fight dispelled their flames and did so immediately. The woman walked up towards the front of the class, her shoes tapping loudly against the stone floor. She started speaking again before she got to the front of the class. "I am Instructor Claire Redheart. I have been assigned as your teacher in the ways of fire mana."

She paused as she walked by Kiru and raised an eyebrow at his Defunct badge. "Despite what some of the staff deem as worthy pursuits, I am not interested in pacifying the interests of some of our more eccentric staff members. If it were up to me, no Defunct would ever be allowed on this campus."

Kiru looked down and blushed in a mix of embarrassment and fear. He said nothing, though, not keen to gain the ire of such a strong cultivator.

Instructor Redheart gritted her teeth together in frustration and spoke. "Unfortunately, it is not up to me," she said, then bent down to Kiru's eye level.

The psion nervously turned to face the fiery woman while sitting still at his desk.

Her eyes gazed directly into his with raw anger. "If you don't keep up, or if you in any way hamper the progress of those truly worthy of being in this class-room, I will not hesitate to have you expelled. Understand?" she asked.

*"Master, if she weren't so scary, I think I would be in love."* William said.

Kiru gulped and promptly ignored his familiar. He quietly nodded to the instructor, indicating he clearly understood her threat.

The woman's nostrils flared and she continued walking forward, once again addressing the whole class.

With such open hostility from the instructor and the embarrassment of being called out in front of all his classmates, Kiru couldn't have gotten out of there faster. It made him extremely grateful to spend time in the library for his internship. Sure, the work could be menial at times but it was a nice atmosphere. The place was quiet, orderly, and had a peaceful nature about it that helped the psion feel naturally calmer and more centered. He surprised himself by remembering the layout of the large structure perfectly, easily navigating around as if he'd grown up in the library. That realization tugged at his mind for some reason, as if a puzzle piece was just out of reach, but he couldn't figure out why his remembering the layout in such minute detail was so important.

He also felt genuinely felt welcome in the library. Niajar was certainly eccentric, but the elf had been nothing but kind and supportive to Kiru. That made a world of difference in such a cutthroat, elite place as the academy. He only had to make sure to leave Niajar alone during his "research periods." He was very strict about not being disturbed during those times. That was fine with the psion, though.

After spending his lunch hour with Brunhilda and cultivating, Kiru's last two periods of the day were both ones that all first-years had to attend: Strategies I and Combat I. Strategies I was taught by a cultivator adorned in a long, hooded black robe. The only physical features of his that were discernable were his pale hands and dark brown beard, which poked out slightly from the hood. He introduced himself as Ivan Zerkoff, a dark mana user and tactician in the Royal Army.

From what Kiru gleaned from the utterings of his fellow classmates, the man was a rumored spy. All of the roguish-looking figures and dark mana wielders looked upon Professor Zerkoff with awe, even though he seemed to have a screw loose, sporadically bursting into paranoid tangents. He would also randomly call on students and ask them questions during his lecture. Whether they were relevant questions—such as the weaknesses of leather armor—or completely nonsensical ones—like comparing the flying speeds of various swallows—was completely up to chance.

More than once, Professor Zerkoff would disappear in a cloud of smoke and reappear beside a student and ask them abruptly what they would do if a spy asked them to kill a professor. Although some students looked visibly uncomfortable at this, the leather-wearing rogues and dark-mana-wielding students frantically wrote down every word the man said. Kiru thought it best to try and not stand out to the paranoid, supposed former spy.

Aside from his library internship, Kiru most looked forward to Combat I class. General Escobert III didn't say a lot during their first lesson. He was clearly less interested in talking about theory and instead was more into practical combat applications. That meant that the students got to spar. To Kiru's surprise, they weren't allowed to use their techniques, either. Since that put him on a more even playing field with his opponents, the psion displayed an ability to dominate the practice arena that few could compete with, especially when placed in one-on-one bouts.

William really liked that class too. Of course, any chance of violence always made the bloodthirsty imp utterly gleeful.

# CHAPTER TWENTY-FIVE

# Stagnation

The first couple months of class went surprisingly smoothly for Kiru, at least in terms of academics. It took Kiru a little under a week to fully realize that he indeed had acquired a unique benefit, just as Niajar had told him: namely, his ability to remember events in complete detail. That explicit recollection hadn't been just isolated to the Beguiler encounter. It also explained why he'd remembered the library's layout so well on his first day. Recalling a familiar that utilized mental mana into his core gave Kiru perfect memory. Since he first recalled William in the library, Kiru could remember *everything* that had happened from that point until now, down to the finest minutiae. When William was out, conversely, Kiru couldn't remember details as nearly as vividly.

In all of his written assignments, Kiru excelled better than he'd ever done before, outperforming many of the so-called "superior" students, which irritated them to no end. He was often receiving perfect scores, which impressed some of his professors, while arousing suspicion in others. More than once, the paranoid Zerkoff had accused him of cheating, forcing him to prove his knowledge via a secondary oral examination. After that, Kiru thought it best to sometimes get a few answers wrong on purpose.

Unfortunately for Kiru, his perfect memory only helped him so far. For his own protection, he still couldn't use his fire mana techniques in front of the others, so when it came to the more practical requirements, he could only do two things: jack and squat. By the halfway through the semester, he was nearly at the top of the class in his Kingdom History and Combat I courses but was severely lacking in his Fire Mana and Strategies I courses. It didn't help that those courses were taught by the two professors who distrusted him the most. Granted, it was for different reasons. Redheart disliked Kiru for being a Defunct while Zerkoff simply didn't trust *anyone*. Still, Kiru did his best to extrapolate the information from those two classes to help him with his mental mana, although he hadn't had any luck so far on that front.

That just left his Library Internship and his Basic Combat I classes. His new memory still made it extremely easy to process the layout of the library, compared to when he first entered; he always intrinsically knew where each text was supposed to go. Transcribing old texts on worn parchment onto new pages took the most time. Kiru thought he was doing well, but his mentor was notably absent for most of his internship periods, so he didn't have any actual confirmations to back this up.

In regards to his combat class, General Escobert III was surprisingly impressed with Kiru's swordplay abilities. With his knowledge of royal elven sword forms from his mother's training and his time practicing against his fellow classmates in their daily sparring matches, Kiru was truly one of the best in the class, particularly now that he had been at Gold for a couple of months, and both his leg and arm meridians were fully activated. With the additional practice over time, he was feeling increasingly confident in his movements.

Just as with his teachers, his combat prowess improved some students' impression of him, while for others, it made things even worse, the latter of whom often made their disdain painfully evident. Whenever certain disgruntled students were assigned to be his sparring partners, they would attack Kiru even after he was down. Escobert also wouldn't immediately stop them, in hopes that it would help "build character" and somehow help Kiru grow. Kiru disagreed on that front, but the cruelty exhibited by some of his opponents certainly did incentivize him to win even more bouts against them.

The arena where they held their class had a special enchantment carved into its walls to prevent serious injury or death. As soon as the students entered, a protective translucent film encased them like a shroud. When the student had taken what the enchantment would indicate to be a fatal amount of damage, it would turn red and force their bodies to go limp for ten minutes. It was an ingenious way to help the students go all-out on their opponents, practicing their combat abilities without the need to hold back. There was a caveat, however. While the shrouds prevented serious injury or fatal damage, it did not prevent pain.

The students weren't allowed to use their techniques in combat class—just pure weapons training. But when Escobert wasn't paying attention, many would illegally utilize them to incinerate, freeze, electrocute, and generally bring Kiru extra suffering. He had never been so grateful for his paralysis. That in and of itself eliminated a large majority of the potential pain. Kiru could still feel from the neck up, however, so someone unleashing a burst of flame onto his face for a minute straight still *really* hurt. Ambrose's harsh laughter ringing through his ears while he was being electrocuted was particularly enraging.

With the overall mixed reviews of his performance from his different profes-sors, Kiru had assessed himself to be just getting by. But he'd take it. It also helped to have both a friend and teammate to hang out with, even if Brunhilda could be heavy on the evangelizing. Many of the other first-years teased and called her Goody Two-Shields, and he could see why.

She was selfless—to a fault. That, partnered with being too trusting, often left her prone to being inconvenienced or manipulated by other classmates. People would ask her for her food, and on more than one occasion, they asked if she would take on their attacks fully for them without her shields in their sparring sessions to "test their abilities." Fortunately, Kiru didn't have to step in when it came to the latter.

There was much of the world he had yet to grasp, but the poor paladin was just so gullible! Without the psion convincing her to refuse some of the more ridic-ulous requests, he was pretty sure Brunhilda would be laying in a ditch, starved and beaten. He did give the dwarf credit, though. She was undoubtedly a devout pupil of her goddess, if not a martyr to her cause.

The entire first-year class all had Strategies I and Basic Combat I, so both Kiru and Brunhilda, as well as the others, were able to work and practice their best team combat tactics. Kiru and Brunhilda had taken time during these lessons to run different formations and stances as well as plan for possible scenarios. One of their preferred formations was called Scorpion's Stance. Unsurprisingly, however, no one else wanted to join their team. Apparently, a Defunct and a paladin who only used shields wasn't too appealing to the other cultivators.

Kiru was growing frustrated. Though he was advancing in knowledge and skill, Brunhilda and would certainly lose the Warrior Games without any team-mates. He could not afford to be stagnant. He needed to get the first of his father's items.

It was infuriating being so close to the artifact but with no chance to attain it. The psion had become able to use his Telekinesis so much more effectively over the recent months, only needing to recover his mana once a day thanks to the high mana potency on the island, but he was still falling behind his classmates. He needed to find an edge. He had a unique power that was once used to rule this kingdom, yet no teacher in the use of mental mana.

It was during one morning that William, being the impatient little imp he was, asked Kiru for the fifteenth time why he hadn't found a way to become stronger already. Kiru groaned as he explained his frustrating situation to William once again. The psion was in one of the library's silent rooms, working on transcribing some severely faded ancient text referring to a minor border skirmish between the Kingdom of Blades and Imakandi. "I need to find a better way to cultivate."

"And a new technique," William added, biting down on a piece of dried meat Kiru was pretty sure he'd stolen from the cafeteria. "Don't get me wrong, Master, your Telekinesis is good, but you should get something that crushes our enemies or makes them succumb to your will!"

Kiru sighed. He had managed to keep the knowledge of his Telekinesis a secret, but it was hard to not to feel a bit jealous at his fellow students' displays of power, knowing what he himself was capable of unleashing. at least he had gotten more used to being called a Defunct, but he still wanted another technique. "You're not wrong, William, but who's going to teach me that here?"

Then, as if in answer, Niajar swung open the door and entered the room. "Ah, my favorite pupil. How goes transcribing some of our older texts?"

"I'm pretty sure I'm your only pupil, and it's fine, just . . . tedious," he answered. Over the months, their relationship had grown less formal to the point where Niajar was like an odd uncle to the psion.

"Pray tell, why do you write in the soundproof room?" the librarian asked.

"It's less distracting."

"You do know that we're in a library, right? Loud noises are not commonplace. You're not going to find another two teammates for the Warrior Games if you spend your entire internship hiding away," the elf said. Over the course of their interactions, Kiru had reemphasized to Niajar his desire to win the first-year Warrior Games. He didn't tell him his true motivations as to why, but the elf didn't seem to be interested. To Kiru's surprise, Niajar was positively elated with his goal, more so than anyone else he'd met so far. Since then, though, the elf had been a little pushy in his efforts to help Kiru, mostly trying to get him to socialize with other students.

The psion sighed. "Niajar, I appreciate your concern, but we've been over this. Everyone is either already part of a team or is not participating at all. If you want to help me, maybe you could find me a Defunct who won the games in the past. I could at least learn something from reading about their match history."

The librarian's grin didn't fade. "Why, what a magnificent idea, my pupil! It's so ingenious, in fact, that I've already thought of it myself."

That got Kiru's attention. He snapped his head up to his sponsor. "And?" he asked excitedly.

The elf pulled out a red book from inside his robes. "I discovered that, in all of the entirety of the games' history, there has only ever been one Defunct champion. For whatever reason, all mention of him has been removed throughout the kingdom, except for one book I found in a junk shop on my most recent trip to the capital. I think it will make an excellent addition to the library, don't you?"

"Yes!" Kiru choked out, looking at the tome like a man in the desert would a cup of water.

He reached for it when Niajar pulled back. "Not yet. I will give this to you on one condition."

"What is it?" Kiru asked, still enraptured by the book in the elf's hand.

"You no longer do your work in any isolated rooms, from this moment on, and I will give it to you at the week's end. First, I must catalog it."

Kiru bit his lip in frustration but nodded. "Deal." Despite it being the beginning of the week, having a tangible goal in sight was much more bearable than fumbling around trying to happen upon a way to utilize his psionic powers.

He recalled William before collecting his things and walking past his sponsor. Ever since the elf's not-so subtle threat to the familiar those months ago, the imp's typical mouthiness had become notably absent whenever the librarian was around.

Niajar's shoulders sagged with relief. After months of intensive research, multiple called-upon favors to be repaid, and the ridiculous amount of coin he'd spent on that old gnome smuggler over in Waketown, he'd finally gotten this information. Even as the head librarian of the entire academy, the one who had access to one of the largest abundance of knowledge in all Alterra, this book had eluded him.

Niajar wasn't a fighter; he was a healer. He couldn't even help Kiru cultivate. He couldn't train Kiru in the classic manner, but he could give the Fist House student knowledge which should serve him in an even greater capacity. The fire in the boy's eyes when they first met, an ambition clearly roiling about under the surface, had only grown with their acquaintance. It was an ambition to match the elf's own—an ambition necessary for them both to achieve their goals.

Thinking about what he'd read so far in the book, Niajar's wide grin returned. The stories about a Defunct winning the Warrior Games had never been confirmed, only mere rumor elevated to the status of myth by gossips and students. It was a source of much contention, and many didn't believe it to be true. It angered the librarian to no end that he could not find any evidence to the story, only the words of a few old soldiers he talked with one night at a tavern.

Then, one day last week, Niajar had figured it out. He suddenly realized why there was no evidence, as if he'd been struck by lightning. The victory had been covered up! Once he determined that, Niajar just needed to get into contact with his less-reputable sources, and the rest was taken care of. "Get ready for a shock, Kiru," he'd said, too low for his words to be heard by his pupil. "The champion has been right under our noses this whole time."

# CHAPTER TWENTY-SIX

# Hearing Voices

Kiru tightened his headband as he sat down at one of the tables in the library. Though he had agreed to no longer do his work hidden away in one of the silent rooms, Kiru had actually made more progress with regards to his mental mana cultivation in the past few days. First, he found a new abundant source of mental mana. It was completely by accident, but it made the psion both giddy with excitement and frustrated that he didn't think of it sooner.

It was fair to say that writing down bland, dull texts could be . . . well, boring. It was during one of those times that he decided to close his eyes and take a break. He had almost drifted off to sleep when the realization struck him. In this state of semiconsciousness, Kiru was alerted to the overabundance of mental mana inside the library. He audibly gawked and nearly slapped himself. *Of course there would be an abundance of mental mana here!* Everyone in the library was researching, studying, or using their brain in some capacity. This building was *crammed* full of mental mana! He quickly began cultivating the mana into his mental core, almost laughing at how rapidly he replenished the spent energy. Instead of the hour he usually needed to provide about six hours of movement in the mana-dense area of the academy grounds, the library was able to do so in a mere twenty minutes.

The second thing he'd discovered was on the very next day, and it was completely by accident. Two days before he was supposed to get his prized book, Kiru was busy organizing a stack of tomes that had been returned, and then putting them back in their proper places throughout the library. It was rather quiet inside the building, aside from the subtle scurrying of the occasional rat sneaking about. But it wasn't that quiet inside Kiru's mind. William was moaning and complaining incessantly in there about how bored he was. Kiru had been spending even more time in the library, now that he found it to be a great source of mental mana, which meant less time that he was sparring with Brunhilda.

He had improved in his overall mana efficiency using Telekinesis, but constantly needing it to move meant there was a persistent drain on him. Also, when he focused more mana to a certain part of the body, that equated to an increased demand on his mana. So, he'd been accumulating extra mana from the library over time in case he was stuck in a pinch. If he kept it up, it would hopefully help give him a large reserve of energy for the Warrior Games.

With the decrease in combat this past week, however, the little demon inside Kiru's brain grew more and more frustrated. *"This is soo boring!"* he complained again.

"Quiet," Kiru whispered harshly at the demon.

*"C'mon, Master, just lemme out for a little bit. I promise I'll just throw a few books at some unsuspecting chumps."*

"The last time I let you out to 'have fun,' you set a Sword House student's jacket on fire!" he retorted, his face an angry snarl.

Another student was looking at him, their face wide-eyed as they watched Kiru seemingly talking to himself. They awkwardly scooted away behind a bookshelf.

*"That was an accident, Master. Besides, that guy called me ugly. I couldn't not set him on fire."*

Kiru's mind reeled from his familiar's incessant babbling. He just wanted some peace and quiet, so he could finish his responsibilities for the day and get the book Niajar promised. He sighed and rubbed his temples. Trying to calm himself, he cultivated as he closed his eyes. *The damn imp just won't stop talking. Why? Why won't he just shut up and give me some peace? Can he not just be satisfied with being quiet for one minute? Heck, I'd be willing to even give him an extra cookie. Sure, he'd be bouncing off the walls later, but it'd be worth it.*

*"Fine, I'll shut up for a cookie, but it better be chocolate chip,"* William conceded.

The imp's words gave Kiru pause. He hadn't spoken those words aloud. He was just thinking. Tentatively, he tried again, forcing his thoughts out. *William, can you hear me?*

*"Is this a trick, Master? You told me not to talk."*

The psion's eyes widened. *Oh, crap. William, you can hear my thoughts?! Wait, no, that's not it!* Kiru suddenly realized that he had a subtle deficit of his mana during his mental conversation with William. Somehow, he subconsciously used some mana when thinking. Quickly, he put together what that meant. *I can use Telepathy now! I think . . . I think it's a new technique. Oh my gosh, I learned a second technique!* he sent excitedly.

It took a few moments for the imp to process. *"Wait . . . Master, summon me out."*

Curious, Kiru did so.

The imp left his body as an orb of red light, then materialized onto the table. William then scanned the area, finding another Fist House student perusing a section of books on geology. When the imp saw the student, a mischievous smile grew. "Master, watch this," he whispered, then stared at the student. *My, don't you look delicious!* He sent his thoughts telepathically to both Kiru and the other student, sounding like some malicious predator ready to pounce on their prey.

The human dropped his book to the ground and scanned the library wildly. "Did . . . did you hear that?" he asked Kiru loudly, a look of sheer terror in his eyes.

"Shhhh!" William hissed at the questioning cultivator, as if he wasn't the cause of his fear.

"Must have been my imagination." The man chuckled nervously and picked up the book, still shaken.

Kiru felt a mixture of annoyance and disappointment. Any technique he had access to, William, being his familiar, did as well. While he was happy to gain telepathic abilities, Kiru bemoaned that the little demon now had access to them too.

*I've always wanted to try man-flesh before. Tell me, do you taste like chicken or bacon? I'm dying to find out.* William sent to the unsuspecting student.

The man gasped and quickly turned his back to the nearest bookcase, frantically scanning about. "Who's saying that?!" he shouted as he nervously scanned the area like a cornered animal.

*No one can hear me, manling, and no one will be able to hear you scream when I eat you. Muahahaha!* William telepathically cackled.

This time, the man didn't stick around. He threw his book up in the air, screaming in sheer terror, and bolted for the nearest exit.

William fell on his back, cackling as only an imp could.

"Really?" Kiru asked. "As soon as you get the ability to use Telepathy, you try to cause more trouble."

"Oh come on, it was funny!" William replied.

Kiru chuckled. "Okay, maybe a little. Before Niajar finds out, though . . ." He recalled his familiar. William protested but couldn't resist his master's will. Now, with a new technique, Kiru felt reinvigorated. He wasn't sure, but he theorized that the high mental mana density of the library coupled with frustration at William brought about the Telepathy technique. He had no way to prove if that was the case, but that was the best he could go on.

The next couple of days after that passed by without issue for him, and soon it was finally time to acquire the book! He went to Niajar's office to get it. Niajar handed it to Kiru without complaint, but as Kiru grabbed for it, the elf at first refused to let it go and instead drew the psion in close. "I believe this information will be very useful to you."

"I think so, too," Kiru replied, not sure where the elf was going with this.

"Strictly speaking, you probably shouldn't have it, nor even know of its existence. A very well-connected individual must have gone to great lengths to have this information removed from the public record. Only my great investigative skills as a librarian were able to uncover it. So, it would behoove us both to not speak of this to anyone, understand?"

Kiru nodded. He needed every chance he could get. If he had to use a potentially not-so-legal method to attain victory, so be it. His mother had taught him that anything worth fighting for was worth fighting dirty for. That was right before she threw dirt in his eyes, then used the distraction to trip him. Kiru had no issues with using insider information to win. He was already at a massive disadvantage, and he'd take every break he could get.

He quickly tucked the small book into his bag and hurried off back to his room. He closed the door behind him, then began frantically reading only to realize it was a copy of a book that he'd already read!

During his time in the library, he'd thumbed through the records of every year of the Warrior Games, hoping to glean some useful information. Kiru now realized that one of the tomes he'd read before was actually a forgery, as this possessed the information that had been edited out.

The book was a complete analysis of the Warrior Games held by the academy thirty-four years ago. The records were almost entirely the same except for one specific person—one of the first-year champions. Where the official copy had a dwarven dual mace wielder who utilized metal mana, this one named him as a half-orc/half-elf Defunct who wielded two hook swords.

Kiru let out a small gasp as he put the pieces together. Those who were half-orc/half-elven were definitely not common, even within the diverse Kingdom of Blades. Those who wielded a pair of hook swords were even rarer. In fact, Kiru knew of only one person who fit that description: *It was Giiyam! The groundskeeper was a former champion!*

Kiru hungrily read every word about the half-orc. There was a whole chapter devoted to each champion, going into explicit detail about each's fighting style. There were even drawings displaying the sword forms Giiyam had used, based off of the author's recollection. Kiru committed them all to his perfect memory.

He even read some of the author's theories about Giiyam being some sort of cultivating genius—that whatever defect he had to make him a Defunct was actually a boon; that he had found a revolutionary way to cultivate, making one not even need techniques. Each theory was pure conjecture, but they were adamant that Giiyam *had* to be hiding something special.

According to the book, Giiyam was relentless, a terror on the battlefield. Despite his inability to use techniques, he instilled fear in many of his opponents and was the main reason for his team's victory, carrying them all the way to victory. In fact, he was so impressive that Kiru's father immediately took him out of the academy and promoted Giiyam to a high-ranking officer in the Royal Army.

That explained why Giiyam hadn't won his subsequent years, but it still left Kiru with even more questions: *If he was in the Royal Army that served my father, how did Giiyam end up here? Is he a traitor like Van Blaine? If so, why would he be a groundskeeper instead of a personal guard to the usurper? Is he hiding from Van Blaine?* More importantly, one thought superseded all of those other questions: *How can I convince him to teach me?*

# CHAPTER TWENTY-SEVEN

# Putting It to Practice

For the next day, Kiru was completely wrapped up in his book, entirely focused on the information pertaining to Giiyam. He studied every word, every picture down to the most minor detail. It didn't state much about his history, just that he was from the Kingdom of Blades. The style of sword fighting he used was a rare one called The Cruel Mantis. Kiru pored over the drawings of the half-orc's sword forms, hoping to be able to imitate them himself. At some point, Kiru planned on talking with the groundskeeper, but he wanted to make sure he gleaned every bit of useful information from the tome first.

Despite his perfect memory, he read through the section over and over again, even sneaking the book into his classes and re-reading surreptitiously. Eventually, one of his instructors noticed. "Oi! Kiru, what're you doing up there?!" General Escobert called up from the arena floor.

Kiru could vaguely hear Escobert's voice in the back of his head, but he didn't pay attention to the general's actual words. He was too mesmerized by the book to make out what had been said his words. Brunhilda, who was sitting next to him, had to elbow him in the side.

Startled, Kiru quickly closed the book and put it in his bag. "Oh! I'm sorry, sir! I was just—"

"You think that you're too good to pay attention to my lectures, aye?"

"No, sir! Sorry, sir!" he apologized. While it was nice to have a teacher like Escobert who actually seemed to favor Kiru, that came with a downside, namely extra expectations. If Kiru didn't know any better, he'd have said the general was a sadist, given how much leeway he seemed to allow others in using their techniques against Kiru after he was defeated and the dwarf "wasn't looking." But because of the half-elf's disadvantages, Escobert pushed him even harder than the rest to make up for it, ensuring that if anything was lacking, it wasn't his training, or to Kiru's chagrin, his durability.

So, with Escobert's extra investment in Kiru's training, the dwarf also got irritated whenever his Defunct student didn't seem to be returning the attention in kind. The gold beads braided into his beard rattled as he shook with visible anger. His face turned red, nearing the shade of the Fist House jackets. "You'd think a cultivator of limited ability getting taught by a decorated general would be grateful! Well, if you don't want to listen to my lectures, it looks like you should have a practical exam, boyo!"

Kiru gulped. The only time the general ever called anyone "lassie" or "boyo," was when a painful lesson was incoming. "Kiru, grab your team and come down to the arena."

The psion turned to Brunhilda, who gave him a frustrated look before sighing and joining Kiru in walking down. The pair then stood at attention by the retired general. Then Escobert projected his voice in a lecturer's tone for all of the first-years to hear. "Now, while I admit you've exceeded expectations in your fighting ability, it's important to *not* get a big head. You need to also learn as much as possible. Knowledge is power, and in battle, power is great. Now, class, can someone who was *actually* paying attention tell me what we were just talking about?"

A hand went up.

"Ah, yes. Zane?"

"It's what to do when you're outnumbered and outmaneuvered in a battle," he answered with a smug smile directed at the psion. Since their first encounter, the two had never spoken again directly to each other. Still, Zane never missed an opportunity to look down on the Fist House student or belittle him during class.

"Correct! Now, since our resident Defunct thinks he already knows enough about this to not pay attention, let's test his knowledge, shall we? Zane, bring your team down to the arena, too."

The elf did, and soon he and his three compatriots were standing on the other side of Escobert. "Now, we will have a demonstration of this very topic for the entire class," the elder dwarf said as he took a few steps forward. Then, he turned to face the six students before him. "We're going to have a fully sanctioned practice match, here and now."

Kiru's heart sank. He turned to look at Zane's group. The elf had a malicious smile on his face, not unlike the smirk he'd seen on Ambrose's. Even his little fairy familiar had that snarl on their face, which looked almost unnervingly unnatural.

Escobert continued, "Unlike in our sparring, where we fight using just our weapons and physical exertion, for this sanctioned match you'll be allowed to use your techniques to your fullest abilities." There were some audible gasps and murmuring from the students. "No need to worry; your innocent little baby faces won't be harmed. The enchantment from the arena will prevent any serious injuries, as usual." He then pulled out a small, round device from his pocket and twisted it with a click. The transparent shrouds that had covered all the students hummed with extra force, indicating that they had just been empowered.

Escobert was an earth mana cultivator on the Path of the Shifting Stone, and he displayed his ability after he tucked his device back in his pocket. With a force of his will, he slammed a booted foot down on the dirt arena floor, directing his mana into the ground. It was some sort of stone-manipulating technique, as a stone ring just a few inches high elevated from the dirt, now encircling the two teams. It was a mini arena, but it was still plenty big.

"Students, move to the opposite side of the practice arena. You will be given one minute to prep. Then, on my mark, you will begin combat until your opponent is fully subdued," the general ordered.

"Kiru, ye be very booksmart, but . . ." Brunhilda sighed, her unbreakable kindness strained in a situation where she should be irate. "Well, but that wasn't very smart at all, now, was it?"

"I'm sorry," he apologized, shamed by her gentle reprimand. "I'll make it up to you. You can practice all of your pitches for serving Hlin on me after we're done."

The paladin positively beamed at that. "Deal!"

"Now, let's go over what we know about Zane and his squad," he said, leaning in as they made it to their assigned spot.

"As ye know, Zane be a nature mana cultivator on the Path of the Warrior Druid. We both know he fancies using that rapier on his belt. That human brute be some barbarian, if you can't tell from the massive axe and his short temper. I don't know any of their techniques, though."

"Same here," Kiru affirmed. "I know his axe can catch fire, but I'm not sure if it's a technique or enchantment."

"Aye," Brunhilda agreed.

"But we can potentially use the barbarian's anger to our advantage. What about the other two?" Kiru asked.

She looked over at the robed gnome. "She be a cleric of Ein, goddess of medicine and healing. She's right shite when it comes to fighting with her staff, but her healing's even better than mine. Lastly, that drakonid fella." She nodded toward the lanky gold reptilian man. "He fancies daggers, so he'll try to get up close and personal with us like he's done during previous training bouts. I don't know what type of mana he uses. Do ye?"

"Likely some sort of elemental type. In my fire mana class, there are a number of gold drakonids there," Kiru answered. "I also read that they almost always use either fire or ice mana and that they share at least one type of technique."

"What is that?"

"Some sort of breath attack," he answered grimly. There was shuffling excitement among the gathered first-years in the arena stands. This was the first time many of them were getting to see a sanctioned match that allowed the participants to use techniques. Kiru would've been excited, too, if he weren't one of the aforementioned participants. The voice in his head, however, was excited. *"Aww, yeah! Let's do this, Master! Grind their bones into dust!"*

Kiru promptly ignored William's hunger for battle and turned to his partner. Brunhilda was muttering a silent prayer to her goddess as she took in their opponents. He put a hand on her gauntleted shoulder. "May Hlin protect us," he said, giving her a comforting smile.

Hearing those words, she smiled back in appreciation. There was still a defeated look on her face, though. It tugged at Kiru. He didn't want his friend to despair. He meant it when he said he was going to win the games.

He looked over to his opponents and grimaced. Both Zane and the barbarian's smug faces promised pain. Those looks stirred up that all-too-familiar anger inside Kiru. This time, though, he let it fuel him instead of take him over. Kiru was tired of these asshats always using their techniques to hurt him; it was time they got a taste of their own medicine. Besides, Kiru needed to learn to fully trust the paladin, anyway. If they were going to win the Warrior Games, he knew he was going to have to inform her of his full capabilities eventually. Pissed off and ready to rumble, he thought now was a good time.

*"Don't freak out, but I've figured out a way to send messages without speaking,"* he sent telepathically to the dwarf.

Brunhilda's eyes widened in shock. She didn't say anything but was notably dumbfounded.

*"Trust me,"* he sent. *"I'll explain after the match. For now, let's go with Scorpion's Stance."* Though Kiru had been unable to find any record about psions or mental mana techniques during his time in the library, he found plenty of books regarding different fighting tactics. Partnering that with his newfound practically flawless memory, Kiru could quite possibly be a genius in combat theory. It was just putting it into practice that he needed to improve upon.

There was a moment of hesitation, making Kiru regret his rash decision to reveal his Telepathy, but then Brunhilda nodded. She would trust Kiru, for now. She knew well the battle formation he had sent; they had practiced it repeatedly. She snapped her arms out, causing her twin round shields to form from her armor. She slammed them together and stood in front of the psion, bracing herself. Each of her large shields were on either side, covering their flanks.

Kiru stood behind her, his pair of short swords at the ready, both pointing forward at their opponents. One was just above Brunhilda's head, while the other was held above his own like a scorpion's stinger. *"We've gone over fighting a barbarian-style opponent before. They're strong, but their forms are reckless. When he exposes himself during a swing, that's when we'll strike. Then, while he's down, we'll try to take out the gnome before they realize what's happened. If we strike quickly when they lash out, we may overcome our number disadvantage."* he sent.

She didn't look back to him, just grunted in acknowledgement.

"Ready!" Escobert raised his hand. "Begin!"

Kiru and Brunhilda braced themselves for an all-out assault by the other team, but it never came. In fact, all four of the opposing squad was just standing there, with a strange nonchalance. Zane gave the pair a smug look, hand on his rapier still in its hilt. "Listen here, class," he said, projecting his voice for all to hear. "My team and I, Team Supreme, are going to win the games. It's indisputable. That wretched defect over there," he said, pointing at Kiru, "and his misfit paladin are a stain upon our fine school. They aren't even worthy of the mantle of cultivator. I won't even need to move from this spot to defeat them. Witness our skill and despair!"

At his words, the gold drakonid drew his daggers, and then, in a flash, disappeared.

The crowd gasped in surprise.

Brunhilda did, too. "Invisibility! Kiru, can you see him?" she asked, scanning their surroundings.

The other three members of Zane's squad just stood there, watching in anticipation.

The psion furrowed his brow. *He* could see the lanky drakonid as clear as day, but based off of the reactions of literally everyone else in the arena, no one else could.

*"Hahaha! The fools!"* William bellowed inside Kiru's mind. *"They think such petty tricks will get past us? No!"*

The roguish drakonid stalked forward slowly, careful not to disturb the sand underfoot and give away his location. Kiru made sure not to stare so as to not give away that he could see the drakonid, but he made sure to never fully keep him out of his vision.

*"William, how are we able to see him?"* he asked.

*"Two reasons, Master. One, because we're awesome, and two . . . probably the mental mana flowing through your body. This is just like with those Beguilers trying to lure you in. This fool isn't using some sort of stealth. He's using an illusion. Pfft! No illusion or enchantment can get past our superior minds!"* he boasted.

Despite his familiar's childish answer, Kiru had to agree. Being able to see through illusions was, in fact, awesome. He then sent another telepathic message to Brunhilda. *"Don't worry, I can see him. On my signal, use your shield to kick up sand to our right."*

She just gave a very subtle nod, almost imperceptible, in response.

Kiru continued his charade of scanning the environment. "Where is he?" he asked out loud, making sure to sound nervous.

Zane and the rest of his team were still grinning on the other side of the arena as the drakonid closed the distance quietly. When the drakonid was right by Kiru's flank, he drew one of his daggers back to thrust it into the psion's side. *"Now!"* Kiru sent.

Brunhilda let out a battle cry and slammed her right shield into the sand at an angle, scattering it out in a wave. The sand flew up into the drakonid's eyes as he began his attack. The drakonid's form phased back into view just as his thrust began. The reptilian rogue's head recoiled and his attack went off-course. That provided an ideal opportunity for Kiru.

Kiru planned to strike using a sword form from Monarch's Razors, but the rogue's forward stab ignited something in the psion's perfect memory. The drakonid's attack reminded Kiru of the Beguilers' thrust attack. He was also reminded of how Giiyam dealt with it. More than once during the past couple of months, Kiru had thought about implementing what he'd seen from the groundskeeper. Noticing the similarity in his opponent's attack to the monster's, the psion made a split-second decision and re-created it.

Using his short swords, Kiru guided the drakonid's thrusting dagger away from his body even further, forcing the attacker to stumble forward. The rogue's eyes went wide as his surprise attack was very much rendered ineffective. Continuing forward to mirror the half-orc's form in his memory, Kiru's swords spread wide in two different directions. He couldn't hook in his weapons as Giiyam did, but they were still both sharp enough to allow the psion to improvise.

One sword struck at the drakonid's neck while the other bit at his ankle. The shroud enchantment of the arena prevented true fatal damage from occurring. It was a good thing, too, because Kiru could tell the lethality of that maneuver even on his first time using it. The shroud blocked the swords from actually penetrating the rogue's scaley flesh, but it turned red, and his body went limp, indicating that Kiru had indeed executed a fatal strike. The drakonid gasped before collapsing at the psion's feet.

The arena was silent, utter shock and surprise permeating the atmosphere. *"Oh! Master, I have a great comeback catchphrase right now!"* William sent.

Kiru lowered his sword, pointing it directly at Zane. "Witness our skill and despair."

# CHAPTER TWENTY-EIGHT

# Round Two

The crowd of first-years roared. Kiru, a Defunct from Fist House, defeated a Sword House student from the top team in a matter of seconds! There were plenty who didn't look on Kiru favorably, but it seemed that Zane's smug arrogance had brought about an even stronger resentment. They cheered in excitement and more than a little amazement at the psion's display. Even Escobert stared slack-jawed.

Kiru didn't look at them, though. His attention was still focused on Zane. Sure, they had fought off the initial attack, but the match was far from over.

Kiru would treasure the druid's dumbfounded look within his new perfect memory for a long time. Clearly, he hadn't been expecting this. The nice part, too, was that, since the drakonid was officially "killed," their healer could no longer aid him. Quickly, Zane's look of shock was traded in for a scowl. "Warren."

The human barbarian, Warren, snapped his attention to Zane.

"Let's show these bastards what true strength is," the druid said as he pulled out his rapier.

Warren had on a mad grin as he grabbed his great axe and faced Kiru's team. He squeezed the weapon tightly and activated one of his techniques. Both edges of the double-bladed weapon erupted in barely contained wild flame. Then, he leaped forward, quickly closing the distance between them with exceptional speed from his single bound.

Brunhilda was prepared. The protection paladin ran up to intercept, raised both of her shields, laying one partially over the other, and blocked the downward strike. Then, she pushed the large man back with a force of effort. Her strong legs were able to handle the barbarian's attack, but raising both of her shields left her body exposed—just what Zane was waiting for.

The druid's entire right arm was now completely encased up to the shoulder in a layer of thick, twisting vines, as if some sort of parasitic infection came from the weapon he gripped. He then activated a technique of his own. He pointed his blade, and his plant arm shot forward, like a snake striking.

The rapier was aimed directly at the dwarf's exposed midsection, looking to impale her straight through the stomach. Despite her plate mail giving a layer of protection, Kiru moved to intercede. He dashed in front of his teammate and blocked the incoming blade with his swords forming an X cross guard. He held back the blade but was caught off-guard by the vines. Some of the vines from the extended arm reached out and wrapped around Kiru's wrists.

They squeezed down on his arms, forcing them to stay in place. Then, like a slingshot, the druid's arm shrank, pulling him forward. Zane flew through the air, closing the distance, and kicked Kiru square in the chest. The psion coughed reflexively as Zane let go, the force of the kick sending Kiru backwards to crash into Brunhilda. The duo hit the sand and rolled a few feet away. They groaned but quickly forced themselves up at the ready and back to Scorpion's Stance.

"Looks like you're a liar, Zane. You *did* have to move from your spot after all." Kiru said, baring a bloody grin at the elf.

The gnome scurried over to the downed drakonid to heal him. It wouldn't allow him to participate again, but it was a kind gesture, as the pain from Kiru's sword strikes likely lingered. "No!" Zane barked angrily at the cleric. Kiru's words had visibly angered him. "If Goldie can get so easily beaten by a defunct, he's worthless to us. He's no longer on our team."

The gnome was startled, but after looking at the elf's threatening stare, she nodded uncomfortably and left the prone rogue. The barbarian, however, did not have such qualms. "Ha! You got that right, boss! I never liked the scaley freak, anyway!" the man mocked as the fire on his ax increased in size with his disdain.

Brunhilda's look conveyed sheer contempt. For one to willingly leave their comrade to suffer went against the core of who the protection paladin was. She snarled at the elf and human, giving the meanest expression Kiru had ever seen on her face before! "May Hlin smite their infernal hearts," she growled.

*Hmm, infernal hearts*, he thought. Those words stirred up some memories in his mind. It felt as if two puzzle pieces were slowly being brought together. Warren was a fire mana cultivator. He was in Kiru's fire mana cultivation class, and the markings on his axe confirmed it. Almost all people who utilized that type of mana had a core influenced from the infernal realm, Muspelheim. If he was not mistaken, then that would mean using an attack from a more divine mana source should do more damage.

Brunhilda had told Kiru she knew two techniques. The first was called Rejuvenation, and it was what she used to help him recover during the Beguiler fight. The second was called Divine Shield. It was a technique that called down holy light, infused with life mana, to make a protective column around its target.

It would burn enemies, but not allies, who touched it, too. The downsides were that, despite it setting the flesh of the opponent who touched it on holy fire, it didn't always prevent physical attacks from going through. It also dissipated after ten seconds.

Kiru smiled as a cunning scheme formed in his head. *Hlin may very well smite our enemies, after all*, he thought. William sensed his master's violent intentions and cooed in excitement. *"It's time to do our special attack,"* Kiru sent to the paladin telepathically.

The paladin knew exactly what he meant. She immediately knelt forward and placed both of her shields above her head.

Kiru ran right up to Brunhilda and jumped onto her shields.

In one fluid motion, Brunhilda launched the psion forward like a missile.

Both Zane and Warren were surprised by the sudden attack but not enough to be caught fully off-guard. The elf and human both blocked his attacks midswing, halting his momentum completely and forcing him back to his feet. There was a sharp popping and Kiru was pretty sure the sudden break in his velocity had caused him to tear a muscle. As his feet landed, the gnome cleric backed up a few paces, while Zane and Warren gave predatory grins.

Kiru matched their grin right back. They thought they'd caught him; they were wrong. *"Do it!"* he shouted telepathically to Brunhilda.

The paladin raised one of her shields in the air and called down her technique. A cylindrical column of divine light shot down from the sky, encircling the psion. Its borders had a two-foot radius from his body in either direction—plenty of room for the technique to make contact with his opponents. Brunhilda's technique protected anyone who she deemed an ally, and it was a good thing, too. If Kiru were an enemy, he had no doubt that the technique would have done him terrible damage.

Zane growled at the Divine Shield and pulled his rapier back as the technique burned. For Warren, it was different. The muscular man howled in pain as his body was lit aflame like dry kindling. His infernally aligned mana core showed its increased susceptibility to the Divine technique. The gnome was just outside the Divine Shield, so she was spared from its effects. Granted, Brunhilda told Kiru that she would have increased resistance due to also being a life mana user and a member of the same holy order as the dwarf, but it was evident that the cleric didn't want to take chances.

Despite the significant damage, the barbarian's pain tolerance was astounding—he was still on his feet. The burning man growled, then swung his great axe once more at Kiru, keeping his body but not his weapon distant from the Divine Shield and breaking it with this attack. Kiru ducked under the wild swing, but Warren quickly closed the distance and followed up with a kick. That move did connect but not on the psion. Brunhilda had run her stubby legs quickly enough to intercept the kick with one of her shields. Warren groaned and hopped back, his flesh still sizzling from the holy fire on his body.

The gnome cleric's hands glowed yellow, and the flames began to dissipate off of the barbarian's body. As soon as they left, his wounds began to heal.

"Oh, no, you don't!" Kiru said and went to strike at the Sword House student. His attack was cut off when what seemed like a hundred projectiles struck both him and Brunhilda in the back, knocking them face-first in the ground. Kiru was getting way too familiar with the taste of sand in his mouth.

The psion's mind went a little foggy. His control on Telekinesis relinquished, and his body went limp. He was picked up and raised in the air, his focus coming back to see that it was Zane's massive vine arm holding him prone midair. The elf scowled at Kiru, a steady flow of leaves coming out from his other palm. He didn't know exactly what had struck him in the back, but it came from Zane, and it likely had something to do with those leaves.. There was a loud crunching sound of metal on metal, and Brunhilda's prone body, completely covered by a red shroud, plopped down beside Kiru. The psion looked down at his friend, the shadow of Warren hovering over her, then back to Zane. The shock brought his focus back full-force.

The elf was still scowling. "You're going to pay for making me reveal my second technique," he spat in the sand, then brought Kiru just inches from his face.

Not wanting to waste an opportunity, Kiru used the proximity to headbutt the elven assface right in the nose. The jewel in the center of his head, covered by his bandana, definitely brought some extra oomph to the attack. There was a satisfying crunch of bone as Zane's nose broke.

Zane cried out in pain, while William let out an uproarious, villainous laugh inside Kiru's mind at the sight. Then, something metal and sharp struck Kiru in the neck, and his vision went black.

# CHAPTER TWENTY-NINE

# Coming Clean

Kiru recovered consciousness while he was being brought on a gurney over to the medical ward. Despite the enchantment on the arena which prevented life-threatening injuries, Kiru's neck felt like a tree that had been assaulted by a lumberjack. William was still conscious, however, and he quickly brought his master up-to-date on what had happened. Zane's team had been declared the winners. Shocker there. After that declaration, the enraged Warren had kept attacking, which was the source of Kiru's current neck pain.

Escobert had to personally intervene to stop the barbarian from breaking through the enchantment and decapitating the psion. The dwarf subdued Warren in a flash with ease, breaking the man's left leg for his insubordination. He then dismissed the class and forced Warren to limp to the medical ward rather than being helped.

William cackled at that punishment because, in truth, what the general did to him was worse than what happened to anyone else. Kiru groaned as he craned his neck to see Brunhilda and the drakonid being carried in gurneys alongside him. Both were unconscious but thankfully only seemed to have minor wounds.

They were attended by the school's physician, a human man who was a cleric of Odin. Brunhilda, during one of her impromptu sermons about Hlin, told Kiru to always be wary of those who follow Odin. They were zealous for knowledge, just like their patron deity, and were prone to doing unsavory things in order to obtain it. All of them had to cut out one of their own eyes, too. When they were brought into the medical ward, the one-eyed cleric looked upon the trio, then zeroed in on Kiru.

"Ooh, a half-elf!" he said excitedly. "It's not often I get to study one of your kind! There are all sorts of things I can learn from your anatomy." The man gazed on the psion with hungry eyes as if he were a slab of meat.

"Eh . . . yes," Escobert answered for Kiru. "These three were injured in part of a sanctioned practice match today. They just need some simple healing, and then they should be on their way. There is one more, though. He's on his way and will need a broken leg mended."

"Yes, yes, of course." The cleric waved the dwarf off. "But first—" He pulled a monocle over his lone eye and began examining Kiru. "—I cannot see most of the body, due to this . . . impressive elven armor," he said in admiration. "I must know, what is it made of?"

"I don't know," Kiru answered.

"Not a problem," the cleric said. "I'll analyze it after my examination is complete." He continued scanning Kiru. "Your body appears to be disproportionately distributed. The musculature of your body under your armor indicates a well-developed form, but your hands and neck have mild-to-moderate muscular atrophy. Maybe you have some rare muscular disease, due to your mixed heritage! Curious," he said with restrained but obvious glee. It was clear that the armor was still doing its job in concealing Kiru's atrophied body underneath. The cleric, however, was determined to study it in its entirety. "We could be on the cusp of learning a brand-new condition! Now, let's take off that bandana and assess for any head trauma."

"No!" Kiru said as he frantically reactivated Telekinesis and pushed himself away from the nosy cleric, falling off the bed.

Instead of seeming put off, the cleric just looked more intrigued. "Oooh, hiding some secret condition, are we? I promise I won't harm you. I just want to learn."

"I'm sorry," Kiru said as he shakily stood up. "It's not that, it's just . . ." He turned to see Brunhilda blinking herself slowly awake. "I already have a dedicated physician!" He blurted out the made-up excuse as soon as it came to him.

"Really? Here at the academy?"

Kiru nodded emphatically. "Brunhilda is a skilled paladin of the goddess Hlin and is an excellent healer. I would feel more comfortable with having her care for me, if you don't mind?"

The dwarf's face was one of utter surprise, her auburn hair now disheveled and partially covering her face.

Kiru gave her a pleading look.

"Your physician is injured. She is not fully capable of taking care of you."

"These are just scratches," she said, voice notably weaker as she gestured at the few not-so-insignificant gashes on her thick skin. "We who follow in the path of Hlin are tough, and so are our charges." She smiled, almost convincingly.

The cleric of Odin began muttering to himself, looking back and forth between Kiru and Brunhilda. "But, but I . . . I want to learn," he pouted. Then his eyes widened, and his predatory grin returned. "To be officially in the exclusive charge of a deity outside of the pantheon in any country inside the Great Alliance, you must be an acolyte of said deity. Curious, are you a follower of this Hlin, half-elf?"

Kiru gulped. He looked over to Brunhilda. She sat there with her mouth open, a look of fear but also of excitement plastered on her face. Kiru had no choice. "Yes. I am an acolyte of Hlin as well," he said.

Brunhilda's grin was so large it threatened to split her cheeks in two. "Well, ye heard my charge. That man be under my care, and by my goddess's will, I will protect him, so leave him to me." She had such vigor and tenacity in her voice, it made the cleric take a step back.

He quickly recovered, however, pretending as if that moment of fear had never occurred and instead masking it with a veneer of annoyance. "Oh, fine! Minor god followers," he muttered. "You two can leave then, if you're so inclined not to share your secrets." They both nodded gratefully and hurried out of the medical ward as fast as they could without overtly running.

They passed by Escobert, who gave them a serious look. "Can't say I blame you lot for not wanting his aid. The lead cleric is a creepy fella, but he's also very good at what he does. So, lass, if you find yourself unable to fix any injuries he's sustained, you bring him back to the cleric, got it?"

"Yes, sir!" she responded with a salute, her earlier grin still plastered on her face.

They continued out of the medical ward.

The cleric of Odin shook his head in frustration. At least he would get to learn about drakonid anatomy some more. From what he heard, the one who had just arrived used a unique type of mana for his kind. Maybe he would remove a few of his scales for testing? He turned to the gurney where the gold drakonid had been placed, but nothing was there. "What?! What's the meaning of this?!" he accused as he snapped his head to Escobert. All he saw was the dwarf's boot as he slipped out of the doors.

The cleric broke the clipboard in his hands in anger before he screamed, "Grah!"

Kiru led Brunhilda to the library, which contained the only rooms with silent enchantments that he knew of. There was one potential obstacle, however. The library was officially closed today for a deep cleaning by some strange constructs that the artificer class had made. They looked like strange lion dogs with large, round mouths like suckerfish. They weren't necessarily sentient, but they were voracious in trying to ingest any dirt, grime, or living being inside the library until dawn—and that included students!

Thus, once a month, Niajar or one of the other staff members would lock the doors and flip a secret switch to turn on the magical constructs. Fortunately, with his privileges of being the librarian's intern, Kiru was able to convince the secretary working at the front desk to hold off on doing so, promising that he would after he was done. Despite them being alone, they still decided to employ one of the silent rooms to be extra careful. He locked the door after the glowing rune of light activated. "I know you have a lot of questions."

"Goddess, yes, I do! What happened out there? How did ye do that during the fight?! Speaking to my mind?"

Kiru sighed as his body collapsed to the ground. He was running very low on mana after the fight, and he still hadn't been fully healed yet from the various injuries he'd sustained during the spar.

Brunhilda gasped and ran over to pick him up. "Kiru! Ye've gone limp, lad! What's going on?"

"It's okay," Kiru answered. "Just set me up with my back against the wall. After that, I promise, I'll explain everything."

Her nostrils flared in a mix of frustration and concern, but she complied.

Kiru took in a deep breath. A flurry of emotions ran through him: excitement, apprehension, fear, doubt, anticipation. He knew that he would eventually have to trust Brunhilda, and she was about as honest and good a person as he'd ever meet. Still, a small part of him was still scared of being exposed. Despite that, Kiru let out a slow exhale and decided to take a chance and finally open up to someone. "It's going to sound strange, but I'm not exactly a Defunct."

She just looked at him expectantly.

"It's true that I have my core can't produce techniques, but I have a second core, a core in my mind. I'm what's called a psion. I can use mental mana." Kiru spilled his story to the paladin. He told her everything: his father and the coup, his paralysis from his fight with Ambrose, how he awakened his mental mana core, what happened to his mother, and his ultimate goals. He even showed her the gem embedded in his forehead. "And that's the truth of it."

Kiru knew Brunhilda was a very trusting person, but it was apparent that even she struggled to fully believe what he'd said. "So, say yer telling me the truth? Yer body be completely unfeeling?"

"Below the neck, yeah."

"And ye use 'mental mana,'" she said. "And ye be out to save all of Alterra from another Draconic Campaign? As much as I want to believe ye, this does seem like a wild story. Can ye prove it?"

He pursed his lips and began to take off his armor.

The paladin blushed profusely. "What're ye doing?! Hlin does not condone this kind of activity! Ye haven't even tried to court me!"

Kiru chuckled. "Relax. I'm just going to show you my torso. My armor hides my actual form underneath."

Brunhilda looked uncomfortable but relented, turning away until Kiru was done. When he was completely shirtless, he told her to look back. She would be the first person to see his atrophied body other than his mother and William.

The paladin's face was that of utter horror. Confidence-boosting, it was not. Confidence-obliterating would be a more accurate description. "By Fenrir's fangs, how're ye? . . ."

"Moving? I told you, Telekinesis," he said, then picked up a small rock on the floor and levitated it in front of her before dropping it back down again.

"No, how're ye even alive? You're practically a walking skeleton!"

"Ah, well, stubborn determination, I guess?" he answered, putting the enchanted armor back on, sparing them both any more awkwardness.

"*No! It is our destiny! You are the Kiru the Conqueror with William, the Breaker of Wills, aiding you. No mere punk and his hired thugs will ever stop us!*" the imp cried out indignantly inside Kiru's mind. He looked up to Brunhilda and could see the doubt had not been fully erased from her face.

He sighed. "Look, I know it's hard to accept this all as truth, so hopefully this next thing will do it. Brunhilda Lightsworn, I swear to you on my soul that what I've said is true. Now, will you help me?"

The paladin's eyes widened as she physically felt the weight of Kiru's words in her own soul. It was clear the dwarf realized that Kiru either fully believed a lie, or he was telling the truth. Either way, it proved that he truly meant her no harm. Plus, he had clearly demonstrated his psionic abilities. Brunhilda's face first showed reluctance, but then her expression softened in concession. He could tell that she believed him. She believed her friend. "Fine, I will help ye, but on one condition."

"Name it," Kiru said, his voice flooding with relief.

She gave a wry smile. "Ye actually have to become an official acolyte of Hlin. If she approves of you, then I will, too."

Kiru sighed. "Fine,"

The psion was quickly informed by William that the imp *really* didn't like that. He began to protest in such a rapid-fire fashion, it threatened to give Kiru a serious headache if he let it go on for long. So, he let his familiar out. The ugly little fiend formed and landed with both feet on the floor. He looked at the paladin with utter contempt. Given the dichotomy of their powers' origins, the two had a pretty rocky relationship.

"Palabitch."

"Ugly imp," she responded.

William turned to face Kiru. "No. You can't do it, Master! I'd rather freeze my butt off in the icy depths of Hel than let you be some holy acolyte!" He sent an extra telepathic message to Kiru: *"I vote we just kill her and hide the body. That is a much better option!"*

"We are on the same side," he said, pointedly looking at his familiar. "Just because I agree to have a patron deity doesn't mean I won't be the same conqueror I was before."

The petty little imp crossed his arms and pouted, but he didn't protest any longer, aside from grumbling under his breath.

Kiru then looked at the dwarf. "That goes for you, too. I will agree to be Hlin's acolyte, but I won't swear to serve as a cleric or paladin. That's not what I'm after."

Brunhilda looked disappointed but agreed to his conditions. Kiru knew she was happy enough at this point to get *anyone* to join her order, even if it was just a mere acolyte versus someone with her level of zeal. She had Kiru kneel before her, then placed a hand on his shoulder.

"Do ye, Kiru, swear on your soul to serve Hlin, Goddess of Protection as her acolyte and ally and bring her glory?"

Kiru felt the heavy weight of the oath on his body like a weighted vest. "Yes." With that, the oath sank into his very being, sealing him to the promise. Then, to his surprise, holy light emanated from her hand. The light was bright—so bright, in fact, that it obscured Kiru's vision. He was forced to blink a few times, and when his vision cleared, he was no longer in the library.

Instead, he found himself in some sort of boundless room of pure, pristine white. There was no telling where it began or ended. He wasn't alone, either. There, standing before his kneeling body, was, without a doubt, a divine being. A woman with pearlescent skin adorned in heavy plate armor made of solid gold looked right at him. She had a face both immaculately beautiful but deadly serious. Her irises were the same color as her armor, and her purple hair was cut short on the sides. She had two shields made from some blue pulsating energy, each the size of Kiru himself.

"Thou claimest to make an oath of fealty, but I see no fervor in thine eyes towards us gods. Why? Why, then, wouldst thou make such a vow?" Her voice was regal and detached.

Kiru swallowed hard. This wasn't his real body, yet it felt very real. This had to be Hlin. He had never given much credence to the Divines before, but having one here before him quickly changed the psion's mind. "Begging your pardon, your holiness, but I swore to serve as an ally, not to blindly obey." It terrified him to correct an actual goddess, but if he didn't say anything, she could misinterpret his words and force him off the path to reclaiming his father's throne.

The stern but beautiful goddess seemed a bit frustrated at his words. She stared at him for a good minute, Kiru not daring to speak again under her gaze, but then, she gave a slight smile. "Indeed. Thy words are true. I know of your identity, son of Chromebane. I dare say that none of your kind have ever dared contract with us gods before. It's . . . intriguing."

"My kind?" he asked.

"Do not play coy with me, son of Chromebane! Thou art a psion, a Herald of Change, one who hath stolen from the bastion of Pandemonium that is the void and somehow survived!" She spoke with such utter authority that the force of her words made Kiru fall completely down on his face. He was too busy trying not to get crushed to paste to think too deeply, but he had no idea what she meant about the "Herald of Change" or that he had stolen from some "bastion."

After a few tense moments, she finally released the pressure she had on the boy.

"My apologies," he said as he pushed himself up.

"I have no time for games, Psion. Why hast thou offered to align with me?"

"I wish for the aid of your paladin, Brunhilda," he answered honestly.

The beautiful, purple-haired goddess scanned his eyes for any falsehood or deceit. When satisfied, she nodded. "Very well then, Herald of Change. Thine words are true. I will ensure thou hast my loyal servant as your ally, but for a price."

Kiru fought not to roll his eyes. There was always a catch.

"Thou hast spoken with my paladin about her quest?"

"She wants to help you get promoted to being part of the pantheon."

"Indeed. It is one of my greatest desires. Join her in this quest, aid her in establishing me in all major capital temples, and thou shall have both her aid and mine."

Hope sprang in Kiru's chest. "Can you fix my body?" he asked.

She shook her head solemnly. "Whilst my healing is strong, I am a goddess of protection, not restoration. Thine injuries are too old and too serious for my hands."

Kiru frowned but nodded. He was disappointed but understood her words.

"But I can give thee a boon," she said and tapped the headband on Kiru's head. His heart began to race in excitement as divine power coursed through the black fabric, enhancing it and giving it golden trimming. Kiru's eyes widened as he felt the power coming off the item. It made him feel . . . strong. Not *only* strong though, but safe too.

"Thine garment now has my blessing. Despite its appearance, my power has blessed the fabric to provide a magical layer of protection for thine entire head. It will serve as a garment worthy of one who is my ally. Go now and spread my path of protection," she said.

"Thank you," he said, bowing his head to the goddess, truly grateful. Before he could raise it again, another bright light flashed across Kiru's vision.

He was back in the room, still kneeling as if nothing had happened. Brunhilda gasped as the glow in her hand faded. "Ye met her?! Ye met Hlin?!" she asked excitedly.

"I did," Kiru said. "And she blessed my headband, too."

The paladin looked at it and noticed the golden trimming that had not been there previously. Then, without warning, she punched Kiru straight in the forehead, or she would have, had her gauntleted fist not struck against some semi-translucent barrier. The barrier around his head shimmered in place for moment before fading. Kiru pulled his head back in response to the strike.

"What was that for?" he asked.

William was indignant. "You see, Master? This dwarf tried to kill you. End her. End her now!" he shouted.

She rolled her eyes at the imp, "I didn't do anything serious, ye ugly demon. I was just testing out yer master's newest piece of enchanted gear."

"Liar!" the imp shouted, but Kiru put his hand up.

"It's okay, William. I'm fine," Kiru said.

The imp grunted angrily but relented.

The paladin gave a toothy grin at William, then looked at Kiru, "Did ye feel that?"

Kiru placed a hand on his head. "N . . . no."

Brunhilda smiled. "Hlin's blessing has graced yer headband, my friend. It now projects a magical helmet made of mana. If someone manages to destroy it, the helmet will take twenty-four hours to regenerate. It be pretty strong, though, as it didn't break even with my punch."

"How do you know that?" Kiru asked.

The paladin smiled and undid the fabric holding her hair in a ponytail. It was purple, but it had the same enchanted golden trimming on it. "Welcome to the order of Hlin, acolyte."

# CHAPTER THIRTY

# Going Rogue

After Kiru's induction, Brunhilda took some time to examine his body for injuries. He had, in fact, torn and bruised his trapezius muscles on the left side. With the uptick in fighting lately and his inability to feel his body, Kiru couldn't help feeling extra grateful to have a healer in his corner.

After that was done, he put his armor back on and recalled William. As he stood to go, the psion noted one more change. Right at the center of his chest plate, a crest was emblazoned into the cinnabar armor: a spear, splintered into multiple pieces as it struck a shield, the symbol of Hlin. The goddess had made his newfound alignment to her cause official for everyone to see. If he was going to help her become popular enough to join the pantheon, being a walking advertisement couldn't hurt, especially after he won the Games.

They walked out of the silent room, and Brunhilda immediately stopped, a look of confusion on her face. The bookshelves had moved and were not where they were when they entered.

"Oh," Kiru said, understanding her bemusement. "When sundown hits, the shelves reorient in the library to allow more room for groups of students to study. It makes finding books more difficult but finding the exit much easier." The dwarf relaxed. Kiru had learned she wasn't a night owl, so she was almost never out of her room this late. They headed in the direction of the library entrance when Kiru's perfect memory kicked in a warning to his mind. He stuck an arm out to halt Brunhilda.

"What is it?" she asked.

"These shelves only activate at night when someone is still in the library. They shouldn't have moved until *after* we exited the silent room."

"Right, because ye said no one can be in here since the constructs are going to clean this place after we leave. So that means—" Brunhilda's face made an O-shape when understanding hit her. They weren't alone.

Goosebumps traveled up the back of Kiru's neck. He slowly scanned their surroundings. There, crouching on one of the bookshelves behind them, was the gold drakonid they'd fought earlier, a pair of daggers at the ready. His body shimmered slightly.

Both the rogue and the psion locked eyes. The drakonid's reptilian eyes conveyed surprise, then ferocity. Before Kiru could shout, the rogue leapt from the shelves. "Spy!" he hissed as he descended toward the half-elf.

Kiru pulled Brunhilda back, narrowly forcing them both out of the way of the assassin's blades. They drew their weapons and faced their attacker.

Despite the miss, the drakonid landed soundlessly on the library floor and did a cartwheel/spin combo to turn back and face them.

"Kiru, where is he?" Brunhilda asked.

"He's right in front of us, about ten feet ahead," Kiru said, pointing at him with one of his swords as he realized the glow he'd noticed was from the cloaking skill. He could have used Telepathy, but the psion was trying to be frugal with his currently limited supply of mana. This guy had tried to kill them! Whether Zane had put him up to it or he had been hired by Ambrose's family, Kiru couldn't let him escape. And since he wasn't planning on letting the drakonid live to tell the tale, Kiru pitched his voice so he could hear him. "I can see you, asshole."

The drakonid hissed and leaped at them.

In terms of pure physical combat ability, Kiru was not lacking, but he knew that he couldn't match the drakonid's speed, going full force. Too bad for the assassin, Kiru didn't need to rely on just his swords anymore. He reached out his hand and activated Telekinesis.

The drakonid gasped and froze in midair, his Invisibility fading, confirming that this was the same stealthy student who was part of Zane's team. The gold drakonid was still wearing his blue Sword House jacket, too. Using Telekinesis on something other than himself was much more difficult for Kiru. It required more mana and weakened the control he held on himself, especially with an unwilling target. It required a battle of wills, his versus theirs. During the past couple of months, Kiru had continued to practice Telekinesis on the rats that William would bring back for snacks. Once, Kiru had tried to use the technique on three rats at once, and the struggle had made him vomit. Still, pushing himself had helped him improve over time. The results were showing in his control over his opponent.

Right now, Kiru was succeeding in subduing him, but the assassin was still violently struggling to break free. He didn't have forever. Kiru had questions, though, and this guy likely had answers.

"Brunhilda, do you have any rope?"

"Aye, in me bag."

"Tie him up," he grunted, his body shaking.

She immediately went to work, pulling the assassin's daggers from his hands and wrapping him up tight with her rope, pinning his hands and feet together.

Once that was done, Kiru lowered the assassin and pressed the point of one of his blades to their throat. "Who are you really, and why did you attack me?"

The gold reptilian rogue snarled. "It doesn't matter who I am, spy. Though I may have failed, New Draconia will never return. We of the Serpent Isles will make sure of it."

That gave Kiru pause. *New Draconia? He thinks I'm working for the chromatic drakonids?* "Why do you think I work for New Draconia? Why do you think I'm a spy?"

"Enough of your questions! I will not betray my people. Just kill me and get it over with, spy!"

Kiru narrowed his eyes at the assassin. This misunderstanding, if indeed it was, might be a fortuitous one. New Draconia was as much an enemy to Kiru as it was to any gold drakonid. They'd been trying to reignite the fires of war for ages, and this could be the opportunity he had been waiting for. He sent a telepathic message to Brunhilda, letting her know of his plan.

She gripped her shields tight, ready to activate Divine Shield at a moment's notice.

Kiru leaned down, looking the assassin square in the eyes. "I am not allied with New Draconia."

"Hahaha! Do you think I'm a fool? You are clearly no Defunct, with that technique you used, and no one outside those influenced by a dragon could pierce my veil."

Kiru rolled his eyes. Apparently, sparing the drakonid's life wasn't enough proof that he wasn't a nemesis. He needed something more convincing. Kiru tugged on the rope and untied the assassin. "Would a spy do tha—!"

The assassin tackled him to the ground. The gold drakonid raised his sharp claws to slash at Kiru's neck, but Brunhilda activated her Divine Shield technique. The beam of light made contact with the drakonid and seared his scaly flesh. He let out a hiss of pain and jumped back.

Brunhilda charged the assassin.

The drakonid pressed his clawed hands together, almost as if in prayer; then his body shimmered, indicating his invisibility.

The paladin immediately stopped her charge, scanning back and forth in hopes of catching sight of her invisible foe.

The assassin didn't have such an issue. Kiru wanted to use his Telekinesis again, but it drained a good bit of mana from him. Kiru wasn't sure if he could pull it off again. He did, however, have no issue using his other technique. *"Brunhilda, duck!"* he shouted inside her mind.

The dwarf, showing complete trust, ducked down and dodged the drakonid's leaping attack, forcing him to fly over her. The drakonid took the miss in stride, rolling on the ground back to his feet and executing a spinning heel kick at Kiru's face. Fortunately for the psion, a semi-translucent helmet materialized around his head, protecting him from the impact. The blow still sent him flying back like he'd been hit with a sack of bricks. The psion crashed into a nearby bookshelf.

The assassin wrenched one of Kiru's shortswords loose as the psion flew back. Brunhilda turned and swung her shields at the reptilian man, but he blocked with his new weapon, then tripped the paladin with his tail.

Kiru forced himself to his feet.

The drakonid deftly spun in a manner seemingly only roguish fighters could and threw Kiru's shortsword like a spear.

The psion leaned to the left just in time to avoid getting impaled, but the distraction cost him. The assassin used his long legs to close the distance and wrap a clawed hand around Kiru's neck, pinning him to the bookshelf. He then used his remarkably sharp claws to knock the psion's other sword out of his hand and shatter the blade. The drakonid snarled, opening his mouth wide to bite Kiru's face off.

Within Kiru's mind, there was a distinct, *"Oh, shit!"* from William, which gave him a desperate idea. Kiru closed his eyes and summoned his familiar, giving him a mental order. The imp floated out of his head as a ball of red light and materialized between Kiru and his attacker.

The gold drakonid's eyes went almost comically wide when the bony, ugly demon appeared out of thin air before him, and he wrapped himself around the assassin's mouth, slamming it shut and holding it closed.

Brunhilda struggled to stand but had a look of determination nonetheless, readying her shields.

Being held up by the drakonid, the psion didn't have to use Telekinesis on his body to stay upright. He had recovered enough during his time talking with Brunhilda to have just enough for an emergency situation, and he thought this situation qualified as one. So he focused most of his mana down his right arm meridian, concentrating it in his arm to punch the drakonid square in the gut with the force of an ogre. The drakonid went flying back, William still clinging to his snout.

Then Brunhilda hit the drakonid square in the back of the head with a forceful swing of her shield, catapulting William off the assassin and into a bookshelf.

The rogue's eyes went distant, and he moaned in pain before dropping like a sack of rocks. Kiru hoped she hadn't outright killed the guy, as he still had questions that needed answers.

William cackled, crawling over to the assassin. He turned and farted in his face before running away, laughing giddily.

Kiru, on the other hand, had lost most of his patience. He pressed his sword under the drakonid's jaw, where, according to a text he'd transcribed, their scales weren't as tough. "Hey!" he shouted.

The drakonid winced and jerked but quickly regained his senses. As his gaze landed on the blade pressed against him, he froze. He regarded Kiru with a mixture of fear and respect in his reptilian eyes.

"Now, as I was saying, would a spy free you? Would he extend trust, when it would be easier to just kill you and let the constructs that clean the library remove all trace that you ever existed?" *"Would a spy be able to speak into your mind?"* he asked telepathically. Truthfully, he didn't know if there were any spies that could use Telepathy, but it was a calculated risk.

The drakonid's nostrils flared. "No." Apparently, his previous harsh tone hadn't been him trying to whisper. His voice just *was* a sibilant hiss.

"I'm going to move my blade back, and we're going to have a discussion like civilized people."

"Yeah, bitch, like civilized people! We've spared you twice; you won't get a third chance . . . bitch!" William added from his perch on Kiru's shoulder.

"I truly do apologize for him, but he's also right. If you try to attack us again, I really will kill you and let the library's cleaning constructs tear you to bits."

"Like a bunch of wild dogs!" William added.

"I understand," the drakonid agreed, and Kiru removed his blade. Slowly this time, the lanky rogue stood up, rubbing at the spot where the psion's blade had been.

Brunhilda stood right behind him, ready to administer a smackdown if he tried anything funny.

"Now, who are you? Are you really a student here, or have you been pretending to be on Zane's team just to find the right opportunity to kill me this whole time? Why did you attack us, and why did you think that I was a spy?" Kiru asked. He knew the rogue had a name similar to Zane's, but he had never heard it clearly, as the gold drakonid had been rather quiet all the times Kiru had been near.

"I am Zhaden of Clan Ironclaw," he answered with a subtle bow. "As to why I attacked you, in recompense for sparing my life, I will tell you. It is because you can see me. This information is seldom known to outsiders, but we of the Ironclaw Clan are a rarity among my people.

"We do not use mana originating from our origin realm of Draconia but rather dream mana instead. This allows us to use techniques not common to other drakonids, even amongst us gold drakonids. This also makes us outcasts, however, looked down upon by our own kin as being unworthy of our dragon heritage and strength. Our techniques fool most, except those with powers originating from the home of my ancestors: dragons, drakonids, and their vassals. When you saw through my technique during our sanctioned practice battle, I feared you were a New Draconia spy sent here to infiltrate the Great Alliance."

Zhaden explained how the cultivators from the Serpent Isles served as proud and deadly warriors. The best among them were part of a group called the Fangs and were also sent on missions to keep peace between the nations of the Great Alliance as well as prevent invasions. Outside the Gold drakonid nation, only the leaders of the other nations and a select few others knew of this. Only a majority vote by the Alliance leaders could dispatch them.

"It is my greatest desire to become part of the Fangs and gain respect for my clan. Our ability for illusions should be considered a strength, not a defect." He then turned to focus on Kiru directly. "In regards to that, I do request that you explain how you were able to see me? Surely, you have some connection to the gold draconic bloodline if you were able to see past my illusions and speak directly into my mind?"

After a moment's thought, Kiru explained who he was for the second time that night. He knew he was in an "all or nothing" situation, so he thought he'd be honest and see how the drakonid reacted. He didn't go into as much detail as he had with Brunhilda, but he let enough out to get the general message across.

Kiru didn't know how the assassin would respond once he learned the truth, so he made sure that, while he was speaking, he was cultivating to regain mana as well. He also made sure to keep his swords at the ready. If Zhaden didn't like his answer, Kiru wouldn't hesitate to end the rogue's life once and for all.

William was clearly thinking along those lines as he glared menacingly at the gold drakonid.

Despite the grim thoughts, Kiru was truly hoping that he might gain another ally instead.

When he was done explaining, the lanky drakonid stood there slack-jawed. "Truly?" he asked.

Kiru nodded.

Zhaden put his hand to his chin and looked down. "This is most unfortunate. If the psions have been falsely accused, then all other nations are being misled. If . . ." Zhaden stopped his musings and looked at Kiru with firm resignation. "Swear on your soul that your words are true."

"I swear on my soul that my words are true." He felt the weight of his oath fall on both Zhaden and him like a heavy blanket. Then, it faded.

Zhaden gave a grim nod. "This is most unfortunate. We must inform my country. Comrades, let us depart and head to the Serpent Isles. We will need to steal a ship."

Kiru was excited to visit the mysterious land of the gold drakonids where few outsiders had ventured, but this was not the time. "I can't, at least not right now. This is the best chance I have to get my father's item."

Zhaden growled. "But my people!"

"If what Kiru's saying be true, then *all* of our people are in danger. We only have seven years left until a new Draconic Campaign is at our doorsteps. Our best bet is to help him," Brunhilda interjected.

Zhaden hissed a little but didn't say anything else.

Seeing an opportunity ripe for the taking, Kiru pounced. "Well, it looks like our goals align, Zhaden. It looks like the best bet for saving all of the Alliance is to work together." That was the obligatory part, tugging on his moral need to save the innocent. Now came the hook: the personal motivation. "Besides that, Zhaden, I also like your drive. I want people like that around me. If you want to be the best illusionist, it looks like you'll have to join our team, because we're going to win the Warrior Games. Surely, whatever treasure you acquire when we win the tournament will help you on your quest."

The drakonid's reptilian muzzle contorted to give his people's awkward equivalent of a smile. "You sure you want me? I was recently beaten by a Defunct," he said wryly.

Kiru smirked back. "Definitely."

"Good! The team's coming together!" William declared proudly. "Team Terror Incarnate will strike fear in the hearts of our enemies."

"By Valhalla's grace, no!" Brunhilda strongly protested. "Why not Hlin's Holy Warriors?"

"I am not of this goddess you profess to serve, so that would be inappropriate," Zhaden said.

"Yeah, I agree with him." Kiru said. "I'm considered an acolyte, but I'm technically just an ally. No need for false advertising."

Brunhilda looked hurt at Kiru's words. She then crossed her arms in annoyance. "Hmph! Well, what do ye suppose, then? We can't just go and say 'Team One True King,'" now can we?" she asked sarcastically.

She wasn't wrong. They couldn't just name themselves something too obvious, but on principle, he didn't want to sound ridiculous, either. He wanted to convey seriousness, something that wouldn't draw too many discerning eyes, but also indicate their intent to change things, to rock the foundations they were fighting against.

Something Hlin said about him stuck out in his memory. She said he'd "stolen from the bastion of Pandemonium that is the void." While he certainly didn't know what she meant, he liked how she said it. He would tear down the usurper's monarchy and avenge his father's murder. He would bring the winged king, Pandemonium.

"Pandemonium," he said. "Our team name is Pandemonium."

Zhaden bobbed his head. "It's not . . . inappropriate for us. This group seems rather chaotic."

Brunhilda sighed. "I guess."

"I like it!" William said. "We will be those who bring ruin and woe to our enemies! They shall hide and fear from the inescapable Pandemonium!"

# CHAPTER THIRTY-ONE

# Sneak Attack

Zane scowled after he left his father's office. It was late afternoon, and the shadows had grown long on the academy grounds as he headed through the stone hallway. Usually, his dad would deal with anyone who defied or challenged his boy with extreme prejudice. He had already done so with a brutish pugilistic orc who had dared strike Zane just days before the semester began. The headmaster said his son was destined for greatness—the king had no children, and both Zane and his father knew that his throne could be theirs one day.

Zane just had to be careful when bringing it up with his father, since Niazen's temper had worsened dramatically since he'd been appointed headmaster. Despite his anger issues, however, he still doted on Zane, and had taken care of one student already this year, after that loud buffoon dared to humiliate his son. *Then why did he refuse to help me take care of that insignificant pest? It must be my uncle's doing.* He squeezed his fists tight in anger. *That Defunct made me look like a fool. He made me break my word in front of the class. I can't believe I had to use my hidden technique on him.* "Who is this Defunct?" He gritted his teeth.

"That mongrel is a cockroach," a voice answered from the shadows.

Zane put his hand on his rapier and turned in the direction of the voice. From the shadows beside a nearby column, a human teenager emerged. His body was in the process of losing its baby fat, but his face was still portly and pockmarked. Most notably, he had what looked to be a mark in the shape of a hand across his cheek. *Is it a birthmark?* Zane thought.

The human wore a Sword House jacket and at least carried himself like nobility. Upon seeing that strange mark on his cheek, Zane recognized who he was. "Ambrose Constantine, am I right?" Zane asked, already knowing the answer. Ambrose was a distant cousin to the king, and one of the few who Zane considered an actual threat to his winning the Warrior Games.

"You are correct," the teen answered, offering his hand. "I understand you have a pest problem."

"I can handle that pest myself," Zane said as he turned to walk away.

"I meant what I said. That peasant is a cockroach. He keeps coming back. Good thing for you, I've dealt with him personally in the past. I know how to deal with him. I've done it before."

Zane stopped and turned. "How?"

The human noble examined his fingernails as if what he was talking about was of little import. "The trash doesn't care about what happens to himself, but if something were to happen to someone he cares about, say a certain paladin who won't shut up, he may be more compliant."

"Say that I agree with that assessment. How much would putting advice to action cost?" Zane asked, keeping his face firm.

"Payment is not necessary," Ambrose answered. "But it has come to my attention that you're a team member short for the Games after you publicly kicked the drakonid out of your group. I believe I could fill in for him."

Zane looked at Ambrose, his expression remaining neutral. There was a heavy silence as the noble waited to hear what the elf would say. Finally, Zane gave a very small grin, "Welcome aboard, Ambrose Constantine," he said, extending his arm and finally shaking the noble's hand. "Once we deal with our pest problem, the Warrior Games will be a cinch."

"And the glory and power that comes with it will be ours," Ambrose finished.


For the next few weeks, things went surprisingly smoothly for Kiru. With Pandemonium now three members strong, they were actually serious contenders. People gave the psion much more respect than before, as well. Being the Defunct who stood up to the headmaster's son made him much more of a polarizing figure. Some came to respect him while others disdained him even more than before.

Zhaden had repeatedly urged Kiru to exercise caution and remain on-guard when it came to Zane. He warned the psion that the young elf would not take the insult of having forced him to break his word lightly, even if it was Zane's fault for being overconfident. Nor did Zhaden think that Zane would be okay with the drakonid joining Pandemonium, despite Zane having been the one to dismiss Zhaden from Team Supreme. The gold drakonid more than implied that Zane may seek some kind of retribution and had discussed a rumor among the Sword House students that the elf had already pulled some strings to make an orc student who stood up to him "disappear" before the first semester had even started.

Kiru wasn't too worried. He didn't put much stock in rumors. He had quickly learned that Zhaden was very much like Professor Zerkov in that he was also quite paranoid. More than once, Zhaden expressed concern that they were being followed when it was just other students on their way to the cafeteria or another class. As for Zane, aside from interacting in combat class and the occa-sional petty insults, the headmaster's son seemed to avoid the psion. So Kiru would be on-guard as he always was, but didn't think Zane warranted any spe-cial concern outside of class.

The newly formed trio fought well together. Having a new and very capable damage dealer who could turn invisible vastly improved their practice fights in their combat class, which were now more focused on team fights. After their first official, sanctioned practice match, more and more students began adamantly requesting times to do the same and train with using techniques in combat. It required a staff member to officiate and sanction and for both sides to agree.

Surprisingly, no one was willing to spar with Kiru's group. For whatever rea-sons, despite their hostility, students refused to rise to the bait of fighting a "weak" Defunct and take him and his team on full force. It was odd to the psion, but nothing could be done.

So, Pandemonium could only spar against assigned opponents in their com-bat class without the use of techniques. They were getting better and better when it came to pure physical fights but still had difficulty when going against teams of four. Not every team caused them trouble, but there were plenty that did, espe-cially Zane's team.

One day, when Pandemonium was assigned to spar against Team Supreme, the cocky elf revealed that they added Ambrose, the absolute worst person, to their squad. The noble wasn't any more of a real threat, but his presence—his *existence*—infuriated Kiru. He focused on not engaging with Ambrose unless absolutely necessary. Even though Kiru's temper had improved, his shared history with Ambrose, the pain the noble had caused him, and the loss of his mother had made his anger more difficult to control.

Because of that, it was quite literally an exercise in restraint when Pandemonium had to spar with Team Supreme. Kiru had trouble focusing, practicing sword forms, and developing strategies because all he really wanted to do was cut Ambrose in two. It was a sentiment that William happily encouraged the psion to act on.

Due to that, Pandemonium didn't fare particularly well against Team Supreme. It was after a fairly significant defeat that Zhaden took Kiru aside after class to speak with him. "May I speak truthfully?" the drakonid asked.

Kiru was a little caught off-guard but nodded slowly. "Yes. I always want you to speak truthfully. What's this about?"

"I know the nobleman from your village irritates you even more than Zane. It is plain for all to see. I have experienced such issues as well when I was a hatch-ling. Many gold drakonids have looked down upon the Ironclaw Clan, and so many of us have faced similar hardships," he said.

*"Where's this guy going with this?"* William telepathically asked Kiru.

The psion didn't reply but was wondering the same.

"A lot of anger accumulates within us from dealing with our drakonid brethren, but we developed a method to help us control it. I would like to teach it to you, as I believe it would be beneficial," Zhaden hissed.

Kiru didn't know if he should be grateful that the often more quiet Zhaden was offering to help or insulted that the gold drakonid was essentially implying that Kiru couldn't control his temper. He decided to go with the former. "Uh, okay, Zhaden."

The drakonid nodded, and he cautiously led Kiru to an isolated patch of grass making sure no one had followed them. Once there and satisfied they weren't being watched, they both sat in lotus position facing each other. "Close your eyes," Zhaden directed.

Kiru complied.

"Now, picture your body as being hollow, devoid of anything."

Kiru thought that was strange but followed. William started to ramble inside the psion's mind, so Kiru summoned the imp and let him munch on a piece of jerky to preoccupy him. Once he was able to fully visualize his body being empty, just a sack of skin and muscle, he nodded to Zhaden to continue.

"Now, imagine all of that anger, all of that fury that appears when you encounter Ambrose. Envision it as a large flame outside of your body," Zhaden hissed. "Open your body, and let that flame inside, but slowly as if through a straw."

Kiru's neck reflexively tensed, and he groaned slightly as he did so in his mind's eye. An orange-red roaring bonfire exploded into life in his imagination.

Zhaden seemed to intuitively know what was going on because he continued, "Now, guide the flames to flow in a controlled pattern throughout your body. Instead of letting the fire rage wildly, channel its flow, let it empower you. Let it feed you instead of you becoming its kindling."

Kiru struggled with this part of the mental exercise. *How do I control fire?* he thought. In his mind's eye, the bonfire extended tendrils of flame. Once they made contact with his hollow body, they began to feed into him as if the flames were somehow liquid. The fires of anger he had visualized began to roar inside his body.

Instantly, the psion felt fury rage inside of him. He wanted to lash out, to cause pain, wanted to cave Ambrose's stupid face in! He began to breathe rapidly as this visualization exercise was working almost too well. "What do I . . . do now?" he asked Zhaden through gritted teeth.

"You already have pathways for the flames to follow inside your body. Use your mind to guide them along where your meridians would be. Then, use the flames to empower your envisioned body," Zhaden said hurriedly.

Kiru gasped slightly at Zhaden's words. To guide them along where his meridians would be in his envisioned hollow body made so much sense to him. His meridians were the pathways for mana, for energy to flow through and empower him. Armed with this new understanding, Kiru guided the flames being fed into his imaginary body to flow in the pattern of the meridians of his actual body. In just a few seconds, the fire obeyed his will and instead of moving about uncontrollably, it flowed in a tight, specific pattern. It reminded Kiru of lava being moved through carved channels.

Kiru's breathing immediately lightened. He still felt the anger, but just as Zhaden said, it was fueling instead of leading him. Despite not having physical sensation in most of his body, Kiru couldn't help but feel invigorated and more "in control" of his anger. Those fiery feelings, when directed as he was doing, empowered his psychological state instead of consuming his focus.

The psion took in a deep breath and smiled. He opened his eyes to meet the drakonids. "Thank you."

Zhaden gave a small grunt and slightly nodded. He stood up and began to walk away when Kiru called out to him. "How did your clan come up with this exercise?"

The gold drakonid turned around slightly. "Most gold drakonids have an innate connection to fire. Though we of Clan Ironclaw cannot use fire mana, that doesn't mean we still don't feel the fire inside, so to speak," he said and then walked away.

Kiru was truly grateful for what the drakonid had given him. Over the next week, he put it to good use. His focus became clearer, and when forced to spar against Team Supreme, he was able to keep his cool. Out of all the sparring matches against Zane's team, Pandemonium almost beat them twice. Kiru was pretty sure that the gnome cleric cheated by using a healing technique when not allowed to, but he couldn't prove that claim. Still, the timing was suspicious when seemingly incapacitated foes miraculously regained energy after being near the cleric.

Now, the only thing that wasn't progressing, aside from practicing with techniques for Zhaden and Brunhilda, was trying to convince Giiyam to teach Kiru. Repeatedly, Kiru had tried to find and talk with the stoic groundskeeper, but the half-orc was either busy or just flat-out refused to engage unless it was about "groundskeeping business." The stoic orc was either single-mindedly focused on his duties while upon academy grounds, or he was intentionally avoiding Kiru.

The semester had just ended, marking just under six months until the Warrior Games. Right now, though, the students had a couple of weeks to relax, train, and do as they pleased. Kiru had been practicing his sword forms late into the evening; he went to bed to bed that night determined to redouble his efforts to convince Giiyam to train him with his extra time off. Kiru was so exhausted after his training, he'd collapsed on the bed with his armor on, still sweaty and unwashed, and he didn't even care. He fell asleep almost instantly, not even bothering to summon William and cultivate.

Hours later in the early morning, Kiru awoke, just before sunrise, to William screaming in his mind, *Master, wake up!*

Heart racing, he activated his Telekinesis and sprang out of bed. It was dark, the only light coming from the moon through a window, but he could make out two hooded, bulky figures standing just inches in front of him. Their forms seemed strangely distorted, but Kiru could make out their silhouettes with perfect clarity. But he was so caught off-guard that he didn't have time to react when one of them punched him square in the nose.

The impact knocked him into the wall. He was about to swing a wild fist in return when a large, heavy weight clinked around his wrists. Immediately, the psion lost all control of his body, his Telekinesis disrupted. He dropped to the ground, bouncing like a pebble on a lake.

The two figures cackled. "Guess the Defunct isn't as strong as he thought," one of them said. "Looks like he dropped from just one hit." One of the shadowy figures picked Kiru up by his black hair. The limp psion panted with fear. The two were now so much more distorted; some sort of veil must have been concealing them. *Why could I discern them earlier? More importantly, why can't I use my mana?*

He had just enough time to move his eyes down to the pair of bulky handcuffs around his wrists before another fist made contact with his face. With a crack and a shock of horrible pain, Kiru's nose broke, and blood flowed down his face. The brute holding him shook him until his focus fully returned.

"Is that all the fight you've got?! Stand up. Come on, Defunct. Don't tell me you can't handle a little trollstone!" The brute let go of the psion, dropping him flat on his face like a limp noodle.

Kiru raised his head to regard the shadowy figure, the reason behind his inability to use his mana suddenly clear. *That guy said trollstone,* Kiru thought. Trollstone was an extremely rare type of rock found in Stonereach. It has been rumored to have come into contact with Yggdrasil's roots, overcharging them with so much mana it disrupted the mana flow from one's core. *That must be what the handcuffs are made from. It's probably why I can't hear William, either.*

"Haha! Wow, how're you so weak?" the second figure asked, then kicked the psion in the side. Kiru didn't cry out in pain, because fortunately he couldn't feel it.

"Guess that's why he's a Defunct," the first one said. "Though I think the boss is giving him too much credit by ordering us to use trollstone," he said, then picked Kiru up by his hair again, bringing him inches from his face. "Apparently, he thinks you're clever, Defunct, so he doesn't want to take chances."

Kiru squinted his eyes, trying to process these words.

It wasn't long, however, before he got an answer to his unspoken question. "Zane sends his regards. You broke his nose; now we break yours." He then let out a cruel chuckle before raising his fist again. "And for an extra lesson . . ."

Kiru closed his eyes, wincing in anticipation of the incoming blow. But the figure suddenly let out a pained growl, and Kiru was flung to the ground. He bounced and rolled until his back was facing his ambushers. He struggled to move, to get up and fight, but he couldn't. But he heard the sounds of a skirmish behind him—grunts, slams, and impacts that thudded for about half a minute until they suddenly stopped.

Kiru's heart raced. Who had shown up and joined the fight, and even more crucially, who had won? A hand grasped his shoulder and turned him around. Relief flooded his heart as he saw Zhaden standing before him. His two attackers were now unconscious, laying on the floor.

"It appears that Zane finally decided to take his retribution, like I warned you," the drakonid said.

"Indeed," Kiru agreed. Zhaden had been insistent about the elf's anger and his ability to hold a grudge. It wasn't that Kiru hadn't taken his ally seriously. It was just that he never expected Zane to send someone to beat him up in the middle of the night months later. He really could hold a grudge! Kiru had thought Zhaden to be too paranoid. Now he learned the gold drakonid was right.

Zhaden cocked his head. "Your nose appears to be dislocated." Without any ceremony, he reached and snapped it back to place.

Kiru let out a grunt of both pain and relief.

The drakonid's eyes went wide. "My apologies. I thought you couldn't feel with your mana flow disconnected."

"You're right, but that's not the case for my face."

"I see," Zhaden said, looking sheepish. He busied himself studying the handcuffs on Kiru's hands. "Trollstone? Impressive. Now I understand why you were so inert."

"Yeah, pretty clever and all, but would you mind getting me free? Kinda prone here," Kiru said, spitting as a fresh gout of warm blood trickled into his mouth.

The drakonid gave a chuckle, flicking out his reptilian tongue, then took a key from one of the attackers and freed Kiru.

Immediately, the psion felt the surge of mana flow through him once more. He used Telekinesis to force himself back to his feet. He looked down to see two figures, an orc and a human, both in blue Sword House jackets, unconscious on the ground.

"Thanks," Kiru said. "How did you know to come here?"

"I was also ambushed by a pair of attackers from my house. But going after someone who specializes in stealth did not go favorably for them. Logically, I concluded that you would likely be targeted, as well. It appears that the headmaster's son has invested some notable resources if he was able to get Trollstone cuffs. Do you think he knows?"

"No," Kiru answered. He had been very deliberate about who had told of his psionic powers. Only his teammates and William were privy to that knowledge.

"Why do you think he was so emboldened as to attack us, then?" Zhaden asked.

Kiru thought about it for a moment, then an answer came to him: *Ambrose.*

"Likely their new teammate," Kiru answered. "Will you store those cuffs? Maybe we can use them to our advantage later."

Zhaden agreed. He placed them in a small pouch, just as they heard footsteps running toward the door. They both stood at the ready when Joseph stumbled in. "What's going on here? Do you know what time it is?" he asked. Then, he noticed the two unconscious students on the floor. His eyes began to glow green. "Explain yourselves immediately," he commanded. Not a trace of his typical mirth could be heard.

Joseph was an overall good-natured guy who'd been nothing but kind to Kiru. He had always had a warm nature. Despite that, what the man was giving off now was nothing but dangerous intent. Kiru looked nervously at the third-year. Despite Joseph only being a Beta Gold, Kiru wasn't sure if he could take him in a fight, even if he'd wanted to. "I was attacked," Kiru said quickly in order to prevent any more conflict. "These two ambushed me in my room, and Zhaden saved me."

"My teammate is correct," the rogue added. "I was attacked as well, so I came to make sure Kiru was unharmed."

The light faded from Joseph's eyes. "Whoa, seriously?"

Kiru nodded emphatically.

"Wow, this is real bad, dudes. I'll have to report this to the disciplinarians. Is there anyone else who's been hurt?"

Kiru thought for a moment, then his heart sank. "Brunhilda!" He took off. Zhaden followed close behind.

"Hey, where you going, brother?" Joseph called out.

"I have to check on our other teammate," Kiru shouted back as he continued to run. The psion instantly regretted that he hadn't thought about the dwarf earlier. He desperately hoped she was okay. Both Kiru and Zhaden sprinted across campus grounds, heading to the Shield House dormitory. The tall, lanky reptilian man quickly passed Kiru as they ran, showing his clear speed advantage, and he made it to the building a good minute ahead of Kiru. They knew where Brunhilda's room was so bolted straight to it. To their dismay, the door was open and there was a trail of blood that continued inward.

Zhaden put a clawed hand up to stop Kiru, then he squatted down to analyze the entryway. He pulled out one of his daggers and cut a line Kiru had not seen. "Enhanced razor wire," the rogue hissed. "Would've inflicted a nasty wound, had we run into it." After that trap was cleared, they went into the room. It was larger than Kiru's humble room—about double the size, in fact—and it was completely trashed.

Books, clothing, and armor were thrown about everywhere, shredded and broken. Multiple gashes were carved along the stone walls like claw marks. The worst part of it was the blood. Red stains littered the walls in a spray pattern. To Kiru's horror, the dwarf lay on her back, a bruised and bloody heap, breathing irregularly. His lip quivered in fear as he saw a large, bloody, clawed toe had been set beside her as well, likely planted as some sort of false evidence.

Kiru went straight to Brunhilda. "Hey, Brunhilda, can you hear me?" he asked as he knelt down and cradled the dwarf's head. Her right eye was swollen shut. There was a gash across her lip, and she was riddled with cuts and punctures.

She grunted, then coughed.

"It's okay. We're here now," Kiru said.

"I'm . . ." she muttered.

"Save your strength," he said, then turned to Zhaden. "Help me carry her."

The paladin mustered just enough strength to say two words. "I'm sorry."

Tears welled up in the half-elf's eyes. "No, I'm sorry. I didn't take Zhaden's warnings enough to heart." Then, exerting more mana, he used Telekinesis to gently lift the paladin up. Kiru's body quivered. She was not resisting, so that helped, but she was a densely muscular dwarf. She was, in fact, the heaviest thing Kiru had ever moved with Telekinesis. His nose even started to bleed again from the strain, but he didn't care.

Quickly, they alerted the student advisor for the Shield House, then carried Brunhilda to the medical ward, Kiru keeping his arms under the paladin to look as if he were holding her with only physical effort. The voraciously curious cleric was more than happy to examine another subject as he assessed her status. "Various bruises. Numerous lacerations in parallel concentric patterns. Patient has surprisingly thick skin, even for a dwarf. The thickened epidermis likely protected her from more serious injury. Will have to collect a sample for analysis," he muttered to himself as he performed his physical examination.

"So . . . she's going to be okay?" Kiru asked.

"Yes, yes, she'll recover. Her body is surprisingly durable, but it'll take time."

"Okay, well, can't you use a technique to help her recover faster, though? You are the head of the infirmary."

"Young man, why would I do that?" he asked, confused. "You and the paladin had stated that my healing was undesirable to that of your deity's. Plus, I need my mana for more valuable things, such as my precious experiments. I estimate your friend will be back to fighting shape in a couple of weeks' time."

"Kiru is not a healer. So, you are satisfied with letting a patient suffer? Do all clerics on the continent think this way?" Zhaden asked.

The cleric shrugged. "They don't, but why should I care? I crave knowledge, and there's nothing new to learn here. She'll be fine, as I said. Now, if you don't have anything else, I'll be going . . ."

"Is there something we could give you? Something that would be valuable enough to convince you to help our friend heal quicker?" Kiru blurted out in desperation.

A crooked smile then grew on the one-eyed cleric's face. "You know, now that you mention it, I do happen to have a special concoction of own design that could accelerate her healing, but in exchange, I'll need something."

"What?" Kiru asked.

"A skin sample, from all of you," he said, looking at both of them expectantly.

Kiru turned to Zhaden. The drakonid was clearly uncomfortable with the proespect but, regardless, ripped a golden scale from his tail and handed it to the cleric.

Kiru pulled out one of his swords and removed a thin piece of skin from one of his fingers.

The cleric's cracked-tooth grin grew even wider, then he ripped a piece of loose skin from one of the unconscious dwarf's wounds without ceremony. "Excellent! I need to go place these in preservatives. Once that's done, I shall return with a . . . special healing potion." He scampered off with something akin to glee.

"That cleric, as you say, gives me the creeps."

Kiru couldn't help but agree. He might regret giving Odin's disciple a piece of his psionic genetics to sample in the future, but at this moment, it was a price he was glad to pay, if it would help his friend. While waiting impatiently, he noticed the symbol of Hlin on one of her shields still attached to her arm. Though he was legally one of her acolytes, he hadn't taken to utilizing it, aside from his divine headband. Time to change that.

Kiru closed his eyes and prayed. Recalling Brunhilda's instructions, he reached out to Hlin with his mind. With his emotions, he conveyed both his friend's situation and his desire to help her. He wished for her to improve and hoped that the goddess would intervene for her head acolyte. To his surprise, he got a response.

*"Fear not. Thy compatriot has mine affection. I will not let the acts of cowardice or even Odin's follower do her harm."*

Kiru opened his eyes and gasped. *There really* is *something to this prayer stuff!*

Just then, the cleric returned. He held a glowing glass vial of purple fizzing liquid. "I have returned with a special brew. This should help the dwarf recover expediently." He poured it directly into Brunhilda's mouth before either Kiru or Zhaden could say anything. "She may grow a new limb, though . . ."

The psion's eyes widened in fear.

*"The fuck?! Oooh, this is hilarious! Wait, no. Master, we can't let her get hurt any further!"* William screeched inside Kiru's mind. It surprised Kiru that the imp was so protective of the paladin for once. Despite that, he couldn't help but feel similar. The damn cleric was experimenting on his friend!

Brunhilda groaned loudly. Purple veins flared and spread all over her thick skin. Then, she suddenly sat up in the bed, her eyes open, sclera black as night. Her voice was deep—monstrous-like, even—and she roared in pain as the effects of the potion coursed through her body. Her body began to stretch as if she were being pulled by some machine. Bones grew and muscles expanded until she was almost as tall as Zhaden. Her pupils glowed an unnatural teal, and the purple veins began to glow as well.

The wounds on her body miraculously regenerated before the psion's eyes, healing as if time were running in reverse. While the magic of healing techniques treated wounds directly with their own power, the potion worked differently. Instead, it enhanced Brunhilda's self-regeneration to a monstrous level.

She looked like a monster. She roared like a monster! Kiru, Zhaden, and even the cleric all had looks of increasing concern. Kiru was honestly afraid Brunhilda would turn into a threat they would have to fight; his fear proved to unfounded, however, thanks to Hlin's timely intervention.

The goddess' symbol glowed on Brunhilda's shield. Immediately, her agony stopped. Her body shrank back to its original state until she a dwarf once more. Well, mostly dwarf.

Her hair was now the same purple that her veins had been. She was also now a head taller than even the tallest dwarf in Kiru's memory. Her arms were a tad too long, proportionately, as well. Aside from that, she seemed to be herself again. She was alive, unharmed, and now she was looking at them in bewilderment, but fully conscious.

"By Hlin's hard helmet, I think I have trollblood."

# CHAPTER THIRTY-TWO

# Called Out

It turned out the now-purple-haired dwarf did indeed have trollblood. Odin's cleric tested her blood and verified it was so. Trolls were tough, brutish creatures with long arms and a ridiculous ability to heal themselves, making them very difficult to fell in a fight. The paladin was not a troll. She was still a dwarf, but it essentially worked like a blood transfusion where *all* of her blood had been replaced. Normally, that wouldn't be possible, but Brunhilda asserted that Hlin's divine intervention must have affected how the potion worked inside her body to give her such a blessing.

After his moment of prayer, Kiru couldn't argue. It appeared that the goddess was able to influence the effects of the potion somehow, preventing it from turning Brunhilda into a massive, mindless monster but retaining some of its benefits. The cleric, meanwhile, was ecstatic, writing his findings on a notepad, and wanted to try some other potions on them. Needless to say, the trio hastily refused.

Kiru desperately wanted to give the cleric a piece of his mind for experimenting on her so dangerously as that. On sensing that the crazed man was multiple ranks higher than him, however, Kiru begrudgingly decided to hold his temper at bay, to William's chagrin. And Brunhilda even managed to take some solace in the fact that she and Hlin now had the same hair color.

After leaving the medical ward, the three of them went straight over to the guard station to see what progress was being made about the attacks, but when they got there, something seemed off. The guards' expressions seemed strangely calm, cold, and calculated. They escorted them to a room where the three waited for a few minutes before Corporal Tavish came in. He sat down at the plain wood table and gestured for them to sit on the opposite side.

"Well, it seems you lot had an . . . interesting night." He read over a few pages, which Kiru presumed were documents detailing last night's events. "Why don't you go over for me what happened, according to your best recollection."

Kiru did and, with his perfect memory, provided the information in exact detail. Zhaden and Brunhilda nodded and added their own personal takes of what they experienced in their own rooms. Brunhilda hadn't seen who attacked her, but she had heard a distinct, snorting laugh. Kiru knew it had to be Ambrose. The corporal wasn't as convinced.

"So, you're telling me that a few students attacked each of you in your rooms. Two of you were able to overcome them, but the lass here was caught off-guard."

"Exactly," Kiru said. He had held off on openly accusing Ambrose and Zane, but he was gearing up for it. The evidence was irrefutable.

"What proof do you have to substantiate your claim?" Tavish asked.

"Kiru's advisor was notified about the unconscious students in his room," Zhaden answered.

"And yours?" the corporal asked the drakonid.

The drakonid's mouth hung open. "I . . . realize that, in my haste to help my compatriots, I didn't notify mine."

"Surely, Joseph's testimony will be sufficient." Kiru jumped in.

"Ah, yes, your house advisor," Tavish said, flipping through the papers. "We spoke with him earlier tonight. He stated that he saw you two bolting out of the half-elf's room, after hours, and shouted something unintelligible to him. Concerned about what was going on, he checked your room, as the door was left open. There, he found the room destroyed with blood and hair scattered about. *No students*," he said pointedly.

Kiru furrowed his brow in confusion, and then he looked down and away, thinking, *No students? How can that be? They were right there when we left Joseph with them.*

William couldn't hear Kiru's thoughts, but he knew what his master was thinking. He put it all together for the psion. *"Master, you understand, right? The human betrayed us."*

The psion's heart sank. William was right. They were being set up. He looked up to the guard expectantly. "He must be mistaken. That, or our attackers fled before he came into the room." Kiru was tempted to have Zhaden bring out the trollstone cuffs, but from how this discussion with the guards was going, he thought that revealing the cuffs would more likely just end up with them in the dungeons.

The bearded corporal tsked and shook his head. "Right, here's what I think. I think the lass here was getting too confident in her skills and decided to sneak out and test herself against one of the sacred beasts outside the school grounds. We already have a record of that kind of reckless behavior before from you, and you wouldn't be the first to try so." Tavish continued before Brunhilda could retort, "To her surprise, she realized that a single Gold couldn't stand a chance against one of the powerful beasts. Pfft, as if that wasn't obvious," he said below his breath.

"You ran, but you didn't realize the beastie tracked you, using whatever method you used to sneak out to follow you in. You thought yourself home-free back on academy grounds, but it kept following you to discover where you live, and that's when it struck. The sacred beasts are a vengeful sort and have been known to stalk their prey over large distances, so it checks out that one would do so to a mere first-year student," the corporal, said then looked back to his papers.

"I'm not sure how, but it's clear that you must've let your teammates know that you planned on such a stupid endeavor. When things went bad, they ran to go save you," he said, his tone giving no doubt that his mind was already made up.

Brunhilda's cheeks blushed in indignation, her new trollblood already showing in the purpleish shade. "What a preposterous accusation, sir!" she replied. "I would never do such a thing. I'm a paladin!"

"Of a minor goddess," Tavish interrupted, knowingly. "And a rather tenacious one at that! Do you know how many times a young cultivator has gotten overconfident, or a minor cleric or paladin has tried some stupid stunt in order to glorify their deity? Too many times to count," he said, then gazed firmly at all three students.

"You should all consider yourselves lucky. We found the sacred beast on the grounds and subdued it before it could hurt anyone else. It was a juvenile raptorcat, and it was missing a claw—a claw that matched the one in your room. To your good fortune, no one has reported anyone breaking the rules and trespassing into the forest. If there had been any evidence to the contrary, I would have been forced to either expel you from the academy or lock you in the dungeon."

The three students shuddered. They'd heard stories about the dungeon under the school grounds. None of them were good. "Now, I appreciate you trying to cover for your teammate, but it was bloody stupid of you to even allow that! Since I can't prove that you did, in fact, let a dangerous sacred beast into campus grounds, and since no one other than yourselves were hurt . . . no charges will be laid on you."

All three of them sighed in relief.

"But neither will I accept your false testimony. Lying to an officer of the Royal Army is a punishable offense." Tavish closed his eyes and rubbed the hair on the back of his head. "You're young, though, and I respect you looking out for each other. Tell you what, why don't you just tell me the truth, and I will let you out of here with just a warning. From what I heard of what happened to you, lass, you've received punishment enough."

Kiru looked to Zhaden, then to Brunhilda. *"Tavish isn't going to accept the truth. I don't like it, but I think we should cater to the man and give him his already-presumed version of what happened. Agreed?"* Kiru asked his teammates via Telepathy.

They both nodded silently. None of them liked it, but it was the only way for them to get out without punishment. William, however, had the exact opposite opinion. He ranted inside Kiru's mind about how the psion should cut the guard apart with his blades instead of spitting out a false story. Kiru didn't follow the imp's advice.

Kiru then told Tavish the exact story he wanted to hear. He said that Brunhilda had been eager to defeat a sacred beast as a display Hlin's power, against her teammates' advice. When Zhaden and Kiru found out, they ran to help their friend, but it was too late. It pained Kiru to tell this false story, as it did the sincere paladin to have to accept the blame, as well. Still, it satisfied Tavish, and the three were let off with just a verbal warning and a promise that if this happened again, he would not be as "friendly" as he had been this time.

After they left the guard facility, Pandemonium convened in one of the library's silent rooms, Kiru letting William out to provide relief from the incessant, irritated rambling inside his mind.

"I can't believe that they'd think I would do something so rash! Hlin be the goddess of protection, not battlelust!" Brunhilda lamented.

"It is strange that the guard did not find evidence to match our testimony," Zhaden added. "Why do you think that Jospeh would have falsified his report?"

"It's obvious, fool," William answered for his master. "That goofy cultivator was bought off by that chunky punk who calls himself a cultivator, Ambrose. It's clear that, since he joined with Zane, they used their money to buy any extra help they could get."

"But what be the point of that? Why would they not just try to kill us?" Brunhilda asked.

"It's to send a message," Kiru said. "Pompous guys like Ambrose and Zane sometimes aren't satisfied with just eliminating their enemies; they wish to crush their spirits." He clenched his fist in anger. "Remember when I told you Ambrose broke my spine?"

They nodded.

Kiru let out a deep exhale from his nostrils before continuing, "That's the kind of people we're up against. They are trying to make us realize that they can hurt us without consequence. They want us to be afraid, the sadistic assholes." Kiru smiled. "You know, it's funny. Them doing this shows me *they're* the ones who are afraid. They're trying to keep their pride intact, putting down anyone who would dare topple the public perception that they're the best."

"Damn straight!" William asserted.

"What do you propose we do, then?" Zhaden asked.

A shit-eating grin grew on Kiru's face. "We play on their pride."

Later that day, Zane and the rest of his proclaimed Team Supreme were out in the main courtyard, regaling their small crowd of admirers, cronies, and suitors with embellished tales of their accomplishments, as was their usual routine.

"The only reason they did any damage to any of us in that sanctioned match was because of that weak drakonid throwing off our routine," Zane said.

"That's not how I remember it," Kiru loudly interrupted. "From what I recall, you overestimated us, and I broke your pretty little nose."

There was a flash of anger on the elf's face, but then, noticing the trio before his team, his smug expression came right back. "Please, that was a lucky hit, and you know it. Besides, you look like the one with a broken nose. It seems one of your betters finally had enough of you not knowing your place, Defunct," Zane replied.

Ambrose gave a nasal laugh at that.

In all the chaos of last night's events, Kiru hadn't addressed his own injury. That wasn't a big deal to him for now. Zhaden had already set his nose, so he just had the bruising left.

Zane then turned his attention to Brunhilda. "By the way, I'd heard that you tried to take on a sacred beast on your own and got the shit beat out of you, Paladin, but it looks like you just got beat by the ugly tree instead. I mean, what happened to your hair and face? Ugh!" The students laughed.

The dwarf blushed in embarrassment.

Kiru had enough. He put a hand on her shoulder and laughed at Zane and his team. He did so until all the other laughter fell silent. "Wow! Man, it's hard to grasp how anyone can stand to be around you asshats. You know what's really funny? How four Sword House students with all the resources and money they could ever want are acting like cowards? You literally have no excuses, yet you're running scared."

"Like a bunch of little bitches," William added from Kiru's shoulder.

"Just like a bunch of little bitches," Kiru agreed, chuckling.

"Careful now, mongrel, we don't want any more . . . accidents to happen to you," Ambrose threatened.

Zane elbowed the noble in the stomach. "Quiet!" he spat. The elf then turned back and glared at the psion. "Team Supreme is second to no one in the first-years, especially not some Fist House Defunct and his team of misfits. Even your top third-year student has *just* made it to tier-one Ruby. And I hear the only reason he got that high was because some anonymous benefactor gave him some rare book to help him ascend." He knowingly smiled at Kiru. "The pathetic fool couldn't even help himself; must've made some sort of deal."

That gave Kiru pause for a moment. The top Fist House student was Joseph! So, *that's* what he had been given to lie about the attack. Though Kiru didn't like Joseph's betrayal, he understood it. Many of the upperclassmen were at least at Ruby level, so being two ranks below had put him at a massive disadvantage. Having a guarantee of ascension would be hard to pass up in his situation.

Kiru decided to ignore the comments about Joseph and pressed on. "Then, how come you haven't requested another sanctioned match against us?"

Zane scoffed, rolling his eyes. "Pfft! Why waste our time? Your little squad can't even get a fourth person to join you, despite your claims of how good you are. Fighting you does us no good. Team Supreme is the best, and we only deal with the best—not some second-rate freaks." he said, his little sprite familiar chuckling at his cruel humor.

"Freaks?! I'll show you freaks!" William hissed, then lunged off Kiru's shoulder. The psion recalled the imp midair, bringing him back into his core, despite William's protests. He felt it more prudent to prevent his familiar from causing trouble. Fortunately, no one commented on William's behavior.

"Though we are more controlled than my familiar, our feelings are similar," Kiru said, keeping his voice neutral but deadly serious. "If you truly think you're better than us, prove it."

"Fine, Defunct. We can get my father to sanction a match for us today," Zane replied.

Kiru shook his head. "No, we'll prove it at the Warrior Games at the end of the second semester."

"Now who's scared, cur?" Ambrose barked out from behind Zane.

"I'm not taking your bit away from you, Ambrose, don't worry," Kiru snarked right back, referring to the noble's cowardly nature.

Ambrose's face turned red. He opened his mouth to retort when Zhaden spoke up.

"Surely defeating an opponent recovering from fresh injuries wouldn't give you the glory you seek," the drakonid said in his harsh, whispery voice.

"You're thinking that kicking your asses again would give us any glory at all!" Zane replied.

"Nevertheless," Kiru said. "We challenge you, here in front of many to see and bear witness that, at the time of the Warrior Games, with us being at one hundred percent, uninjured and *unharassed*, your team will be laid low by Pandemonium.

"If, for some reason, our team is beset by *accidents* or *injuries*, and you somehow win, your victory will be a tarnished one. Everyone will know that you only won because you were too inept to actually beat us fair and square. They will know that Team Supreme is just a bunch of posers who had to rely on outside help to win," Kiru added. He had planned to do this callout intentionally to ensure his and his friends' safety from whatever Zane and Ambrose could concoct to hamper Pandemonium's chances of success.

Finally, Zane's smug look cracked, replaced by an angry scowl even uglier than William's face, which was impressive in its own right. He stood up and stomped toward Kiru. "You peasant, low-class, no-potential, Fist House scum! How dare you accuse us of needing outside help!"

Both Kiru's teammates tensed, but with a telepathic message from him, they regained their composure.

The psion kept his smile. "On the contrary, Zane, I'm merely giving you the opportunity to publicly back your claim," he declared. "We swear on our souls right here that we will not interfere with each other team's growth or cause them injury, either directly or by association. Then, when the time comes for the Warrior Games, we'll see who's right. It's a simple agreement, anyway, as those are the rules of the academy. It's a no-lose agreement for you to prove your words true, Zane. Unless you're afraid?" Kiru asked, sticking out his hand.

The elf's nostrils flared, but then he looked around. Everyone in the court-yard was staring at them—dozens of students, mostly humans, from every house and every year all focused intently on this conversation. He was caught. If he backed out now, he'd look weak and afraid. He quickly came to his senses and snarled at Kiru. "I agree to your terms, and I swear by them," Zane said and grabbed Kiru's gaunt hand. Despite the lack of musculature on the appendage, he gave a grunt of surprise at the half-elf's surprisingly strong grip.

The rest of Team Supreme echoed their leader's words, solidifying the oath.

"As do I," Kiru said.

Zhaden and Brunhilda repeated Kiru's words, making the oath binding between all the members of the two teams.

A weight settled inside them, the feeling of their oaths taking hold. Kiru's smile grew even wider as he let go, and they left Zane and his minions. Now that any harassment had been dealt with, they needed only one more thing: proper training.

# CHAPTER THIRTY-THREE

# Ballroom Blitz

Niajar was the one who'd recommended that Kiru see Giiyam for training, so Kiru thought the librarian would be the best one to ask about the inconveniently absent groundskeeper's whereabouts. The final exams for the semester were complete, and it was the second day of the allotted break time before the new semester would start in a couple of weeks. The eccentric elf seemed to have gathered that Kiru—now that he had more free time—would indeed come to him for aid, because when they got to the door of his office, there was a note hanging off of it:

*Kiru, you're a bright boy, and your persistence is admirable, but to some it may seem . . . infuriating. Though I prefer a fine glass of wine, many others have ale as their drink of choice, those of orcish ancestry particularly so. They prefer their cups to be rather sturdy. They have some strong jaws, after all! See you next semester!*

*Your illustrious and beloved sponsor,*

*Niajar*

Kiru was pretty confused. Was Niajar saying he was annoying and it drove people to drink? Apparently, he led Giiyam to go drink some ale? *How did that help him?* The psion showed his teammates the note.

Zhaden couldn't make out any pertinent information, but fortunately, Brunhilda did. "I forgot ye two haven't left the academy grounds since ye got here." she said, rubbing her forehead. "There be a bunch of taverns out in Waketown. I spend a lot of my time talking to the drunkards there. Ye'd be surprised how willing they be to share secrets once ye buy 'em an ale! Anyway, there be a dive bar hidden in a corner of Waketown called the Strongjaw. Clearly, the groundskeeper has been spending his time there."

Both the psion and rogue made an "Oh!" face in understanding. The trio made their way across the forest and massive bridge toward Waketown. Guided by the dwarf, they passed through some rather seedy alleys to eventually arrive at a large tavern built inside the rocky cliffside. The Strongjaw was completely made of stone, carved clearly from the cliff it was set into. The entrance was rather small and shabby-looking, but once the trio entered, they realized the interior was anything but.

The main floor of the tavern was large, with an impressive bar, many tables, and even an expansive dancing floor with a stage where a bard could play music. Since it was early afternoon, the tavern was mostly empty. There were still enough patrons present to keep the staff from suffering too much boredom, though. With his mother having worked as a barmaid all his life, Kiru felt very comfortable in the tavern. He knew exactly what to do.

He went up to the bartender, tossed him a silver coin, and asked him where a rather quiet half-orc liked to spend his time. Without a moment's hesitation, the barkeep took the coin and nodded to a dark corner of the bar.

Kiru did his best to act subtly, but he seemed to be drawing attention with his bright red jacket, nevertheless. When he turned, he saw the groundskeeper looking directly at him, a blank expression on the half-orc's stoic face. Trying to exude confidence, Kiru gave a friendly nod of his head.

The half-orc just raised his pointer finger and gestured for him over.

Kiru raised a finger in response, conveying that he'd be over in just a moment. He looked back to the barkeep who was all-too-happy to take his next silver coin. Kiru smiled, as his frugal nature was helping him at the moment. The coin he'd just given up was from the collection that William had stolen from the merchant back in Fox Hollow. It helped that the academy required no direct payment for the various supplies and services provided there such as meals. "Say, that half-orc over there, what does he like to drink?" the psion asked the barkeep in a hushed tone.

The mustached bartender gave a wide smile, revealing a glistening gold-capped tooth. "Oh, that old lad fancies a good flagon of Soulcrusher. Terribly strong stuff. I only keep it in stock 'cause he's a long-time customer. If you're looking to talk with him, a pint of the stuff will go a long way."

Kiru smiled. "We'll take four, then." The bartender poured four pints of some dark, foamy ale with a strong, bitter aroma. After Kiru paid him, the trio, with their ales in tow, headed over to the half-orc's table.

"Good afternoon, Giiyam, fancy seeing you here. Soulcrusher?" Kiru asked, sliding over a pint.

Only the groundskeeper's eyebrow moved as he looked down at the pint offered before him. He took the cup from the psion, and his face became neutral once more. "Thank you for the round. I admit, I'm impressed by your taste in beverage. However, I must ask, why have you come here?" Only the bulging veins of his hand squeezing tightly on the mug betrayed his anger.

Kiru gulped. The half-orc was sitting with a neutral face and tone of voice, but he felt as if he were just inches from a hungry lion! Despite that, Kiru was fairly certain that Giiyam wouldn't kill them. "Th-thank you for speaking with us, respected elder," he said, bowing his head to the gray-haired groundskeeper.

"Thank ye, sir," Brunhilda added, copying Kiru's motions.

Zhaden didn't say anything, but he also bowed in respect, as his allies did.

William seemed to be intimidated by the groundskeeper as well, because he was notably silent in Kiru's head.

The psion then took a deep breath to muster up his courage before speaking again. "I believe you know why we've come here," he blurted out before he could stop himself. "My team needs you to train us . . . Please!" he asked, bowing his head once more.

Giiyam let out a deep sigh as he stared Kiru down. After a few long moment, the psion looked up to meet his eyes.

"No," Giiyam said simply as soon as their eyes locked. "The academy's training should be more than adequate. Besides, I am a groundskeeper, nothing more."

"But you're also a past champion, and you're . . . like me," Kiru said in a low tone.

The half-orc's eyebrow raised up once more. "How do you know this?"

Kiru shrugged. "Library internship. I get to be privy to some more . . . rare information." he answered.

"Please, sir," Brunhilda added. "The fact that ye both be Defuncts cannot be mere coincidence. This must be divine intervention."

"I admit that the odds are rare, Paladin, but I will not train you. Any of you." Giiyam said sternly.

"But why?" Kiru asked.

"For starters, I'm forbidden from training anyone in the art of cultivation on academy grounds. I will not tell you why. It's just so."

The trio cocked their heads. They wondered why Giiyam would even bring that up. He was a Defunct. No one would seek out his knowledge about cultivation, especially when they had an entire academy of teachers to choose from.

Giiyam didn't acknowledge their unasked questions and pressed on with conviction, "Secondly, there's no point. If I just train you and you win, what will that grant you? Respect?" he asked, looking at Kiru. "Status?" He turned to Zhaden. "Glory?" That time, he was looking at the dwarf.

All three of the students broke eye contact with the half-orc. Though he wasn't completely accurate, he was close enough. Brunhilda wanted to glorify her goddess. Zhaden wanted to be elevated to elite warrior status amongst his people.

Kiru . . . Well, Kiru would be lying if he didn't admit that, aside from acquiring his father's item, he was also fighting to be respected.

His time in the academy so far had shown him that too many people clung onto preconceived notions of who was valuable. He was classified as a Defunct, so many deemed him worthless. Though Kiru hadn't seen much of the kingdom, he assumed the mindset was much the same for those of low cultivation rank and skill. He not only wanted to help protect the people of the world, he wanted to help their minds grow. Winning as a labeled Defunct would be a great start.

Giiyam continued, his contempt unrestrained. "Those are all selfish goals. Cultivators are supposed to make the world a better place, not just for themselves, but for others. To protect and uplift the weak, to raise each other up, to help each other manifest their destinies. You clearly have not looked past your own personal ambitions, so you are not worthy of being trained. Now, leave me." He dismissed them and began drinking his ale, no longer looking at any of them.

Kiru wanted to protest, to say that he was indeed fighting to do just that— to save all the world, to help people grow past their biases, as well as to earn respect for his skill in combat—but he couldn't. He'd already taken a chance telling both of his teammates. His mother had warned him that he couldn't just go blabbering to everyone about his ability to cultivate mental mana, and there was clearly some odd reason that Giiyam couldn't teach them on the academy grounds. *Maybe he'd made some sort of oath?* That made Kiru even more wary to tell the elder groundskeeper, despite his anger at being rejected.

He ground his teeth together but forced himself to remain respectful. "Thank you for your time, respected elder," he said with a slight bow, then left, his teammates doing the same.

"That man doesn't sugarcoat nothin'!" Brunhilda said as they were walking toward the door. Most of the other taverngoers were gone now, save for a table of rowdy dock workers, based on their look and strong fishy smell.

"It seems to be in line with his serious countenance," Zhaden replied. "What do you propose we do next, Kiru?"

Kiru didn't hear the words, though. He was too lost in his own thoughts. He even ignored William's angry muttering inside his mind. He was just dwelling on what Giiyam had said. *Was* he being selfish? Had he lost sight of his goal? Had Kiru gotten so focused on just winning the tournament that he hadn't put enough thought towards how his strength could help others? His musings were stopped by a flash of motion in the corner of his vision.

He raised his head to see a group of five men laughing loudly and making the barmaid very uncomfortable. She was a human—blonde, and looked to be in her early twenties. She gave an uncomfortable laugh and took a few steps back. Then, one of the men grabbed her by the wrist, tugging her back to him.

"Why're you in such a hurry, love? Come on, just a little kiss?" the drunkard asked, making a kissy face and forcefully pulling her toward him. The man's compatriots laughed again at that.

"My good fellows, I'm so glad you're enjoying yourselves all in good fun, but I do need to have my barmaid back," the skinny barkeep said as he came up behind the table, nervously wringing his hands.

"Ah, piss off, Marty!" Another one of the drunks, a black-haired dwarf backhanded the man, forcing the bartender square on his back. The group laughed maliciously again.

"No! Marty!" the maid cried out, managing to slip free of the laughing man's grip and running over to the assaulted bartender. She knelt over and cradled the man's face, his left eyelid quickly darkening into a bruise.

"Don't worry, love." The drunk man stood up out of his chair with a crooked grin on his face. He was bald, covered in tattoos, and had some large muscles, despite a notable layer of fat on top. "Why don't you spend some time with a real man?" he asked, reaching a hand to her neck, but then, he was suddenly stopped by a hand tightly gripping his arm. "What the?" he asked in shock.

Kiru hadn't thought about going over to intervene. The academy had a policy against fighting outside of training matches on their grounds. That didn't stop Kiru, though. That was because he moved on instinct. These bar workers needed help, and some primal part of his brain needed to protect them. Using Telekinesis, he forced more mana into his palm as he squeezed down onto the man's forearm.

"Grah!" the tattooed man growled. "Beat it, kid!" He swung a fist at the psion's head with his free hand. Kiru didn't move. He didn't need to. A loud, metallic *clang* rang out as the man's fist connected with one of Brunhilda's shields. The man cried out in pain as his hand recoiled, and that's when Zhaden struck. The rogue stabbed one of his daggers straight into the man's foot, pinning him to the ground.

"By the will of Hlin, begone, villain!" Brunhilda pronounced with righteous fervor, then used her disproportionately long arms to hit the tattooed man square in the jaw with a shield. Kiru knew from his time fighting with Brunhilda that the kind-hearted paladin meant to hit him in the chest, but she was still getting used to her new body. So, she her coordination wasn't perfect yet. A few teeth went flying, and Kiru let go of his arm. The dagger in his foot kept the man's body pinned to the ground, causing him to dislocate his leg in his struggles and forcing him to land against the stone floor on his back. The man groaned, and Zhaden ripped the dagger out of his foot.

The three students braced themselves in between the men and the Strongjaw staff. The fight was over in mere seconds, so the seated men blinked in astonishment before they could fully process what was happening. Quickly, they all stood up and brandished their weapons, an assortment of cutlasses and daggers, with one wielding a rusty trident. "You kids just made a big mistake. You may have your fancy academy, but we know how to really fight," a black-haired dwarf threatened, smiling maliciously.

Kiru *really* didn't like bullies. Add his familial affection toward tavern workers, and he was ready to throw down. He would protect the weak and help those in need. If that meant beating the snot out of these brutes, Kiru was all too happy to do it.

Faster than anyone was expecting, the psion flew forward. In one quick motion, he unsheathed one of his swords, but instead of cutting his opponent, he slammed the pommel of his weapon square in the dwarf's temple. The dwarf's eyes rolled in the back of his head as he slumped unconscious from the single blow.

*"Haha! Yes! Show these fools their folly, Master!"* William cheered inside Kiru's mind. This time, the psion didn't argue.

*"Stay out of this. They're mine,"* he telepathically sent to his friends, his mental voice cool and calculated. There were four remaining, all of which were at Gold rank. Two had daggers, one wielded a cutlass like the unconscious dwarf, and the other pulled out a trident that had been laying on his lap. All of them were human, but they were also all larger and more muscular than the psion. Despite their size and number advantages, they looked at him with a mixture of fear and anger.

Anger won out as the first of them lunged at Kiru with a dagger aimed at his gut. He side-stepped the attack and drew out his second blade in one quick motion, slicing the man's thumb right off of his hand. Following up, Kiru kicked the man square in the groin, and the attacker crashed to his knees, thoroughly incapacitated.

The trident wielder stabbed at Kiru, yelling incoherently. On instinct, the psion responded with one of the forms his mother taught him. Instead of blocking the strike, he gently guided the trident away from him, using his swords. That allowed him to close the distance with his attacker. The drunk man, reeking of fish, went pale as Kiru was on him before he could react. With a flick of his wrist, Kiru sliced the tip of his sword across the man's left eye. A gout of blood and ocular fluid gushed out.

The man dropped his weapon and clutched his eye, wailing in pain. Kiru then spun and kicked the man in the side of his leg. There was the loud crunch of bone as his kneecap shattered from the impact. Kiru turned back to see the last two attacking him at the same time. Using a technique from Giiyam's Warrior Games bout, the half-elf caught the cutlass with his blades in a cross guard, then used it to block the dagger from the other man. Then he pivoted to trip the dagger wielder, and WHAM! The cutlass wielder backhanded Kiru across the face. Kiru spun from the impact.

"We may not have any fancy schooling or techniques, boy, but we're still Gold-rank cultivators, same as you" The cutlass user gave a wicked grin. "And we know just how to deal with shits like you."

Kiru's eyes went wide as the man brought down his blade, only for it to be intercepted by his purple-haired friend stepping in front of him. There was a loud clang of metal on metal as the sword struck her shield. "Too bad for ye yer not only fighting him! We're a team!" she growled and forced his cutlass back. The dagger wielder flung his blade at the paladin, but Zhaden's dexterous hand caught it before it could reach its mark.

The drakonid adjusted the weapon in his grip and threw it back at the assailant, embedding the small blade in his shoulder.

"Why you!" the cutlass user shouted and swung his blade at the rogue. Zhaden ducked low under the blow and drew one of his own daggers. In a swift motion, Zhaden stabbed into the man's ankle and sliced his Achilles. No longer able to stabilize on the limb, he staggered. Brunhilda used that to her advantage, bashing him in the face with her shield, knocking him straight on his ass.

Kiru forced himself up, now behind his two friends. All the men were incapacitated and moaning on the ground. For his part, Kiru's mouth was bleeding slightly. "Leave, all of you, now. Never come back, and be grateful that you remain mostly intact." The drunks moaned and nodded in agreement, then staggered, limped, or crawled out like terrified insects. The guy missing his amputated fingers grabbed them on his way out. If he got to a healer quickly enough, he might be able to get them repaired.

Some could say that amputating limbs, removing an eye, and slicing a tendon were an extreme way of kicking someone out. They'd be right. Kiru did not feel even one scrap of remorse, though. The drunks had been clearly willing to kill, so they got off lucky with just some body parts missing and damaged. For as cruel as they were, sometimes only a cruel response got the message across. They would not come back; they'd learned their lesson.

Once they scurried out of the tavern, Kiru let go of his tough visage. "Thank you," he said to his friends.

They both turned to face the psion. Neither of them looked pleased. "My words were for ye, too, Mister Leader," Brunhilda said. "We're a team. Ye don't get to go off and play hero on yer own. When ye be part of a team, we go through things *together*," she emphasized.

"I concur with the paladin's assessment," Zhaden said. "I agreed to join as equal part of the group, not a lesser member, like before. I know sometimes one may have to undergo personal trials, but a tavern brawl is not one of them."

Kiru opened his mouth to protest, then promptly closed it. He sighed. "You're right. I'm sorry. Thank you for dealing with my . . . headstrong nature." Kiru wasn't completely sure, but he thought a bit of his anger may have been influenced from his fire mana core, even with it being broken. "I just—I just got so angry and caught up in keeping you two safe as well, I didn't want to risk you getting hurt."

"Headstrong is one way to put it . . ." Zhaden smirked as much as his reptilian face could allow. All three of them gave slight chuckles at that jest. "You need not worry, Kiru. It's honorable that you wished to keep us from any harm, but we can handle ourselves in situations outside the academy."

Kiru nodded in agreement. The Pandemonium trio then turned back to the barmaid and bartender, who were staring at them in awe.

"Thank you all!" the mustached man said, gratefully. "As far as I'm concerned, you're welcome to as much Soulcrusher as you'd like, on the house!"

That was when Kiru realized that he hadn't even had a sip of the ale he'd ordered. Giiyam, who apparently had been watching their fight with interest, was up and walking toward them. "You know, it is forbidden to have altercations outside of academy grounds?"

"Why, there's no need for that, old Giiyam," Marty said. "We didn't see anything, did we, Mary?"

The blonde barmaid—Mary, apparently—nodded emphatically in agreement.

The stoic man didn't turn to face them. While looking at Pandemonium, he just raised a hand up to them, and both of the tavern workers went quiet. He turned his focus directly upon Kiru. "It appears you took my earlier advice to heart, Kiru. You've surrounded yourself with good people. I approve. I have two questions. The first is for you," he said, nodding to the psion. "Why did you interfere, when you know the illegalities of your actions?"

Kiru was tempted to lie and say he had forgotten, but he was tired of faking it. Either Giiyam could handle the honest truth or he couldn't. "Those people needed help," he said simply. "And those guys didn't look like they were going to stop. Somebody needed to do something. So, I did."

The half-orc's face remained neutral, showing no evidence as to whether he approved or not. "And for your team, why did you insist that you and they not kill those men, Kiru? Certainly, you realize they would not have treated you he same in return?"

"*Yeah! Why didn't you kill those whiny bitches?*" William asked Kiru inside his mind.

Kiru gave a smile and answered. "I'm not opposed to killing when needed, but they were just drunk assholes. Despite them being clearly dangerous, killing them was unnecessary. If we ended people's lives just because we didn't agree with them, we would've been no better than the countless bullies and cruel-hearted nobles out there. After all, you told us that cultivators are meant to make the world a better place. I think teaching those jerks a lesson helps make it at least a little bit better."

Giiyam gave a rare smile and an even rarer chuckle. "Well said, Student. I concur with that assessment. I wish to recant my previous statement. Your team, Pandemonium—I find you worthy of my training."

# Tag Team

Niajar was enjoying a particularly interesting novel. When he had not been about the kingdom searching for rare texts, he had been searching the writings inside his own library in a frantic bid to find ways to help his Defunct pupil soar above his counterparts. It was exhausting and to the librarian's frustration, it had not bore much fruit. He was, however, glad that he had sense to set the boy to transcribing; he was astoundingly fast. While that would eventually make Kiru a capable librarian, it did not, however, help in terms of combat.

Still, that didn't mean Kiru was without *any* progress in the matter. Niajar was particularly happy to hear how the teen had acquired two competent teammates as well as breaking his cocky nephew's nose. That was no mean feat, especially given Kiru was a Defunct. Niajar had been going almost nonstop to help his pupil and had taken the week to care for his mental health. Even now, the librarian was sitting on a comfy chair with a cup of Earl Grey tea beside him as he read a tale about a company of dwarves on a quest to best a dragon hidden inside a solitary mountain.

"I can see why this is considered a classic," he mused. His relaxation time was cut short, however, when a loud knocking came from his condominium door. He set down the novel down on a stack of books full of stories and lore from Alfheim that he had previously gone through. He tied his floral gi so that he would be presentable, then went over to the door. Looking through the peephole, he smiled. His gentle pushing seemed to have borne fruit.

"Why, Master Giiyam, what an unexpected surprise! What can I do for you?" he asked as he opened the door.

The half-orc was nonplussed. "It seems that you shared more with your pupil than just your tenacity in bothering me. I hope that information about my time as a student here was not shared with any others?"

Niajar gave a toothy grin. He had once pestered the half-orc so much about adding ornamental flowers to the library that Giiyam had actually yelled at him, threatening to let Odin's cleric sneak into his library. The cleric and Niajar had a fairly antagonistic relationship, second in animosity only to the elf's brother. The greedy cleric had been caught on more than one occasion trying to "borrow" rare information that Niajar had painstakingly collected, leading to him finally banning him from his sacred facility. Niajar would have petitioned to have the cleric fired had the one-eyed man not so obviously been one of his brother's most loyal lapdogs.

"I currently have not, and if my student's team wins, no one else will need to," he answered, patting Giiyam on the shoulder. "Come, come in. There's much to discuss. Would you care for some tea?"

The half-orc grunted and followed Niajar in. The quiet man took the tea and sipped. "What do you want?" he asked, getting straight to the point.

"It is as I said before. I want my Defunct pupil to win the Warrior Games for the first-years. Seeing as you're the only Defunct to have done it, I figured you were the ideal candidate for the job."

Giiyam took another gulp of the tea. Apparently, he liked Earl Grey. "Why?" the half-orc asked.

"Well, you must know that we sponsors get a large profit if our student wins—much more than just a mere recruiter. Yes, we have to take time away from our own personal growth for that of our recruits, but I've found it to be a quite profitable endeavor."

"You like to gamble, but I can see right through that farce. You don't really care about profit. You never have. All you do is obsess over your books and your library."

Niajar chuckled. "Indeed. You could say I'm an open book." He winked.

Giiyam continued to stare blankly.

"You're no fun. Fine, yes, there is a more personal stake, but it doesn't concern you. All you need to do is help him and his team win. You can do that, yes?"

"I can, but why have you not helped?"

Niajar's grin cracked a little at that question. "I have, in my own way. I found *you*, didn't I?" When Giiyam didn't say anything in reply, Niajar begrudgingly continued. "I am . . . not much of a fighter. In truth, I am better at surviving than anything else. My path is called Nature's Gift, and it is focused on healing. While that makes me an effective healer, it also makes me hardly qualified to serve in the capacity of a combat trainer." His smile returned. "I can still hold my own, mind you." He winked again.

Giiyam didn't acknowledge it, rather just continuing to take in the elf's words. "Understood. I will help the boy and his team. I find them to be worthy cultivators, and that is a rare thing. However, I will only do so if you agree to destroy all evidence of my participation in the tournament, and if you will actively help me in their training. As a Defunct, I am a poor instructor in the art of cultivation."

Niajar stroked his chin in contemplation. "Hm, I suppose I could lend my knowledge to aid my pupil's allies. Though, I can't officially give any of them direct aid, aside from Kiru. I normally don't care about the minutiae of academy rules, but currently, one of my wagers is reliant upon the boy's obedience."

One of the half-orc's eyebrows raised. "And blackmailing a fellow staff member is allowed?"

"Oh, come now, Giiyam. We both know there would be no other way you would accept. Do you know how hard it was to even procure the information about your enrollments?"

"Not hard enough," he muttered, taking another sip of tea.

"Well, it looks like we've come to an accord, then. Is there anything else we'll need for our training venture?"

Giiyam sighed after finishing his tea, his emotionless face making the gesture look very fake. "Just one thing."

# CHAPTER THIRTY-FOUR

# Private Tutor

After their tavern brawl, the members of Pandemonium were offered free drinks at the bar. Giiyam had left but not before telling the group to meet him at the library entrance tomorrow night. Apparently, he was confident that Niajar would provide him and the team with some sort of training space? The party wasn't sure, but they didn't protest. In the meantime, they decided not to refuse the free booze. Kiru hadn't left the island for half a year, so he thought a little revelry was earned. With their mission a success and the brutes gone, they actually had time to enjoy a pint of Soulcrusher, too! It was too bitter for Kiru's taste, but Brunhilda downed them like a champ.

The alcohol also helped ease some of the paladin's anxiety, and she spoke more comfortably with others around than she ever did previously. Of course, Hlin came up, but unlike usual, her words weren't in the form of a pushy sermon, rather just a tale of her strong, honest belief. It may have been the alcohol or perhaps even just the more relaxed manner with which she spoke, but her words seemed to actually move both Mary and Marty.

Grateful for the party's service and admitting that they and the Strongjaw could use some more protection, both of the humans decided to become official followers of the goddess. Kiru had never seen Brunhilda so giddy before. Moving unbelievably fast for a dwarf in plate mail, she zoomed across the tavern to a section of stone wall. Before the humans could stop her, she had pulled out some tools from her satchel and began carving into the wall at a prodigious rate. Dwarves were natural diggers, and it showed.

In minutes, she had carved out a small depression. She only stumbled once as she accidentally took a larger-than-intended chunk of stone with her newly elongated arms. Still, the carved-out area was uniform . . . mostly. Above that was now the symbol of Hlin. The paladin quickly pulled out a statue of pure marble, lit a few candles, and uttered a small prayer over a blank book she set before the statue.

The carved symbol in the stone flashed once, then the flames of all the candles grew in intensity. The book suddenly glowed with holy light. After a couple of seconds, the candles settled, and the book stopped glowing, revealing that the pages were now full of text. Just like that, the paladin had set up her first shrine in the Kingdom of Blades. Marty and Mary stared in a mix of awe and shock.

They looked like they wanted to say something like, "A tavern isn't the best place for religion," or "Why didn't you ask permission to do that?" but a few extra silver pieces from Kiru, and a quick reminder that they did, in fact, say the Strongjaw could use some protection, stopped them from saying anything.

Kiru smiled as he looked over at his ecstatic friend. He thought he had been happy about getting Giiyam to train them, but it didn't compare to the joy now etched on the dwarf's features.

"Brunhilda, are you not worried that your goddess' statue will be stolen? That much pure marble will certainly be tempting to many," Zhaden brought up.

She shook her head and smiled. "Nay, Zhaden. Ye can't remove a statue in a shrine sanctified by a Vasir. The holy power of the gods binds it to the place it's in. The statue can only be removed if the entire shrine is destroyed or if the building it's in collapses."

"So, if they're so sturdy and durable, why not make them everywhere, and why not just ask for forgiveness rather than permission?" Kiru queried.

Brunhilda downed an entire mug of ale in two large gulps and beamed. "I'm glad ye asked, Acolyte. It's good to see yer interest in aiding our goddess further." She patted him hard on the back. After she imbibed yet another large mug, she answered. "Ye see, shrinecraft be a very precise thing. I don't know about other pantheons such as the Beast Gods, but the Vasir be very strong and very particular.

"Unless ye seize a place in battle, they won't sanctify the shrine you erect. The exception be that you can if ye've got permission to put one there by the owner. So sneaking a shrine in won't work. The Vasir also have precise specifications for their shrines."

Though Kiru would often nod along and not pay full attention to Brunhilda's religious ramblings, he actually found this information rather interesting. Maybe it was the alcohol, or maybe it was that it had to do with a tradeskill? Either way, he was fully focused on what the dwarf was saying.

She raised up a finger to count. "First, they need a statue of their likeness made of smooth stone such as marble, jade, or granite. Next, they require candles made from Valhallan beeswax. It's not easy to procure, but I have a cousin back in Stonereach who can get me some. After that, all ye need is a blank tome, and to carve out yer deity's holy symbol. Once that's all done, and ye pray to yer patron, the god will sanctify the shrine with their holy mana, bestowing blessings upon all within the building, especially their followers, thereby bringing themselves glory."

"That . . . sounds difficult to procure," Zhaden said.

Brunhilda nodded emphatically, a slight purple tint to her cheeks from the ale she'd been knocking back. "Oh, yeah! Ye can't just go 'round making a shrine all willy nilly. The only reasons I can are 'cause I'm from Stonereach, and my beekeeper cousin. Stonereach has an abundance of high-quality stone and is one of only a few places where Valhallan bees live. Paper is rare there, so that's the most expensive for us, but that issue's all . . ." She paused to gulp down another ale. "Taken care of." She finished, accidentally letting out a belch. The purple shade of her cheeks intensified with embarrassment.

"What blessings will Hlin bring to our place, High Paladin?" Marty asked excitedly, not minding the burp in the slightest.

"Ye give me another mug, Acolyte, and I'll tell ye," Brunhilda replied, her speech slurring a little bit more.

The bartender did just that and handed her another full mug.

Brunhilda gulped it down, then threw the mug at Marty without ceremony. He raised his arm up to protect his head, and the wooden mug shattered against his forearm, spraying foamy ale residue all over him.

At that, there was a stunned silence from the crowd as the bartender's face turned red. "W-What was that for?!" he sputtered in anger.

She pointed a finger at the man's arm. "Hlin's the goddess of protection. Despite yer thin body, ye were able to get hit by a throw from a Gold-rank culti-vator. That's me. Hehe!" She giggled before continuing. "And ye don't even have a scratch."

Marty looked at his wet but uninjured arm, then back to Brunhilda a couple of times before laughing loudly. The others joined in response. Both Marty and Mary were thrilled that their bodies were now more durable. It could help them with difficult customers. Well, more difficult than a typical, respectful bar-goer but less than the group that Pandemonium had to deal with.

After the festivities, they returned to the academy and retired for the night. Despite the two dozen ales that Brunhilda drunk, she was, impressively, still in control of her faculties. Sure, she slurred and was a little giggly, but she only had a good buzz. Kiru was grateful. He hadn't wanted to have to carry the metal-clad dwarf all the way back to her rooms. Dwarves weren't known for being light-weights, and though he wasn't going to say anything directly, the muscle-bound, armored paladin *definitely* fit that description.

The next night, after taking some time to rest and cultivate back in his room, Kiru met up with his friends, and they all headed to the library as Giiyam had instructed. That the groundskeeper had suggested that particular location had sur-prised Kiru, but he went along with it. But what surprised him even more was that it was Niajar, not the groundskeeper, who was standing outside, expectantly waiting for the trio to arrive.

"Ah, why, if it isn't my beloved pupil and the rest of his team! I see you took my wise advice to heart and found a skilled mentor."

"Niajar." Kiru nodded. "What are you doing here?"

"Me? Why, this is my facility. Why shouldn't I be here?"

Kiru squinted at the librarian.

"Follow me," he said, not elaborating any further. Suspicious, but still trusting his benefactor, Kiru followed with his teammates close behind. They walked dutifully behind the elf through the winding twists and turns of the library's halls. Kiru quickly realized that the bookshelves were arranged differently than their usual pattern. Sure, they would move, but he had never seen them in this particular arrangement before. After getting so used to how things were inside the magical building, it disturbed Kiru to see them out of place.

Eventually, they made it to the southeast corner of the library, where they faced a blank wall. The librarian then felt along the stone until his fingers reached a slight depression, which he pressed. There was a click, and the stone began to sink inward. More stones in the wall followed, silently, eventually revealing a secret hallway.

Niajar gave a confident smirk, then disappeared into it. The party was a bit nervous, not knowing where the librarian was leading them. Their curiosity outweighed their trepidation, however, and the trio followed the librarian inside. After they crossed the threshold, the stones quickly re-formed into the wall behind them. The party turned back reactively, all of them submerged in complete darkness. That is until a torch was lit.

They turned to see Niajar ahead of them. "Come now, we haven't got all day."

"It's night," Kiru replied.

"Don't be coy. You know what I mean!" The librarian continued walking, Pandemonium close behind. The stone path quickly led to a downward spiraling staircase. The air was damp and grew chillier the farther they descended. Moss and a few fungi were growing amid the cracks in the stone, too. Eventually, their nostrils picked up a stale and slightly foul odor.

Kiru suspected he knew where they were going. His suspicions were confirmed when his ears picked up on the sound of flowing water as the party hit the bottom. Sure enough, there was a rusty metal door labeled "Sewage System." Either Niajar didn't notice the students' disgusted faces, or he just plain ignored them as he grinned and opened the door. They recoiled in response to both the light from the room as well as being hit by a concentrated wave of the fetid sewage, no longer held at bay by the door.

After recovering their wits and wiping the tears from their eyes, all three of them noticed that Niajar had vanished. The door was still open, however. So, groaning at the librarian's antics, they went through, finding themselves in a large stone chamber, well-illuminated by ensconced glowing crystals and lichens stretching across the ceiling. The artificial light was so good, it practically rivaled that of the sun at midday!

It was utterly massive, at least a mile in all directions, to Kiru's eyes. There was even a streaming river which flowed out of a hole in one wall and into another on the other side of the chamber. The water was somehow covered with a film of green moss with discarded trash and other refuse intermittently popping out. Yeah, it was a river of sewage.

Along the river's perimeter was a slim stone walkway, as well as a bridge from the doorway the team had come out of, leading to a conspicuously large stone island in the middle of the flowing sewage. There stood both Niajar and Giiyam, waiting on the trio expectantly.

All three of them scanned the suspicious area, then glowered at the staff members ahead of them. Was their primary intention to train their immune systems, because Kiru felt like they would all contract a respiratory disease from breathing in this foul air. Still, he kept quiet. Someone was willing to train them in using their techniques in combat, which was more than any of their fellow classmates or teachers were willing to do.

"Niajar, may I ask where exactly you brought us?"

"Why, the sewer, of course."

"Now who's being coy?" Kiru replied.

"Well said," the elf conceded. He opened his mouth to answer, but Giiyam beat him to the punch.

"This is a decommissioned section of the academy's sewage system. I know not why it was abandoned."

"Some report of structural instability or some other nonsense," Niajar couldn't help but add as he popped his head up and put a hand on the groundskeeper's shoulder. "I suspect some ruins may be nearby, from the remains of the building the library was built on. I assure you three, it's completely safe. Giiyam and I discovered this place by accident after I kept getting reports of a nasty odor in my library. We've done a thorough search and have found no evidence that this place is in any danger of collapsing on us. We've even been able to reconnect it with the main sewage system to help drain out some of the more stagnant debris. Haven't we, Giiyam?"

Giiyam turned his head, looked down at the hand on his shoulder, then stared intensely at the librarian.

Niajar chuckled nervously and apologized as he removed his hand.

Giiyam grunted before turning back and addressing the students again. "It is as he said. The place is isolated, and only Niajar and I have knowledge of it. As I told you before, I'm expressly forbidden from teaching within academy grounds. You do not need to know why," he added, cutting off the question that had already built up in Kiru's mind. "I also have no interest in teaching where I can be publicly observed. Here, though, is the perfect place in which to train you. We are not technically in academy grounds, and we are safe from prying eyes."

"Now," he said, unsheathing both his swords. "Show me what you can do."

"Wait, do you mean you want us to go all-out? Here?" Kiru asked. He still knew he couldn't reveal his psionic nature, but that didn't mean he couldn't fight with greater zeal nor that his friends couldn't use their techniques.

His question was immediately answered by a prompt fist to his gut. The air swiftly left his lungs as he went flying across the small stone island. Kiru's teammates quickly ran to his side, standing at the ready to protect the psion. The unexpected hit almost made Kiru lose control of his technique, but he eventually forced himself up, coughing and wiping the drool from his face.

He looked back at the half-orc, Niajar somehow now a standing on the other side of the massive chamber across the river of sewage. The librarian waved cheerily before sitting in the lotus position to cultivate.

"Our opponent is fast," Zhaden said, brandishing his pair of daggers. "Even faster than you, Kiru."

"What do you suggest?" Kiru asked, pulling out his twin short swords.

"In a pure fight of physical might, we cannot win, but . . ." The drakonid activated his Invisibility technique. "We can use more than our brute strength." Zhaden lowered his lanky form and sprinted toward the groundskeeper.

Giiyam closed his eyes and took a deep breath.

Zhaden, still invisible, leaped up in the air, both his weapons poised to strike.

The half-orc simply took a step to the right, dodging Zhaden's attack with minimal effort. The drakonid landed on the ground, kicking up a small bit of dust. Giiyam's eyes opened with what looked like deadly intent. Before Zhaden could respond, Giiyam spun and did a roundhouse kick, hitting the invisible drakonid square in the jaw. Zhaden's technique dispelled as he was knocked unconscious and sent skidding across the stone.

With one opponent down, Giiyam sprinted toward Brunhilda and Kiru. The psion took a step forward, but he faltered as his diaphragm spasmed. Though he had no physical sensations in his limbs, he still needed to breathe. The paladin, however, was still fine, and she charged the incoming half-orc with both shields raised and managed to deflect two of the hook sword strikes before Giiyam began to get a sense of her timing.

Unfortunately for Brunhilda, Giiyam's odd swords seemed specialized in dealing with a shielded opponent. He swung his blades for a third time, knowing exactly where the dwarf's shields would be. The hooked portions of both blades snapped tight around the lip of both shields. In a display of sheer strength, the half-orc heaved the armored dwarf off her feet, spun in a circle, then slammed her back down to the ground again. She bounced like a ball. Giiyam spun and kicked her in midair and sent the dwarf crashing into the unconscious Zhaden.

With his breathing finally stabilized and seeing an opportunity, Kiru flooded his leg meridians with more mental mana. He surged forward at high speed, using one of his favorite sword forms his mother had taught him. It was the same one he used on the orc back at Fox Hollow: the Demon's Inciting Strike. Both his short swords struck, but not against flesh. With a loud clang of metal, Giiayam blocked both of his blades with just one of his swords. Kiru groaned as his momentum ground to a sudden halt.

Giiyam, a good head above Kiru's height, was now looking down at him, staring directly into the psion's eyes. The groundskeeper then took his free sword and thrust it at Kiru's face. The psion deflected and riposted, and the sword fight began in earnest. Kiru was a good swordsman, one of the best first-years in all of the academy, with really only Zane rivaling him on that front. As impressive as he was, thanks his mother's training, he could still quickly tell that Giiyam was on another level. Despite that, Kiru refused to give up. He fought with as much tenacity as he could muster.

The chamber echoed with the sounds of metal on metal. Giiyam's stoic face indicated no effort or strain on his part, which frustrated Kiru even more than the bloodthirsty little imp in his head. Kiru had never fought against an opponent wielding hook swords before. Even though he'd read about them, actually fighting against them was difficult. For almost the entire battle, he was on the defensive. More than once, the blades wrapped around his own and diverted his body, putting him at increased risk of being hit. Before coming to the academy, Kiru would never have been able to stand even the most meager chance of overcoming such an opponent. Now, however, he had learned how to recall his familiar and had acquired perfect memory from it. As they fought, Kiru was able to grasp the half-orc's movements, his footwork, and his sword forms. Giiyam was repeating the same four attack patterns with Kiru. *Is he testing me?*

The psion waited, predicting the patterns and desperately defending himself, biding his time for the right moment. Then . . . *there!* There was a moment where the half-orc's guard was vulnerable. It was a gap in Giiyam's form, an opening where both his weapons were spread wide, leaving his torso exposed. With violent force, Kiru used a form he hadn't tried since he had trained with his mother, Stag's Desperate Charge. He lunged at Giiyam with the points of both swords aimed right at his heart.

That was when Giiyam did something different.

The groundskeeper leaned back, narrowly avoiding Kiru's blades, and spun, catching both of them with his right-hand weapon. Giiyam cartwheeled, spinning and guiding Kiru's blades straight to the ground. The groundskeeper was back on his feet, directly facing him once more. Before Kiru could free his weapons from the odd hook blade, Giiyam took his free sword and swung. He did not swing at Kiru, though. He swung at the student's pinned weapons.

The half-orc's hooked blade shattered Kiru's short swords into multiple pieces. No longer stuck in place, the psion staggered backward with the hilts of his blade in each hand, uneven nubs all that remained attached to them. He landed square on his ass before being promptly kicked in the forehead. His headband's divine enchantment kicked in, protecting him from the damage, but he was still knocked back and slammed into the ground.

Kiru had to take a couple of seconds to blink his vision clear. When he finally did, Niajar was channeling with his familiar floating above his shoulder, funneling some sort of green-colored technique through his palms and into Kiru.

"A strange situation we find ourselves in," he said. "The first time I encountered you, you were beaten and on the ground. Now I've gotten you a trainer, and you've gone and done it again."

Kiru groaned. He had cultivated more often and for longer periods of time to compensate for these training sessions, so he still had enough mana to once again activate his Telekinesis on himself. He noticed that Niajar was standing on his foot. Concerned that the elf would suspect something, he tried to play it off. "Maybe I would get off my back if my sponsor would get off my foot," he said through gritted teeth, pretending it actually caused him pain.

The librarian put a hand to his chest and sighed in relief. "Oh, good! How your body looked after being kicked, I was afraid you had lost sensation in your nerves once more."

Kiru forced himself to remain calm, but on the inside, he was greatly concerned. *Does he suspect something? Wait, did he just admit that he was testing my body?!* Kiru thought. He then realized that the librarian's curious nature must have led him to wonder how Kiru could have recovered from his initial grievous wounds those years ago.

Kiru fought to keep a scowl from his face. *I should've known better.* While Kiru trusted that Niajar was interested in Pandemonium's success, he had forgotten that the enigmatic elf had his own hidden motives. Kiru had also lost sight of the librarian's inquisitive nature. He would have to be better about concealing his secret in the future, especially since it seemed that Niajar would be healing them of any injuries during their practice matches with Giiyam and thus more focused on their bodies. Kiru forced himself up and created the illusion of limping over to his friends, who were now standing as well. He wanted to maintain the charade for the time being.

Once they were all together, Giiyam addressed them. "Hmm, despite your youth and only a semester's worth of training, I can see true promise in each of you."

The three students brightened at the praise.

He had his weapons sheathed on his back and his hands clasped behind him. He walked in front of the three with the bearing of a military leader. It reminded

Kiru that Giiyam had served. *Why was he a groundskeeper? Why did he want to hide his previous enrollment at the academy?* he pondered.

"However," Giiyam continued, interrupting the psion's train of thought, "it is clear that while each of you have individual skill and martial talent, you lack in experience using your techniques. Even more importantly, you failed to fight as a group using those techniques at all."

"*Hey! No fair! He did a sneak attack! We weren't prepared!*" Willliam complained in Kiru's mind.

Kiru bunched his lips in self-recrimination. Hearing William's complaints, Kiru realized that he had forgotten his mom's first lesson: *Always fight dirty.*

Despite not hearing the imp, the paladin agreed. "With all due respect, sir, ye attacked us by surprise. We were caught off-guard. Ye can't blame us for fighting as we did. We did our best."

"Wrong!" Giiyam said with some actual heat in his voice. "In the Warrior Games, do you think your opponents will give you the chance to prepare for them? Do you think that such a public event where the professors and nobles wager, that there won't be cheating? That, in order to protect their investments, the patrons and families of the students won't give them a competitive edge?"

"He's right, you know," Niajar added needlessly.

Kiru lowered his eyes in a mix of anger and disappointment as the groundskeeper's words reminded of his mom's first lesson and his own failure to act on it.

All three students' faces flushed in embarrassment just now realizing how much more difficult their predicament was. Not only would they be facing talented cultivators but ones who would have no compunctions about manipulating the fights in their favor. Kiru, in particular, had been so caught up in improving his own strategy, he wasn't thinking about what shady things his opponents might have planned to win. He needed to account for that, and the first step to overcoming scheming opponents was to have skilled teammates he could trust to get the job done.

He looked over to his friends, whose faces betrayed wavering confidence. That would not do. If they were going to win, they were going to need to believe in themselves and each other. He needed to help them overcome this mental hurdle of knowing that their opponents would try to cheat them out of victory.

Kiru walked in front of the dwarf and drakonid. "I have bigger goals than just this tournament, and I know that the odds will never be in my favor. That doesn't matter. What matters is that we win. I know we can do it, and I don't want to quit. Do you?"

His two teammates both gave him a warm smile and shook their heads.

Kiru smiled back, then looked at Giiyam. "We're not gonna quit just because it's hard. You won, despite being a Defunct. Will you teach us how to win?"

Giiyam actually gave a toothy grin, the biggest smile Kiru had ever seen on his face. "Good. You have resolve. You'll need it. As for how, there are two things. The first I've already shown you." He put a finger up. "You must become strong, so strong that they can't stand a chance unless they give you their best." A second finger went up. "The second is that you must be clever."

Kiru nodded, grasping the connection with his mother's second lesson about hiding your strengths. The sudden reminders of Surturia brought up a pang of guilt inside his chest. His lip quivered and his right arm trembled slightly from his lack of focus. Kiru closed his eyes and let out a deep exhale, letting go of the feelings of shame accumulating inside him. When he opened his eyes once again, Giiyam was just staring blankly at him. The groundskeeper raised an eyebrow in curiosity at Kiru's sudden distraction.

When he didn't explain but just nodded for Giiyam to continue, the half-orc obliged. He wasn't going to press Kiru. "Being unable to use a technique puts you at a particular disadvantage. So, your team must possess knowledge about your opponents' weakness and conceal your strength. That way, they will have no way to fully prepare for you."

He faced Zhaden. "That information-gathering should be your job, rogue."

"I believe I am up to the task," the drakonid replied.

Giiyam nodded. "Good. Think on what I've said, all of you, on how to use your techniques in sync. Together instead of one at a time." He turned his back to them. "Come back in two days. We will resume training then."

# CHAPTER THIRTY-FIVE

# Fu Tao

The trio sighed at the half-orc's words but nodded. They began to follow Niajar toward the exit, but Giiyam stopped Kiru. "Stay."

Trusting him, Kiru waved to his friends and waited on the island with him. Giiyam did not speak more until the door closed behind the librarian and students. "You managed to predict my movements from our fights. Impressive."

"Thank you, sir." Kiru bowed his head in respect. "I've also studied your sword forms . . . from what I remember from your fight with the Beguilers and what I've put together from the book regarding your championship run in the games."

The groundskeeper raised an eyebrow. "Hm, show me."

Kiru raised his two stumps of swords up. "Uhh . . ."

Giiyam unsheathed his weapons and handed them to Kiru. "Show me."

Surprised, Kiru set down the broken short swords and took the two hook swords from Giiyam. They were odd weapons. The protective guard covering his hand was sharp and slightly curved, like a small ax blade. With the hooked tip of the weapon's extra weight, its balance was slightly top heavy in comparison to the short swords he'd been using before. Again, Kiru couldn't truly *feel,* per se, but he'd developed enough familiarity with swords to grasp the differences.

Kiru spun the weapons, familiarizing himself with them. After getting a bit more comfortable with the blades, he backed up a little, then showed Giiyam what he had learned. First, he demonstrated the form used against the Beguiler, swinging his weapons together and spreading them out to strike at two different spots. He then used three different forms he'd picked up from the books: a sideways slash and upward slash with one blade followed by a downward slash with both blades, and a wrist-flicking form to spin the blade. Kiru then followed up with the four forms that Giiyam had just used on him, based off his recollection.

"You grasp the basics very well, but your understanding is not perfect. Your mind is sharp, but while you understand *what* the sword forms are, you don't understand *how* to do them."

*"What's this jerk saying? How dare he say our memory isn't perfect! Master, let me out of here. I'll give him a memory he'll never forget!"* William promised.

Kiru did not indulge his familiar. Instead of getting mad, he understood what Giiyam was implying. There was book knowledge, and then there was practical, experiential knowledge.

"What style were you trained in?" the half-orc asked.

"Monarch's Razors," Kiru replied.

Giiyam raised an eyebrow. "Monarch's Razors? That's a rare style. It's very aggressive and usually reserved for . . . elven royalty."

Kiru opened and closed his mouth a few times, realizing that he'd just let slip a major secret.

To his relief, Giiyam actually laughed, full and heartily. "So, that's your story, young one. You're a bastard from Anor'Voren! I've never seen such a terrible poker face in all my life! Hahaha!"

Kiru decided not to correct the man. Technically, he *was* a bastard whose family hailed from the elven capital . . . on his mother's side.

"Haha, you got me." Kiru chuckled along, playing into the half-truth.

Giiyam put a hand on his shoulder. "Not to worry. The Kingdom of Blades is where everyone can belong, even the outcasts of other countries." He looked up at the ceiling, as if recalling a fond memory. "This land is a place where even Defuncts like us can become more."

"I agree," Kiru said, completely honestly this time.

The half-orc then looked back at Kiru, his neutral visage returning. "While you are familiar with Monarch's Razors, you are still a novice. Sure, you are more skilled than most, but I can tell you have not spent enough years practicing. Why have you not continued your training?"

Kiru stayed quiet for a while, wrestling with his painful memories. He opened and closed his mouth a few times before any words came out. Even then, his voice grew shaky as it always did at the thought of his beloved mother. "My . . . master died before she could fully teach me."

"I see. My condolences," Giiyam replied. "I cannot make you an expert in Monarch's Razors, but I can teach you to branch off of it, using it as a base, if you're willing to leave that path behind?"

Kiru was conflicted. On the one hand, he was truly ecstatic at finally getting to learn from a master swordsman. On the other, it meant he would truly have to forsake mastering the form of fighting that his mother had intended for him. He would be diluting his style if he truly integrated another. Sure, he'd been attempting to mimic what Giiyam had done before, but now he realized that he had been using that to supplement what he'd already learned. If he accepted to be trained under Giiyam officially, his path to true mastery of Monarch's Razors would be gone forever. *Will I be abandoning Mother if I do?*

William seemed to understand what was going through his master's head—maybe because he literally lived inside there. *"You're not abandoning Flamebringer's fight, Master,"* he sent. *"She would want you to use what she taught you and build off it, just like the green man offered."*

*"Thanks, William. That is very wise,"* Kiru sent back, clearly surprised by the imp's words.

*"Of course! Whatever helps us crush our enemies is what Flamebringer would want. Also, all my words are wise! Duh! You should listen to me more!"* the petulant imp answered.

Smiling, Kiru looked to Giiyam. "I accept. Please teach me your ways, Master," Kiru said and handed the hook blades back to him.

The half-orc nodded and officially accepted the psion as his pupil.

For the next couple of hours, Giiyam taught Kiru about both his weapons and the style in which he used them. First off, the hook blades were known as Fu Tao. They originated from the remnants of one of the human civilizations that survived Ragnarok. Secondly, the half-orc confirmed that his sword form was called the Cruel and Cunning Mantis or the Cruel Mantis for short. It was an aggressive but semi-defensive form that focused on disabling an opponent, targeting exposed weaknesses, and incapacitating with devastating damage. It was aptly named, as it was cruel by design, but from what Giiyam had displayed, it was clearly effective. A true master of this style of fighting would be a dangerous foe indeed.

William practically purred in delight.

After learning all of this, there was one thing Kiru still needed to know. "Wait, does this mean you're giving me your swords?" he asked, unable to hide his excitement. The blades were clearly of good quality. The metal had no dents or scratches, and the bladed handle guard was serrated to ensure severe injury to an opponent.

The half-orc stared at him with a deadpan expression. "No."

"Okay, then. Does the school have a Fu Tao for sale or on lease?"

Giiyam didn't say anything but just stuck his hand out expectantly for his blades to be returned. Kiru began handing the weapons back when the groundskeeper suddenly turned his palm upward and gently pushed the Fu Tao back to Kiru. A wry smile grew on the half-orc's face, indicating he was messing with the psion. "I'm giving you my *practice* swords. My actual weapons are much better."

Kiru looked at Giiyam, dumbfounded. The stoic bastard had actually made a joke! For the second time, Kiru heard a real laugh from the man, too, and he couldn't help but join in.

For the next three weeks, leading into the first week of the semester, Pandemonium dedicated their focus into training and improvement. To their relief, Team Supreme kept their word and there weren't any more "accidents" like what had happened with Brunhilda.

Unfortunately, the assigned sparring matches in their combat class were more rough-going than expected. The sparring sessions without techniques against some of their classmates became more difficult for numerous reasons. The first was that, while they were still skilled, Pandemonium was always outnumbered three to four in every fight. While they had always been outnumbered before, their opponents were now improving—finding even more effective ways to kick the members of Pandemonium when they were down.

The second reason was Kiru. Picking up not only new weapons but a different fighting style forced Pandemonium to readjust a number of their already-trained tactics such as Scorpion's Stance, putting them behind their classmates. His perfect memory helped, but as Giiyam had pointed out, there was a difference between book knowledge and practical knowledge. Practical knowledge required physical experience and practice. There was no way around it.

Meanwhile, the rest of their classmates were improving as well, also increasing the gap. Those who had generous benefactors or overly invested sponsors in the academy began showing the results of having friends in high places. Students returned with improved equipment and combat prowess. Kiru even thought some of their tools were enchanted, like his headband.

A few notable professors were taking what seemed to be too much of an interest in their sponsored students' success. Of them, there was the Fire Cultivation I instructor, Claire Redheart, the always-hooded dark mana master, Ivan Zerkoff, and of course, headmaster Niazen J'sarko himself.

All of those staff members' sponsored students and the teams they were on were noticeably better equipped and prepared than before. Apparently, they also had taken their winter break to improve. It seemed that their sponsors really didn't want to lose their wagers and any other side bets this year. There were five teams made up of the staff members' sponsored students, and they all glared at Pandemonium, exuding much more power than before.

Despite the newfound challenges, Kiru was still confident that Pandemonium would overcome in time for the Games. However, that confidence was shaken a couple of weeks into the semester when they had their first sparring match against Team Supreme. Not only were their rivals all decked out in new pristine equipment that provided even better protection and worse damage against their opponents, but both Zane and Ambrose were exuding a strange new confidence and sense of power. Kiru's heart sank when he realized what had happened: both of them had ascended from Gold to Ruby.

The psion gritted his teeth. He made sure to spend extra time in the library every day to cultivate and accumulate enough mental mana to help him in the prolonged training sessions. He even made sure to let William out every night as well in order to get more mental mana while the imp was dreaming. Still, from what he understood about what happened when people ascended from Gold to Ruby from his experience at the academy, Kiru knew he was not ready. It wasn't just about sheer mana quantity, mind you, but techniques. From the standard method known at the academy, the first thing a cultivator required was five techniques. With so little access to information regarding mental mana techniques, Kiru knew that first step was going to be very difficult. With their team outnumbered and outclassed by Team Supreme, Pandemonium would have their asses firmly handed to them.

"Don't bother getting up, mongrel," Ambrose spat. "Just stay down in the dirt where you belong."

Kiru didn't respond. He instead kept his head down and waited on his knees after Ambrose beat him. Kiru wondered if Team Supreme no longer felt that Pandemonium was worth the worry, completely ignorant of the fact that Zane was still keeping a cautious eye on the psion.

Later that night, Kiru was at Giiyam's barn training with the groundskeeper. Pandemonium would practice with the Defunct swordsman in their makeshift arena four nights a week, Niajar keeping an eye from a safe distance in case they needed healing. For an hour before every session, though, Kiru would receive personal training from Giiyam.

The training was significantly different from the group sparring or even how his mother had taught him. The most striking aspect was that Giiyam didn't actually spar with the psion. He didn't even teach him sword forms!

Every night that he came to Giiyam's home for his hour of individual training, the groundskeeper had Kiru do a variety of menial tasks around the barn. Kiru protested that this wasn't training, but the stern half-orc's serious gaze silenced him. In the past six weeks, the psion had done all sorts of odd, simple tasks. He cleaned horse hooves, removed dirty hay with a pitchfork, used a scythe to cut grass, swept the floor, then removed rotten wooden boards and hammered new ones back in place. None of it seemed to have anything to do with Fu Tao. The groundskeeper just instructed the psion in his tasks and insisted he follow his strange methods precisely.

Giiyam had Kiru flick his wrist frequently when using his tool to remove dirt from the horses' feet. He told Kiru to use both his shoulders and wrists when removing the dirty hay. When using the scythe, Giiyam instructed Kiru to turn the blade at the end of each swing and use the tool to cut grass on the backswing. Last of all, instead of directly facing any given nail he was meant hammer like every other person in the world would do, he would have him stand to the side of the board and nail and swing the hammer laterally.

It was after that last job that his frustration finally began to break through its restraints. Once he was done, he left the barn and made his way to the library. As he stomped through the building, all dirty and sweaty, and past a group of students who openly recoiled at his stench, he gritted his teeth and began muttering to himself.

William fully agreed with him, egging him on. Kiru made it through the hidden corridor and eventually down to the hidden sewer-chamber-turned-arena. His friends and the groundskeeper were already there. The half-orc had left Kiru to finish nailing the boards a half-hour prior, and he was now standing there nonplussed. Seeing Giiyam's stoic face seemed to rile Kiru up even more.

"What is the point of all of this" Kiru asked. "I thought you were going to be training me. Turns out, your 'lessons' are just your way to trick me into becoming your farmhand! I fail to see how any of this is helping us improve our odds at winning the Games!"

Brunhilda and Zhaden stood there in stunned silence.

Giiyam's expression didn't change. "You think that my training is lacking?"

"Pfft! I struggle to call it training at all. While I'm shoveling horse crap, other teams are getting better gear and ascending in rank. I don't want to be a liability for my—"

Giiyam put a palm up, silencing the psion. "Come," he beckoned.

Kiru's nostrils flared, but he did as he was told.

Giiyam then unsheathed his blades—his *real* blades: ornate, enchanted with runes, and somehow managing to exude a sensation of pain to the psion. "Draw your swords."

"What?"

"Now!"

Kiru complied, startled by the harshness of his tone.

"Hammer The Boards," he ordered, then lunged a blade at the psion's gut.

Kiru's enhanced memory—coupled with the fact that his Path of the Puppet Master had grown to grant him a stronger grasp of the energy that he used to move his body—allowed him to perfectly recall how Giiyam had taught him to hammer the boards. He swung his right Fu Tao out to the side, catching the half-orc's blade and redirecting its trajectory away from his body. Giiyam lunged again, and Kiru did the same with his left blade.

Giiyam gave an affirming grunt and nodded. He deftly freed his weapons and posed once more to strike. "Good. Now, remove the nails." This time, Giiyam swung horizontally, directly at the psion's chest.

Kiru held his right blade up and met Giiyam's weapon with the clash of metal. Remembering the wrist motion, Kiru wrapped the hook of his Fu Tao around his opponent's and forced Giiyam's wrist into an awkward position. Giiyam swung his other sword in the same way, but lower than his first weapon. Kiru repeated the motion to intercept, swinging his weapon upward instead, forcing both of Giiyam's weapons to press against each other.

"Good," he said again, and Kiru released his weapons.

They repeated each move until they had gotten through all of Kiru's lessons together. The psion felt goosebumps on his neck as he processed what had happened. He couldn't believe it! Giiyam had, in fact, been training him, after all.

"Do you still think my training is lacking?"

"*Oh shit, Master! You're a badass again!*" William said.

"No. No, sir," Kiru said, now with complete respect for the groundskeeper's unorthodox methods. "Please forgive my rudeness. I was . . . arrogant and impatient."

"You were, but you are forgiven. Just show trust in my methods. Don't forget, I am a former champion."

Kiru bowed even lower in appreciation, then regrouped with his friends, who themselves weren't quite over the shock of what they had just seen. Once Niajar joined up, they began their training together in earnest.

# CHAPTER THIRTY-SIX

# The Beast

Father!" Zane called out as he hurried through the large doors of the headmaster's office. The elf was in the lotus position, hovering over his desk, his eyes closed in meditation. Zane didn't understand why he insisted on wearing those ridiculously tall, cylindrical shoulder pauldrons wherever he went, but the last time he'd questioned his father about it, Zane had been promptly backhanded into a wall.

Niazen groaned at the interruption, then floated down to the ground. "What is it, son?" he asked, not trying to hide his irritation.

"You know that Defunct kid? In these recent couple months, his team has gotten good—too good. I figured something was awry, so I followed him to the library. I saw the punk go through some secret room there. I think Uncle Niajar's doing some extra training."

Niazen raised an eyebrow at his impudent son. "And?"

"And . . . he's clearly cheating. No way that worthless Fist House student can get as good as he's gotten—not without help. Give me artifact-level gear or get my team and me to Sapphire-rank! That way, we can crush them."

"You worthless whelp!" Niazen shouted at his son with such force, the boy fell to his knees. In that moment, his dad reminded him of some kind of monster. It was almost as if his words had gone directly into his mind!

"I give you every advantage that you could possibly imagine—rare techniques, high-quality pills—and called in multiple favors to raise not only you but one of your companions as well to Ruby-rank as simple first-years! Even with all that, you have the audacity to demand more?!"

Zane collapsed to the ground, now lying flat on his belly, forced down by his father's aura.

"If you cannot defeat a boy who cannot even use a technique, even with all the resources at your disposal, you deserve to lose! Well, what do you have to say?

Can you, the top student in the world's most prestigious academy, not handle a Defunct?!"

The ground around Zane started to crack from the pressure as Niazen's grip on his power slipped, letting out more than intended. Realizing his mistake, the headmaster regained control and withdrew it.

Zane gasped as if he'd been held underwater. "Gah! Yes, Father!" He panted a few more times. "Sorry, Father! I will make you proud, and I will win for you!" the young elf said as he pushed himself up, then left as quickly as he could.

Niazen ground his teeth, his bet with Niajar drawing circles in his mind. Until now, he had felt nothing but secure, despite his soft-hearted brother's insistence that he not intervene on Zane's behalf. The headmaster had found those terms tolerable. Instead of dealing with Zane's opponents directly, Niazen had just over-invested in his son's growth instead.

If Zane was concerned, however, even after all of his boosts, that worried Niazen. He wanted to eliminate this pest of a student, but he couldn't break his oath to directly intervene. The voices in his head groaned in displeasure at that. Closing his eyes to concentrate, Niazen wracked his brain for a loophole in his deal with his brother.

If a cultivator swore an oath on their soul, their bodies allowed them to actually feel the weight of those promises via their core. Because of that, they could probe whether or not something they wanted to do would violate said oath. The more complex and secure the oath's stipulations were, the more difficult it was to find a loophole. This, however, wasn't the first time Niazen had tried to find some sort of workaround to a soul oath, and he knew how to test his theories securely.

Sure enough, when he probed at the soul-binding agreement he'd made with his brother, Niazen had found that Niajar had been too lax in what "breaking the rules" meant. The headmaster gave a cruel smile. His brother had seriously messed up, and he would ensure that Niajar's pet Defunct would pay the price. The elf then swiftly ran and jumped out of his window from his high tower.

He channeled his faerie fire mana, and fuchsia flames surged out of his palms and feet, giving the headmaster the ability to levitate. Niazen descended to the medical ward. Just like Zane, he was too focused to notice the small floating creature following him from a distance. "Carl!" he shouted as he opened the doors. No one was present. The headmaster strode into the ward and pressed the secret panel hidden under one of the cots. A stairway appeared in the floor, and Niazen wasted no time going down it.

"Carl!" he shouted once more as he descended.

The one-eyed cleric of Odin met the elf at the bottom of the stairs. "Yes, Headmaster?"

"There are some students breaking the rules, going into forbidden grounds on campus. I think it's time to show them some . . . extreme discipline. How has the most recent pest I brought you been coming along?"

"Ah, yes! Subject 626. He's provided me with much valuable data!"

"Is he fully functional?" Both cleric and headmaster grinned maliciously. "It's time to unleash the beast." The two cackled as a small familiar flew off to warn his master.

Within minutes of Giiyam opening Kiru's eyes to what the psion had learned, Pandemonium had shown significant improvement. Bolstered by Kiru's new skills over the months, the team had their best match against Giiyam to date! Now with Kiru being able to adequately contribute and using Zhaden's Invisibility along with Brunhilda's Rejuvenation and Divine Shield techniques, they were able to damage Giiyam and force the half-orc to go on the defensive. Working in tandem like that also helped them better understand how their techniques worked in sync. For example, they discovered if Zhaden used Invisibility while Brunhilda was using her Rejuvenation on him, his form would be highlighted, rendering his technique useless.

Kiru also secretly implemented his Telepathy too over months, figuring that neither Niajar or Giiyam would be able to notice. With improved communication, improved physical fighting, and the use of techniques, they felt much more confident in fighting full force.

That didn't mean Giiyam wasn't a fierce opponent. More than once, the ridiculously fast swordsman managed to dispatch each of the three members on his own. But fighting full force allowed the trio to vastly improve their skills. And it also had another benefit, albeit at a cost. The hidden chamber had no protective enchantments on it, so the wounds were actual wounds. With both Brunhilda and Niajar present, the injuries were never long lasting, but they could definitely be serious, Giiyam had amputated more than one of Kiru's fingers to emphasize that the psion needed to focus on his wrist movements. Zhaden was once eviscerated by the half-orc's Fu Tao as well. Aside from the horrendous wound, the smell of spilled bile made Kiru vomit.

Though the training Giiyam implemented was cruel to an extreme that would bother some cultivators, it helped Pandemonium sharpen their battle instincts even more than in the arena. Their senses were much more ready. All of their speed, strength, and intelligence in combat improved. They had a much better idea of what they could take and what they couldn't in terms of damage, and after repeated injuries and fights, that threshold grew. All three of them—Brunhilida most of all—could take serious wounds and keep going. It wasn't the most enjoyable way to grow, but it was undeniably effective!

After their final bout for the day, all three of them collapsed to the stone ground, breathing heavily. "Well done, all of you!" Giiyam praised with his monotonous voice. "You should be proud, and you will no doubt be amongst the top performers in the Games."

"Quite right!" Niajar called over. The elf then jumped across the large gap with casual ease, demonstrating the capability of such a high-ranking cultivator. "You are one of the best first-year teams," he said after he landed by the half-orc. "But that is the crux of your issue. While you certainly *one* of the top teams, you are not *the* top team."

That brought down the team's spirits. He was right.

There was, however, a mischievous glint in his eyes as he continued. "Now, what would you say are your two biggest obstacles in this competition?"

"Missing a fourth member be a big one," Brunhilda said.

"Our current repertoire of equipment, techniques, and cultivation ranks have also fallen behind the more elite competitors," Zhaden added.

"Correct! Ah, right on the money! It's truly remarkable how insightful you youths are!" Niajar beamed at them. Just then, Nicodemus came zooming in. The little familiar orb of light turned into a hummingbird and began chirping enthusiastically to his master. Niajar nodded, somehow able to understand the unintelligible noises. "Mmm, I see. Oh! Oh, my!" The librarian recalled his familiar, then looked back at the party.

"What is it?" Kiru asked.

"It seems that there are some in the academy who are . . . less enthusiastic about Pandemonium's progress. It would be wise for the three of you to remain here for the time being."

"But I have a midterm exam in my Life Mana class I need to study for!" Brunhilda protested.

"Stay here," Niajar said with strong intent. His trademark charm disappeared from his face.

Understanding the gravity of the situation, all three of them agreed with no more protest.

"Good." The librarian faced Giiyam. "Groundskeeper, there appears to be a situation in which your aid is needed."

The stoic orc grunted in response, sheathing his Fu Tao. The two promptly left without another word, leaving Pandemonium in the underground training arena. Hours went by, and the trio pondered as to what could've shaken Niajar so much. Had Zane decided to break his word and buy off more students to send a message? Had some of the other students gathered outside the library to ambush them, or had someone gone through their belongings and planted some sort of incriminating evidence?

Ever since Joseph's betrayal, Kiru had been more defensive and paranoid. He often matched the caution that Zhaden displayed now too. He made sure to avoid engaging with Joseph, all trust with the guy now gone. He had tried to speak with Kiru a couple of times, but Kiru always made an excuse not to, despite noticing that Joseph had a sad look in his eyes. He assumed he wanted to apologize, but the psion wasn't willing to give him a chance. William had recommended that Kiru make him cry blood instead of tears, but he felt avoidance would be more low-profile.

Kiru made sure to always keep everything important on his person at all times. That included his mother's storage ring. There was no way he'd leave it for Joseph to potentially steal! So, he at least felt confident that nothing of great value would be lost. He couldn't say the same for his classmates.

Given their theorizing seemed to be getting them nowhere, they decided to do at least something productive, and so they cultivated. Kiru was also pretty low, since he hadn't taken time to bring in more mental mana inside the library. He summoned William in order to let him stretch his legs, which helped with the composition of the ambient mana around them. The little imp's exposed brain wasn't *that* big, but any extra influence of mental mana was beneficial.

A rat was crawling about on the congealed piles of sewage below their island. The ugly imp licked his lips and rubbed his hands together. "Ooooh! Dinner!" he proclaimed, then used Telekinesis and brought the rat to his hands. Before the rat could crawl away, William opened his mouth and promptly bit its head off.

The party scowled in disgust and then did their best to ignore the crunching. A couple of more hours went by, though it was difficult to tell exactly how many, with them being underground. Kiru had managed to resupply his body with more mental mana, packing more into his meridians for extra storage than he typically did, leaving him feeling renewed and refreshed. He'd even been able to successfully block out William's eating, whining from boredom, pouting at being ignored, and more eating. It wasn't until the imp came to physically slapping the psion across the face that Kiru's focus was finally broken.

"What?!"

"Master, something's coming." The imp pointed to the wall on the other side of the chamber. There was a crack in it, and it bulged out slightly. Kiru watched as the bulge momentarily grew larger, then retracted, like a bird trying to force its way out of its egg.

*"We've got company!"* Kiru shouted telepathically into the minds of his comrades. Startled by the sudden noise in their heads, both Brunhilda and Zhaden were quickly broken out of their own meditation. Both of them scrambled to their feet and turned to the psion.

Kiru tightened his enchanted headband, then pointed to the wall where the bulge was still expanding. All three equipped their weapons and braced themselves for a fight. In a matter of seconds, the wall shook, bulged even more, then *BOOM!* The section of stone burst open, sending rock and dust flying out.

Automatically, the three members of Pandemonium pressed their backs to each other, just as they had trained, protecting their blindspots as the dust obscured their vision. A spine-chilling howl rang out through the large chamber. The students focused and hurriedly scanned their surroundings in the dust cloud. Even as the debris settled, however, they still didn't see anything.

Kiru hadn't yet recalled William; the imp was sitting on his shoulder, scared shitless and scanning even more frantically than the others. Then William looked up. "Above us!"

Processing the warning in milliseconds, Kiru shouted his order. "Scatter!"

Trusting in their training, all three jumped in different directions. They narrowly dodged the creature that was currently descending. With a resounding thump, something heavy hit the ground. It was a four-legged beast completely covered in brown hair, obscuring any eyes and ears from sight. It had a strange metal contraption with tubes of glowing green liquid connected to its skull. Its mouth was large, with a prominent underbite. Though Kiru couldn't see the creature's eyes, it seemed to stare directly at the psion with distinct intelligence. Despite the heavy layer of dirt in its coat, the beast's senses appeared to be unbothered, and it gave off a focused, predatory desire. The psion had the distinct feeling that whatever the hairy creature was, it was an alpha predator not to be trifled with.

"I believe this is the situation Niajar was referring to," Zhaden hissed.

"No shit!" William angrily replied.

"No shite!" Brunhilda echoed. "For once, I've got to agree with the imp. What in the world is this hairy thing?"

At her words, the creature snapped its head at the purple-haired dwarf and gave an angry roar before sprinting at her.

Kiru wondered where the librarian and groundskeeper were, because it seemed they had failed to find the thing they had been trying to protect the students from. *"Shit! Pincer Method!"* Kiru sent telepathically to his team. Brunhilda charged forward while he sprinted to the right, and the rogue went left.

The paladin met the beast head-on. She managed to block a claw swipe with her left shield, but it still forced her back. That bought Zhaden and Kiru enough time to flank the beast on both sides. The drakonid threw a couple of daggers, which hit their mark, embedding just barely in its thick hide. The beast turned its head toward Zhaden and growled. Somehow, though, it still managed to jump back and dodge Kiru's sword strikes, despite its back facing the psion. *Are its reflexes that good?*

Emboldened by his previous successful hit, Zhaden pulled out two more daggers and hissed, "It's mine." The drakonid then activated his Invisibility, instantly disappearing from sight. Then he charged across the shallow water, his rogue training making his steps almost imperceptible.

Kiru was able to follow Zhaden as he charged but noticed that the snarling beast seemed to be able track him as well. Before Kiru could send out a warning, Zhaden closed the distance. The drakonid was about to thrust both of his daggers at the beast's neck when it ducked at the last moment and bit his left calf. The beast's large canines clamped down through his thin armor and reptilian scales and began to swing him around like a shoe in a dog's mouth. Blood poured readily from Zhaden's leg.

Before it could do more damage, however, Brunhilda was ready. *"Divine Shield!"* Speaking the name of a technique out loud typically seemed to solidify it more in the cultivator's mind and seemed to make the effects stronger. Brunhilda certainly ascribed to that mindset. A beam of holy light miraculously surged down from the ceiling of the cavern and engulfed the drakonid. Immediately, the technique's defensive measures kicked in and lit the hairy beast aflame. The beast cried out in pain and dropped Zhaden. It backed away and began rolling in the shallow, fetid water to put out the fire.

The stench of burned hair filled the air, but Kiru put it out of his mind. He and Brunhilda ran over to their friend, who was clutching his injured leg. Blood was still oozing from it, but not as profusely as before. Kiru looked to Brunhilda. "Can you heal him?"

"Aye, but not completely. I'll need more time to fully–"

"Do it," Kiru interrupted. "I'll buy you time." He rushed off with his Fu Tao at the ready. The beast, now no longer on fire, shook its head as smoke rose off its burned fur, exposing green and blue flesh underneath. The Cruel Mantis specialized in fighting bipedal humanoid opponents, focusing on striking the weak points of those types of foes and dealing crippling blows. Since it wasn't currently standing on its hindlimbs currently, Kiru decided to face this particular four-legged foe using a form from Monarch's Razors instead. Deciding to go with Demon's Inciting Strike, Kiru surged forward with a burst of speed, his swords crossed in an X-formation.

As if expecting the attack, the beast jumped over the psion and took a swipe at both him and William on his shoulder. Kiru reacted on instinct and raised his right blade to protect his familiar. The Fu Tao blocked the beast from striking the imp, but it left the psion's back exposed. The beast raked its claws down his back. Kiru groaned in pain as the claws scraped against his neck. Fortunately, his armor prevented them from doing further damage as the beast continued its downward swipe.

The creature landed on its back legs. It stood a good foot taller than Kiru and growled menacingly.

"You'll pay for that," Kiru muttered angrily, undeterred. Then he turned and used a newer maneuver from the Cruel Mantis style, a particularly nasty attack called the Thief's Punishment. The swing from his turn allowed his right Fu Tao to go straight into the beast's left palm. He then twisted his blade to jerk its arm upward and expose its wrist. Kiru's other sword then rose and slashed the beast's wrist in a move designed to cleave the hand off the opponent's arm.

William cheered. "Yeah! Take that you big, ugly . . . Oh, shit!"

The Fu Tao had simply cut across the beast's wrist, not removed it. The beast recoiled in pain, then clamped his mouth over Kiru's head!

Thankfully, the enchantment on Kiru's headband kicked in, divine intervention alone protecting his skull. Kiru screamed from the intense pressure, crushing him much like when the circlet his mother gave him fused with his body.

The beast let out a whine like a hurt puppy and backed away from Kiru. The psion shook his head and glared at the beast, confused at its withdrawal.

"Master, you get it, right? The hairy thing is blind, but it's sensitive to sound. Make its ears bleed for crossing us!" the imp cheered. Kiru could've slapped himself for not realizing it earlier. Instead, he channeled that frustration into attacking the beast. This time, he would follow William's advice. He unleashed a power he hadn't used directly on an opponent before: Telepathy. He used no words, just unintelligible screaming that focused he directed straight into the beast's mind. In response, it stood on its two hindlimbs and grabbed its hairy head, roaring in pain and shaking, as it desperately tried to banish the screams invading his mind. Unprepared for this kind of assault, it staggered about, still clutching at its head. It clawed and squeezed at the metal headpiece it wore as if the device were causing the noise, breaking and shattering it into pieces. It ripped out the tubes connected to the headpiece and spilled the green fluorescent liquid all over the ground in the process. The rest of the headpiece then followed.

Within seconds, the beast went slack and fell to its knees. Kiru stopped his Telepathy, as the creature no longer seemed to be a threat. Before Pandemonium's eyes, the beast began to shrink. Its long hairs regressed until they were indistinguishable. The roars also changed, turning into screams. In less than half a minute, the monstrous creature went from being a huge hairy beast to an ordinary orc. He was wearing tattered rags as well as a severely shredded blue Sword House jacket. Kiru gasped in surprise. The beast was . . . *a student*!

The orc dropped his hands and gave a relieved sigh before passing out and collapsing in a heap.

# CHAPTER THIRTY-SEVEN

# Mutt

Once the group had processed what had just happened, they tried to help the orcs regain consciousness. Kiru opened the unconscious student's eyelids but, to his shock, found both pupils to be milky white. The orc indeed was blind, just as he had suspected of the beast.

Numerous scars covered his body. Some were crooked and jagged, as if from animal claws and teeth, while others were very smooth and precise, perhaps from a medical procedure. His left arm, in particular, had some grotesque scars running from his shoulder to wrist. A long, thick, brown mohawk extended past his shoulders, and the only clothes he wore were a busted pair of shorts and his shredded Sword House jacket.

The orc opened his eyes and groaned as consciousness returned. Not sure if he was truly friend or foe, the party still kept their weapons at the ready.

He yawned. "Good fight."

"E-excuse me?" Kiru asked.

"That was a good fight! Hahaha!" The orc sat up quickly, making all of Pandemonium flinch. "Whoo! How long was I out?"

"I believe it is we who should be asking the questions," Zhaden said, rubbing his partially healed left leg. "More pressing, who are you, and what is a Sword House student doing attacking us?"

The orc didn't seem bothered at all by the drakonid. He gave a big, toothy grin. His milky eyes didn't lock onto Zhaden directly, but it was clear that he knew where the rogue was, even without sight. "M'Baku M'toon, first son of Chief M'Baku Sartall, but you can call me Mutt. I'm a first-year here at the academy. My dad sent me here because he got annoyed with me—which is fine 'cause I *love* to fight! As for why I'm in this specific place . . ." He trailed off casually while scratching his cheek. ". . . I guess it's 'cause I reached Ruby-rank."

That caught the trio off-guard. "You've reached tier-one Ruby already, as a first-year? How?" Zhaden asked.

Mutt scratched the back of his ear, reminiscent of how a dog would. "Well, after I beat the piss out of the headmaster's snob of a son when he was picking on some quiet gnome girl, the elf brought me to his office. He thanked me for the humility lesson for his son and said he wanted to reward me. Then some strange guy with an eyepatch brought me down to his lab and said that he would help me get to Ruby.

"I was initially doubtful, seeing as we beast mana users need to ingest sacred beast cores to ascend, but since this is the best place to help cultivators, I thought I should give him the benefit of the doubt. He gave me a special pill, and . . . well, the rest is a bit hazy. It was like I was there, but not there. That's how I knew we just had a good fight! Hahaha!"

"Wait, wait, wait," Kiru said. "Why do you need to consume sacred beast cores? How does that help you ascend in rank?"

Kiru had read about sacred beast cores in his duties as a librarian's assistant. Sacred beasts didn't possess an actual core like regular cultivators. Instead of an organ that took in mana, they compressed mana into their bodies and laced it with their blood to form a crystalized core made of the two substances. They could be used for a variety of purposes, including enchanting, creating mana-enhancing potions or pills, and even developing poisons.

Mutt chuckled. "I'm a beast mana cultivator. Unlike most cultivators, we ascend based on the number and quality of sacred beast cores we ingest, becoming like the sacred beasts themselves." The others' eyes widened. They had clearly never heard of such a wild method before, either.

"How can you see us?" Kiru asked. "If you don't mind me asking."

Mutt clicked his tongue. "Many a dangerous beast does not require their eyes, and neither do I. My senses are enhanced enough to know I'm talking to a drakonid, an elf of mixed heritage, and a dwarf who smells like a troll."

Brunhilda blushed a little at that.

Kiru's perfect memory finally put together who exactly Mutt was. "You're the orc who stood up to Zane and was sent to the dungeon and never heard from again!" The other two went a little slack-jawed at the revelation. *This guy was practically just a rumor! He was on the school premises so little, no one actually remembered who he was.*

"Um, Mutt, you've been gone for a very long time. It's been at least a semester and a half."

He didn't seem bothered at all. "Really? Huh! Time flies when you're having fun! Well, guess it's time I make my return." He stood up and turned his back to the trio. "Thanks for the good fight."

"Wait there!" Brunhilda called out. "Ye realize ye were set up, right? It looks like they intended for ye to be some mindless beast forever, not to help ye actually ascend."

Mutt grinned. "Well, it looks like I got the better end of it. No one can tame this beast. I am the strongest student in our class, and I intend to prove it."

The orc began walking away when a spark of inspiration flashed in Kiru's mind. "Then join us," he said.

"Oh?" The orc turned his head to the side.

"We are going to compete in the Warrior Games. You won't win without a team, and we won't win without a strong fourth member. Besides, if you join the team that defeated you, you can still say you really are the strongest."

The orc's toothy grin widened.

"Uh, Kiru, shouldn't we talk about this first?" Brunhilda asked nervously.

Zhaden nodded. "I agree with the paladin's words. We should exercise caution in sele—"

"First thing, Sword Guy—" Mutt interrupted Zhaden, not giving either Brunhilda's or the drakonid's words any notice. "That was an undisciplined beast you fought, not my true strength." He chuckled. "Second thing, despite that, I like your cunning. You're clearly a strong fighter, Sword Guy. So fine, I accept your offer."

With that, Pandemonium accepted their fourth member.

After taking time to fully heal Zhaden, the team learned more about their newest teammate. Mutt was apparently royalty himself. He hailed from the orc homeland of Imakandi, and his father was the high chief of the country, which was divided into various regions governed by subservient chiefs. The orc was born blind, but he relished a fight and was kind of ditzy. That, or he just didn't care about the grave severity of events around him. William and the orc immediately hit it off with their mutual love for battle.

"Let's get out of this place. It reeks!" Mutt said.

"Nay, we're supposed to stay until our instructors come back and tell us we can leave the safety of this place," Brunhilda retorted, ever the obedient one.

"While that may have once been the best course of action, I think our most recent fight is evidence that our location's safety has been compromised," Zhaden replied.

The paladin sighed. "I suppose yer right, Zhaden. Then, if someone's after us, I don't think we should go out the way we came in. So, how do ye reckon we leave?"

Mutt clicked his tongue loudly a couple of times, then turned his head to the hole he came through. "Oh, that's easy, let's just go through the way I found you."

"Do you think it's safe?" Kiru asked.

The orc ran over and jumped off the island, flying straight into the dug-out hole. The others stood there in stunned silence before Mutt stuck his head out. "Nobody else here!" He jumped the impressive distance back, displaying the power of a Ruby-rank cultivator. "Let's go," he said, sticking his muscular hand out for Brunhilda to grab.

She crossed her arms. "Hmph, nobody tosses a dwarf!"

"Oh, well, in that case . . ." The blind orc wrapped his arm around her waist.

"What in Hlin's good grace are ye doing?"

"I'm gonna carry you," Mutt replied matter-of-factly.

"No! Wait! This is all happening so fast!" she said, frantically trying to squirm out of his arm. She pressed her hands against the orc's muscular body, and her face went purple. *Was she . . . blushing?!*

Before she could escape his grip, however, Mutt had already leaped, easily carrying the armor-clad dwarf across the cavern. Not trusting in their own ability to make the leap, Kiru and Zhaden let Mutt carry them as well. It was admittedly embarrassing, but they preferred that to falling into the disgusting sewage water below. Before Kiru left, though, he put the shattered headpiece that Mutt had worn into his storage ring. He had a feeling it could be useful, despite its wrecked state.

Pandemonium began their trek through the small tunnel, forced to crawl on all fours. Kiru had recalled William earlier to ensure the little imp couldn't cause any trouble for him. While they crawled, Kiru thought about whether or not he would divulge the truth about his psionic powers to the orc. He'd done so for his other teammates, and that had worked out well. Mutt seemed like an overall good guy, if a little daft and gullible.

Kiru was leaning more toward telling him but, after consideration, decided to hold off on it, just in case. The orc had literally been experimented on, and Kiru had only just met him.

The dark, rocky tunnel smelled of newly churned earth, meaning the entire thing was freshly made. Mutt had clearly dug through solid stone and dirt to find them. The darkness eventually faded as a subtle light appeared. All four of them made it through the tunnel and into a stone room about twenty feet by twenty feet and half as tall. The light was coming from a hole in the ceiling above, and the party quickly discovered that it was moonlight. They were still underground, but only just.

They also quickly discovered that this was no mere stone room. No, it was a tomb! There was a large stone coffin lying in the center of the room. Stone statues of skeletal bodies lay on each of its corners, modeled to look as if they were desperate to keep the coffin lid closed.

"Ugh! It smells just as bad here, only instead of waste, it's like . . . death!" Mutt scratched his ear like a dog. "Anyway, the way out is right up there." He pointed to the hole up in the ceiling.

Kiru took a step toward the coffin. There was something odd about it. Although it exuded a sense of inherent creepiness, something silently drew Kiru closer to it. As he neared, words carved into the stone lid appeared, legible despite their apparent age:

*Great power is placed inside*
*Only for the strong of mind.*
*Often held but rarely touched,*
*Always wet but never rusts,*
*Often bites but seldom bit,*
*To use me well, you must have wit.*

He read aloud. He found a small square depression under the riddle. *A keyhole, perhaps?*

"A riddle? Ooh! I love riddles!" Brunhilda beamed. "But do ye think we should even try to solve it? I mean, this be—"

"Unsettling," Zhaden hissed, agreeing with the paladin. "Perhaps, the best course of action would be to come back after we find the librarian and groundskeeper? That way, we can ensure the threat to our party has passed."

"Come on, you have me now." Mutt pointed to himself proudly. "I don't know who's after you, but they'll have to go through me first. Hey, Sword Guy . . ."

"It's Kiru."

"Oh, yeah. Sorry." The orc chuckled nervously. "You said that we're gonna win the Games, right?"

"Yeah."

"Well, then we're going to need as much power as we can get. So, let's open this sucker!"

While he was apprehensive, Kiru didn't disagree with Mutt. The voice of the overconfident William inside his mind was also cheering for more power. While that would usually inspire Kiru to do the exact opposite, there was something about this tomb . . .

"Fine."

"Yes! So, does anybody know the answer?" Mutt turned back to Zhaden and Brunhilda. They didn't have one.

"It's a tongue," Kiru answered. All of them looked back at him in surprise. He shrugged. The scrolls and tomes he transcribed and sorted while working in the library weren't always related to cultivation or higher forms of education. One such book was *Stubbelfield's Punitive Puns and Ridiculous Riddles: A Book on How to Embarrass Your Teenager.* This exact riddle happened to be in there.

Kiru was truly starting to grasp how powerful a tool his perfect memory could be, in terms of sheer knowledge retention. He'd been focusing on the physical—learning sword forms, battle patterns—and his assigned studies. Now, he more fully realized he needed to get his hands on every bit of knowledge he could. Knowledge was power, and learning more could prove vital in his journeys to come.

Mutt cocked his head. "Hmm, tongue, huh? Okay." The simpleminded orc stuck out his disproportionately long tongue and walked over to the coffin. Before anyone could stop him, he stuck it into the depression. The stone shifted with a click.

"Uh, guyth, my tongue ith thtuck."

A green glow shot from the skeletons' orifices, the carved riddles, and the depression in which Mutt's tongue was stuck. The statues moved on their own, pulling away from their positions. They knelt by the coffin as the light faded from the words. Then, an orb of light surged through the depression and into Mutt's mouth! Whatever had been holding his tongue let go, and the orc coughed and recoiled.

Then, as if an off-button was pressed, Mutt stopped mid-movement. His milky white eyes glowed the same green. "Ahh," the orc sighed. He stood up straighter, popping his spine, and examined his body. "A Ruby with strong physical features and a weak mind. What a perfect vessel!" No longer was he speaking with the harsh and toothy voice of Mutt. This was deeper, smoother, and more masculine.

The orc flexed his muscles. "Oh yeah, it's all coming together!"

Ever the protector, Brunhilda got out the first word. "Who are ye, and what have ye done with Mutt?" she asked with a fierce gaze.

The glowing-eyed orc turned and seemed to realize he wasn't the only one in the room. "Oh, new subjects! How delightful! I apologize, but I don't really have time for this. Now, bow to your new master." The orc's green eyes flashed, and all three of the students collapsed to their knees.

Kiru groaned. The force pushing down on him felt strangely familiar: it was none other than mental mana! Realizing what was happening, Kiru was able to manipulate the mana around his body to allow himself to stand, but only *just*. That was better than what he could say for the rogue or paladin. He was the only one equipped for this kind of fight, and he was barely keeping it together! It was understandable that the others were doing much worse.

"Oh, another psion! It's been a while since I've put my skills to the test. Let's dance."

Kiru's eyes rolled back momentarily, and he almost fell into unconsciousness as he felt the more targeted psionic assault. He regained his composure and visibly shook as he stared the other down. Whether intentionally or not, memories from the being inhabiting Mutt began to leak into Kiru's mind. He began to get an idea of who this was.

It was the spirit of a psion from before the time of Kiru's father—a psion gone rogue, corrupted by his own power. Against the advice of his allies, he had begun experimenting with new ways to use mental mana, many of which were morally dubious, to say the least. After experimenting on a large enough number of unwilling subjects, he'd managed to create his own personal mental mana technique, which he called Subjugate.

Kiru let out a small gasp as realization struck him. Van Blaine had claimed that all psions had the power to dominate minds. He had used that reasoning to commit genocide. Kiru had thought that claim unfounded, but this spirit had indeed created the very technique Van Blaine accused all psions of having. "Subjugate" was, in truth, the power to dominate a mind. This person used that ability and had started a cult that worshiped him. Once this was discovered, his goals were quickly thwarted, and the psion was mortally wounded. Before death could take him fully though, he had escaped with a few of his followers and set up this secret trap room so that his mind could fully subjugate and inhabit another's.

That's what he'd done to Mutt, and he was using Subjugate on Kiru right now! Kiru groaned as blood flowed from his right nostril. *I must resist . . . but how?* He was cycling mana in a protective dome around his mental core, but it appeared to be in vain; the spirit's technique was too strong for Kiru to handle alone.

Luckily, however, he wasn't alone.

*"Fuck off, asshat!"* Wiliam spat to the malevolent spirit, and the familiar inside Kiru's core manifested itself as an orb of red light. William used his own mana to wrap around the psion's core in a protective layer, effectively preventing this spirit's mental invasion.

Kiru groaned in relief at his familiar's aid. With his eyes closed and his focus inward, he noticed a tether of the spirit's mental mana wrapped around his core, trying to break through William's layer of protection. The tether was a slight shade of green the same color as the orb and the glow of Mutt's eyes. The young psion also felt a strange . . . *connection?* He snarled at the possessed orc as he realized it. His face promised retribution. What this spirit had used to tether others could become his own leash.

Kiru began flooding the tether with his own mana.

The orc's glowing eyes widened. "What are you doing? No, you will submit!" More of the malevolent spirit's mana surged forth, siphoning from his orc host and using it to fight against Kiru's. Though the tendril of mana was invisible, occasional green sparks flew between them. It looked like their battle would be a stalemate, but then the spirit's power began slowly gaining ground.

"Hahaha! Imbecile! This dance has been fun, but your fledgling power can't compete. You don't have enough mana!" the spirit gloated.

Kiru's head ached from the exertion and the worsening drain on his body's energy. The exertion grew even worse as he continued to siphon his mana to use his Telekinesis.

*"Master, give him all you got! Crush this fool! You're the king of all the psions!"* the imp cheered.

The familiar's words sparked an idea. "You . . . will . . . submit!" he shouted at the spirit. The golden gem embedded in his forehead flashed, and he stopped using his Telekinesis. Kiru's body went limp. He couldn't see Mutt's face, but he did hear him speak.

"Huh! The king's jewel? No! No, it cannot be!" The spirit's voice trembled with fear.

Now that Kiru no longer needed his mana to fuel his technique, he flooded the tether with even more of his power. It wasn't much more, but it was enough to turn the tide, "I am the rightful king, and *you will submit!*" he shouted.

With a majestic burst, his mana overtook the tether entirely, wrapping around and subjugating the spirit inside the orc's mind.

The orc howled before going suddenly silent. Kiru undeniably held the spirit in the palm of his hands. Unlike a physical mind, the spirit was entirely composed of mental mana. With a flick of Kiru's will, the spirit could be crushed. The green eyes flashed once before the orc fell to his knees. He shivered in fear despite Kiru's limp body splayed out before him.

No longer under the mental exertion from the possessed orc, Brunhilda and Zhaden slowly pushed themselves back up. "Kiru!" the paladin shouted in concern. She ran over to him while Zhaden pressed a dagger to Mutt's throat. "Oh, Kiru! By me granpappy's pickaxe! Are ye alright?" she asked, cradling his head.

"Phew! Yeah, that one took me by surprise." His breath was heavy, but he smiled now that he'd freed his friends. Still, keeping Subjugate intact was causing a constant drain on his mana. He was uncertain whether he'd be able to keep it up if he tried to use Telekinesis again. "Could you lift me up to face him?"

The paladin quickly nodded and did so.

Despite the blade pressed to his throat, the spirit possessing Mutt showed no fear toward the rogue. Instead, he was breathing rapidly, his glowing green eyes staring directly at Kiru, effectively trapped in a prison from Subjugate.

Kiru looked to Zhaden and gestured for him to back off. Zhaden pulled his dagger away and took a step back, still keeping an eye on the orc before them. The orc didn't budge, eyes still locked onto Kiru. "P-P-Please, spare me. I was unaware that I was in the presence of the king of psions."

"Bow."

The orc immediately fell to his palms, pressing his head to the floor.

"You took control of my ally's body and attempted to make my friends and me your slaves. Give me one good reason why I should allow you to continue to exist," Kiru demanded.

"I-I can make you stronger!" the spirit pleaded. "My king, in possessing this orc, I have learned from him about this new era. There are many things that have been lost. I can teach them to you. If you only let me continue controlling this simple buffoon's body, I will gladly enlighten you!"

"Imbecile!" Kiru shouted, mocking the spirit with its own previous insult against him while squeezing and squeezing it with his mana.

The being coughed and whined within Kiru's clutches. "I'm sorry, my king!"

Lips tight with anger, Kiru growled, "This is your last chance. Enlighten me." With a predatory smile, he slightly loosened his mental grip on the spirit.

"Uh- yes! Of course, my king. It is clear you possess the strength of mind and will to overtake my technique. It is my honor to give you the information in its entirety. May you learn my Subjugate, and may it bring you glory." The spirit used the link to gift some mental mana and send every scrap of information he could compile from the recesses of his memory, including conveying how sensitive that information was and how reluctant he was for anyone else to know it.

Kiru's eyes widened as he instantly absorbed the spirit's years of data on the technique. The torture, the horrors, the precision, and utter control the man had achieved in his previous life. Kiru's lips quivered as he saw the countless atrocities the spirit had callously performed, all for the sake of increasing his own power. Tears welled up in his eyes. It was almost too much for him to bear. The only way Kiru could deal with it was by focusing on the technique itself, not the unfortunate victims so as not to be overcome by despair.

Within seconds, he'd taken in all of the information. William was overjoyed.

*"Yes! Master, this is great! Now, no one can dispute that you are the king and that I am William, Breaker of Wills! It doesn't even require much mana for more simple-minded oafs. We can use this technique on the entire school, and your father's hidden item will be ours!"*

*"No, William,"* the psion sent back with an anger that he hadn't felt since he'd seen Ambrose for the first time at the academy. This anger was the only thing helping the psion keep it together, and he used it to fuel himself via Zhaden's visualization method as he continued his telepathic conversation, *"One, if and when we dominate someone's will, it will be an enemy, NOT an innocent. Second, we don't have nearly enough mana to pull that off. Do I make myself clear?!"*

For once, Kiru had managed to genuinely intimidate the imp, and it showed in his response: *"Um . . . okay, Master. Uh . . . we're still gonna crush this jerk, though, right?"*

*"Definitely."* Kiru glared into Mutt's glowing eyes. The spirit had indeed kept his word . . . this time. He had gifted the psion with a technique—sure, a

technique that had and could be used for evil purposes, but a powerful technique, all the same. Kiru didn't want the panicked spirit to feel more secure, though. No, he wanted to keep the malevolent being on the back foot. Copying the scowl he'd seen on many an indignant noble face, Kiru took a page from Ambrose's playbook and took up the role of a tyrannical ruler.

"Do you think that *this* was a worthy tribute to spare your life, mongrel? I already figured out how to use Subjugate. Your information was worthless! Now, this is your final chance. What can you give me so that not only I, but my entire party, will become stronger?"

The spirit possessing Mutt still had his head pressed to the floor. "My king, I know exactly what will aid you in this endeavor. I will gift you with lost knowledge on a better method to ascend to Ruby-rank than the method most use. Please, if you will spare me, I will grant you this information."

"If it is as great as you say, I will spare you," Kiru replied.

With a smile that revealed how confident the spirit felt that he was about to buy his way to safety, he transferred a bit of knowledge. It was the Ruby ascension method used by the lost civilization of Ippo Ogres. Once again, Kiru's eyes widened with the new information he was granted. He gasped as his mind took in the ascension method.

Apparently, before Ragnarok, there was a clan of ogres called the Ippo Ogres living in Jotunheim. During Ragnarok, they had allied with the giants of Jotunheim in a battle against the gods. Their civilization was decimated, and most of the remaining fragments devolved into simple-minded brutes such as trolls and cyclopes. What made them so formidable in their time was that they had discovered an efficient way to outproduce mid-level cultivators to make up the bulk of their army. An army of mostly Ruby-rank cultivators would easily defeat one of Silver and Gold.

The spirit didn't share with Kiru how he'd uncovered such rare information, but the half-elf could tell that it was true. The spirit had even used it himself in his previous life. The most widely used method inside the Great Alliance was a three-step process. The first was to acquire five techniques. The second was to be able to use all five techniques at once. The third was to meditate and accept that those would be the only techniques you would use for the rest of your life. Kiru hadn't put much focus on finding a way for himself to ascend due to his limited number of techniques. Now though, there was more hope.

Unless you had access to the knowledge and resources, you could be forever stuck at Gold- rank this way. The first and biggest barrier was gaining five techniques. Techniques were jealously guarded. Unless you had access to specific manuals, scrolls, or tomes, or were one of the elite students fortunate enough to get a sponsor, you would be stuck trying to create new ones based of pure experimentation. Forging a new technique could be advantageous, but it came with high risk as well. If a cultivator wasn't careful, they could end up doing irreparable harm to themselves while trying to create a technique.

Zane had basically confirmed that that was how Joseph had been bought off. The student had known only four techniques for years, but then "miraculously" learned a new one in order to reach Ruby. Now, while one could do the other two steps without any aid, it definitely didn't hurt to have some mana-restoring and fatigue-dampening pills at the ready. Kiru had learned that was why more of the wealthy, upper-class cultivators ascended higher in rank. The method that the spirit just imparted to Kiru, though, revolutionized the step from Gold to Ruby! There were now only two steps. The first was to acquire just four techniques instead of five. With fewer techniques to spread attention between, the ones the cultivator did know became more focused and powerful while still having enough variety in techniques.

The second step: instead of doing them all at once, the cultivator performed a meditative ritual and accepted the techniques as part of who they were—part of their very being, not just mere tools they could use. This method helped the techniques not only become stronger but easier to wield and manipulate.

Kiru instantly saw the benefit of such a method. It relied far less on financial resources to get stronger. Sure, you still had to learn four techniques, but none of the expensive pills would be required! If such knowledge were commonplace, the rank for the average cultivator within the Alliance would likely be one tier higher at least. The Ippo Ogre army must have been impressive indeed. Being able to field such a large number of higher-rank cultivators was a huge advantage!

"My king . . . is that gift acceptable?"

"It is, and as promised, I will spare you," Kiru answered. Then, with his mana fully wrapping the spirit, he squeezed. It was akin to slowly squeezing a grape in the palm of his hand.

"Grrrraaaahh! You gave your word!" the dying spirit growled at Kiru.

Kiru stared furiously back into the spirit's green eyes. All the horrors, all the terrible things that this thing had done in its life . . . Kiru had never seen a clearer manifestation of evil in his entire life. He knew he couldn't live with himself if he let this spirit threaten any more innocents.

"I spare you from the concerns of this life. Now die, you evil piece of filth!" Kiru spat. With that, the psion clamped down completely, and the evil being possessing Mutt was no more.

*"Master, that was so cool! I have to say I've never been prouder ! Hahaha! Do it again!"*

Kiru didn't acknowledge his bloodthirsty little familiar, instead focusing on his orc ally. The green glow faded from Mutt's eyes, returning them to their familiar milky white. Mutt blinked and resumed his normal hunched-over posture, sniffing and jerking his head up as if he'd been asleep.

"Mutt, you there?" Kiru asked.

The orc was facing one of the walls, scratching the back of his head. "Yeah, I'm here. I . . . saw it all, somehow. Though I have never been able to use my eyes before, the thing controlling me made me watch somehow. I couldn't control my own body." He turned to face the psion. "I know what you did, and I . . . understand what you are, psion."

Kiru's heart raced nervously.

Before he could respond, Mutt zoomed right over to Kiru, picking him up and holding him in a tight embrace.

"Hahaha! I owe you big time! Thanks, Sword Guy!"

"It's . . . Kiru," he groaned in response as the orc's hug limited the expansion of his lungs.

"Oh, yeah! Kiru! Thanks, pal!" He let go of the psion, who dropped to the ground like a limp noodle. "Oh! My bad there."

"It's fine! It's fine!" Kiru replied, activating his Telekinesis on himself. He was terribly low on mana, but he didn't want to go through another hug session with the brutish orc.

"Good to know! Still, Sword Guy—I mean, Kiru . . ." he corrected himself with a toothy grin. ". . . I owe you. If it wasn't for your big brain, I'd still be some sort of puppet. We of the M'Baku Clan repay our debts." His expression turned serious, and he dropped to one knee. "I, M'Baku M'toon, by the laws of my people set by the alpha beast god, Fenrir, pledge my life in your service. I will assist you in your endeavors and keep you from harm. As long as you will have me, I will be a loyal member of your pack. My alpha."

Kiru wanted to tell the orc that was unnecessary, that he didn't need to make some sort of formal pledge to him. He felt, though, that doing that would be some-how wrong. That denying this intense oath would offend Mutt and possibly insult his honor. So, he decided to respond to his words in kind.

"I, Kiru Chromebane, accept your pledge, M'Baku M'toon, with the same gravity with which it was given, but on one condition. You now know that I am a psion, a user of mental mana. I am also the son of a wrongfully convicted father and the rightful ruler of these lands. I am on a quest to recover my father's items, reclaim my kingdom, and save all of Alterra from another Draconic Campaign." Kiru gestured to Zhaden and Brunhilda. "My pack are my friends. My pack are my family. If you swear to aid me in this quest, or if you cannot, swear that you will keep my identity and plans a secret. If so, I offer you my hand in friendship."

"Of course!" Mutt exclaimed, gripping Kiru's hand tight and shaking it emphatically. "How could I say no? If that is the caliber of enemies we'll be fac-ing, we have so many good fights ahead of us! It's gonna be so much fun!" With that, Mutt became a full-fledged member of Pandemonium.

# CHAPTER THIRTY-EIGHT

# Technicality

R*elease us!*" one voice said.

"*Kill!*" the other demanded.

Niazen glowered as he tried to fight off the voices in his mind once more. If Van Blaine found out what he had done, the king would kill him. Now, dealing with the consequences of his actions, the headmaster was almost wishing he would. What would his family's founder think if he knew? No, morality was a weakness. Only power mattered. He had made his sacrifices to acquire this power, and he would damn well keep it. By his strength, he would bring glory to the J'sarko house, and he would force those weak idealists like his brother to serve him, as they should.

As if summoned by his thoughts, Niajar burst through the doors of the head-master's office. His trademark grin was completely gone this time, replaced by an uncharacteristic scowl. Niazen placed his drink back on his desk and raised an eyebrow. "Librarian."

"Niazen," the librarian growled, intentionally ignoring his brother's title.

Niazen's face grew stern as he waited for his brother to tell him why he'd barged in.

"You broke your oath! You've sworn that you wouldn't interfere with my pupil, yet that's exactly what you did!" the librarian shouted.

"How so, Librarian? In case you've forgotten, I said I would not interfere, unless your latest protégé broke the rules. He did so by intruding into an unchecked section of school grounds without proper permission. So I acted, and you can easily confirm for yourself that our soul-binding agreement is still intact."

Niajar ground his teeth. "That area *isn't* school grounds. It is an abandoned part of the sewage system."

"I disagree. It's under the library, which is part of the academy, so there it also is part of the academy."

Niajar pinched the bridge of his nose in annoyance. "You know, Brother, acting coy is my thing. It really doesn't suit you at all." His look of annoyance changed to a scowl. "You damn well know what you did and why. You had the cleric send out one of his science projects to assassinate my pupil because you got scared."

Though his outer expression was neutral, the headmaster was temporarily overcome with paranoia. His brother had discovered his secret? How?! He held his breath, ready to eliminate Niajar from the world.

"You know, in different circumstances, I simply would've reported you to the authorities for allowing that cleric's malevolent experiments on students, but I'd wager your acquaintance, Van Blaine, knows all about it."

"That's *King* van Blaine, and don't you forget it!" Niazen barked angrily, his expression covering his relief. Good, his brother didn't know the true extent of what he'd done. He needed to keep it that way.

"*Yes! Kill!*" one of the voices howled.

Niazen tensed his hand like a claw, then recomposed himself, changing it to a pointing finger. No, even though he could squash his brother, it would still take a lot out of him. Plus, the pleasure of rubbing Niajar's smug nose in his failures was much more satisfying. "The king is aware that I've allowed the cleric to indulge in his . . . curiosities," he admitted.

"Well, I would try to appeal to your morality on the issue of students being kidnapped, tortured, and experimented on, but clearly, morals are low on your priority list. So, let me communicate in a manner that you *will* listen to." He furrowed his brow at his dark-haired brother. Despite that, a confident smirk appeared on Niajar's face. "I was too cocksure and didn't take enough time to ensure our oath was rock solid. You took advantage of that and tried to manipulate the arrangements of our agreement to cheat your way to victory. Now, clearly your relationship with the king has afforded you some protection from harm within the Kingdom of Blades." He held a finger up. "But, what if, the other countries found out? What if the powerful rulers of multiple nations found out that their dead and missing children were actually secret playthings for some deranged, one-eyed madman?"

Niazen snarled. "Get to the point!"

"Call off all efforts in trying to harm my pupil and his team. I will personally oversee the rest of their training, and they will remain unharmed in my care. After you agree to that, then we will add additional amendments to our original agreement to prevent any other . . . *misinterpretations*. Do that, and I will continue to keep your cleric's curiosities secret."

The headmaster's scowl deepened. The voices moaned in defiance of his grip. If they couldn't gain control, they would make their jailor feel their anger.

Niajar's eyebrow quirked as he looked at his brother. Despite Niazen's still form, his strange shoulder pauldrons seemed to . . . move?

Before Niajar could say anything about them, Niazen lashed out. Without words or motions, Niajar was flung into the wall with violent force. Though Niajar was not a fighter, he was undeniably a strong cultivator. He and his brother were the only Emeralds in the entire academy to reach the top tier, Complete Emerald. Yet the ability Niazen was now displaying was unlike anything the librarian had ever experienced before!

Niajar coughed blood, eyes bulging with panic. Meanwhile, Niazen floated effortlessly out of his chair, none of the typical purple fire around him, and flew over to his brother. "Do you honestly think you can threaten me? I am the headmaster!" His voice was somehow coming from multiple different directions, despite him being only inches from Niajar's face. "Give me one good reason I shouldn't rid myself of your constant annoyances."

"If you kill me, I've ensured that the leaders from all of the other nations will know of your deeds. They will demand your head, and the king will give it to them to preserve the peace," he choked out. "You may not fear me, but you do fear him and what he'll do to our house if you're caught!"

Niazen flared his nostrils. Niajar was right. Even though Niajar hadn't discovered the full extent of Niazen's experiments, his damnably persistent brother still had enough evidence to damn him and the J'sarko house. He couldn't risk it.

Shaking, the headmaster wrestled back control from the voices in his head, easing the pressure off his brother. "Fine! I will no longer look for any loopholes in our arrangement to stop your precious Defunct." He turned his back and waved off his injured brother, who fell to his knees. "It matters not. Your team of three Golds cannot hope to defeat a squad possessing two Rubies."

Niajar winced in pain as he stood. "Agreed." His face conveyed a mixture of pain and, for the first time, doubt. Niajar channeled one of his healing techniques. and his bruised, damaged skin turned into pieces of bark and fell off the elf like shed snakeskin.

"Ah," he sighed in notable relief. "See you in three months, Brother," he said, flashing his trademark grin once more.

Pandemonium clawed their way up to the hole at the top of the underground tomb, finding themselves right by the wall at the edge of the campus. Mutt scouted around first, using his attuned senses to check for enemies. After he gave the all-clear, he helped the other three up.

"Where should we go?" Brunhilda whispered. "Sword House?"

Kiru shook his head. "The hidden training room was our best bet. They're not likely going to help us in Sword House with . . . you know . . . *me*," he said, pointing to his red, dirty Fist House jacket. "We've established the security of Fist and Shield House aren't good enough. So, there's only one place I'd recommend." He pointed to a familiar shack and barn not far off in the distance. Giiyam's place.

When they arrived, the stoic half-orc was there and on edge. They found him following a set of tracks on the ground for what turned out to be Mutt. He almost attacked the party outright when he noticed the new addition to their group. It was fair to say with his scars, completely white eyes, unkempt hairy appearance, and partially hunched-over posture that Mutt didn't look like an average student, so Giiyam's response was understandable. After the groundskeeper learned that the blind orc was not a foe, he quickly ushered them into his home. Giiyam did, however, raise an eyebrow upon seeing Mutt following them with no need for assistance at all.

"Forgive my bluntness, but how are you able move about with such ease?" he asked Mutt.

The blind orc cocked his head in confusion, "Uh, with my legs?"

Brunhilda sighed and rolled her eyes, a slight smile on her face, "He be meaning how can ye move even though ye be blind."

"Oh! My other senses are enough. I also can feel vibrations in the ground," he said and lifted up one of his bare feet, wriggling his toes.

Shortly afterwards, Giiyam brought them some tea, and they informed him of what had happened since they last had seen each other, leaving out the psion stuff, merely saying they'd found a tomb.

Not long afterwards, Niajar arrived. He was a little thrown off by the dirty, wild-haired, blind orc sitting with them and tried to politely exclude him from the conversation. "I think it may be best for our new hairy friend to head back to his dormitory," the librarian said to the three other students. "I have news that's more, *er, hem*, sensitive."

"Oh! You talking about where I was sent to kill Kiru here? Hahaha! We've resolved that, buddy! We're friends now!" That shut up the talkative elf. He just blinked, dumbfounded for a few seconds, processing Mutt's words.

Giiyam explained what the party had told him, only much more concisely.

"Well, this is an exciting development! I knew you could make friends, no matter how many hours you hid in my library!" Niajar said, putting a hand on Kiru's shoulder.

"Hey! That's where I have to be for my internship!"

The blond elf waved off Kiru's very valid point, then readdressed the party as a whole. "In regards to any future threats, that time has passed. I've ensured your safety. Nevertheless, your proclivity for making enemies has made the academy . . . *unsafe* until the Games. So, you will be under my direct supervision until then."

"Where are we staying?" Brunhilda asked.

"I have a few guest rooms inside my library. Giiyam will fetch your things. You'll be living there until the semester's over."

The half-orc's nostrils flared, the only sign of any agitation at being volunteered for such a task.

Niajar paid him no mind. "As long as you're within the main building, no one will touch you."

"But what about our studies and the shrine to Hlin over at the tavern in Waketown?" Brunhilda protested.

"A shrine in a tavern? Odd place, but I assume the workers can take of it." He waved it off, clearly not concerned. "As for your studies, I will be taking over as your substitute instructor for all your courses. Now, I am no paladin, but my library has a plethora of knowledge on numerous subjects, so I shall be a sufficient first-year's instructor for your more general courses. As for the more advanced things. I should have some books that will help," he said, not very confidently.

"Fine. I won't make a fuss, as long as ye allow me to build a small shrine in the library. Ye be preventing me from cultivating inside the school's chapel. That place has plenty of life mana, the holiest of all mana types. If I can't go in there, that'll really lengthen the time I'll need to cultivate."

Niajar sighed and pinched the bridge of his nose. "Very well, you may make a small shrine in your guest room."

"Yes!" She clinched her gauntleted fist in triumph. With the immediate threat now past, the team of four was escorted back to the library. No longer would they be able to go outside or even to their secret training room. The large chamber full of books would be their only home for the next few months.

# CHAPTER THIRTY-NINE

# Research

Over the course of the next two months, Giiyam continued to personally instruct the four members of Pandemonium three nights a week inside the library in secret while Niajar taught them during the day. Escobert was furious. He stormed into the library and threatened to raze it to the ground, but upon Niajar showing a scroll signed by the headmaster, the dwarf stopped his tirade. He was still mad, but his hands were clearly tied.

Before he left the library, Escobert found Kiru and all but threatened the psion that he better continue his combat studies. Kiru quickly nodded his head in agreement. He had planned to anyway, and he wanted to make sure that the angry dwarf had no reason to doubt that. The boy had no illusions that the retired general couldn't crush him like an insect had the dwarf wanted to. Seemingly appeased, Escobert abruptly stomped off and left the library.

Though Niajar was eccentric, the elf was actually a competent instructor in the numerous varied subjects the four were learning. He did, however, provide *a lot* of reading assignments. The others moaned, but for Kiru and his perfect recall, it was a piece of cake! Mutt crossed his arms, giving a smug grin. Being blind meant he couldn't read books, he said

The librarian wasn't foiled. He brought a little construct for the beast mana cultivator. Kiru's eyebrows raised as the elf handed Mutt a stone tablet, and a familiar small construct appeared on top.

"Hello, there!" Daisy Directory cheerily said to the orc.

"Ugh! Not again! More audiobooks!" the orc moaned.

"Oh, don't be such a sourpuss!" the construct rebuked.

"Quite right!" Niajar added. "Audiobooks are a lot of fun! You can not only learn but be taken to new worlds. Once you're done with your studies today, I recommend listening to the one called *Dr. Druid*. Fantastic trilogy!"

Kiru admittedly found the idea of those audiobooks appealing, but he needed to focus. Fun was lower on the priority list, especially when he was so close to his goal. Armed with new knowledge on how to ascend to Ruby-rank, the psion did more of what he should've done when he started his internship. He read. And he didn't just simply read. He ravenously absorbed every single piece of parchment he could get his hands on.

His main goal was to find any lost, hidden, and/or misplaced information regarding ascension or techniques. If he could find a mental mana, life mana, or nature mana technique so he or his friends could have four in total, they would have another Ruby-ranked cultivator in their squad along with Mutt! Unfortunately, he was unsuccessful in finding any helpful manuals for him or his allies, since techniques were so jealously guarded.

However, the psion truly did learn *a lot*. Being from a quiet, isolated mining town, his overall knowledge had been lacking. His entire journey leaving Bristleton and getting to the academy had been a huge culture shock. He had seen and learned so much, and he'd only traveled within the small kingdom he lived in! It was fair to say he had been naïve to say the least. Now, though, even if a book he picked up didn't have the information he'd been looking for, it was still of use.

The tomes spanned a wide variety of topics. Kiru read history books, mining charts, maps, a bestiary, a monster manual, a book on the intricacies of both chess and pai sho, and eight different books on the main dialects found about Alterra. Using the information from the language books and listening to students speaking in their native tongues around him, Kiru was able to fully grasp the different dialects he listened to. His accent was rough, but if he were to visit foreign lands now, he would be able to generally be understood.

He now knew Common, Elven, Orcish, Draconic—which was hardest of all, since his mammalian face couldn't fully do what a reptilian one could—Gnomish, Dwarven, and a few different variations of some of them. Those variations were High Elven, a speech pattern used primarily by nobility, Coastal Dwarf, which used laughs and many more "Arrs" in their speech, and a strange human language from a dusty book he found hiding behind some others.

It was an ancient tome from a time pre-Ragnarok. It contained an old human language called "Japanese." That one was fun! The language was dramatic and relied on inflections. The first time Kiru went "*nani?*" his friends gave him a curious stare, so he decided to keep that joke to himself. The reason he was able to learn this dead language was that it had a primer comparing it to another dead language, English, which the Common dialect everyone spoke was based off of.

Kiru also found multiple books and scrolls recounting battles, war strategies, and fighting tactics. He even managed to find a copy of *The Art of War*, just like the one his mother had given him! Re-reading that book brought a smile to his face as he relived fond memories of her. The psion even found the *Dr. Druid* book Niajar had mentioned. The librarian had been right. It *was* a fun read!

Going off to the Sciences section, Kiru read a few books on physiology and botany, learning about cells and how blood flows, specifically the importance of mitochondria in increasing the efficiency of absorbing mana into your body. The book also listed a few different foods to help boost someone's mitochondria. Someone had taken a quill and actually underlined some of them with a hand-written note that promised, "If eaten daily, it will help provide up to a five percent boost in cultivation uptake over time."

That was huge! After reading that, he had his friends make sure they ate a portion of blueberries, beef, and spinach daily—anything to help them absorb more mana easily. Though the party was growing in a lot of respects, they were still lacking a major component to help get any of them to Ruby-rank: techniques. Kiru had hoped having access to an entire library of one of the world's most prestigious academies would've given him at least *some* enlightenment for his path. Unfortunately, this was not the case. Kiru knew it had been a long shot. With the taboo status on psions, it made sense why no evidence of mental mana techniques were available. The only book the library had regarding the subject was Van Blaine's biography. It talked about how brave and selfless he had been as he purged the mental mana cultivators from the kingdom. Truth was, it was genocide, simple as that. Instead of any valuable information, all the book gave Kiru was a feeling of disgust.

Brunhilda didn't have much luck, either. The Order of Valhalla tightly regulated technique information for their followers only, and anyone who wished to follow a certain path as a paladin or cleric had to get approval from them first. Once approved, Brunhilda said that most often, technique acquirement was a matter of politicking. It was a field that she was notably lacking in given her overly zealous nature and the fact that her deity wasn't a major god. So, it wasn't shocking that no random glowing divine tome had leapt out at her from a shelf.

That left Zhaden's dream mana. There *were* some tomes on that subject, but they were mostly full of conjecture, as well as recommendations on how to combat it. There were no technique manuals.

Reading up on dream mana did, however, spark Kiru's memory that it was a variation on nature mana. There may be some connection there he could exploit.

*"Master, learning stuff is great and all, but all we do is that and fight that half-orc guy. When are we gonna kick some baddie's ass again?"* William asked, interrupting his train of thought.

*"Maybe when I can find two more techniques for Zhaden to learn,"* Kiru replied.

*"Pfft! That's easy. He uses that nature crap, right?"*

*"Yeah."*

*"Then go ask that scary librarian. He uses nature, too. He's bound to have some books on the stuff somewhere,"* William said.

Kiru's eyebrows raised. A genuine smile grew on his face. *"You know, William, that's a great idea!"*

*"Duh! I'm full of great ideas! That's why you should listen to me more!"*

Recalling that the imp liked to store things between his skull and exposed brain, Kiru decided not to challenge his familiar's assertion, instead just letting William feel good about himself. Pressing past a pair of Shield House students doing some research, Kiru quickly made it to the section where he found his monster manual. He then found an old scroll labeled *"Jotunheim & Its Inhabitants."*

Sure enough, there was a chapter on ogres in there. Only a few sentences were dedicated to the Ippo Ogres that he'd learned about from the spirit he defeated. It was remarkably sparse when it came to pertinent information, however. He then went over some basic cultivation manuals. He found one that had a rubric and graph detailing ascension within a humanoid body.

Kiru had an idea.

He grabbed ink, parchment, and quill and scurried over to an isolated room to put his plan to action. None of his friends would like it, but if he didn't take a risk, it would mean this whole year was wasted. Neither he nor the world could afford that!

Thinking on risks, Kiru again considered confessing his secret to the librarian and Giiyam but decided again that it was better not to. With how quiet and secretive Giiyam was, Kiru couldn't be sure he wasn't oathbound to report him or something. And while Niajar had been a good ally to Kiru, the psion still wasn't ready to trust him in that capacity. While more open with Kiru than Giiyam, it was evident that the enigmatic elf had his own secrets and was clearly not helping him out of altruism. The librarian was looking to profit from Kiru in some form or capacity.

Kiru began frantically transcribing the Jotunheim scroll but decided to add a new section not previously there before. By the time Kiru was done, there was a nifty new chart on the "Ippo Ogre Ruby Ascension Method."

Next, Kiru needed to get rid of the evidence. Niajar was very attached to his books. As such, he allowed no open flames within the library and he tried to recycle any parchment he could. "William?"

"Yes, Master?" he answered as Kiru summoned him out of his core.

"I need you to go find and catch a rat for me."

"A rat? Why? You hungry?" William asked.

"What? No!" Kiru said in clear disgust.

The imp just shrugged.

"I need you to get a rat and bring it here so it can destroy this old scroll."

The ugly little demon's beady eyes widened. "Uh, Master, while I love unnecessary destruction, I think that's a bad idea." He quickly looked over his shoulders as if someone were in the small, enchanted room with them. "You know how the weird book guy is. He'll kill me!" he whispered in genuine fear.

"Relax. He won't know about it. Trust me, you do this, and we'll get back to kicking ass real soon."

"Promise?" William asked.

"Promise," Kiru assured his familiar.

"Fine, but you gotta sweeten the pot some more. I'm all about beating some people up, but if I'm gonna risk my neck, I need something in return," The imp said.

Kiru sighed. "What?"

William gave a toothy grin and cackled, rubbing his hands together in glee. "You know how Palabitch likes to take naps sometimes?"

"Yeah."

"And how she snores really loud?"

"Yeah."

"You have to let me draw on her face next time she snores during the day."

There was a heavy silence as Kiru thought about the offer. He didn't prefer pissing off the dwarf, but the benefits far outweighed the risks. "Hlin, I hope you understand," he said, looking up. "William, you got yourself a deal."

"Aw, yeah!" After that, the imp scurried out of the room. William came back a few minutes later, munching loudly, and presented a headless rat to Kiru.

Kiru's eyebrow twitched in annoyance. "I need it to be alive, William."

The imp grinned. "Just messing with you, Master," he said and held another rat out in his other hand. This one had its head intact. It was notably malnourished and looked hungry. That worked for Kiru. The psion had laid his body against a wall and gone limp, halting his Telekinesis so he could better focus on the rodent and not split his focus on keeping himself up. Whenever he tried to do something like that, his control was at risk of being sloppier, and Kiru didn't want sloppy.

Kiru restarted his Telekinesis but this time focusing on the rat. He carried it over to the scroll and set it atop the table. The psion had sprinkled some crumbs on it earlier. The rat at first clearly wanted to bolt but, upon seeing food, it ravenously began consuming every scrap. When there were no more crumbs, it began eating the scroll. Kiru let the rodent eat its fill until a good fourth of it had been consumed.

"All right, that's enough." Kiru said. He was about to pick up the rat with Telekinesis once more, but William beat him to it. The imp flung the rat directly into his mouth and bit down with a satisfying crunch.

"Hm, the paper adds a new consistency to the dish. I like the texture," William said with a mouth full of rat, critiquing it like some connoisseur of raw rodent.

Kiru opened his mouth to say something, but sheer disgust and shock kept any words from coming out. He needed to read a book on teaching manners to children, to the imp. William was in firm need of some instruction. Putting the little demon's disgusting food choices out of his mind, Kiru grabbed the ruined scroll and his forgery and began making his way to Niajar's office.

"Niajar!" *Knock, knock, knock.* "Niajar!" Kiru said excitedly.

The eccentric elf opened the door. "Why, if it isn't my favorite pupil! How may I be of assistance? Your training with Giiyam isn't for another couple of hours . . ."

"Have you read this before?" Kiru asked, making sure to sound shocked.

"*Jotunheim & Its Inhabitants,*" he read. "No, it was a donated piece written by the patriarch of a noble family two hundred years ago, I believe." His eyes widened. "Yes! Yes, that's right. His name was Jayson Ronald. Nice human. Fascinated with pre-Ragnarok history. Why do you ask?"

Kiru pressed it into the elf's chest. "I just finished transcribing it. You need to read it."

"All right, all right. I'll do it after I finish my work."

"Now!" the psion interrupted.

Startled, the librarian obliged. He led Kiru into his office and opened the scroll on his desk, then began reading. Kiru pointed to the section he'd added. Niajar's mouth began moving, muttering under his breath. "Ippo . . . Ogres? But, but how? Oh! In-Incredible!" he said in disbelief. "What a spectacular find!" He put a hand on Kiru's shoulder, like a doting parent. "I knew you'd make a phenomenal librarian! Research and discoveries like this can change the world! That's why our work is so important, gathering knowledge for the benefit and enlightenment of all! I dare say, you are on the fast track to becoming the best librarian in the kingdom. Well . . . second best." He winked.

Kiru felt a pang of guilt for lying to Niajar but managed to suppress it. "You're right! Sharing knowledge to help all, not just nobles, is what we all should strive for."

"Indeed! Well said, my boy! Now, can I see the original document? I need to verify your findings."

Kiru braced himself. This was the linchpin of his plan. He put on a pained smile. "Ah, about that. Before I could come over to tell you—"

"A rat ate some of it," William finished. He had followed Kiru over to the elf's office, keeping to himself until that moment so as to not draw the librarian's ire.

"It's true," he lied, then showed the ruined scroll.

"You let a rat in my library?" he asked Kiru with a touch of anger in his voice.

"No, no, sir! They were already here!" Kiru noticed that they really were, but they were scarce.

"Really? I have a hard time believing that, since we have constructs that remove any and all pests from this facility."

"I know what you mean, but I think the secret chamber we had trained in has . . . rats." He shrugged.

The librarian pressed the bridge of his nose. "I trust you at least disposed of the vermin."

"Oh, yeah! I ate it!" William finished the statement by belching loudly.

Before the elf could go off on a tirade, Kiru decided to distract him and dangle the bait of the offer he had come up with. "Do you know what this knowledge means, Niajar?"

"Well, if this knowledge is accurate, it could revolutionize cultivation as a whole! Thousands of people will be able to reach Ruby where it was once impossible," the elf answered.

"Yes, including my team!"

Niajar's eyes widened, then narrowed, a sly grin on his face. "Indeed, my pupil. May I ask, have any of your allies acquired four techniques?"

"Ah . . . no."

"Then, pray tell, how can your team use this?" the elf asked.

"Well, I was thinking. You're the head librarian, and you told me you're the head of your entire family."

"Yes."

"So, you must have access to plenty of rare books, such as some technique manuals . . ."

"Kiru, we've been over this."

"But!"

"I cannot allow you access to the library's restricted section," Niajar interrupted. "For starters, it is wildly reckless. If you were to read a book beyond your level, you could do unnecessary, irreversible damage to yourself and others. Some of the magic inside those tomes is very dangerous even to an expert. Also, since this method you've discovered is untested, it would be wildly inappropriate." He put a hand on Kiru's shoulder. "I've placed my faith in you and bet on your success. I don't want to take any untested risks right now."

Kiru sighed and squeezed his right hand into a fist, his resolve not broken, despite his sponsor's resistance. "Unless we find a new way, our growth will always be controlled. In order to advance, we have no choice but to put ourselves in the debt of others. Even this academy that helps its students far surpass the abilities of a mere common cultivator has a high cost.

"If you don't have the gold, you must pledge servitude to the army or become indebted to an organization like the religious Order of Valhalla or one of the guilds." He remembered how Joseph had mentioned that his uncle had advanced through serving in the army, then being placed as the head of a mercenary company. Likely, that mercenary group was paying for his schooling in some form or fashion.

Kiru looked to his mentor, a serious expression on his face. "Please. You don't have to let us in there. From my studies, I've learned that dream mana originated from Alfheim, just like your nature mana. Dream mana also just so happens to be what Zhaden uses. You have to have some books regarding that in your personal collection." The eccentric elf had one particular interest, and that was Alfheim, the original home of the elves. Niajar had even said that was their family's original patriarch's passion. Kiru had a strong hunch that the librarian had to have related tomes tucked away somewhere.

"Perhaps I may have the items you're referring to. Still, it would go against the rules. I cannot provide direct aid in rank-ascension to a student who I am not the sponsor of. Now, I'm not always the biggest rule-follower, but circumstances have changed that, for the time being."

Kiru smiled. He'd prepared for this line of defense. "Good thing he's from the Serpent Isles, and as a student from another nation, he has no official sponsor. So, if he were to 'happen' upon some new techniques, rather than be taught them by someone, it wouldn't be against any rules, now, would it?"

Niajar put a hand to his chin in thought. His face was at first contemplative, then surprised. Then a scheming smile grew that matched Kiru's. "My boy, you really have done your research. I'm impressed! You really will make a fantastic librarian! On your graduation here, I will personally refer you to the Grand Hall of Studies at Anor'Voren."

Kiru smiled. He didn't intend on graduating, so he was fine with that. "Deal!"

# CHAPTER FORTY

# Ascension

Ye sure we should be doing this?" Brunhilda asked, being the cautious mother hen of the group.

"Oh, yeah! He'll be fine!" Mutt answered, not concerned at all, before scratching the back of his left ear with his foot. "That's the spot!"

"I know it's scary, but Niajar should be able to better guide Zhaden as he ascends. Niajar is an Emerald, after all. I have the base knowledge from reading the ascension method, but I don't have the experience of ascending that high yet. Like it or not, this is our best chance. His powerful healing should help rectify any unforeseen side effects, too," Kiru explained.

"And if he can't fix 'em?" Brunhilda interjected.

"Then it's a good thing we have a paladin and skilled healer on standby. Hahaha!" Mutt chuckled, putting his arm around the dwarf.

Her face flushed in embarrassment. She had told Kiru that dwarves considered lots of hair and a muscular body *very* attractive, and the orc had both in droves, though his oblivious nature made him completely unaware of Brunhilda's feelings in that regard. It did, however, bring a smile to Kiru and Zhaden, who understood the paladin's plight.

It was midnight, and Pandemonium's members were in the back of the library. Niajar had started closing the place down for eight hours during the evening so he could ensure that the place had been cleared out for Giiyam's training and could reorient the bookshelves to make a large training arena. That was where the elf was waiting on the drakonid expectantly.

"Zhaden, if you really don't want to risk it, you don't have to do this," Kiru said. "I respect your choice, and don't want to impose something untested on my friends. This is my burden. You don't need to put yourself at risk for my quest."

"*Yes, he does have to do this!*" William asserted. "*We need to figure this shit out!*"

"However, I do trust the information I was given. Will you trust me?"

"Hlin knows I trust you, Kiru, but it seems too risky. Who knows what this method will do to him?" Brunhilda asserted before the drakonid could answer. "Ye said that the spirit claimed this method came from ogres, right? What's to say it doesn't turn him into one? I say we be getting plenty strong enough on our own. We be so much stronger than we were before."

Zhaden shook his head. "Unfortunately, our opponents are as well, and if Kiru is to be believed about the state of the world, our fellow classmates will be the most minor of our enemies to come."

"Oh, man! I mean, I hope the world doesn't go to war, but if we fight a dragon? Awesome," Mutt smiled.

The others didn't share the orc's optimistic opinion. Reminded of the more serious threats they all faced, both the paladin and psion's faces quickly went from concern to resolved. "Still, this isn't without risk. Do you trust me?" Kiru asked.

Zhaden wagged his large tail in a display that Kiru had learned meant he was happy. He gave a hissing laugh. "I appreciate your concern, but the fate of Alterra involves us all. Besides, we gold drakonids are especially involved in protecting the world from our chromatic brethren. The risk this imposes doesn't change that. Your quest is still mine as well, my friend. I trust you."

That made Kiru pause. He had considered his teammates his friends, but the drakonid was more serious, objective, and analytical. Not once had he ever expressly called Kiru more than an ally, until that moment. The psion smiled. "Thank you."

Zhaden nodded and the party left the silenced room in the library to go to where the bookshelves had been specifically oriented to give them a makeshift training area. It was night, and Niajar had instituted a new strict curfew nearly every evening to allow the students time to train. They could no longer use the sewer training arena as that was breaking the rules, so the library itself was their next best option. After a couple of minutes, they made it to the area and found both Niajar and Giiyam waiting. Kiru was personally glad to see Giiyam again because he knew the half-orc would have to leave soon to prepare the arena for the Games.

Niajar had been specific that he couldn't directly help the drakonid ascend, but if Zhaden said a specific set of phrases, the librarian would have to make sure Zhaden was okay. He didn't go into it, but the elf told Kiru that he had made a *particular* agreement to keep the members of Pandemonium safe, and the elf needed to make sure he did nothing to break it.

"Er, hem," Zhaden cleared his throat. "I am going to attempt a new way to ascend to Ruby under no coercion. No member of the academy can stop my attempt at this even though it is very dangerous," he recited the memorized lines.

The librarian grinned and put a hand to his chest in false exasperation. "Oh, my goodness. I cannot advise you to do such a thing, student. If I cannot convince you to stop, then as a member of the Royal Academy I cannot in good conscience let you attempt this without staying as a means to ensure you don't hurt yourself."

Giiyam rolled his eyes, clearly annoyed with the whole farce.

Niajar stuck out his right hand and tapped the ring on his pointer finger. Immediately, as if out of thin air, an old, ragged purple tome appeared right above the ring. It was obvious that it was an enchanted storage device like the one Kiru had. The librarian caught the book, then delicately dropped it just a couple of inches to the floor. He repeated that three more times: two more books appeared, one green and the other black, and then a scroll.

"When you do attempt this reckless, untested method, please let me know so that I can work to ensure you are unharmed," Niajar said, promptly turning away from the pile of reading material and examining some other books on a nearby shelf as if they were suddenly extremely interesting to him at the moment.

Wanting to see what happened, Mutt, Kiru, and Brunhilda stayed to watch. If this worked, the paladin and psion could use this method, too!

Zhaden hurried to the piled-up books and tome and sat in lotus position. First, he opened the scroll and studied the Ippo Ogre ascension to Ruby method. Once done, the rogue quickly took the three tomes and eagerly began scanning through, muttering to himself. Not wanting to waste their time, Brunhilda, Kiru, Mutt, and Giiyam decided to cultivate. Niajar continued to keep an eye on the gold drakonid in case something were to happen.

Kiru wondered idly why Giiyam was cultivating. Sure, there were the typical reasons that many people cultivated: helping to prevent impurities from building up, and providing the body with some energy. Giiyam was anything but typical, though. The groundskeeper was strong, ridiculously so. *I'll have to do some more research on Giiyam. There's more to him than meets the eye*, he thought.

Everyone sat in the lotus position while Kiru laid on his back. That way, he could stop using Telekinesis on himself and restore more mana instead of getting a zero-sum gain. It also helped when he cultivated in the library proper, as the mental mana density was so much thicker there. The stoic half-orc looked at Kiru but didn't say anything before going back to cultivating.

After a few more hours, Niajar finally announced that it looked like Zhaden was now three techniques stronger. The three opened their eyes to see the lanky rogue standing beside the elf with his tail wagging happily side-to-side like a dog. "Well, let's see 'em, then!" Brunhilda said excitedly.

Mutt began sniffing loudly.

Kiru's eyes narrowed. Something seemed odd about Zhaden. His silhouette seemed to shimmer slightly.

"What're you doing?" Mutt asked behind the party. "He's right here."

They turned and saw the blind orc pointing . . . at Zhaden! There was another Zhaden standing right behind them.

"By Hlin's mighty shields!" the paladin exclaimed in fear.

The tall assassin was hissing in laughter.

"Duplication," Niajar called over. "The user manipulates dream mana to form an illusory duplicate of themselves." He then waved his hand through the duplicate, causing it to fade into mist. "A great tool for a roguish fighter, but clearly ineffective for those who do not depend on sight, like Mutt. Next is . . ."

With a snap of Zhaden's fingers, Niajar abruptly fell silent, despite the fact that his mouth was still moving.

"The Silence technique. My mana distorts the sound coming off a source, muffling and dispersing it so much that it eliminates all noise," the drakonid explained.

Realizing that he was not being listened to, Niajar tapped his foot and looked at him expectantly. Zhaden snapped his scaly fingers, and the elf's voice instantly returned.

"The last technique is . . ."

"One that shouldn't be done here. It's a powerful one that shouldn't be tested on allies," Niajar interrupted, clearly uncomfortable with the idea.

"Well, what's it do?" Kiru asked.

"Well, there are good dreams, and then there are nightmares. That technique feeds on those nightmares and . . . let's say, brings them to life," Niajar explained.

Giiyam gave a subtle eyebrow raise at that, while both Brunhilda and Kiru stared at Zhaden with a mixture of both awe and newfound fear. Anyone who could bring nightmares to life was someone you didn't want as your enemy. Aside from the awe and fear Kiru felt about this final technique he also had to admit that he felt strangely excited. Even though he had not personally seen the Ippo Ogre Ascension Method firsthand, he knew that it would work. The spirit had been utterly positive that the information he'd given Kiru was accurate. Kiru had no reason to doubt it. Even Giiyam gave a subtle eyebrow raise at that. Kiru was especially glad Zhaden didn't know that technique when he'd ambushed them back in the library.

"So, is it time for him to ascend?" Brunhilda asked.

Niajar grinned. "Yes, but I suggest you keep your distance. Ascending to Ruby is a more volatile step in comparison to the previous steps, and I'm unsure what performing this new method of ascension will be like."

Taking his warning to heart, the others made sure to stand near the very edge of the makeshift arena. Zhaden sank into the lotus position in the center with Niajar standing nearby. "Now, from what I've gathered, you need to accept these techniques as part of your identity. You must attain enlightenment and make these four part of your very being. Think of your goals, your dreams."

The gold drakonid closed his eyes, conjuring his desires before his mind's eye.

"Speak it into being! Make it real!" Niajar ordered with fervor.

"I wish to join the Fangs. I wish to gain esteem for Clan Ironclaw. I wish—" His reptilian eyes opened, locking onto Kiru's. "—to ensure another Draconic Campaign never happens again on Alterra, as all gold drakonids should."

Giiyam's eyes widened in shock momentarily at his words. Before anyone else could notice, they returned to his regular neutral look.

"Good! Excellent! Think about those now, my boy! Your goals will require dedication and hard work. What must you become to attain it?" the librarian asked, following the guidance of the ascension method he'd read.

"I must be deadly. I must be a killer."

"Well, yes, the Fangs are a deadly group, at least according to the information I've been able to gather about them." The librarian said that last bit more to himself. "But think harder, Zhaden. *How* will you be deadly? *How* will you be a killer?" Niajar was trying to help guide the rogue to a revelation, but Zhaden needed to figure it out himself.

The drakonid cocked his head to the side and his nostrils flared in frustration. "I will use my techniques . . ."

Niajar nodded enthusiastically and waved his hand for him to continue.

"I must become invisible." A palpable flash of power flushed out of the drakonid as his body turned invisible for a moment. Zhaden's tail wagged happily as he finally understood what he needed to do. "I must be silent." Again, another pulse of power flushed out of him, but this time, there was no noise, despite the wind.

Zhaden looked down, thinking about how to verbalize his next affirmation. "I must be an illusion—one of many." Another wave of power roared from his body as ten more sitting duplicates appeared beside him before fading away. Finally, his eyes took on a menacing look. A low growl rumbled from his maw. Goosebumps ran up everyone's backs they were gripped by an unidentifiable fear. "I must become a nightmare."

At his words, the glowing orbs of light mana began to flicker. A dark shadow emerged from Zhaden. It quickly coalesced into a large, draconic being of pure menacing power. Everyone reactively took another step back from the nightmarish creature, their minds assaulted by unnatural terror. They trembled in fear— all except the psion. Feeling some sort of mental attack, William had instinctively shielded Kiru's mental mana core and thus his mind.

That was the only reason Kiru wasn't quivering along and falling down to the ground like the others as the shadowy nightmare let out a bellowing roar along with a pulse of dark power. Instead, Kiru crossed his arms defensively. To his surprise, in a flash, Giiyam had rushed out to stand between the three students and Zhaden, his Fu Tao at the ready, a bead of sweat trickling down his temple. The fact that a Defunct could show such bravery was still both remarkable and inspiring to Kiru.

As fast as the shadow appeared, though, it regressed, seeming to be drawn into the rogue. Zhaden's golden eyes flashed once, going through all the hues of the rainbow in just a second. Then, his body collapsed from exhaustion. Immediately, the unnatural fear fled all of those who had been affected. Niajar forced himself back up, coughing in embarrassment that a first-year student made him stumble, and he self-consciously brushed off his blue robe.

As soon as the librarian noticed his unconscious charge, he scurried over to him, scanning his body. Being the skilled healer that he was, he quickly identified the issue. Then he pulled out a small vial holding a viscous, translucent liquid and administered it to Zhaden, saying as the others rushed over, "He's fine. He's fine. Just a case of severe mana deprivation is all. Apparently, this is one of those potential side effects the old manual didn't mention."

"By my mother's meat tenderizer!" Brunhilda exclaimed. "Be that what I think it is?"

"You certainly do have a healer's eye, my dear. Yes, this is concentrated mana, specifically nature mana which Zhaden's dream mana is a subset of," Niajar answered.

"Eh? What's so special about that?" Mutt asked.

"Have ye not been paying attention to our lectures, ye flea-ridden brute?" Brunhilda said.

"No. Wait, I have fleas? I thought that special shampoo you gave me dealt with them." He scratched his wild hair.

The paladin sighed. "No, ye don't have fleas anymore, gullible idjit. Well, if ye had paid attention, ye would've learned that making mana both concentrated into a liquid form and purified of any residual types be an extremely difficult and costly method."

"Oh, well thanks, Robe Guy!" He gave a toothy grin.

It was clear that Niajar didn't fancy being called "Robe Guy," but he visibly shook it off. "Not a problem. I needed to ensure his safety as a staff member of the Royal Academy anyway."

After a few minutes, Zhaden slowly began to stir and blink his eyes.

"How're you feeling?" Kiru asked.

"My head hurts worse than when I drank that rancid alcohol at the Strongjaw." Zhaden groaned and put his hand to his head. "What was it called?"

"Soulcrusher," Giiyam answered with one of his rare grins.

"Right . . . that," he hissed.

"Well, do you feel any stronger?" Kiru asked the question on everyone's minds. Zhaden now seemed to emanate the sense that he was at Ruby level, but Kiru wanted to make sure.

"What is it your familiar likes to say?" Zhaden asked, a mischievous glint appearing in his slitted eye. Then two duplicates of the drakonid appeared, but they were standing, not mirroring his body like before. "You bet your ass I do!" they hissed in unison. That brought chuckles out of all of the party members. Though William was recalled inside Kiru's core, the imp was especially happy for the shoutout and laughed along with everyone else. With that, Pandemonium was now two Ruby-ranked cultivators strong! It was a good thing, too, because Giiyam had to go prepare the school grounds for the Games and could no longer train with them.

With just one month to go, it was time to practice with their new powers, finalize their plans, and get ready to rumble.

# CHAPTER FORTY-ONE

# To the Games

All of the schools and minor academies in the Kingdom of Blades set their finals to finish before the Warrior Games in order to ensure that everyone was available to either attend the Games in person or—as most couldn't afford such an endeavor—travel to the capital to watch them there. There was a unique set of crystalline constructs connected between the colosseum to the city which allowed the former to send moving images to the latter of what the audience members in the coliseum were seeing in person, which were then projected onto a huge section of the capital's inner wall, allowing countless crowds to watch the event live.

The month-long preparation for the Games led to a huge, week-long event in the capital. Foreigners from all across the Great Alliance would travel there and cause a huge economic boom for the kingdom.

The Royal Academy in the Kingdom of Blades, however, was not *most* academies. All studies and finals were put on hold until *after* the Games were finished. That led to virtually no students spending time in the library, as almost all of them were in the practice arenas refining their strategies and techniques. Thanks to this, Niajar was able to institute even more limited hours for the library. The more it was closed, the more Pandemonium was able to get practice time in, honing their strategies and fine-tuning their teamwork, especially now that they had their fourth and final member.

Though not the most book-smart, the bestial orc was a very competent combatant. In conjunction with Zhaden, who was now also now a tier-one Ruby, it would be fair to say that Pandemonium was now truly a very formidable team. The drakonid's improvements were incredible, as well. Granted, they had only seen him use his new techniques once, but the difference was significant. First off, as long as he didn't attack, his Invisibility technique used to last half a minute at most. Now, its limit was doubled to a minute. Secondly, he could use it on an ally now, instead of himself. It only lasted five seconds, but in battle, five seconds could be a long time.

Additionally, instead of only one duplicate, Zhaden could now make two. They also didn't have to mirror his form, as they used to. The drakonid's Silence technique, like Invisibility, had also improved. It could now be used on another, also only lasting five seconds. Another bonus: despite the improvements to the techniques, both Kiru with his mental mana and Mutt with his enhanced senses of smell and hearing weren't affected. That helped their team fight with better coordination. And Zhaden's Nightmare technique . . . Well, he hadn't used that on anyone, so the team hadn't seen it, but they had glimpsed its power during Zhaden's ascension. That scary display had been evidence enough for them that they were okay with trusting that the rogue would use it only when necessary.

The month passed by quickly, and finally, it was time for the Games. Niajar had all their items immaculately cleaned for the event beforehand. William fortunately provided enough distraction for the elf that he didn't seem to notice Kiru's severely thin body outside of his magic armor or even his enchanted headband, for that matter. After examining their returned items, the psion was extremely glad for both the immaculate care and minor repairs Niajar must've performed to allow their armaments to be in such pristine condition. His cinnabar armor had no chips or cracks, and was so clean it glistened; meanwhile, both of his blades had been sharpened so that, aside from the grip, any part of its surface could cut an opponent.

None of their gear had so much as a dent, nor a single thread out of place! Based on what Kiru knew about dealing with smithing and gear maintenance— which was now a good bit from all the reading he'd done, not to mention his time as a smith's apprentice—he could tell that ensuring their equipment was this flawless was no small feat! Dealing with his enchanted armor and headband on top of that would have been difficult in ways he didn't want to contemplate.

Kiru honestly had wondered beforehand if they were going to have to wear different gear than what they had been training in, like generic matching armor. He was glad that wasn't the case. There was, however, one change. All of their jackets now had a large, gaudy flower in bloom embroidered on the back. It was white and . . . bedazzled? William was irate at how unthreatening it looked, and the imp went on a tirade inside Kiru's mind. Kiru let out a subtle groan as the familiar kept ranting. Finally, Kiru threatened to verbalize what the imp was saying aloud. William was still pretty scared of the librarian squashing him, so that threat shut him up.

Kiru wasn't thrilled with the designs, either, but on seeing Niajar's outfit, he understood why they wore embroidered jackets. The librarian was in some sort of custom robe, the same blue as he always wore, but made of silk and covered with numerous small, bedazzled flowers on it. It made the elf hard to look at. Clearly, he was showing that *he* was the sponsor and benefactor of Pandemonium. That gave Kiru a feeling of relief. Like it or not, the librarian would be with them until the end. Kiru decided not to complain and just say "thank you."

As the party exited the library, guided by Niajar, they took in their first direct rays of sunlight and fresh air in the three months they'd been living in the library. It was a bit of a shock to their systems at first, but soon they were all reveling in the warmth and comfort of the early summer sun. They had been isolated within the library, so they hadn't been able to fully appreciate all the goings-on at the academy. It had been hard to have Niajar in charge of their curriculum, meals, and lodging, but given the stakes, all four of the young cultivators believed it was worth it. The most challenging part was keeping Brunhilda from going back to the Strongjaw. She wanted to check on her fellow Hlin followers. She was able to settle for sending letters back and forth. All that was over now, as the surrounding din hit their ears.

The entire school was abuzz with activity. People were moving about hurriedly in all directions. There were now many more people than before, and not just students and staff, either. More kingdom guards than Kiru had ever seen before had congregated on the grounds. They all wore the same armor as Tavish and Keaton had, except without the academy's insignia emblazoned on it. They were stationed at every corner, preventing any fighting, guiding traffic along, and packed tightly, standing atop the walls around the academy. Not only were there guards, but carriages kept streaming in, many of them rolling across the grounds and heading into the dark forest.

A line of people were also trying to gain entrance to the island, as multiple large barges carried passengers over. The carriages themselves were also dazzlingly unique. Kiru was pretty sure one was made of either pure ice or glass. They were also pulled by a variety of different creatures. There were horses, large reptiles, a strange, one-eyed bipedal bird that looked at Kiru too long for the psion's liking, and even a couple of tenk duos. The passengers and guards around the carriages were also a varied and diverse set of peoples. Wealthy dwarven merchants, human dignitaries, and representatives from countless guilds made up only some of those visiting campus grounds.

Some of the most distinct were the elves. Under the banner of Anor'Voren's academy, two of them followed behind a human carriage. They seemed alien to Kiru. He'd met elves—his mother was one, Niajar was one, Giiyam was part elf, and the academy certainly wasn't short of them—but this pair were like none he'd ever witnessed. Their features were fine, as if chiseled from stone; somehow, though, they looked frail at the same time.

Their white hair was shoulder-length, and their skin was almost translucent, more like a thin membrane, similar to frogs. One of them seemed to be covered in a layer of sweat. Kiru honestly wondered if they were sick. Oh, and they were riding atop a pair of massive white tigers.

Reactively sensing another predator in their midst, the tigers jerked their heads toward Mutt and growled. Niajar tucked the hood of his robe to obscure his features and stood back from the party. To Mutt's credit, the orc didn't back down from the large cats. The blind orc snarled right back.

"Oh look, Tryndelion," one elf called over to his sweaty comrade. His tone sounded detached and otherworldly, matching his alien appearance. Kiru's pointed ears twitched. His speech was High Elven, one of the dialects he'd learned!

"It appears that this is the best the Alliance's great academy has to offer: a child who confuses himself with a beast."

"Hm, indeed," Tryndelion agreed. "It would seem that the standards of this so-called 'Grand Hall of Learning' have fallen even lower than rumored!" They laughed in condescension.

Mutt growled loudly at the offense. The orc didn't have to understand exactly what the elves were saying, as the intended insult was unmistakable in their tone and bearing. The two tigers started to growl right back. Then the sweaty elf, Tryndelion, noticed Kiru. Specifically, his armor.

"It can't be," he muttered, pulling on the reins of his tiger, creating some distance between it and Mutt. "It appears the half-breed has some Bronzium armor."

The other elf glanced over to Kiru before looking away. "It appears so, Brother. We need not worry, though. His red jacket indicates a low rank. He will no doubt die. We can just buy it off of his corpse later. Accidents do happen after all." They didn't even bother lowering their voices as they rode away.

Kiru didn't know what Bronzium was exactly, or if that's what the cinnabar-colored armor he'd inherited from his mother truly was, but these guys had personalities even more revolting than their skin. Kiru had never been able to stomach a bully, but over time, he'd been able to harness his anger and not allow it to take control. Kiru would remember these two; his perfect memory would ensure it. When the time was right, he would let that justified anger out on them.

There were sometimes freak deaths during the Warrior Games, and a pair of sweaty, shady elves plotting would just cause more difficulties for the psion. Kiru wasn't going to fight them now, but he could still get his point across. "There are occasional accidents in the Warrior Games, but it would be unfortunate if something were to happen to me," he called out to the elves, speaking in their native tongue.

The elves stopped their mounts and turned their heads back to the psion, shock evident in their expressions.

"Someone may suspect that you had something to do with it. We wouldn't want to start an international incident, would we? I'm sure Queen Armenia wouldn't be very happy about that."

The elves' translucent skin began to turn red with indignant anger, but before they could respond, the rule-following Private Tavish came to the rescue, to their surprise. "Hey, you two, quit holding up traffic. Either take to the sky or keep moving!" he called out from one of the rooftops.

Kiru wondered what he meant by "take to the sky," but that was quickly answered when the tigers sprouted long, white wings. The two large felines went airborne with one mighty flap of their feathered appendages. Kiru's headband and jacket whipped from the gust of wind.

His gaze followed the predators in awe. First, he was struck by the fact that he actually got to see one of the flying tigers native to Anor'Voren that he'd read about. Second, his eyes widened even more to see that there weren't only flying creatures filling up the clear blue sky. There were also a couple of chariots pulled by pegasi along with multiple balloon vehicles, propelled by some sort of flame device.

Kiru looked up in dazzled awe. He'd learned so much from the massive quantity of books he'd read, but he hadn't lost his sense of wonder. There was a difference between knowing something existed and experiencing it in person. He watched in fascination for a few moments, until finally being whisked away by Niajar's firm hand on his shoulder. He turned to see the elf pulling the hood off his head and looking at the flying felines.

"Kiru, my boy, when I found you, you were in a backwater mining town." He turned to face Kiru and raised an eyebrow. "When in the world did you learn High Elven?" the eccentric elf asked. His expression seemed stunned, matching that of Kiru's teammates.

Kiru scratched the back of his head and chuckled nervously at the attention that the elf was paying him. "Haha, um, I learned it during my studies."

Niajar's trademark grin came back, the elf beaming with sheer pride. He put his hand on Kiru's shoulder. "Discovering a long-forgotten ascension method and learning Anor'Voren's persnickety variation of Elven? I dare say, my boy, you're on the fast track to outdo even me, if you keep this up."

Smiling, the party joined the line of traffic en route to the games. They stopped by Giiyam's on their way. Unfortunately, the half-orc was not there, but that was not why Niajar brought them.

They went over to the stables to find a strange, small carriage. The thing was shaped like an onion but with a gigantic purple and yellow flower on top. Niajar waved with a flourish. "Ah, here it is. This, my lovely students, is our ride."

Mutt sniffed loudly. "This carriage smells nice. Most smell like dung from the mounts pulling them."

"Speaking of which," Zhaden hissed, "where are the mounts?"

The librarian beamed. "They come included." He let out a loud whistle, and the carriage started to shake. Then, suddenly, two large wolves jumped out of the flower's yellow center, landing right in front of the carriage. They had gray fur and a ring of purple petals around their necks exactly like the carriage. Kiru realized that the arrangement of petals matched their jacket's floral embroidery, as well. Clearly, Niajar had a preference for flowers.

"Lady and gentlemen, I present to you, flower wolves. For those who are sensitive to smell," Niajar said, giving Mutt a friendly pat on the back. One of the wolves then promptly squatted to defecate. A single, large seed fell out of its rectum and quickly grew into a small patch of grass as soon as it touched the ground. "No dung smell."

The blind orc gave an appreciative nod. Quickly, the four members of Pandemonium hopped into the onion-shaped carriage. Niajar took the driver's spot outside the vehicle. The nature mana cultivator then grew green vines from his palms, seamlessly wrapping around the pair of flower wolves' necks to form into makeshift reins. The canines didn't seem to mind that at all, and the team quickly rejoined the line heading toward the Games.

The path through the dark forest was fortunately uneventful. Despite the dangers, the presence of military forces and powerful cultivators served as an adequate ward against any monster or sacred beast threat. In only half an hour riding along the trail through the dark forest, the party made it to the other side of the island for the first time. They'd seen it before from a distance atop the large bridge connecting to Waketown, but this time, it was vastly different.

Where there was once a ring of water, an utterly gargantuan colosseum of stone stood. It was still clear that the arena spent most of the year underwater, as there were still noticeable areas covered with sections of algae and pockets of what looked to be coral observable even from a distance. Kiru hoped some of the spectators brought towels. The stadium itself was on a peninsula connected to the island.

All the party's mouths were hanging open in wonder. Well, other than Mutt, who remained rather nonplussed. "Hmm, sounds impressive, but not as big as the one back in Imakandi."

"You have an arena bigger than this in your home country?" Kiru asked.

"Oh, yeah! It's in the center of a dormant volcano. I've been there a couple of times. Trust me, this place ain't got nothin' on that stadium!"

Before Kiru could ask more, Niajar leaned his head inside and spoke up. "Pardon the intrusion, but we're here." The cart came to a halt at his words, and the party realized they were third in line at a metal gate. A contingent of at least one hundred armored guards were stationed there, permitting only those allowed to enter, leave, and do security checks to pass. There were strange stone, multitiered stables on the other side of the gate with a sign indicating it was something called a "Parking Garage."

Those with flying mounts and airborne means of transportation drifted down to the top of the garage, the guards managing the traffic showing surprising coordination in how well organized it all was. There was also a smaller entrance at the gate on the left side labeled "Contestants."

"Alas, this is where we part," Niajar stated. "I dare say, I am proud of all of you. Though Kiru is my only official pupil, I've grown fond of you all."

"Even me?" William asked, crawling up Kiru's shoulder.

"Well, most of you," he clarified, then proceeded to change the subject. "You've all shown great growth and potential. Just think about where you were at the beginning of the year."

When Kiru had first arrived, he was alone (besides William) with not much more than the clothes on his back. Now, he had real friends, people who trusted and believed in him, despite his status as a Defunct. At first, his quest to save the world had given him purpose. He still had that purpose, but it had evolved and carried more weight now because he had true companions he cared deeply for. Now he'd fight to save the world to help both him *and* them not just survive but thrive. Kiru would get his father's items, and he would prevent the next Draconic Campaign in order to ensure that would happen.

His musings were cut off when Niajar continued, "I believe in you. All of you. Now, go kick my nephew's ass."

Pandemonium cheered at that and headed out of the cart. They moved over to the contestant entrance and were surprised to see General Escobert stationed right outside. "Oi, well if it isn't the aptly named Pandemonium. Yer team sure caused a ruckus this year. Glad you didn't cause too much trouble and could still make it," the dwarf said. He then noticed Mutt. "And you have a fourth member! Who might you be?" he asked, putting a quill to the paper on his clipboard.

"M'Baku M'toon, sir. First-year."

The general muttered and scanned over multiple pieces of paper. "Ah, there you are. . . . Yer attendance is terrible! There's no way you've been to enough classes to be allowed to participate. I'm afraid yer gonna have to—"

"He was in the school dungeon," Kiru lied, cutting off the dwarf. "After he was let out, he participated in private tutelage for the last few months with us, under the direct supervision of Niajar." He indicated the librarian in the nearby carriage.

The chipper elf waved over to the general.

Escober's nostrils flared at seeing the librarian.

"He even made sure the headmaster approved him joining us too, and you know how those two feel about each other," Kiru added, whispering the last words for emphasis to the elder dwarf.

"Really?" Escobert asked.

Kiru nodded.

Having a bit of a soft spot for Kiru, the dwarf relented. "All right, you can enter, but if yer lying to me, Kiru, I'll make sure yer out of the academy and go straight to latrine duty in the king's army."

"Understood," he replied, not phased by the threat as he had no intention of actually serving in the military. He took a step to walk past the general, but Escobert didn't like Kiru's response.

"Hmph," the dwarf scowled, then stomped an armored foot on the ground. The power of an Emerald-rank cultivator made itself known as the general used a technique. In the blink of an eye, an entire bodysuit of stone shot up from the ground and encased Kiru completely, stopping his movement mid-step. "I know you spent months under the tutelage of that flowery elf and his fast talkin', but don't forget what we in the military expect in terms of decorum."

A predatory smile grew on the dwarf's face. "Now, understood?"

"Understood!" Kiru replied with gusto. He would've saluted if he could have moved his body.

"Understood, *what*?!"

"Understood, sir!" Kiru shouted.

Some of the nearby people chuckled at the display, but Escobert was satisfied. He exhaled and stomped his left foot once more, causing the stone to sink back down to the ground with no evidence that it had ever moved. He then stomped his right foot, making a large tunnel appear in the ground behind him. "Go through this path. You'll be directed to your quarters until it is time for the Games to begin."

The party, wanting to avoid causing another scene, promptly headed down the dark tunnel. Their path descended but quickly leveled out, heading in the direction of the colosseum. The party was completely quiet as they walked down the pitch-black tunnel. Only Zhaden couldn't navigate in the darkness, so he took up the rear, placing a hand on Brunhilda's shoulder for guidance. They continued on until they noticed a subtle, orange light at the end of the tunnel that grew brighter as they got closer. After a few minutes, they made it to the end.

There was a step down where the path forked in a semicircular pattern. There was also a familiar face there. Sitting on a box under one of the torchlights which illuminated the pathway was Giiyam. "Giiyam!" Kiru said excitedly, glad to see their mentor once more.

The stoic half-orc's face didn't betray any excitement, but he did give the party an approving nod. "It is good to see you all again. I am sure you will do well."

"Fuck yeah, we will! We're gonna win it!" William asserted.

Giiyam just blinked, staring blankly at the imp.

"Well, we are." William crossed his arms, pouting.

"Follow me," the groundskeeper said, grabbing one of the torches and heading off to the right. They trailed behind him.

"Are we beneath the stadium?" Kiru asked.

Giiyam grunted, nodding in affirmation. The large stone hallway had multiple ensconced torches which helped illuminate it much better.

Mutt sniffed loudly. "It smells like fish here."

Giiyam grunted again.

"Why?" Mutt asked.

"This place be underwater for most of the year," Brunhilda answered.

"I'm confused. What's the point of doing that? It must be annoyingly tough to dry up this place."

"Mmhm!" The groundskeeper grunted with much more enthusiasm this time. Clearly, he agreed with Mutt's assessment. As they were walking and talking, Kiru felt something. It was faint, but there was a familiar resonance somewhere off in the distance. For lack of a better word, it seemed to hum, keeping in sync not only with the jewel and circlet embedded in his head, but his core as well.

Kiru grinned stupidly. His father's item was near; he could feel it! He'd actually become a participant in the Warrior Games. Now, he just needed to win it.

"It's because of the prizes," the psion answered Mutt. "Some truly awesome items found nowhere else in the world are in the hidden storeroom here in the stadium. Keeping them deep underwater is only *one* layer of protection. I know for you, Mutt, a good fight is its own reward, but the prizes are the main appeal of the Games for most participants. It's a chance for the cultivators who win to reach higher than they ever could have otherwise and to bring honor and prestige to their family, country, or guild."

"Oh! Well, that makes sense. Maybe they have a really good comb. Nothing's really worked since I lost mine." The blind orc's teammates chuckled at that. "Oh! I know! Maybe they will have some technique manuals, Shield Girl. That way, we can get you to Ruby, too!"

"I don't know. The Order of Valhalla is pretty strict about who can learn their techniques. I'm not sure if they would allow any of their sacred manuals to be in there."

"If the rumors are to be believed, then it's a strong possibility that there are indeed some rare technique manuals within the treasure room," Zhaden hissed.

"Well, that settles it, then! When we win, you and I will find a couple of technique manuals for our prizes and get you to Ruby!" the orc said.

"You'd do that?" the paladin asked Mutt in disbelief.

"Of course! Now that me and Stabby are already at Ruby, we need to make sure our Shield Girl and Boss get there, too."

Brunhilda blushed and gave a lighthearted jab to the orc's shoulder. "Well, thank you, ya brute."

He good-naturedly punched her back, causing her to accidentally stumble a few steps. "Haha! You're welcome, Brunhilda."

The paladin, rogue, and psion all started in surprise. Mutt was pretty bad at names, even having difficulty calling Kiru by his real name—and he was his team leader. Case in point, Mutt calling Kiru "Boss." The fact that he called Brunhilda by name showed he was actually developing a real connection with the team. It helped the others feel more confident in their squad and reaffirmed their bond.

As they all walked, there came to a set of large metal doors on both sides of the damp, fishy hallway. Eventually, they stopped by one on the left. "Room 730," Giiyam said. He then spun the door's large wheel handle. The moaning of barely used metal being forced to move hit their ears. Then, with a large clang, it had opened fully, revealing a simple stone room. There was no light within; a simple, unlit candle and match had been set on the floor in preparation.

"Um, Giiyam . . ."

"This looks like a prison cell," William finished.

"Do not worry. The stone will lift up on the other side when it is time for you to enter the arena. Now, in you go."

Uncertain about the room, but trusting the man who'd trained them, Pandemonium entered. There was one small rectangular opening in the top right corner of the room, revealing nothing but darkness and stone. They figured it was to allow fresh air in. Once they entered, they turned back to the groundskeeper.

Though they'd seen no one else, Giiyam looked both ways, making sure there wasn't anyone who could listen before looking back at the students. "Sit, do not stand."

"Wha—"

"Shh! After you enter the arena, and they announce the start of Round One, jump forward." Kiru was about to ask again, but the half-orc raised a finger before he could. "Jump forward," he repeated, then slammed the door shut, closing the team in complete darkness.

# CHAPTER FORTY-TWO

# Round One Begins

The party wasn't sure how long they had been in in the dark room. They had lit the candle as soon as Giiyam had slammed the door, but without a stable, flat surface to place it, it didn't take long for it to fall over onto the rough stone and go out. After that, still trusting Giiyam, they all sat on the ground in lotus position, trying to pass the time by cultivating but without any real success.

Now that they were at the arena, the gravity of their situation truly hit them. They not only needed to defeat some of the best and brightest young cultivators in all the world, but they also had to do so while being watched by representatives of some of the most powerful organizations in the world. They would be scrutinizing his every move, so Kiru knew he had to make sure to not to show off any obvious displays of his psionic powers. He would have to be extremely focused in order to not let his secret slip.

"Remember, only one of us needs to make it through for our whole team to qualify," Brunhilda said, trying to reassure everyone. The first round of the tournament was a free-for-all between all of the four-person teams. Once there were only eight remaining, the round would stop. The remaining rounds were bracketed team-versus-team bouts, eventually leaving only one. Just as the dwarf had said, to win—or qualify in the case of Round One—there only had to be one person left standing from the team. The kingdom would have plenty of healers on standby to help the participants recover before the next round to ensure that every member of each squadron would be ready to proceed.

Having the patience of a toddler, William quickly grew bored and frustrated. He kept sending telepathic messages to Kiru with different ideas on how to prank the purple-haired paladin. Brunhilda, ever the zealous pupil, continuously muttered prayers to her goddess. To keep the imp occupied so he didn't interrupt Brunhilda's holy communion, the psion let William munch on the candle as a snack. He was pretty sure the little demon ate half and stored the other half between his skull and brain.

All four members of Pandemonium breathed meditatively, trying to control the tension building up in their bodies. On the one hand, a small degree of tension helped them stay prepared. On the other, too much could inhibit them. They needed to loosen up. Fortunately, a distraction soon came to draw their focus. The stone room they were in began to move. the momentum pulled all of their torsos backward as the stone room slid forward.

There was a loud "Errh!" from the tiny imp, who was flung against the stone wall, slamming into it like a rag doll. "Owww," he groaned.

Deciding William was in danger of getting crushed into paste if he weren't kept in a safe place, Kiru recalled his familiar back into his core. Then the stone room stopped moving. Well, at least it stopped moving *forward*. From outside the small airhole, the team could hear the repeated sounds of stone crashing against stone. They were tempted to look out to see what was happening but thought better of it.

It was a good thing too, because something crashed against their room's right wall, shifting the squad in their seated positions on the floor. Immediately afterwards, their momentum was halted again as they hit something else—likely another stone room—to their left. After a few more seconds, the crashing noise stopped. All of them took a deep breath, and then the stone room was propelled upward. Kiru was glad they'd taken Giiyam's advice and remained seated, because they were all been thrown about like a cup full of dice.

Then the dark airhole began to let light into the room. It was faint but eventually grew brighter until the room finally stopped moving. None of them dared stand, though, half-expecting this torture room to spring yet another surprise at them. It wasn't until the stone door on the opposite end began to rise that they felt safe enough to stand.

Nearly all of Pandemonium's eyes squinted at the sudden surge of bright light, except for Mutt, who yawned and stretched on all fours like an animal waking up from a nap. "It's time," Kiru said and unsheathed his Fu Tao. The others did the same with their weapons. Brunhilda bowed her head and muttered a prayer to Hlin as they stepped forward.

Kiru was glad she did; they were going to need every bit of help they could get. He even sent a quick *Keep us safe* to the goddess since that's what she excelled at. To Kiru's surprise, he somehow felt more reassured. His enchanted headband felt more comfortable and secure around his head, too, making him feel more protected. *One of the perks of being an acolyte,* he mused.

They all left the dark room and entered the arena. Just as their eyes were beginning to adjust to the light, they suddenly widened in amazement. The cheers of the crowd around them rang in their ears. They were now undoubtedly at a point of no return.

The team was in the vast sandy battleground where countless gallons of blood had been spilled over the years in the pursuit of glory. The center ring was at least a thousand feet wide and across. The ground below them, while mostly covered in sand, had a few splotches of grass. The only other notable landmarks inside the arena were six stone columns placed evenly across the ground as well as a few others placed across the perimeter of the arena. There was one on each side of Pandemonium. What truly caught the students' attention, however, was what was above the arena they were in.

One hundred concentric rows of rising seats surrounded the arena pit. Each and every one was filled; there was hardly so much as an inch of space or any shoulder room to speak of. There were also a number of ornately adorned booths where the wealthy and well-connected sat. There had to be at least ten thousand people up there! Kiru had never seen so many people together . . . well, *ever*! The crowd roared as all the students entered the arena. It was an exhilarating feeling that none of Pandemonium, barring Mutt, had ever felt before.

All the other teams had come out at the same time, all from entrances spread along the perimeter of the arena. A few of them hobbled out and sported a few cuts and wounds. They clearly hadn't taken a seat before their liftoff and had paid the price.

Kiru caught sight of a few more pristine, walled-off booths set into the stands closer to the arena sands. From inside one of them to the left of Pandemonium, placed centrally in the stands, Headmaster Niazen J'sarko stood up and walked forward, where he could be seen by the entire arena. He was wearing a gaudy, bejeweled robe, primarily black rather than the customary blue; he still, however, retained his awkward shoulder pauldrons—certainly a style clash, but few dared to make a public comment on that. The elf raised both hands out magnanimously, and the crowd quickly fell to a hush.

Smiling, Niazen pulled out a strange stone and pressed it to his neck. "Welcome, one and all, to the five hundred and eighteenth annual Warrior Games!" His voice, amplified by the undoubtedly enchanted rock, projected loud and clear throughout the entire arena. The crowd cheered enthusiastically at the headmaster's words. Niazen continued, "Thank you, everyone, for coming out for such a momentous event. We have so many noteworthy people here today. While I can't list all of you, there is one in particular who deserves our recognition and praise."

He cleared his throat and gestured to the booth beside his. "Introducing the leader of our kingdom, the slayer of the mad tyrant, liberator of our minds, King Swain Derollo van Blaine!" A skeletal monster of a man emerged from the booth. He was short and thin, his skin pulled too tight across his face. His teeth were too large for his mouth, making them look artificial. His long, brown hair was thick and tied in a ponytail. The king wore a strange, conical helmet made of a maroon-colored metal that covered most of his head, a pointed tip on the top. His golden crown appeared to have been sealed over it.

At some point, he must have lost his left eye, because he wore a patch there. Although he had been far away at the time, the psion instantly knew this was the same man he'd seen flying in the air the day his mother died. Van Blaine's armor was unlike any Kiru had ever seen before. It was a rich navy and appeared to be made of scales. The psion had seen scalemail before, but it was always metal that had been crafted that way. The king's armor seemed to be made from genuine, massive scales. *What sort of creature that large had scales? A large snake? A dragon?*

That last thought sent a pang of fear through Kiru. It made perfect sense! That man had killed his father, and if nothing was done, would cause the dragons to invade once more. Without a doubt, the armor was made from dragonhide. Possibly a relic from the last Draconic Campaign? The damn noble had been bought off, somehow!

Kiru gripped his fist tightly as he scowled in anger. His father's murderer was right there, but he was nowhere near strong enough to bring about justice. That point was made even more abundantly clear when the man's most distinguishing feature made itself known. Two gargantuan, sky-blue wings unfurled from Van Blaine's back, releasing a powerful gust of icy wind that tore through the entirety of the huge arena.

All of Pandemonium crossed their arms reflexively as they were buffeted by the cold air. Kiru even swore he saw his breath for a moment! The wings were feathered but glistened in the sun as if they were made of ice. The crowd, mostly comprised of Van Blaine's loyal subjects, went wild at the display and began cheering his name: "Van Blaine! Van Blaine!"

While the crowd rejoiced, Kiru breathed deeply and closed his eyes, trying to compose himself. He'd come so far, from being a quadriplegic commoner to an alpha-tier Gold-rank cultivator leading an impressive team. He was playing the long game. He couldn't let his anger overcome him now. He had to keep his friends safe, too. Kiru finally got control of his anger, but the urge to attack the usurper was still there.

The crowd continued cheering for another half a minute. Kiru's heart rate settled as the crowd did, and the king nodded for Niazen to continue. "Now that we're fired up, let's commence the first round of the Games!" The crowd gave another loud cheer in response, ready for the fighting to begin. "Now, this is only an appetizer, but it should still provide some excellent spectacle for you. During the course of the school year, we have our students spar in enchanted training areas for their protection. It is a very clean way to handle injuries, but it fails to compare to true combat. The enchantment prevents any gruesome wounds from besetting the students, but there shall be none of that today! I bring you *blood*!"

The crowd roared in approval, eager for bloodshed. "Yes, the injuries will be real, and the contestants will know what it feels like to experience true pain from a gruesome wound. Do not worry though, while no enchantment is placed to prevent injury, death is prohibited. We have many clerics and paladins from the Order of Valhalla on standby. When they judge a student no longer be able to continue, they will use their skill to remove them from the fighting and heal them. Their speed and skill will ensure that any wounds are repaired." He gestured to the numerous holy warriors standing right at the edge of the arena, all wearing gold and white armor and pristine white capes, ready to remove and heal any student too hurt to continue.

The elf then glanced down to the arena of students. There were a little over one hundred squads of four on the ground with Pandemonium, and they all were first-years. "Yes, this is the first match of the Games, and each one promises to be even better than the last. We'll start out with the first-years. We have one hundred and two teams below. They have trained all year to bring glory to themselves and the Royal Academy. They will fight in a free-for-all battle. As soon as only eight teams remain, Round One will conclude, and the victorious squadrons will recover for their next round."

Niazen raised his right hand, purple flames of faerie fire surrounding his palm.

The students below braced themselves, anticipating his next words.

"*Get ready. Remember, jump forward*," Kiru sent telepathically to his friends.

"Begin!" the headmaster shouted and slammed his palm on the stone in front of him. There was an audible boom of shattering stone all around them. Trusting Giiyam's vague advice, Pandemonium all jumped forward with haste, giving them plenty of time and space as the columns around the perimeter crashed to the ground. A few pained screams rang out from unlucky students who weren't quick enough to avoid getting crushed by the columns.

Kiru hoped that the healers truly could repair the likely devastating damage the fallen columns had caused to the contestants, but he couldn't dwell on that thought. Combat had started in earnest. Kiru's status as a Defunct was well-known amongst most of the academy. All of his fellow first-years undoubtedly knew of his status after their impromptu match with Team Supreme in the first semester. Thinking the Defunct student would be an easy target, two teams focused on Pandemonium at once.

To the team's left, a squad of four slow-moving, heavily armored dwarves advanced with their shields lowered and maces at the ready. To their right was a gang of sickly-looking cultivators wielding sickles. They cackled insidiously, a mad look on their visages. It was easy to tell from the latter's appearance and strong smell of formaldehyde that they used death mana.

*"Scorpion's Stance!"* Kiru sent telepathically to the group. The team quickly formed up, able to perform the maneuver more effectively now that they had a fourth member. Brunhilda braced her dual shields, one facing forward and the other above. Zhaden and Mutt stood slightly behind and flanked the paladin. The drakonid's blades were at the ready, and Mutt had focused mana into his fingers, toes, and teeth, elongating them with sharp, deadly tips.

The psion took up the rearmost position of the group with his Fu Tao at the ready, poised with one raised high, as if it were a scorpion's stinger. The necromancers struck first, targeting Mutt. One raised a palm and fired sharpened fragments of bone from their hands directly at the orc.

"Sheesh! Is that all?" Mutt responded casually and crossed his arms over his body. The cultivators' already pale faces seemed to go a shade lighter as they saw that the technique couldn't penetrate the orc's hide-like skin. His enhanced Ruby body was paying off.

Another one sprang at Mutt, showing surprising speed despite their thin frame.

"Divine Shield!" Brunhilda shouted.

Mutt's body was instantly covered in a column of protected light, intercepting the sickle's blade before the orc could be harmed. The retaliatory effect of the Divine Shield activated and ignited the cultivator in holy flame as the column dissipated. He fell to his back and writhed on the ground. Enraged, the necromancer's allies charged Pandemonium, focused on retribution over helping the injured cultivator.

Thankfully for him, one of the clerics above used a technique to encase him in a protective dome of light. The technique instantly quelled the flames and began healing the necromancer on the spot.

While that was happening, the dwarves were still approaching from the left. Zhaden hurled one of his daggers, but it was deflected by one of their shields. The four dwarves raised their maces and performed the same technique in unison. "Stone Wave!" they shouted together, then slammed their weapons into the ground. A wave of stone approximately ten feet tall and half as wide across, surged toward the party as if it were rushing water.

*"Split!"* Kiru mentally ordered. On that silent cue, Pandemonium broke into two teams of two. Brunhilda and Zhaden leaped forward while Mutt and Kiru hopped back, letting the wave of stone roll between them.

The necromancers' recklessness and singular focus on Mutt became their downfall as their charge toward the orc brought them too close to the incoming wave of stone to dodge. The three were quickly buried beneath the stone, the rock muffling their screams as their bodies were overtaken. The only indicators that they had indeed survived were orbs of protective light bursting out of the stone; they had been defeated.

The necromancers now clearly down for the count, Pandemonium turned and faced the four dwarves. The now-split team charged their opponents, flanking them in a pincer formation. The dwarves were strong but too slow. Pandemonium had come for them.

After months of practicing against Giiyam's high speed, the party was able to make quick work of them. Zhaden leaped over one dwarf, and in an impressive acrobatic display, flung a dagger midair. With the improvements his Ruby body provided, the rogue's aim was true and hit the dwarf right in the right eye slit of his helmet. The warrior cried out in pain, dropping both mace and shield and clutching at the knife in his eye.

Mutt caught the mace with his jaws, which had grown more prominent since the match had begun, stopping his opponent's attack mid-swing. The dwarf's eyes bulged at Mutt's power before a punch from the blind orc broke his nose and knocked him unconscious.

During Pandemonium's time with Giiyam, they trained for shielded opponents as part of their regime; having someone on their team who used them proved invaluable, as well. Brunhilda's insights on shield types, weak points, and positioning helped Kiru learn how to effectively deal with shield-bearing foes. His hooked blade caught the edge of the dwarf's shield, and the psion heaved, forcing the shield to move. As a result, the dwarf's mace swing was disrupted, and he exposed his left leg.

Utilizing the Cruel Mantis Style, Kiru swung his right blade. The dwarf's leg was heavily armored but not behind the knee, in order to allow mobility. Cruel Mantis Style capitalized on those weaknesses. Kiru knew that all too well from the times he'd literally been butchered by Giiyam's blades during training. Kiru's Fu Tao bit into the back of his opponent's leg, piercing through the muscle, tendon, and bone, bursting through the dwarf's kneecap. Not giving his opponent time to retaliate, Kiru continued through his form and sliced across the dwarf's neck with his other now-free blade.

A spray of warm arterial blood covered his face from the attack. The dwarf no doubt would've died in a matter of seconds, had a cleric not used another protective dome. Brunhilda was having the most difficulty against her opponent in a battle of two shields versus shield and mace. Fortunately, Mutt came to her aid and tackled her opponent from behind, pinning the other dwarf to the ground and breaking their elbow and leg with consecutive sickening crunches.

*"Aww, yeah! Hahaha!"* William chortled inside Kiru's mind. *"That was great, Master! Do it again!"*

Kiru didn't respond to his familiar, the rush of battle hitting him all at once. There was no protective enchantment, no professor looking out for them during training, just a group of holy cultivators using their judgment and trying their best to keep everyone alive. Pandemonium couldn't rely on others to make sure they were safe; they would need to ensure that their own skill kept them from harm. Still, Kiru had a subtle grin of exhilaration on his face.

He wiped the blood away from his eyes and looked at his party. All of them, his friends, gave him firm looks of resolve. They were with him to the end. He tightened his grip on his blades and turned his gaze to the chaotic battlefield full of hundreds of cultivators before them. They would fight, and they would bring pandemonium.

# CHAPTER FORTY-THREE

# Round One Concludes

*Ding!* The sound of the arrowhead rang out as Brunhilda's shield deflected it. The fighting had been going on for about half an hour. For the first fifteen minutes, it had been pure chaos, many of the four hundred and eight cultivators being eliminated in that timespan alone. Afterward, the remaining fighting became much more coordinated, demonstrating the remaining contestants' prowess.

Pandemonium had decided to play defensively, bracing their backs against a wall to prevent being surrounded. Unfortunately, another stone mana cultivator, a friend of one of the dwarves they'd defeated at the beginning, had decided to strike at that very moment. Using a technique similar to Escobert's earthen armor trap, the cultivator caught Mutt unaware and pulled the orc into the wall. At the sight of their friend being swallowed up, the rest of the team ran away from the wall to ensure they wouldn't fall victim to the same technique. Unfortunately, however, when Mutt burst through the stone seconds later in a display of profound strength, they were now separated from him. Despite being weakened from the effort, the beast mana cultivator roared, activating a technique that grew his hair out as an extra protective barrier.

That's when the stone mana user's teammates struck. From both sides, two people clad in black, tight-fitting garments appeared. Before Mutt could react, they had buried their short swords deeply into his abdomen. The orc's roar was cut short, and he coughed blood. He would've been instantly eliminated had he not used his defensive technique right before. Pandemonium cried out to their friend but couldn't run to him as the earth mana cultivator suddenly used another technique to surround them in a torrent of sharp sand.

They couldn't get to Mutt, but the cavalier orc didn't mind. He groaned, then growled as his two assaulters twisted their blades, in the hopes of actually killing him. Mutt channeled more of his beast mana into his claws, both sharpening and elongating them even further, and backhanded the left assassin. They were sent flying, gushing streams of blood from their slashed face and neck.

Then Mutt grabbed the other assassin's neck and began to squeeze. The cultivator coughed, dropping his sword, still embedded in Mutt's chest, and trying to free his throat. If Mutt hadn't been injured, the man would've been finished, but he was indeed hurt. Thanks to the rapid blood loss, Mut's grip weakened, and the assassin was able to free himself and kick Mutt in the chest. The blind orc fell on his back, unconscious, and a paladin used a healing dome technique to cover him, signaling that Mutt was out of the fight.

Meanwhile, the others were being cut and buffeted by the twister of sand. They were so beset, they couldn't even see that Mutt had been eliminated. The cultivator who'd used the technique was trying to administer death to them by a thousand cuts. Brunhilda raised her shields and covered her teammates, allowing herself to take the brunt of the assault. Meanwhile, the fourth and final member of the opposing team kept firing arrows into the tornado.

Zhaden, kneeling in the sand, looked up to the paladin and noticed the blue sky directly above, the eye of the storm. "Brunhilda, launch me!" he hissed loudly, trying to be heard through the storm.

The paladin nodded in understanding. She stepped back and lowered her shields, giving the drakonid room to stand. The sand started to assault him once more, but he powered through and focused. He dodged an arrow, took a few running steps, and jumped on her shields.

Brunhilda then raised them and tossed the gold drakonid into the sky. Right before his feet had left the shields, he'd jumped, propelling his upward ascent even higher. To the awe of the crowd, Zhaden crested above the tornado, three daggers in each hand. The crowd was even more impressed as he activated Duplication, making two more drakonids appear in the sky.

The three attackers had noticed Zhaden, and the bow-wielder had aimed an arrow at the airborne rogue—only now there appeared to be three airborne rogues! The stone mana cultivator was too focused on keeping the sand tornado active, while the assassin swordsman had no ranged abilities. The bowman fired at the rightmost Zhaden, but it went right through him. That allowed the *real* Zhaden to hurl all six daggers at the stone mana user. Two of his small blades were deflected, but four hit their mark, stabbing just above the collar bone. One actually went into the cultivator's jaw.

Startled by the pain, the cultivator spat blood and reflexively grabbed at his ruined face, disrupting his technique in the process.

When the sand dropped, both Brunhilda and Kiru were ready. Both of them noticed Mutt encased in a healing dome. Then, they turned upon the team of attackers, promising retribution. As Zhaden descended, they charged.

The bow user looked up, but the airborne drakonid was gone. Since there was no longer a target in the air, the bow wielder and assassin went after the dwarf and half-elf, leaving their bleeding ally to recover. They didn't see him being tackled to the ground by the descending meteor that was Zhaden, who turned visible right as he made contact. The crowd roared at the display, but the bow wielder and swordsman paid it no mind.

The archer fired a shot at Kiru, but it was Brunhilda's shield's deflected once more. Kiru snarled. He needed to close the distance. He also noticed that the swordsman used some sort of dark mana, as their body became enshrouded in shadow, blurring their form as they charged. Or would have if they hadn't been facing a psion. Their opponents' plan was simple: pepper them with arrows from a distance to keep them on the defensive while the assassin took them out up close.

*"Cut them down!"* William asserted.

*"Gladly,"* Kiru sent back. Concentrating more mana into his legs, Kiru used Demon's Inciting Strike from the Monarch's Razors style. Then in one swift motion, the psion used Telekinesis to propel himself with supernatural speed. He flew past the swordsman, slicing through his cloth armor easily with both of his Fu Tao. He wasn't done, though. After he cut down the assassin, he continued toward the archer, switching to Giiyam's methods to help him slice straight through the cultivator's bow and his fingers.

The archer fell to his knees and cried out in pain as he grabbed his injured hand. Kiru gave him no respite. He spun and kicked the kneeling archer square in the temple with the heel of his boot. The archer fell unconscious, and a pair of protective domes appeared around Kiru's two opponents.

One more team eliminated.

The three remaining members of Pandemonium regrouped and scanned the colosseum grounds for Mutt. Due to the sand tornado, they had been unsure what had happened to him. Brunhilda was the first to spot the orc now encased in an orb of healing light. All three of them looked at their incapacitated friend with a mixture of sadness and gratitude, but they could only do so for a moment. The chaos and violence around them demanded they keep their attention on the fighting.

The crowd continued to chant madly, captivated by the constant warfare. As Pandemonium looked about, they realized they were close to the center of the arena. They also saw that there weren't many people still left standing. It was hard to tell exactly how many teams were represented by the number of remaining contestants, but they guessed around eight.

After a bit more scrutiny, Zhaden's reptilian eyes determined that the number was ten. Like them, the other teams each had matching patches on the backs of their jackets or pieces of armor. To Pandemonium's surprise, they noticed that there were two different coalitions of different teams, as evidenced by them all being grouped together and not fighting each other. There was a group of five squads, and another group of three with only two other independent squads like the trio remaining.

To their chagrin, Team Supreme was part of the coalition of five teams. Ambrose gave a malicious smile, and Kiru could see the noble's mouth forming the word "mongrel." Kiru's neck shivered. He'd trained and cultivated exhaustively for this, but he didn't feel confident that he could survive a prolonged battle being so outnumbered.

Seeing Pandemonium, the squadron of five ceased hunting the other teams, and they all focused on Kiru and his friends. Ambrose conjured a lance of lightning in his hand and hurled it at Kiru. The psion ducked, narrowly avoiding the electrical technique.

"Shit!" Kiru cursed.

"*Run, bitch!*" William pleaded inside Kiru's mind. He didn't need to tell the psion twice.

"Run at the three-team group!" Kiru shouted aloud, echoing his familiar's sentiment. He then turned away from the others and sprinted away from Team Supreme.

Brunhilda and Zhaden quickly turned and followed the psion. "Are you sure about this?" Zhaden asked. "That group has eight members, and there's only the three of us."

"Watch out!" Brunhilda shouted as she shoved the others out of the way of a geyser of flame that erupted from the ground. They all stumbled, nearly falling over, but they were okay.

"I retract that line of questioning," Zhaden said, now convinced by Kiru's logic. They didn't have time to avoid the mega group while trying to defeat the other independent squads. They needed to eliminate three more teams as fast as possible in order to make the top eight. They didn't need to defeat Team Supreme at this exact moment; they just needed to qualify.

The three-team group was focused on another independent squad, so they weren't giving Pandemonium any attention. Kiru glanced back. He shouldn't have. The mega-squad was gaining ground. Brunhilda noticed, too. The paladin stopped running; her heavy armor and short legs weren't doing the others any favors in gaining distance. Her trollblood gave her longer arms but not longer legs, unfortunately.

Kiru opened his mouth to ask what she was doing, but quickly figured it out. Brunhilda turned away from her friends and shouted, "I'll hold 'em off as best I can, lads! Now go! Hurry!" She clanged her shields against each other in challenge before charging at their pursuers.

Kiru gritted his teeth but didn't try to stop her. If he ran to Brunhilda, both of them would be overwhelmed by the incoming mega-squad. So, he honored her wish and continued running toward their intended target. He wouldn't let her sacrifice be in vain. The psion gripped his blades tight, about to concentrate more mana in his legs and arms to accelerate his speed. He bent himself low to propel himself, but Zhaden spoke up. "Not yet, my friend!"

"You serious?"

"Indeed! None of them are Ruby, and I have one more trick they haven't seen." He hissed, and his reptilian eyes flashed black. "When I'm done with them, I'll be too low on mana to do much more. So that's when you strike them." The drakonid's voice became notably more menacing. A bead of nervous sweat ran down Kiru's temple, and he nodded. Instinctive fear clawed at his heart, and he cautiously agreed.

There was a loud clanging of metal behind them, no doubt Brunhilda's shields facing off against the mega-squad's overwhelming force, but they didn't look back. Instead, they focused forward on their target. The three-team group had just eliminated two out of four from another independent team, leaving only two remaining.

Zhaden let out a haunting roar, and a shadowy wave of blackened dream mana leaked out of his body. The mana rushed from between his scales and surged toward the other cultivators as if it were a living shadow. The technique coalesced into a large, shadowy dragon that let out the same roar Zhaden did, only louder and more terrifying. Much of the crowd grew silent or gasped in fear as the technique even affected them from a distance.

The eight-member, three-team squad and their two remaining targets also snapped their heads, faces turning visibly pale as they fully grasped what was charging at them. Some tried to run, but it was too late; the Nightmare was already upon them. The incorporeal technique overtook them, enshrouding them all in complete darkness. Cries of panic and terror echoed from the darkness as Zhaden's technique somehow assaulted their minds with their own fears, their own worst nightmares.

Kiru kept running with his blades ready, but Zhaden could no longer keep up, his mind and body taxed from the drain to his mana reserves. The gold drakonid slowed, then collapsed to the ground, unconscious. Kiru didn't look back. He had one chance to get this right. He had to focus on his targets. Ahead of him were ten haunted-looking students in various stages of mental breakdowns. Two had visibly soiled themselves while another was in the fetal position, muttering and rocking themselves back and forth. Kiru was both impressed and a little afraid of the power Zhaden's technique had unleashed. He felt bad for his fellow students, but he didn't have the time to waste.

His mother's words echoed in his mind, *Lesson number one: Always fight dirty.*

Kiru charged through, dealing crippling blows to the incapacitated students as quickly as possible. William cackled madly in glee inside the psion's mind as

Kiru sliced through their exposed limbs and weak points. As he sprinted through, he used more of his mother's fast, sharp sword style to take them out in haste. He had developed a hybrid of both Giiyam's and Surturia's styles; not having time to completely master either, he had decided to fuse the two together. The result, coupled with incapacitated opponents, made the psion seem like a ruthless butcher as he tore through them. With the speed of his Monarch's Razors and the brutal targeting of Cruel Mantis, Kiru cut throats, eviscerated bellies, and sliced groins, causing a terrifying display of blood and gore to erupt around him as if numerous geysers had been set off at once.

There was a mixture of cheering and booing from the crowd above.

"No mercy!"

"Have you no honor?!"

"Yeah! Cut 'em down!"

Apparently, Kiru was a polarizing figure. Some loved how mercilessly he eliminated his opponents, while others viewed him as a bully, picking on the helpless. Those who knew combat, true warfare, gave the Fist House student a modicum of respect at his tactics. War wasn't fair, clean, or pretty. Warriors needed to get the job done, and that was what Kiru was doing.

Just as Kiru finished off the last member of the three-team squad, he was struck by a crossbow bolt to the shoulder, followed by a javelin made of electricity through his ribs. He couldn't physically feel the bolt in his shoulder, but he heard the loud crunch of it breaking through his armor and scapula bone, and it knocked him forward. He did feel the electricity, however, as it coursed through his body and to his brain, causing him to fall on his back.

He looked up to see both Ambrose and Zane were only feet away, with weapons drawn, their scowling faces promising pain. The rest of their allies were not far off. They drew back, preparing to lunge and pummel Kiru when a loud voice shouted out.

"Stop!" Headmaster Niazen's voice blared throughout the entire stadium. A cacophonous boom of purple flames erupted from the ground, cutting off the remaining members of the eight qualifying teams from each other. More importantly, it kept Kiru safe from another incoming attack. The flames shifted and forced some students to move. After a few seconds, the purple fire died down, and the teams had been fully separated.

Niazen continued, "Ladies and gentleman, I present to you, the members of the eight remaining teams!"

The crowd cheered at his words.

Kiru called on some of the residual mana he had stored through his extra meridians and activated his Telekinesis once more. The psion was grateful to his mother's advice so long ago to form some extra meridians to allow him to hold in more mana. It really came in handy now. He groaned as he got up, the crossbow bolt still embedded in his shoulder, right under his pauldron. Warm blood ran down from it.

"Daisy Directory, will you please project the names of the eight remaining teams for all to see?" Niazen asked.

Subtle runes carved in the upper edge surrounding the arena glowed white and hummed with power for the first time. To Kiru's surprise, light emerged from the runes, coalescing to create a ten-foot-tall projection of Daisy Directory floating above the arena grounds right in the center. "Of course, Headmaster!" the chipper construct answered. "Here are the names of the eight remaining teams with their contestants." She opened her arms, and a list of four team names appeared on each side of her.

Kiru smiled and sighed in relief. There, by Daisy Directory's left foot, was Pandemonium. They'd done it!

*Mom, thank you*, he thought in gratitude. He didn't know if his mother could hear him, but he hoped so. Kiru then scanned the audience to see more than a few people, likely gamblers, servants of nobles, and guilders, frantically writing down the names of the winners on small notepads. Most of them were likely keeping an eye out for potential future recruits to take under their employ.

Kiru and the other students still standing were escorted by a few of the clerics and paladins who jumped down from the edge of the arena. The holy cultivators began immediately healing and tending to the students who had made it through. One gruff man unceremoniously ripped the bolt from Kiru's shoulder without warning as he led him out of the arena. Obviously, it hadn't hurt him, but he was starting to feel a little lightheaded from too much blood loss.

To his benefit, the paladin began immediately healing his wound, quickly removing his lightheadedness and helping him recover his strength. Reminded of the gods, Kiru sent a quick prayer of thanks to Hlin. He didn't have the same fervor as Brunhilda did, but he was grateful to her nonetheless.

The psion smiled and looked up, just happening to peer into one of the isolated booths from which he saw Niajar J'sarko, gazing back at him with a large, boyish grin on his face. The librarian in his floral robes seemed rather composed, unlike most in the arena. He nodded and raised a small cup of tea toward the psion in a toast of approval.

Kiru nodded back in appreciation before being led out of the arena to the medical ward.

Meanwhile, Niazen was baring his teeth, almost frothing from the mouth in rage. Niajar looked over to his brother's booth. He locked eyes with his dark-haired counterpart and gave him a mischievous wink as someone place a large bag of coins in the librarian's hand, winnings from his betting on his team.

At that, Niazen's turned his face away and scowled to himself, at which point the voices attempted to attack his psyche for control once more.

*"Kill!"*

*"Destroy!"*

*"Attack!"*

*"Free Us!"*

Niazen's body shook as he wrestled back control. A trickle of blood started flowing out of his nose. "No, I will not free you. But soon, I will give you the violence you so crave," he uttered.

One of the voices whispered in pleasure, *"Yes!"*

# CHAPTER FORTY-FOUR

# Major & Minor

Kiru was guided through a centralized gate into a wide infirmary. Large numbers of congregated clusters of cots were spread about a massive chamber underneath a section of stadium seating. The infirmary was so big, in fact, that it spanned all the way to the edge of the arena, a contingent of Royal Guards and large metal gates keeping anyone from exiting or entering unauthorized.

Kiru was impressed by the operation. Most students were injured, some rather seriously, but none appeared to be dead. The strong iron scent of blood mixed with burned flesh permeated the infirmary. Groups of cots appeared to be organized by team, as indicated by the matching embroidered insignias.

The injured students were being tended to by robed servants, low-level cultivators of Bronze or Silver-rank serving within the Order of Valhalla. They were doing so while being carefully scrutinized and evaluated by true healers, in hopes of gaining favor from a deity and becoming an official acolyte. The true healers would then take on the patients that required more serious effort.

Kiru could tell the robed servants' abilities to perform strong techniques was lacking, with only a few performing any semblance of magical healing. Their medical knowledge, however, appeared significant, rivaling any other that he'd seen or experienced growing up in Bristleton. Most were cleaning wounds, suturing lacerations with medical thread, or bracing broken limbs with wooden splints with remarkable efficiency.

The injured cultivators, though shielded from fatal wounds by the protective Healing Dome technique, weren't completely spared from serious injury. As such, though they were all stronger than the aiding servants, many were too hurt to physically resist the healers suturing their skin or realigning their limbs, no matter how painful those treatments were. Once the healing work was done, the students either rested or were escorted out of the arena through the back gates, depending on the severity of their injury.

Kiru winced as he saw the state some of his classmates were in, despite the fact that their wounds would heal relatively faster than most cultivators at lower ranks. He could tell that, without magical or pharmaceutical aid, it would have been an unpleasant road to recovery for most of them. Compared to the near-instant healing talented clerics, healers, and paladins possessed, natural recovery was slower, and far more painful.

The servants had their gray robes, now stained heavily with blood, embroidered with two separate insignias on their chests. The right insignia was always the same: a radiant sun made up of two crescent moons, the symbol of the Holy Order of Valhalla. The left one varied, but there were three predominant ones that the psion noticed. The first and most popular was a heart whose borders were made with exaggerated golden thread stitching. It was the symbol of Ein, goddess of medicine and healing, the same deity who the gnome on Team Supreme served.

The other two were also for deities officially accepted within the Pantheon. There was the crow, a symbol of Odin. The one-eyed servants who hoped to be officially recognized by the knowledge-obsessed god put Kiru on edge, but they didn't seem to notice him, fortunately. The other was a small angel wielding a large greatsword. Brunhilda had told Kiru about that symbol before. It was of Frigg, the major goddess who Hlin served as protector.

Aside from Kiru and Brunhilda, only Team Supreme's gnome member had officially accepted patronage from a divine. That made those three particularly popular figures amongst other hopeful future acolytes. More than a few of them noticed Kiru, taking special notice of the subtle rune in his headband. They gave him eager waves and nods of approval. They were impressed by those who had aligned with the minor goddess, and Kiru could tell that some were considering doing the same in hopes of being fully accepted as acolytes.

The psion smiled. His promise to Brunhilda was coming to fruition. From their victories, Hlin would gain glory. The more glory and fame the goddess attained, the more likely she would be to get an altar within the capital. That would put her one step closer to being fully accepted into the pantheon and Brunhilda achieving her goal.

The paladin escorting Kiru gestured to a nearby doorway to the right. Kiru took the hint and started walking in that direction. It led to a cobblestone passage with thick metal doors on each side, with no slit to see what was on the other side. At first, Kiru was on the defensive as to why he had been guided there, but then he noticed that the passage had a total of eight doors, four on each side. Each door had a team name written on it. This was where the winners were escorted, to be healed away from the prying eyes or envy of the defeated cultivators.

The paladin brought him to the room to the right, at the end of the passage. Kiru's focus clouded, and the dull headache he had due to his mana usage during the first round started to intensify. He practically ran to the door the paladin gestured to. There was his team's name, Pandemonium, written in chalk on the door. Kiru was exhausted.

The prolonged fighting and danger had taken a great toll. While others' bodies were shaky from physical exertion, Kiru's mind was fatigued. It was a product of moving with mental exertion versus stamina. *Damn, that fight took a lot out of me, and I'm really low on manna. I need to get somewhere where I can rest and cultivate without risking giving my secret away*, he thought.

As he opened the door, there were his friends, in a single cozy stone room, sitting in a section of beds, and being tended to by a gentle-looking nurse. Smiling, Kiru tried to look strong, not wanting to go limp in the sight of any strangers. He stumbled over to the nearest bed and laid down with his head on the pillow. With no need to move his body, he stopped using Telekinesis. He sighed in relief. By just releasing his technique, the growing headache dramatically lessened.

For a few seconds, Kiru fell asleep. That was until William started talking in his head. Kiru grunted a little in frustration. He opened his eyes to see that the cleric was too busy focusing on Mutt's injuries to pay him any mind at the moment. Now that he no longer needed William's immediate aid, and due to the restless imp wanting to get out, Kiru summoned his familiar from his core.

"Hahaha! That was bitchin'! Oooh! I can't wait for the bloodshed we'll bring next round! Ooh! Cookies!" The imp cheered and ran over to a tray of food.

The rest of Pandemonium grinned as they looked to their leader, proud of him and their accomplishments. They were also amused at his distress at the risk of having an imp on a sugar rush. The nurse turned out to be a cleric in service to Ein, as evidenced by her insignia and skill. She was using a healing technique on Mutt, reinforcing that the winners were getting more rapid and specialized care. She had a hand placed on each side of his body, where he'd been stabbed. Holy light glowed from her hands over the bloody bandages covering the wounds.

The orc's body also glowed where her hands made contact. Mutt groaned, but then let out a moan of content. The cleric with round cheeks smiled, then pulled out a bulky round green pill. "A mana restoration pill for you, dearie. You're gonna need it for the next round," she said, not giving any more explanation to the vague warning.

"That makes sense." The blind orc shrugged casually and gave a toothy grin, not seeming to be concerned in the slightest. The cleric let out a cry of surprise when, instead of taking the pill from her with his hand, he just opened his big mouth and chomped down on it. She wasn't hurt but was definitely startled.

"Right, well . . . who's next?" She chuckled nervously, turning her attention to Zhaden. He had some spots of swelling under his scales and more than a few cuts and abrasions, but pure fatigue was the worst of his problems. After tending to his external injuries, she handed him two pills. "Take the blue one first. It will replenish your stamina. Then, take the green one. It will provide your core with a supply of pure mana. Cycle the mana through your core for at least five minutes in order to change the mana to your particular mana affinity. Then, you can cycle it through your meridians. Understand?"

"Gratitude," the drakonid hissed before taking the blue pill and closing his eyes. He chose to sit on the bed and rest his head against the wall versus lying on it in the standard fashion. The orc and drakonid were so exhausted they fell asleep almost instantly, which was advantageous for Kiru. Their dreaming minds would give him a more active source of mental mana, allowing him to cultivate and restore some desperately needed energy.

The cleric then went to Brunhilda. "Well, look what we have here, a fellow holy cultivator. Who's your patron?"

The dwarf, right eye swollen shut and lips bruised and cut, held her head up high and declared proudly, "Hlin, goddess of protection."

The cleric's head tilted in confusion. "Hlin?" Her eyebrows then raised as understanding hit her. "Oh! Oh, dearie, you serve a minor goddess, don't you? Oh, bless your soul for your bravery!"

The paladin crossed her arms and pursed her lips at her condescending tone. "It be an honor to serve Hlin, thank you very much," she said. "I'm the ordained high paladin in her service, and one day, I'll—"

"Being in the favor of a minor god is just that—minor," the cleric interrupted. "I mean, look at you, lass. You're clearly a capable cultivator, but you're wasting your talents in a pointless endeavor, stifling your growth. Now, you seem like a good person. The pantheon accepts if a cultivator renounces their oath from a minor to a major god. There's no shame in it."

She then pulled out a small scroll from her satchel. "Ein welcomes all healers, and if you'd declare your allegiance to her, you can have the information on the Healing Hands technique. There's a reason Ein is a major deity. She has the respect of other major deities like Frigg who your minor goddess serves, and those who follow Ein faithfully will reap the rewards."

The dwarf's eyes widened. Healing Hands was a powerful technique that the order had decreed would only be allowed for those serving in the official pantheon, beneath the major gods. Having the technique would put the paladin at a total of three, just one away from being able to ascend to Ruby. It would also allow her to help her friends more easily.

She instinctively reached her hand out for the scroll, but then retracted it. She gasped slightly as realization struck her. "Ye be just trying to fill your quota," she accused. "These events be huge draws for hopeful future acolytes that wish to find a patron. Ye be trying to eliminate the competition by converting me, the high paladin of Hlin. Ye be a skilled cleric, but I'll be the judge on whether I'm wasting my talents." She crossed her arms once more. "Besides, I couldn't call myself a paladin if I could so easily be dissuaded from my holy calling by a simple bribe."

The cleric's kindly face turned into an ugly scowl in a flash. "Bribe?! How dare you! I offered you a chance to get out of your pitiful—"

A loud belch came from behind the round-cheeked woman, cutting her off. "Ah, shut up, will you? I'm trying to eat some cookies here. Just do your healing and get out of here, you passive-aggressive wench." William ended his statement with another resounding burp.

The cleric stood there, jaw dropped. A demon—an unholy vermin to the devout Vasir worshippers—was casually relaxing mere feet away from her, lying in a bowl of crumbs with a half-eaten cookie in each hand, like he was lounging in a pool. Enraged, the cleric took out her mace with her free hand and wordlessly attacked William.

The imp let out an "Eeek!" as he leaped from the table to dodge her. The cleric's strength was evident, as one strike was enough to break the table in two, sending food and beverages flying about. William quickly ran over to Kiru's bed and made a fart noise with his mouth while sticking his tongue out to antagonize the cleric.

"I don't know how you got here, demon filth, but by the gods, I will smite you!" she growled, raising her mace, seemingly not caring that Kiru's head was right next to William.

That's when Brunhilda very pointedly cleared her throat.

The cleric jerked her head to the paladin, a feral look in her eyes.

"That be his familiar, ma'am. Now, you wouldn't want to go and hurt a student's familiar without just cause and lessen his chance in the Games, would you? That may be looked down upon by the clergy. Who knows, maybe they would demote you and replace you with, how'd you say it? Someone who's wasting her talents?" A wry smile grew on the dwarf's face.

With a disgusted look, the cleric turned back at the psion. "Is this true?"

"Indeed," Kiru answered.

She scowled, and her nostrils flared. "Hmph," she grunted as she shoved her scroll back in her bag, then reattached her mace to her belt. "Ugly demon pig," she muttered as she went back over to the heavily bruised Brunhilda, who stood up and spread her arms expectantly. It wasn't for a hug, but to allow the now-very-angry cleric to use her Healing Hands on the paladin's injuries as she was assigned to do.

It was obvious she *really* didn't want to heal the uppity dwarf, but she still did her job, even repeating her technique on some broken ribs that weren't completely healed after Brunhilda pointed them out. Once she was done, she shoved her hand in her satchel to get out the same two pills she'd given the others. While doing so, she also jostled the various scrolls and pieces of parchment inside, possibly more bribes in service to her deity. Finding the pills, the cleric yanked them out, then practically shoved them into the paladin's hands, nowhere near as gently as she'd treated Mutt and Zhaden.

Then she unceremoniously turned her back to Brunhilda, letting out a loud breath through her nostrils, and approached Kiru. "You're next, kid. I'm going to need you to take your armor off, though. I need to examine the extent of your injuries. Also, keep your demon away from me."

William pulled down an eyelid and stuck his tongue out at the cleric.

Kiru's heart began to race. He couldn't show the woman his body. It would reveal his secret. Fortunately, Brunhilda, always his protector, came to the rescue.

"Actually, he is an acolyte of Hlin as well. So, I will be in charge of his care."

"You can't be serious?" She laughed.

The paladin crossed her arms and smiled.

"You would allow someone associated with a demon into your goddess's service? To think that a deity would stoop so low." She shook her head, tossed two more pills onto Kiru's bed like the others, and marched toward the exit.

"*Master, keep her here,*" William sent to Kiru.

"*What? Why?*" Kiru asked. He assumed the imp was still hiding somewhere as he couldn't see him anymore.

"*Just do it!*" The imp demanded.

There was something in William's tone that indicated more than his usual childish scheming. Kiru didn't know what he was up to, but he decided to trust him.

"Hey! Wait a minute there, lady!" he cried out in indignation. Kiru proceeded to rant loudly and make a scene about how honorable Hlin was and how she'd protected them and even saved Brunhilda's life. He couldn't see what William was up to, but he hoped the little demon would hurry. He didn't have much left to say without repeating himself.

Finally, William sent him a mental message that he was done, so Kiru abruptly ended his tirade with a "You're dismissed."

The cleric, whose face was now beet-red at being berated by some acolyte, gave Kiru a very uncleric-like gesture before leaving the room and slamming the metal door shut.

The purple-haired dwarf began to sniffle. "Kiru . . . did ye mean those words?" She looked as if she was about to cry.

The psion's mouth opened. He was an official acolyte of Hlin, but his relationship was more like a formal agreement rather than holy dedication.

William answered for him, emerging from under his bed. "Nah, I just had him make that shit up to distract that rude woman."

The dwarf looked shocked. She glanced up to Kiru, and he gave an uncomfortable shrug of admittance, blushing with guilt. "And why would ye do that? Hlin doesn't need us provoking clerics of a major deity unless we're truly intending to spread her faith!"

"Whoa, whoa! I'm holding up my end of the agreement. Our success will be spreading the knowledge of Hlin to all of the Alliance. I'm just not the preachy type." The psion put his palms out, trying to placate the paladin as he gave his defense.

Brunhilda huffed but still seemed to be mollified by his explanation.

William spoke up. "Yeah, and besides, he did it for your goddess' benefit."

"How in the bloody abyss was that for Hlin's benefit?" She glared down at William.

The imp gave a toothy grin, then stuck his hand straight into his brain. His face contorted as he moved it about, finally pulling out a scroll. It was covered in a healthy layer of his slimy brain juice, but it was unmistakably the scroll that the rude cleric had offered Brunhilda earlier—the one that contained the Healing Hands technique.

Brunhilda's eyes widened in surprise. "Ye . . . why?"

"Well, the wench wouldn't stop talking. Then, she tried to squash me like a bug. Also, only I get to make fun of you, not some sarcastic cleric. I only want to deal with one palabitch."

Brunhilda let out a chuckle. "Well, I guess I can deal with that, ye smelly little demon." She took the slimy scroll from him.

*"Look at you being a good teammate. I'm proud of you, William,"* Kiru sent telepathically.

The red-skinned imp's face seemed to turn a shade darker as he scowled. *"Yeah, well . . . whatever. She better use that to help us stay strong and beat up our opponents."*

Kiru couldn't help but laugh.

# CHAPTER FORTY-FIVE

# The Top Eight

After Brunhilda studied the scroll and learned the technique within, she quickly ripped it up in order to destroy the evidence of William's theft. The last thing they needed was that cleric coming after them. Once that was done, she practiced the technique on Kiru's injuries. Unlike tomes containing information on techniques, scrolls only provided a more basic understanding. Most of the books, like the ones Zhaden used, had specialized rune patterns to accelerate learning the techniques, giving students the ability to go through the voluminous pages and gain an adequate grasp on how to perform them in minutes. Scrolls weren't like that. Instead, they just gave the reader a basic understanding of how to direct and control one's mana to produce the intended effect. Still, it was better than trying to figure out a technique on one's own from scratch. So, Brunhilda needed to practice, and it just so happened she had an injured ally to use as a test dummy.

Kiru was a little concerned about the technique potentially backfiring, but the dwarf was utterly convinced by the quality of the Order's scrollwork. Trusting his friend, Kiru relented and let her practice on him. It took her half a dozen tries, but by the end, she was finally able to use her Healing Hands technique on him successfully.

After Kiru's body was healed, and they had all ingested the stamina and mana pills, Pandemonium spent their time using the wash basin to wash off any excess blood and gore they had gotten on them during Round One. Kiru, in particular, practically looked like he'd butchered a whole village.

They also spent time discussing the other remaining teams and their potential weaknesses. They also took turns looking out the small window up top to view the upperclassmen's other two free-for-all matches. The differences in power was immediately apparent. Most first-year students were considered Zeta Gold, meaning they had only one technique. Scattered amongst them, there were about ten or so Rubies, and not many cultivators fell in the "in-between" categories of either a Beta or Alpha-rank Gold. By contrast, about half of the students in the second-year round were Alpha Gold, while most of the others were either tier-one or two Ruby. Kiru knew little about the different tiers for Ruby aside from that tier-one was the lowest tier and that a higher tier indicated a higher power level. With more time and training, they were far faster and deadlier than their first-year counterparts. The small percentage of Sapphire-rank cultivators were obvious, as no one else could touch them. They didn't even look tired or at all put out during the fighting.

While the second-years were impressive, the seniors were astonishing to the psion. Not as many teams participated in their round, but with most being a mixture of tier-two Ruby and tier-one Sapphire, the fighting was even more intense. What was even more extraordinary was that there were two Emeralds present, and they happened to be on the same team! They were a pair of halberd wielders, one human and the other an orc. Kiru knew of them. The human was named Tess and the orc, Thurman. They were called the "Two Towers" due to them standing a good seven feet tall; they were the top students in the academy. Kiru hadn't engaged with them ever on account of them both being third years and from Sword House, but everyone knew of their skill.

The crowd cheered, despite the fact that the cultivators fighting at such a great speed, it was difficult to even track their movements. If the difference between a Sapphire and Ruby was a wide road, the difference between an Emerald and a Sapphire was a canyon. Watching them competing against their classmates, their peers, it couldn't be called anything less than utter domination. The senior class fights were the main events, and the Two Towers were the headliners. Kiru was glad *they* didn't have to face them!

Once the senior class fights were finished, the headmaster declared what the format for Round Two would be. It was fairly simple: the fighting would start up again in half an hour and consist of a team-versus-team matchups, rather than the free-for-all from earlier. The contest was single elimination, and the first-year victors of the Warrior Games would be the team that achieved three wins.

Pandemonium was called first. Kiru wondered if it was arranged that way due to the merciless reputation he'd gained when he'd cut down the dozen or so prone opponents affected by Zhaden's Nightmare technique.

The audience began chanting something he couldn't quite make out. His pointed ears twitched as he tried to grasp the words. Then, they hit him. They'd given him a nickname. "Blood Elf! Blood Elf! Blood Elf!"

The first team they faced was called the Crushers, one of the ones that had refused to spar with Pandemonium all year. It was made up of four humans, two wielding a pair of small warhammers like they were hand axes, and another two so large, Kiru genuinely wondered if they had Giant blood in them. Each of those two held a massive maul in one hand and a kite shield in the other. Kiru was aware they used a rare type of mana called force mana. The psion knew little about it other than that it was very good at breaking things, which explained why their opponents favored hammers.

The two teams stared each other down as the headmaster made introductions. As they did, one of the shorter Crushers began loudly talking to his allies, not even seeming to consider lowering the volume of his voice. Brunhilda, Zhaden, and Mutt were all confused by the man's strange dialect, but Kiru smiled, recognizing the language immediately. It was Japanese.

He was impressed. Learning and using a rare dialect in order to be able to communicate tactics without fear of an opponent listening in was a very clever tactic. No wonder they'd made it to the top eight. Kiru also realized that their usage of the language was slightly off, but he got the gist of what they were saying. The Crushers' plan was simple: all four of them would target Brunhilda. With Pandemonium's healer gone, they would proceed to isolate each other member of the team one by one. It would've been a good plan, had they not been facing Kiru.

Kiru sent telepathic messages to his party, informing them of The Crushers' plan. *"We're going to go with the Sneaky Turtle plan,"* he said.

*"Really? Ha! Sure thing, boss,"* Mutt said.

*"It will be done,"* Zhaden added.

*"They will see that I will not be broken,"* Brunhilda asserted.

*"Do you have to do this plan, Master? It leaves all the blood-spilling to the others,"* William said.

Kiru didn't reply to his familiar as the bell for their quarterfinal match had just rung.

At that noise, both Zhaden and Mutt dove under Brunhilda's shields, completely obscuring them from the Crushers' line of sight. Kiru hopped over the dwarf and pointed his hooked blades at their foes.

The force mana wielders braced themselves. They didn't expect Kiru to rush in front. Their leader, one of the maul-wielders, was an abnormally large, tan-skinned elf. When she saw the Defunct student rush in front, she smirked. She said in Japanese, "Change of plan, break the Defunct with our Pure Force techniques from a distance, then rush the paladin."

Kiru's eyes widened. Then he changed his blades' positions to form an X in front of him and hurriedly sent via Telepathy: *"Brunhilda, Divine Shield me, now!"*

"Divine Shield!" she shouted just as all four of the Crushers lowered their weapons and swung them in unison, shouting "Pure Force!"

A dark green glow came from all of their weapons and shot forward as beams of mana toward Kiru, combining into one giant ranged attack. Kiru heard an *"Oh, shit!"* from William right before the Divine Shield fortunately intercepted, slowing the technique and fighting back against the mana. It still wasn't enough, and the weakened-but-still-very-strong Pure Force technique came right for Kiru. The psion was able to block with his blades but was quickly sent flying backwards over Brunhilda.

Kiru crashed into the sand, coughing and wheezing as he tried to breathe. He'd been blown back but wasn't out of the fight. He looked up to see the four Crushers rushing towards Brunhilda, quickly closing within ten feet of her. *"Zhaden, Mutt, now!"* he sent.

Right before the four could bring their weapons down on Brunhilda, Zhaden and Mutt appeared behind the Crushers. Zhaden materialized out of thin air while Mutt surged up from the ground underneath. The rogue's daggers bit into one's neck while Mutt's claws pierced into the back of another's, instantly halving the number of opponents they now faced.

Kiru smiled as he stood up. Sneaky Turtle was about baiting opponents into coming close so that they could flank and entrap them. With the gold drakonid and orc hidden from view, none of the Crushers could able tell if they were still behind Brunhilda's shields or not.

The two maul users slammed their weapons against Brunhilda's shields. There was a loud clanging of metal on metal as the troll-blooded dwarf withstood the blows. To the remaining two Crushers' surprise, Kiru rejoined the fight.

The psion jumped over the dwarf and hooked his Fu Tao on the elf's shield. His opponent gasped in surprise as he forced her shield down, then promptly amputated her left arm at the wrist, with Hammer the Boards making her lose her shield.

William cried out in glee in Kiru's mind while the elf cried out loud in pain. Fueled by adrenaline, she desperately swung her maul at the psion.

Kiru ran inside her guard and hooked his blade in her right armpit. In a flash, he cut through nearly all of the muscle in that area; blood instantly gushed out of the wound. As Kiru turned to finish her off, he saw he didn't need to as Brunhilda smashed the elf's face with a shield bash. The fourth member of the Crushers had been taken care of in a matter of seconds by Mutt and Zhaden; orbs of protective light surrounded both maul wielders at the same exact moment, signifying Pandemonium's victory.

The crowd roared while Kiru and his friends looked at each other, smiles growing on their faces. With full foreknowledge of how their opponents had planned to fight them, they had overwhelmingly defeated them in under thirty seconds! They had truly become strong. The cheers for "Blood Elf" grew even louder. Also, to Brunhilda's delight, when it was announced that they were the winners, a small congregation of hopeful acolytes sitting around the booth reserved for the Order of Valhalla's representative began cheering loudly to get her attention.

They congratulated and encouraged her. They also asked which deity she served and if her patron was looking for followers.

The rest and recovery time until their next fight was notably shorter. Their semi-final round then put them up against a team sponsored by Kiru's Fire Cultivation I professor, Claire Redheart. The team was called Perpetual Flame, and true to form, they were a squadron of four fire mana cultivators. All were in Sword House and had a flame embroidered on their backs that was nowhere near as gaudy as Pandemonium's glittery flower. Perpetual Flame was also one of the teams that had formed the mega team with Team Supreme in Round One.

They consisted of two dwarves, a gold drakonid much shorter that Zhaden, and a human who wielded a falchion. The drakonid brandished a whip, and the dwarves actually wielded no weapons, preferring to fight with their bare hands. One of the dwarves, their leader, was shirtless, and the entirety of his torso was covered in flesh permanently marred by severe burns. He didn't even have any hair left! Seeing a male dwarf without a beard took some getting used to.

None of them were Ruby-ranked, but they all shared the same technique, Boiling Blood, gifted to them by their sponsor, Instructor Redheart, who was favored by the headmaster and thus given more slots for students to recruit and sponsor. She had described the technique to Kiru and the rest of his class during their first semester. It was one of her own design, so she was rather proud of it. Since Kiru and most of the class were not her sponsored pupils, she didn't give them every detail, but it essentially made the cultivator a temporary berserker. Fire mana literally coursed through their blood, enhancing their speed, strength, and healing ability. They also became utter savages. The members of Pandemonium had watched the fire cultivators' quarterfinal match from their recovery room. It was the first time the team had actually used the technique for the members of Pandemonium to see. Throughout the entirety of their training, none of them had witnessed them use Boiling Blood. Perpetual Flame had kept it as a secret trump card up until that point. During that match, the members of Perpetual Flame had to be forcefully removed from their unconscious opponents to prevent them from killing the students. They won in brutal fashion, despite there being two Ruby-ranked opponents on the other side.

Of course, the crowd had loved it.

Pandemonium had a general plan as to what they would do if they needed to face Perpetual Flame. After actually seeing them fight, however, Zhaden pointed out some distinct insights that helped the team refine their strategy. First, when Perpetual Flame used Boiling Blood, they seemed unable to use any other techniques, opting to fight with their bodies and weapons. Second, when they were forced to stop and Boiling Blood faded, they moved with obvious lethargy. Apparently, the technique had a steeper cost than others too.

"I believe we can use their own strength against them." Zhadene proceeded to tell them his idea. They didn't like it, but in the limited time between their next fight, they had no better option.

The two teams lined up against each other, about thirty feet separating them. "Hey, Defunct boy," the burned dwarf called out. "Yer luck's run out. Once we're through with you, you'll be nuthin' but a bloody pulp. Then, your nickname will stick, Blood Elf."

Kiru smirked. He'd heard worse. It was his turn to provoke his enemies. "I'm the one who'll be a bloody pulp?! Ha! You're funnier than you look, and let's be honest, you look fucking hilarious without a beard." He had heard someone mock the dwarf before their previous match with a similar jab.

The dwarf scowled. It appeared that insult still stung.

"You think you're so strong just because Instructor Redheart gave you some powerful technique," Kiru said mockingly. "Well, I've seen it. It's nothing special. At least, it's nothing special in your pathetic hands." This time, he made sure to look at all of the members of Perpetual Flame. Kiru knew firsthand that the fire mana inside them lowered their anger threshold, and they all took the bait, the drakonid even snarling at the psion.

"If you think you're so strong, prove it. Use your oh-so-powerful technique!" A mischievous grin grew on his face. "Unless you're all scared of being embarrassed by a Defunct boy?"

"Pathetic?! You're the one who's pathetic, boyo! We were handpicked by one of the greatest fire mana cultivators 'round. You're just some weirdo's pet project. You asked for it now. Lads, let's show this piece of shite how far out of his league he is."

Kiru kept his cocky grin but tightened his grip on his blades, betraying his nerves.

As soon as the headmaster signaled the start, all four cultivators activated their Boiling Blood. They roared in fury as their eyes, nostrils, and mouths gave off a bright orange glow. They charged recklessly at Pandemonium.

Kiru and his friends braced themselves, then initiated step two of their plan. They ran. Zhaden turned invisible while Kiru took off like a madman. Meanwhile, Brunhilda was much too slow in her armor so, to her embarrassment, Mutt carried the paladin on his back. The orc's high strength allowed him to hold her and keep up a good speed.

"Ha! Big talk, coward!" The burned dwarf sprinted toward Kiru. His drakonid ally joined him in chasing the psion, while the other two focused on Mutt and Brunhilda. Pandemonium's plan was simple: Force the fire mana cultivators to use their Boiling Blood all at once, then outlast them until the technique faded and the lethargy set in. Since they most likely couldn't physically endure a straight-up brawl against them, they instead decided to run.

The crowd was vehemently against this plan. As they registered that Pandemonium was running away and not bringing them the carnage they came for, the boos and insults started flying. Many even started throwing their food down on the arena floor. Niazen laughed loudly and let the match proceed. Normally, such a display of cowardice from academy students in the arena wouldn't be tolerated, but the worse his brother's team performed, the more Niajar would be shamed.

The crowd continued their insults. Fortunately for Kiru, he was a pro at ignoring verbal abuse. They continued their pace, keeping their distance from their opponents and dodging the food and debris being hurled down toward them. After two minutes straight of running, however, Mutt eventually fell victim to having his attention pulled in multiple directions and tripped on a small rock hidden in a patch of grass. In so doing, he knocked into Brunhilda and the two were overtaken by the two fire mana cultivators.

Smelling blood in the water, they had jumped forward, weapons poised to strike at Mutt's exposed back. Both Kiru and Zhaden were far off as they had spread out to help keep their opponents from grouping them together. In response, Brunhilda jumped in front of her teammate and raised her dual shields. The shields' metal groaned as they met the enhanced fist and falchion strikes, but the paladin's strength and fortitude made itself known as she withstood multiple blows from her foes.

Finally seeing some actual combat, the crowd cheered Brunhilda as she activated her Divine Shield technique, encasing herself in protective holy light. Both of the enraged cultivators struck at the beam of light their blood-fueled rage, their bodies soon becoming engulfed in flame from the technique's retaliation. With the regenerative effects of Boiling Blood, however, the fires dissipated within a matter of seconds, and their bodies began to heal.

The dwarf and human growled and redoubled their attacks. Mutt got back to his feet but stayed hunched behind Brunhilda's shields. The metal began to dent and bend from the repeated assaults, but to everyone's surprise, the paladin continued to withstand their strikes. The troll blood flowing in her veins enhanced her strength to that of two dwarves at her rank. That, plus the abnormally elongated muscular arms she sported, provided a huge advantage in this war of attrition.

"Look! She's holding those fighters off with only her shields!" one robed servant of the order shouted out from the crowd.

"Her goddess must be giving her the strength to fight!" another replied.

"Well, what do you expect? She serves the goddess of protection."

"Is the goddess looking for new followers?"

There was still a lot of booing and cheering from the crowd as a whole, but the section of servants began chanting the name of Brunhilda's goddess in excitement for all to hear. Invigorated by their words, the paladin let out a mighty shout and raised her shields higher in defiance of her enemies. Suddenly, however, there was an audible crack of bone as something in her left forearm broke under the sustained strikes. With a low moan, she channeled Rejuvenation to her arm. It wasn't as effective as Healing Hands, but she didn't have a free hand, and using Rejuvenation was much better than nothing. She would hold on, but not for much longer.

Kiru wanted to rush over across the arena and help but kept to the plan. The psion continued to run, doing his best to not engage any members of Perpetual Flame until he had to. Thanks to his mental mana, Kiru could still see Zhaden who had gone invisible. The rogue was keeping his distance but was trailing the two still in pursuit of Kiru. Perpetual Flame's whip-wielding drakonid came close to stopping Kiru. Their whip connected under his shoulder pauldron where the armor was thinnest. Lacking the ability to feel there, Kiru was spared from the pain, but the impact almost made him lose his footing.

After about thirty more seconds of running, Kiru started to get another headache. He had been exerting his mana to a more extreme extent than usual. Normally, just running wouldn't have been as draining, but he had to invest extra mana in order to increase his speed while keeping up the charade that he was running via natural means. *That* in particular was taking its toll. Fortunately, he didn't have to do so for much longer. Boiling Blood's timer had run out. At once, Perpetual Flame became sluggish. Their steps were slower and their breathing more difficult.

The crowd's raucous cheering quickly turned into murmurs of confusion.

Kiru spared a glance back and saw the cause. He'd gained ground from his pursuers. "Now!"

From behind the pair that had been following Kiru, Zhaden materialized, twin daggers at the ready. The dream mana user struck, slicing his blades across the backs of their legs. In one quick motion, he cut through the flesh behind their knees. They fell forward, and as they did, he stabbed them in their sides, then in the back, leaving his knives in the cultivators.

On the other side of the arena, Brunhilda heard Kiru's words and the power of the strikes from her opponents notably decreased. She finally relented and dropped her shields like an oyster forced open. Instead of a helpless ocean creature, though, out came an angry orc. Mutt had bided his time, waiting to strike. Brunhilda had had to face their opponents all alone for too long and now Mutt was determined to honor her strength.

He jumped out and elongated his claws, slashing down as he landed. The human blocked with their falchion, but Mutt's nails gouged the barehanded dwarf. The dwarf coughed blood as he pressed his hands to his wounds, desperately trying to staunch the bleeding. A backhand from Mutt quickly knocked him unconscious.

"Flame Geyser!" the man shouted.

Mutt's enhanced senses helped him feel the subtle heat and trembling coming from below him. He jumped to the side, narrowly avoiding a column of flame erupting from the ground.

Desperate, the man put all his energy into a final lunge.

Despite the speed of his attack, the orc was faster. Mutt managed to step to the side and bite down on the man's wrist. The fire mana user let out a cry of pain and dropped his blade.

"H-how?" he asked in shock.

Mutt growled and activated a technique to empower his jaws. He clamped down harder, shattering the bones of both his wrists into multiple pieces.

As Mutt unlocked his jaws, the man cried out in terror. Blood shot out from the puncture wounds on his wrists. His cries were cut short when Mutt grabbed him by the throat and lifted him up in the air. Mutt's milky white eyes seemed to stare directly into the trembling cultivator's. "Good fight, but you gotta pace yourself next time." Before his opponent could reply, Mutt threw the man into the wall.

It was a good thing the clerics and paladins were still on duty, because if they hadn't used the protective healing dome on the man before he made contact with the stone, he would have been crushed to paste.

# CHAPTER FORTY-SIX

# Pep Talk

The crowd roared once again, relishing the violence. They still weren't thrilled with how Pandemonium had beaten their opponents but they were satisfied nonetheless after they had brought them their "pound of flesh." After the semifinal round, the students were escorted back to their rooms once more. No healer was present this time, but there were three more high-quality pills on each of their beds, one each for health, mana, and stamina accordingly. All of the team members were tense, except for Mutt. The only time he was ever *not* calm was when he needed to fight.

*So close.* They were so close to the finish line. Brunhilda would bring glory to her goddess, hopefully gaining more followers and making it easier to get Hlin established within the pantheon. Zhaden would gain respect for his skills, making him a top-tier candidate to join the Claw. Mutt . . . well, Mutt would get to enjoy some more "good fights," as he called them. And Kiru was just one fight away from getting the first of his father's items. One step closer to achieving his destiny.

They watched the next round. It was Team Supreme against a team led by someone Kiru had not given much thought to since early in the school year: Genevieve. The dark-skinned ice mana cultivator from Rowe who had rejected Kiru's offer to form a team had managed to get past the first round. She wielded a spear made of solid ice and had a pretty impressive squad behind her. Her team was aptly named Blizzard Dawn, and Kiru assumed it was because they consisted of two ice mana and two light mana cultivators.

Both of the light mana wielders were clerics. From what Brunhilda had told Kiru, light mana wasn't great at healing, but it did help with methods of conjuration. The two clerics manipulated light in such a way that they could produce semi-transparent walls from it. They wore the typical robes of the Order of Valhalla and hefted heavy crossbows. The other ice mana cultivator was a human in his early twenties. His breath was visible and his body partially covered in a layer of frost taking the place of armor. Instead of a weapon, he just held his fists up; he clearly favored the pugilist approach.

"Ranged damage and magic shielding from the clerics while the two ice mana fighters engage up close. It's an effective plan," Zhaden said.

"Ye be right that they can bring the punishment, but they not be built for prolonged fighting," Brunhilda countered.

Kiru raised an eyebrow. "Why do you say that?"

"They have no healer," she answered.

"*Pfft! Even I could've told you that*," William sent telepathically to Kiru.

The psion rolled his eyes at his overconfident familiar.

Unaware of the telepathic conversation, Brunhilda continued, "Since they got no healer, they focused on defending the spearwoman and the martial artist. If any of 'em get hurt, though, they be done for. Those clerics don't seem too confident in their crossbow-wielding skills either."

Kiru looked to where she pointed. Sure enough, the two robed clerics' arms were trembling slightly.

"Though it may be just cause they're so close to their cold teammates," Brunhilda added.

When the headmaster signaled the match to begin, each cleric moved to be directly behind one of the ice-mana wielders and quickly fired their crossbows.

Zane stuck a hand out with practiced ease and leaves zoomed up from the ground, intercepting the bolts. Meanwhile, Warren and Ambrose ran forward and engaged their foes.

Warren's axe head burned as he swung his blade downward at Genevieve. Before it could reach her, a wall of light appeared between them, blocking the strike completely. Warren recoiled from the impact, and that's when Genevieve struck. She thrust her icy spear forward to stab the barbarian's neck. His reflexes were top-notch, though, and he managed to swerve just far enough away that she hit his trapezoid instead.

Ambrose's bout was totally different. Ascending to Ruby had enhanced both the power of his body and his techniques. While he was still a bit pudgy and had the old burn mark on his cheek, the improvements were undeniable. As he ran toward the other pugilist, he jumped in the air and pulled his right fist back.

The cleric behind the ice mana wielder conjured a shield of light, just the same as their counterpart while his teammate readied his own fist to strike back at Ambrose.

That was when the noble smirked. "Air Push," he said. Just as Ambrose was descending toward the conjured shield, his body abruptly shifted to the right. He landed beside the ice mana cultivator, avoiding the shield altogether. Before his opponent could respond, he lifted a hand and said, "Electrocute." A blast of electricity shot out from his palm and instead of striking the other pugilist, he struck the cleric head-on. He was taken out in a literal flash. Smoke trailed off the cleric's form, and a protective dome of light formed over them before they hit the ground.

Ambrose avoided a retaliatory strike from the ice-covered pugilist and laughed condescendingly. Rather than engaging his frosty opponent, he quickly sped off to eliminate the other cleric. Though the second cleric had erected a shield in front of them as well, Ambrose just used Air Push instead to shift them away from the cover of their shield. With an expeditious use of Lightning Limb, half of Blizzard Dawn had been eliminated.

Genevieve and the other ice mana user fought valiantly but were getting overwhelmed by Team Supreme. She did, however, nearly take out Warren, managing to slash him across the chest with her spear and forcing him to back away, at which point she surprised him by throwing her ice spear and impaling him through a thigh, the weapon's tip embedding itself in the ground.

Warren nearly dropped his axe and screamed in pain as he clutched his injured leg.

Genevieve ran up to finish the job, but that was her mistake. Warren, being a fire mana cultivator, quickly melted the spear with his mana, leaving him free to move again. With Genevieve within striking distance and sans another conjured weapon at the ready, the barbarian struck her in the chest with the full force of his fiery axe, nearly bisecting her. Blood spewed from her mouth just as the protective orb of healing light surrounded her.

With her gone, the pugilist ice-mana cultivator didn't last ten seconds. Sure enough, Team Supreme emerged the victors. Despite only using his Razorleaf technique a few times, Zane actually seemed pretty exhausted from the fight. That gave Kiru some hope that they would be at a disadvantage.

The headmaster seemed to notice it as well and, without warning, granted a thirty-minute intermission before the final fight would commence instead of the expected fifteen. Hearing that, Kiru let out a frustrated huff. After all this time, people manipulating systems to take advantage of and hurt others still really bothered him on a deep, personal level.

At first, he was just plain angry and wanted to shout at the injustice, but he quickly realized that was the old Kiru. That was the boy who simply wanted to lash out, not actually make things better. Instead of allowing his anger to consume him, the psion closed his eyes and used what Zhaden had taught him, visualizing that as fiery fuel to empower him.

It was easy to picture as he still had inklings of fire mana inside him from his fractured core. He fed that to his envisioned hollow body. Kiru smiled. Instead of becoming subservient to rage, his anger would serve him, fuel him to help achieve his destiny and remove the corruption that had taken root in his home.

Achieving his goal no doubt called for violence, but he would use violence as a tool, not for its own sake.

Niajar actually came to see Pandemonium during this break. In his floral robes, the elf was practically beaming with joy. He also sounded like he was carrying a bank's worth of coin on him from all the jingling he made with each step. Apparently, he'd bet a lot on Pandemonium's success, and he'd been winning, too.

"Oh, where are my manners? I have a gift for each of you." He raised four bags and handed one to each of them.

All of them reached in and pulled out fresh new school jackets. While their current ones had gotten ripped and stained with blood and dirt during the fighting, none of them were particularly enthused.

Niajar seemed to already be prepared for their responses. "Now, I know what you're thinking, but trust me, they're improvements."

Kiru looked at the front of his jacket. It looked similar to the one he had on. The fabric seemed to be of a higher quality, but that was it. He then turned it around. There, once again was the bedazzled flower symbol of Niajar, but on top was the word "Pandemonium" sewn into the fabric. Below the flower were the words, "Blood Elf."

The others had similarly styled jackets, with Brunhilda's saying "Shield Maiden," Zhaden's "The Unseen," and Mutt's sleeveless blue jacket "The Beast.". The blind orc had to run his fingers along the embroidery to read it, and he gave a toothy grin in approval. Kiru gave the elf a questioning look.

"Some of the bets I made were for favors," Niajar answered the unasked question. "These jackets not only signal that I support you, but they also give you the dramatic flair that'll help you win the crowd over in these situations. Trust me, if they're completely behind you, it'll be much easier to find the ideal guilds and groups who will be willing to pay for your years of tuition to join them instead of serving in the military after you're finished with the academy if that's desired."

A mischievous smile blossomed on the elf's face as he looked at Kiru. "And I know those pompous asshats from Anor'Voren will have no choice but to allow you into their hallowed libraries." He winked before addressing the group as a whole. "Plus, these jackets are made from crystal spider silk. I made a wager with one of the dwarven mining company heads from Stonereach, and he wasn't too happy to part with the amount he'd gambled, so I allowed him to keep some if he could assign someone to make these as quickly as possible."

Being from Stonereach, Brunhilda understood the value of the material. "By Hlin's armor! Crystal spider silk be very rare! You must be paid very well at the academy!"

He gave a wide grin. "My dear, if you know anything about teachers, it's that we're criminally underpaid. No, I've accumulated most of my wealth through wagers, and more often than not, I wager information. You see, being a researcher and librarian gives me knowledge. Knowledge is worth far more than gold to most. So, when I offered up information about an abandoned gold mine on the borders of the kingdom, the greedy bastard took the wager, and as you can tell—" He nodded toward the jacket in her hands. "—I won.

"The coats are also inscribed with runes on the inside. Nothing world-changing, but it will allow the coats to keep you warm when it's cold and cool when it's hot. They will also adjust to always perfectly fit."

Now, Kiru was grateful for the jacket. It would be extremely useful for his journey. He just wished it wasn't so gaudy. He wasn't going to say that to his bene-factor, however. Niajar had looked out for him when no one else would. The librarian also brought some pristine shields and daggers as replacements for the ones that Brunhilda and Zhaden had damaged and lost. "Thank you, Niajar, for everything."

The eccentric elf put a hand on Kiru's shoulder. "Kiru, my boy, you're going to make one damn fine librarian one day. Good luck." With that, the elf left, leaving the party a little sad in his absence. Niajar had no idea that they didn't plan on returning. That this exchange might be the last time they would ever speak.

The psion was hopeful that wouldn't be the case. The librarian was clever and mischievous. He bet that wasn't the last they'd see of Niajar J'sarko.

# CHAPTER FORTY-SEVEN

# Final Round

The party put on their new jackets. Niajar hadn't been wrong about the enchantment on them; they fit like a glove! Pandemonium spent the remaining time cultivating, Kiru in particular trying to absorb as much mana as possible. The pills already provided a great amount of mana; essentially the difference was night and day. Without the surplus they gave him, there was no way he would have been able to fight at full capacity.

Despite that boon, Kiru continued to cultivate with fervor. He wanted to milk every last drop he could get in order to have as much of the magical energy as possible. The fact that Mutt had fallen asleep certainly helped in this endeavor.

It wasn't long before they were being escorted out to the arena, nervous but prepared. They had a few plans to take down Team Supreme. The first involved a war of attrition while Zhaden used his Invisibility to sneak-attack one of their weak spots when it was exposed. The second was to break into two groups of two with Mutt and Zhaden going after the Ruby Ranks while Brunhilda and Kiru faced the Golds. He and the paladin would try to take down their opponents as quickly as possible to help Mutt and Zhaden overwhelm the others.

Both the cleric and barbarian of Team Supreme had only two techniques, based on what the party could glean from their past interactions, making the pair Beta-Gold-rank. However, if Ambrose and Zane went with the standard method of ascending to Ruby, then the two would be hiding a few techniques. Kiru knew of four of Ambrose's from personal experience and observing their other fights. The noble knew Overload, Electrocute, Air Push, and Lightning Limb. That left one he hadn't displayed.

Zane was even more of a mystery. So far, he'd only shown three of his five techniques. The first was Root Manipulation, which he liked to use as a sort of extension of his body. Next was Barkskin, which gave his and his teammates' skin an extra layer of thickness to resist slashing and piercing. The last was an offensive technique called Razorleaf where Zane's mana created and sent up a hail of blade-like leaves to slice up his opponents. That meant two were still hidden. Kiru didn't like that, but if Zhaden could help them get the drop on them, they wouldn't have to worry.

"The first team to make it to the finals is Pandemonium," Headmaster Niazen announced for the crowd in as neutral a tone as possible. "Their sponsor is Niajar J'sarko."

Despite his lack of enthusiasm, the crowd still gave a loud set of cheers for the first-years. It was evident that both Kiru and Brunhilda were crowd favorites, with chants of "Blood Elf" and "Paladin" going back and forth. It got even louder when the people saw their jackets.

Wanting to nip this excitement in the bud, Niazen channeled his mana, causing a ring of tall, purple faerie fire to erupt from the arena's border. "And their opponents!" he shouted, overtaking the noise of the arena with his enthusiasm. "It's Team Supreme!" More purple flames burst out, this time around the entrance where Team Supreme emerged and also on the ground, creating a trail for them to follow.

Kiru was a little confused at this spectacle. Was this supposed to impress anyone? They had to know that the members of Team Supreme weren't the ones doing this. He shrugged. It was simply more fuel to add to his fire.

After the conjured spectacle died down, the two teams faced each other. "Nice jackets," Zane scoffed. "It seems that the only thing my uncle was able to teach you was his horrible taste in fashion."

Kiru smirked. "Did your dad spoon-feed you that line like everything else in your life? His back must really hurt from carrying your useless ass up the ranks."

"Shut it, trash. Unlike you, Defunct, cultivators of true talent like us don't settle for flowery jackets. We deserve the best," Ambrose asserted.

"Indeed," Zane added. "Just like these." He and the rest of his team all snapped on a pair of bulky goggles.

"Dragon piss!" Zhaden hissed under his breath.

"What is it?" Kiru asked.

"Those things are illusionist goggles. It means they can see through my Invisibility and Duplication techniques. All I have left is Silence."

Kiru's expression dropped as he realized the full implications of this. Zhaden couldn't use Nightmare again for another day since he'd already used it before.

Zane's lip curled in a cruel smile. "Ready to get embarrassed in front of all these people, Defunct?"

"Yeah, peasant! We'll make your ugly whore of a mother regret that you were ever born, just like your father did when he ran out on you!"

Kiru squeezed his blade handles tight. Last time Ambrose said a statement like that, Kiru's anger had made him reckless. This time, he inhaled and used the visualization technique Zhaden had taught him. Kiru was now using the noble's words to fuel the "fire" coursing inside him even further, giving him a focused clarity. He would not be a rash opponent but a focused force of retribution incarnate toward Ambrose.

*"He said what now?! Oh, Master, cut him open and spill that asshat's entrails in front of his father!"*

*"You know, William, normally I find your taste for violence to be too much. But today, I'm starting to reconsider."*

*"Yessss!"*

Kiru would not be stopped here, and he would use everything at his disposal to ensure that. In fact, Surturia's second lesson was coming to mind. He had kept his strengths hidden. Now, with his enemies not knowing his true capabilities, it was time to strike. Kiru had to suppress a bloodthirsty grin. The woman Ambrose continued to slander would bring about his doom. *"Change of plans. We're going with the Magic Missile Strategy,"* He sent telepathically to his party.

*"You sure about this, boss?"* Mutt asked.

Kiru nodded. "Undeniably. We're taking them down," he answered aloud. He wanted his opponents to hear him.

"Ready?" Niazen raised his hand. "Begin!"

The barbarian surged forward with his greataxe, flying forward in a great leap. His technique lit his weapon aflame as he raised it.

But Brunhilda's defensive capabilities were up to the task. She lay one of her shields over the other and raised them up. There was a loud clash of steel on steel as the man's greataxe crashed into her overlapping shields. A wave of heat erupted from the point of contact, rippling out to the entire arena. More than one person in the stands broke out in a sweat.

The paladin clenched her jaw as steam started coming off her body almost instantly, her armor threatening to cook her from the inside. "Kiru, do it now!" she shouted.

Immediately, the others got in formation, forming a single file line behind the dwarf. It was Kiru, then Mutt, then Zhaden. Unlike plans such as Sneaky Turtle, this was a secret strategy they had not tested in front of Giiyam for fear of exposing Kiru being a psion. He would stop his Telekinesis technique on himself, temporarily making his body go limp, and he'd use it on his friends, with their consent, of course.

As soon as they all lined up, Kiru stopped his self-Telekinesis, and Mutt caught him, placing an arm under each of the psion's armpits to make it look less obvious.

The rest of Team Supreme didn't remain idle after the barbarian struck. Zane and Ambrose split off to either side and ran at Pandemonium, intending to flank them from both angles while their cleric took a few steps back, keeping her distance from the enemy.

Zhaden, both the tallest of the party and standing at the rear of the formation, was on protection detail. The gold drakonid began expertly hurling his daggers simultaneously at the elf and human, forcing them to dodge or deflect the blades and slow the pace of their charge.

That bought Kiru enough time to enact his part of the plan. With no mental mana being drained on all of his limbs, head, and spine to keep his body standing in a normal manner, he was able to force a huge surge of it out on the dwarf. Like a blast from a cannon, Brunhilda was launched forward just as the barbarian dislodged his flame-covered weapon and raised it for another strike.

The metal-clad dwarf flew at the barbarian like a cannonball, her shields plunging into the barbarian's midsection and forcing him backward. Even though the cleric had moved back to try to keep her distance, the barbarian still collided right into her. All three of them continued to soar for a couple of more seconds before crashing to the ground seventy feet away. A tall plume of dust surged from the ground with a resounding *boom!*

The crowd sat in stunned silence at the sudden attack. Even Ambrose and Zane hesitated for a moment before quickly resuming their charge.

Pandemonium stuck to the plan.

*"Now, Mutt!"* Kiru sent.

The beast mana cultivator spun and hurled Kiru with all of his considerable might. The psion soared through the air towards Brunhilda, the cleric, and barbarian. Mid-flight, he restarted his Telekinesis on himself, unsheathing his blades and holding them in the same position parallel to each other, just inches apart.

Suddenly, the barbarian's gnome ally jumped out of a small crater below. She was dazed, but definitely not out of the fight yet. The barbarian growled as he glared down at the prone cleric. He gripped his greataxe and set it aflame once more.

He should've looked toward the fighting.

Kiru soared right at him. With both Fu Tao at the ready, the psion sliced straight through the barbarian's exposed neck. Kiru's blades and momentum wrought devastation on the man as the force of his strike threw him back and carved such a deep chunk out of his neck, he was nearly decapitated! The barbarian's head was left hanging just by his vertebrae. He was just barely saved by the protective dome that suddenly rose up around him.

Meanwhile, Kiru landed on his feet and turned toward the semiconscious gnome. He was inclined to spare him, but he could not trust the gnome to be honorable enough to accept defeat. He would not leave a potential enemy to come back and bite him in the ass.

Before the gnome could fully recover from the disorientation of her concussion, Kiru sliced her throat, his face liberally sprayed with her arterial blood. The paladins and clerics of course couldn't ignore such a serious inury and cast another protective dome. The rabidly cheered at the merciless violence of it all. The excited chants for the Blood Elf redoubled.

Amidst the cheering, his half-elven hearing did pick up the occasional "boo!" or "honorless scum!" Some still disliked how Kiru did things, but their jeers were much less noticeable. It didn't really bother Kiru anyway. It was easy to judge when not in the midst of serious combat. Combat isn't pretty, and he would get as ugly as he needed to in order for his team to win.

By the time he turned around, Brunhilda had gotten back to her feet. She flinched away from his blood-covered face but didn't say anything after seeing the two protective healing domes. They began sprinting toward their friends. Despite Mutt and Zhaden being the same rank as their opponents, they were not faring so well. After Mutt had thrown Kiru, the orc had charged at Ambrose while Zhaden focused on Zane.

It was clear that Team Supreme had strategized to take advantage of their opponents' weaknesses, just as Pandemonium themselves had done. Mutt had ridiculous strength, dexterity, speed, and enhanced senses, making him a cultivator to be reckoned with, despite his blindness. The team hadn't found a way to compensate for his one clear disadvantage though. The orc was an extremely up-close-and-personal combatant.

Now, Ambrose was normally a close combatant as well, favoring a pair of brass knuckles, but he didn't have Mutt's complete dependance on close-ranged fights. Mutt was only able to claw a gash into Ambrose's shoulder before the noble activated his Air Push technique, hitting the orc in the gut and forcing him back. Then Ambrose set upon him with his Electrocution technique.

The fight between Zhaden and Zane was similar. With his Root Manipulation technique, the elf had formed a protective covering of vines over his entire right arm. He then used the vines to grip his rapier and repeatedly thrust at Zhaden. The drakonid was tall and had a good wingspan, but with his daggers going up against a rapier wielded by an arm that extended out fifteen feet, he stood no chance of getting close enough. The rogue was blocking the sword strikes with one of his small blades in one hand and threw the others at the elf. Zane simply sent his Razorleaf technique to intercept the knife.

The nature mana cultivator spared a glance to see Brunhilda and Kiru charging back. That allowed Zhaden to actually hit him with a throwing knife. The blade would've embedded itself in his neck had he not used Barkskin earlier. Instead, it barely nicked him, causing a small trickle of blood as it bounced off his body.

The elf scowled. This was the first time anyone had seen him get injured the whole tournament! "Enough of this!" He retracted his vine limb, revealing his actual limb under the surface.

Slamming both palms to the ground, Zane shouted, "Wooden Column!" Zhaden had been charging at Zane, trying to close the distance, but a ten-foot-wide column of wood surged out of the ground beneath his feet. Most people caught off-guard would've been launched through the air to land off-balance or fall prone. But Zhaden was not most people.

The rogue quickly composed himself as he was flung across the sky, doing a backflip and staring down at Zane. Gravity took hold, and the drakonid descended like a vengeful meteor. Zane reactivated Vine Manipulation, sending his rapier forward to impale his opponent. Zhaden used the momentum from his deflection to roll to the side. This time, Zane was ready. He flung his arm to the right, and it slammed into the rogue's side, smashing Zhaden to the ground.

The elf reversed the grip on his rapier, then retracted the vines, yanking the weapon down. The wind escaped Zhaden's lungs in a whoosh as his body bounced off the hard ground. The incoming blade seemed to come from nowhere, burying deep in his back before he could register it, let alone parry the blow. In a sudden burst, the blade sank through his leather armor and scaly flesh to pierce his abdomen and pin him to the ground. Blood shot out of both his nostrils and mouth as he gasped in pain and surprise.

Zane slung his vine arm like a whip and simultaneously kicked the rogue. A loud snap shot through the ring as the drakonid's jaw broke, and he fell unconscious. As soon as Zane pulled out his rapier, a protective dome bubbled around Zhaden. The elf glanced around nervously, his eyes scanning back and forth rapidly, and his breath notably shaky. Kiru would be on them any moment with the paladin trailing behind him.

Using his free arm, Zane focused the majority of his remaining mana on the empty space around him until he was almost bone-dry, sending out a call. A large, vibrant green portal appeared beside him. "Forest Stag, I summon thee." He clapped his hands, and a massive stag stepped from the swirling portal of teal light. It seemed to be a mixture of fur, exposed muscle, leaves, vines, and wood. The crowd gasped at the display of such a rare and high-level technique.

Zane hastily hopped on top of the creature's back and it charged the orc, keeping Ambrose busy.

Meanwhile, Mutt's senses were on overload. He reeked of burned hair—getting electrocuted for three-to-five second bursts would do that to a guy. Mutt figured the coward facing him would run out of mana before his stamina ran out. He planned to endure, and through that, he would win. Then, his keen sense of smell picked up something new. A strong aroma of flowers overpowered the burnt hair scent just as his bare feet picked up the vibrations of something large moving nearby.

The blind orc was nearly hit by a burst of air due to the distraction. As he dodged the attack, he could hear the hammering of hooves growing louder and louder. He could tell some beast was trying to get him from behind. Mutt gave a crooked grin. He was ready for it.

The stag lowered its sharp antlers in an attempt to gore Mutt. Not even facing them, however, the orc jumped up in the air, dodging the attack. He spun, hoping to bite the face off of the elf riding the creature. It came at a cost, though. To target Zane, he had diverted his focus from Ambrose.

With his opponent finally in the air and unable to dodge, the noble sent five beams of electricity from his fingertips, hitting the orc.

Mutt's body convulsed, halting his attempt to attack the elf, and he fell. Just like with Zhaden, Zane thrust his rapier straight through Mutt's stomach right as the electrocution stopped. The crowd roared at the display, equally excited for Zane's violence as much as Kiru's. Zane lowered his blade as the stag continued on, Mutt sliding off the rapier from his own weight. The orc groaned loudly in pain as he clutched his wound.

Seeing the paladin and Kiru nearing them, Zane quickly stabbed the orc in one of his already functionless eyes, forcing one of the clerics stationed around the arena to intervene and use their Protective Dome technique. Now, with his bestial mount, the number advantage was on their side. Zane sidled up to Ambrose, and they both charged at their incoming opponents.

# CHAPTER FORTY-EIGHT

# Settling the Score

Kiru regretted launching Brunhilda so far. One, despite her impressive constitution and ability to heal herself, it clearly still hurt the dwarf, which Kiru hadn't intended. Two, it made it harder for both of them to rejoin their allies. Their distance had prevented them from helping their friends in time, but Kiru would avenge them. He just needed to figure out how, especially now that Zane had summoned some sort of behemoth nature mount.

With that creature aiding Team Supreme, the two remaining members of Pandemonium were outnumbered. Despite that, Kiru would use every tool at his disposal, short of exposing himself as a psion to the world, in order to win. *"Master, crush these punks!"* William cheered inside the psion's mind. *"Though he's big, that dumb buck's brain is smaller than mine, and* I'm *an imp!"*

As Kiru ran, he jolted with surprise. The thing had a brain? *Of course* it did, and that brain was susceptible to Kiru. He'd been holding back on using one of his techniques against his opponents as he felt it would have too obviously indicated he was using mental mana on them. Now with the stag present though . . .

*"William, you're a genius!"*

*"I am? I mean, of course I am! I am William, the Breaker of Wills, after all!"* he declared.

Kiru smiled as a plan formed in his head. The forest stag's size made it pull out far ahead of Ambrose as it charged forward. By this point, they were now a hundred feet apart.

On the other side, Kiru was ahead of Brunhilda. "Oi, Kiru!" she shouted. "I can't keep up! Go on. I'll get there when I can."

To her surprise, Kiru actually slowed down to run beside her. "No, I have a plan, and it requires you. Can you meet that thing's charge head-on?"

She tensed but nodded. Before he could give her any more specifics, the stag was on them. Brunhilda slammed her two shields together and blocked the creature's antlers. As a testament to her trollblood-enhanced strength, she only slid back a couple of feet before managing to completely stop its momentum.

Zane was almost knocked off yet managed to maintain his balance, thrusting his rapier at the dwarf's exposed head. Kiru came from behind Brunhilda and deflected the blade with one of his own as the stag lifted its head and sent her flying once more. This time, she crashed into the stone wall, rendering her unconscious. That freed up Zane's rapier. The elf reoriented his blade and thrust it once more at Kiru, but the psion rolled under the stag, getting to its other side before its hooves crashed down.

Before it was able to thrash its sharp antlers at him, Kiru pressed his palm against the creature's head and muttered, "Subjugate." Through his palm, he sent mental mana into the stag's head. William was right; this thing *did* have a small brain. The tether of mana flowed fast and with purpose. Within milliseconds, it found the relatively small brain of the stag, began wrapping itself around the organ, and then tightened. It took just a moment, but Kiru felt a *pop!* as his mana took control of the creature's mind.

It was remarkably easier than dealing with the psion spirit earlier. Kiru figured less intelligent beings were just easier to dominate. Before he could give it another order, however, Zane thrust his rapier at him, making him jump back, creating some distance between them right as Ambrose arrived. It actually worked to Kiru's benefit that he showed up, as that made his contact with the stag's head so brief, no one noticed what he had actually done. He mentally commanded the creature to move as normal, its tiny brain allowing him complete control over it.

"It's the end of the road, you trash. You're outnumbered, and you've got no friends to pull any tricks for you. Surrender, and I'll make sure my stag ends you quickly."

"Oh, you mean that stag?" Kiru pointed at Zane's mount. "Counteroffer: you surrender, and I won't embarrass you too much in front of your daddy."

"You're dead, scum! I'll kill you before the clerics can stop it!" Ambrose scowled as he raised his hands and began to declare his technique. "Revenge of the—"

Kiru cut him off. With a mental command, the stag whacked the snotty noble in his face and side, sending him skipping along the ground like a rock on water, interrupting his technique.

"What?!" Zane shouted in surprise. Kiru wasn't done, though. He ordered the stag to flail and buck the elf off. Zane was thrown from the cervid's back. To his credit, after he bounced once, he did a backflip and landed in a three-point stance. It was cool . . . for about one second, until Kiru ordered the beast to kick him square in the chest. The elf was caught unaware and was flung back a few feet. He coughed blood as a number of his ribs shattered, some likely penetrating his lungs.

The crowd went silent, stunned at what had appeared to be Zane's ineptitude. Everyone watched the eerie sight with bated breath. It seemed like the elf couldn't control his own mount. *Was he not trained enough to use that technique?* many in the crowd wondered. Kiru spared the elf no reprieve. He made the stag lie down, as if it had done so of its own volition. Then, he charged.

Zane wheezed as he forced himself up. He glowered at Kiru. No matter why the beast had suddenly freaked out, he still clearly believed himself superior, and that Kiru was trash and beneath him.

Zane coughed up more blood, his legs shaky and his every breath labored. He still maintained his grip on his rapier, however, although the scores of vines he had wrapped around his right arm fell in thick clumps like shed snakeskin as his focus wavered. His vision cleared in time to see Kiru mere inches away from him. Still, his overconfidence didn't waver.

The psion intended to keep his word. He would beat Zane in undeniable fashion. The elf could barely even lift up his sword. Kiru tensed. He wanted to exact vengeance, to humiliate the pompous elf, but that was not the type of man he wanted to be. He didn't want violence for violence's sake. Instead, it was just a means to achieve his goal. Kiru would bring justice and retribution, and he would do it without sinking to the level of the foul people he despised.

That's when Zane lunged to pierce Kiru's heart. The elf was too slow.

Now, with his mind and heart in sync, Kiru reacted to the attack on instinct. Using Giiyam's methods, he deflected the rapier with his right blade, forcing it down and away from him. Using his left Fu Tao, Kiru then swiftly swung down and sliced the four exposed fingers off of Zane's sword hand, leaving only the thumb attached. Following the motion of the sword form, Kiru took a quick step forward to finish the fight. In one swift action, he angled the hooked end of his right blade through the elf's chin. It burst through the soft flesh and out of Zane's mouth, hooking him like a fish.

Kiru screamed as he heaved Zane into the air by the hook in his mouth. He slammed his bleeding body to the ground with a resounding boom, knocking him unconscious and breaking his Forest Beast technique. Another portal opened and the stag departed through it before it closed behind him.

"Noooooo!" A loud shout erupted from one of the arena booths. Kiru didn't have to look to know who it was.

It almost seemed as if there were multiple voices at once in that shout. A burst of strange energy seemed to disrupt Kiru's Telekinesis. For a heartbeat, the psion's body went limp. Drips of blood fell from his face. *Why is my nose bleeding?*

A protective dome went over Zane's heavily bleeding body. At the same time, Kiru, as well as most of the entire crowd, looked in the direction the scream had come from. There, glaring hatefully at Kiru and gripping the stone boundary so tight cracks were forming was Headmaster Niazen J'sarko in his booth. Kiru felt a pang of genuine concern looking at the man. His expression said that if these witnesses weren't present, he would have reduced Kiru to a smear on the wall for what he had just done.

Even Van Blaine and his queen—who was taller than the man and far too beautiful for theirs *not* to have been a political marriage—stepped into view from their own booth. Van Blaine glared at Niazen and flared his wings once more, a twisting spiral of frigid air coalescing around his booth. The message was clear: this may be your son, but you *will not* interfere.

Blood also flowed down the headmaster's nose as he scowled, quickly composing himself. He nodded toward his liege, then went back into his booth.

Kiru's heart skipped a beat. *I almost watched an Onyx fight an Emerald*, he thought in amazement. A loud crackle of electricity hummed to his left, and he turned to see Ambrose. The cultivator hadn't been taken out of the fight from the surprise attack. His armor was dented and his face cut and bruised, but he was still able to scowl at the psion.

His hands were raised in the air, and a raging torrent of electricity stormed between his hands. "Die! Revenge of the Living Lightning Leviathan!" He then threw his hands down.

Kiru actually hesitated for a moment. *No technique could have that ridiculous of a name, right?*

As Ambrose's arms dropped, the electricity between his palms disappeared, only for four discs of electricity to appear beside Kiru. From each disc, a tentacle of mana and crackling lightning surged out, wrapping around both his arms and legs.

Pain racked through him as he was electrocuted. This wasn't just a few seconds, as with the Electrocution technique. No, this kept going. Kiru's body convulsed, and froth bubbled out from between his lips. His enchanted headband gave off a subtle glow, and a translucent helmet over his head, protecting the outer portion from magical damage. Unfortunately, that didn't stop the electricity from spreading and doing damage *inside* his body. Even on the brink of unconsciousness, he was pretty sure he smelled smoke coming off him, too.

Help came in the form of a bloodthirsty imp. *"I got you, Master!"* William shouted as he began wrapping his mana around Kiru's brain and mental core, protecting them both from the electricity's harmful effects. Kiru shook his head as he was suddenly freed from the pain, but his body was still shaking violently. That didn't prevent him from hearing Ambrose's malicious words.

Ambrose began cackling madly. "Just like before, mongrel, I win! Last time we fought in Bristleton, I broke your core and body. Now, I'm going to finish the job!" He laughed as he held his palms out, continuing his technique.

*"This asshole! This coward!"* William screamed inside Kiru's mind. *"Master, avenge the Flamebringer! Undeniable victory!"*

Kiru snapped his focus to the cackling noble. The psion growled and reactivated his Telekinesis once more. While he could've sent Ambrose flying by using his technique directly on the noble, he would be outed as neither a fire mana cultivator nor a Defunct. He needed to maintain the ruse until he at least acquired his father's artifact. So, he once more used Telekinesis on his burning and shaking body.

He forced his body to take one step, then another. He tugged on his arms, pulling against the tentacles. The tendrils elongated, stretching thinner as they resisted the psion's efforts.

Ambrose's eyes widened in fear and his voice shook. "No. How are you doing this?" His arms trembled.

The electricity coursing through Kiru's deadened nerves caused him to urinate himself, but he didn't know or care. He just kept pushing his body forward, using his mental mana to tug harder and harder against the magical restraints harming him.

"No! Stop this!" Ambrose cried out. Panic was consuming him as Kiru continued to press forward toward him. He desperately started rambling, "You cannot defeat me. I'm a noble. You wouldn't dare strike a cousin of the king!" The fear was overtaking Ambrose, his mind unable to fathom what was happening. He wanted to run, but his technique had him rooted to the spot.

"Shut up!" Kiru shouted. A stray spark of electricity made it past William's barrier, so Kiru faltered slightly. Before his opponent could capitalize on that opening, however, he immediately refocused.

Seemingly empowered by the electricity that struck his core, Kiru quickly gathered every bit of mana he could safely use, every dream, every thought from the past two days—he collected it all and concentrated into his fist. Cocking his arm back, he punched Ambrose square in the face. The electricity coursing through his body followed the concentration of mana as soon as his fist made contact, directing all of that power through the appendage and sending the noble punk flying. Its impact echoed with a roaring thunderclap, and many in the audience covered their ears and winced at the sound of the mighty *BOOM*.

Struck with the force of a lightning bolt, the noble crashed into the wall, sending up a large cloud of dust.

Kiru fell to his knees, exhausted from the injuries he'd sustained and the severe mana drain on his body. He only kept up enough Telekinesis to stay upright. He looked down at his right hand in surprise. Small flashes of electricity still pulsed between his fingers for a couple of seconds more before fading away. *How did I do that?*

When the dust settled, there was Ambrose. The noble was actually embedded in the wall, his body twitching, with his mouth agape and his eyes rolled back. He was unconscious and out of the fight. When a cleric cast another healing dome on the human, the crowd went ballistic with cheering. The Blood Elf, the Defunct teen who couldn't use any techniques, had torn through his superior foes in a path of gore and blood to obtain victory.

Eventually Kiru finally processed what had just happened. *He'd won!* His team, Pandemonium, had won together! A chill creeped up his neck, though, when Van Blaine started walking straight toward him.

# CHAPTER FORTY-NINE

# To the Victor

Kiru went stiff. Swain Derollo van Blaine, the man who had killed his father, was walking toward him. A couple of Royal Guards and a small contingent of high-ranking paladins marched in his wake. Once, Kiru's life's ambition had been to be one of the Royal Guards, to be bound in servitude to the very man who murdered his dad.

A swell of emotions ran through Kiru's mind. *Has he figured out who I am? Is he upset that I defeated a noble and is now coming to punish me?* The wiry, winged man smiled confidently and walked in a casual manner. No hostility was detectable in his display. To further emphasize that, when he locked his one eye with Kiru's, his smile widened and he began clapping.

Kiru forced himself to unclench his jaw, then looked down in order to avert his gaze. *Calm. I need to stay calm.* Van Blaine was walking toward him, Unarmed. *If I'm quick enough, I could slice his neck and avenge my father. No, no, that would be stupid and reckless.* The man was an Onyx-ranked, near the absolute pinnacle of cultivation ranking. One step higher, and he could literally become an immortal. Kiru had a better chance at succeeding in a fight against the entire assassin's guild at once than the winged noble.

He had to act as if he had no idea about the truth, like he was that same kid from years ago, eager to become a Royal Guard. After steadying his shaky breath, Kiru stood up and saluted the king, as would any military member upon seeing their leader. Van Blaine's smile broadened. "Impressive," he said as he walked closer to Kiru. "You put on quite a show, boy."

"Thank you, sir," Kiru replied, holding his salute.

"I admire your respect, but put your hand down. This isn't a coronation."

Kiru complied and looked at the king. He was more than six inches shorter than Kiru's six feet in height, but the power coming off the man was undeniable. An icy chill radiated off of him in all directions, and it made Kiru's neck shiver a little. Van Blaine's smile seemed to come more from narcissistic self-satisfaction at the effect his power was having on Kiru than genuine warmth or congratulations. "To think that someone who cannot use a technique was able to defeat such a skilled opponent . . . It is quite remarkable. The crowd certainly thinks so," he said, gesturing to the crowd still cheering all around them.

"It is my dream to serve you in the Royal Guard one day, sir. I hope this proves I am up to the task." Kiru shivered despite himself, then decided to play off of the conceited asshole's ego. "Though, one as strong as yourself must rarely ever need it."

Van Blaine gave a shrill laugh as he smacked his knee. "Hahaha! Right you are, boy!" He then put a bony hand on Kiru's shoulder. "Normally, I wouldn't even consider using someone who can't use a technique, but I have connections. I'm sure we can find a way to help you overcome your . . . eh . . . deformities." He said that last word with poorly concealed disgust. "Nevertheless, you clearly show promise, if you could defeat my cousin's petulant bastard son."

Kiru laughed along uncomfortably.

"Those weapons, those hooked blades, I've only ever seen a few use them. They were either monks or elite swordsmen. It's been some years since I've laid eyes on them. What style do you use?"

"Cruel Mantis," he answered immediately, then chided himself for giving his father's killer any information that could possibly expose a weakness. He then reasoned that a few bits of truth sprinkled in could be helpful, so the man wouldn't get suspicious.

"Hmm, and your instructor?"

Kiru gulped. For some reason, Giiyam had been very clear that he was never to be seen training Kiru and the rest of Pandemonium. Something had clearly happened in his past that he wished to remain hidden. Kiru would honor that. "In specific sword fighting, I had none. My instructors taught me fighting basics and sparring, but no one taught me this style. Well . . . not directly."

The man raised his eyebrow over his one good eye. "Go on."

Kiru took a deep breath to give his brain time to formulate a story. "I read about it."

"You expect me to believe you gained all that ability from simply reading?"

"I know it's odd, but my sponsor at the academy could also be called rather odd. He's the school's librarian, and my internship with him meant I had to read *a lot* of books."

Van Blaine gave a look of acknowledgement. "Oh, that's right! Your sponsor is Niazen's brother! That makes sense." He laughed, then looked around. "That also explains why the headmaster disliked you so much. I thought it was just because you beat his boy, but his own brother's pupil doing so . . . You may just be his least favorite person in the whole world!" He cackled again. "Not to worry, though, after you receive your prize, you will join me in my booth. After the rest of the Games are complete, I will take you back to the capital myself. You'll be under my protection."

Kiru's face went numb with shock. "I . . . I beg your pardon, sir?"

The king gave a toothy grin. "How else will you receive your training to join the Royal Guard, Blood Elf? Sure, the academy can make *great* fighters. Many of them become distinguished warriors after their tenure, but to serve in my personal guard, you have to be *elite*—the absolute best. That requires special training. Training that *any* cultivator would envy," he boasted.

Kiru was stunned. This was *definitely* going to throw a wrench in his plans. Being stuck inside the literal belly of the beast, it would be impossible to travel around Alterra to get his father's other items. He was falling down a rabbit hole. *Just play along for now, and go one step at a time.* "Thank you, sir! It's an honor!" he said in an excited tone, bowing until he was lower than the winged man. A narcissist like Van Blaine would definitely enjoy feeling taller than his subjects.

"It is, isn't it?" he muttered, smugly. He then placed his wretched hand back on Kiru's shoulder and squeezed. It felt almost hard enough to crack bone. The unnatural chill flowed through Kiru's body. He coughed reflexively as his lungs spasmed. William activated his protective shield over Kiru's brain, keeping it safe from whatever the king was doing.

"Know this though, boy. I expect complete allegiance. I personally rooted out the infection of the Mad Tyrant from these lands, and I will not tolerate dissention within my ranks. If you plan to betray me, I will personally ensure all within your bloodline are eradicated. Do I make myself clear?"

Kiru began to breath rapidly as his body temperature dropped, but he managed to nod, his head still down in a bow. Then, as quickly as the cold had entered his body, it left. Kiru gasped. He would've fallen, had the king let go of his grip on his shoulder. Van Blaine's power was undeniable. The psion breathed and slowly raised himself back up, keeping his face neutral more out of fear than respect.

The king didn't seem to pay it any mind. He gave a toothy grin once more, his one brown eye shining in the sunlight. "Good," he said, then let go of his grip and gave Kiru a firm pat on the back. "I expect great things from you, Blood Elf."

William was uncharacteristically quiet inside Kiru's mind. Kiru could sense his familiar's nervousness and unease from within his core. The fear William displayed was a testament to how afraid the imp was of Van Blaine's power. Kiru felt the same, but this only redoubled his determination to eventually kill this man. He had to show his father's killer that he had a spine and wasn't afraid. Before he could talk himself out of it, he spoke.

"Oh, don't worry, King. I will bring about many great and terrible things for the good of this kingdom, or die trying. And I don't plan on dying anytime soon." He locked eyes with his father's murderer.

For a moment, Van Blaine looked bemused. There was palpable sense of tension as the two silently faced each other. Then, the king cackled again, taking it not as a threat, but as a promise for his benefit. "Well said, boy."

Before he could say more, his contingent of guards and paladins joined them, the members of Pandemonium following closely behind. They were all free from any blemish, their wounds healed and their robes completely restored. The work of the healing domes in conjunction with the power of high-ranking paladins' techniques had brought the team back to one hundred percent!

"Ah, paladins, I see you've finished your work with the other victors. Have your lesser clerics tend to the losers." He casually waved his hand to the high-ranking paladins as if they were simple peasants. His orders were clearly unnecessary, based on their paladins' facial expressions, but they did not dare point that out.

They nodded silently at the order before gesturing to some of their subordinates at the arena's edge to tend to the members of Team Supreme. A paladin then walked over to Kiru. He was blonde, muscular, and had a mustache on his upper lip. Although he was only in his twenties, his face wore the hardened look of a far older, grizzled veteran.

The paladin put his hands out to begin a healing technique on the psion, but Brunhilda interrupted, stating that Kiru was an official acolyte of Hlin and had elected that she be in charge of his medical care. Kiru added that he would, however, happily accept more of the recovery pills they'd had back in their room, along with any magical help to repair their gear.

The grumpy-looking paladin muttered something about minor gods before instructing one of his men to use a technique called Prestidigitation on Kiru. To Kiru's amazement, the dents in his armor snapped back in place, the dirt and tears on his clothes instantly disappeared. Even the blood and gore on his skin disintegrated and floated off his body in flecks. Within moments, the paladin had finished; Kiru now looked pristine. He was still injured, his skin still cut and burned in places from Ambrose's technique, but just wearing clean clothing that fit so well managed to make him already begin to feel better.

Then he took a mana regeneration pill, and Brunhilda started using Rejuvenation on his body. He was grateful for her aid, and that she had remembered to not reveal that she knew Healing Hands in front of the holy warriors who served within the official pantheon. No sense in making even more enemies. While she was healing Kiru, the king addressed the crowd, silencing their cheers with an outstretching of his wings.

Van Blaine first sang his own praises, going on about how, through his reign specifically, the Games had flourished. He also pointed out how most of the top teams were primarily made of citizens of the Kingdom of Blades, in order to assert his country's superiority (many took that with a grain of salt, because the number of foreign students allowed into the academy was drastically lower than the Kingdom's citizens). After his short speech, he finally praised Pandemonium, introducing each one of them by their embroidered nicknames.

At Brunhilda's introduction, many cheered the name of her goddess, to the clerics' chagrin and to the dwarf's sheer joy. But, as expected, the bloodthirsty crowd cheered the loudest for the Blood Elf. Looking around, Kiru actually caught sight Niajar up in a booth. The elf was surrounded by countless bags of coins and was no longer wearing his typical floral robes. Instead, he was wearing the bejeweled black robe . . . of the headmaster! *Wait, is Niajar the headmaster now? Did he bet for his brother's position?* If so, Van Blaine was definitely right. Kiru was certainly number one on Niazen's most-hated list! Where were those ridiculous shoulder pauldrons, though? Were those things not actually a required part of the uniform? Why would someone willingly make such a terrible fashion decision?

His train of thought was cut off when the king summoned a key to his hand, likely from some storage device like Kiru's ring. "And to the victors go the spoils!" The crowd applauded, and he basked in their adoration. He pulled in his wings, kneeled, and wiped some of the sand off of the floor before him, uncovering a small keyhole, easily missed. Van Blaine placed his simple bronze key within it and turned. There was a loud click, and the ground opened up, sinking down and revealing a spiraling, descending pathway to the treasure room.

Stale air rushed out from the descending stairway, and Kiru's heart began to race as he sensed something else rush out along with it. With no magical barrier inhibiting Kiru's connection to his father's item, his mind was suddenly beset by a wave of longing. One of his father's items was down there, and it was calling to him!

Entranced, he was barely able to acknowledge the king as the man handed him a gift token enchanted with runes, which he could use as payment for one of the items down below. Kiru nodded and began to descend the stairs to the treasure room. He could feel his father's item pulling him closer all the while, as if he were a fish on a lure. His friends followed, yet he was so entranced, he hardly noticed. It wasn't until Mutt deliberately passed in front of him that his mind snapped back to the present moment. "Oh . . . uh, what?"

"Um, Boss, we've been trying to get your attention for the past minute. Everything all right?" the orc asked.

"I'm sorry. It's just—"

"The item you're looking for—it's actually here, isn't it?" Zhaden pointed down to a dark hallway, the gateway into the treasure room.

He nodded in answer.

"That's good to know. If possible, let the rest of us to get our items first. I suspect that, if the item is indeed linked to your heritage, once you try to claim it, more pandemonium may occur," the drakonid said.

"Haha! Good one, Stabby!" Mutt bellowed out. "It's because that's our team name, Pandemonium!"

Everyone else had a good chuckle.

Kiru looked to Zhaden. "That's a good idea, my friend. Let's go get your rewards first." The others took another step down, when Kiru suddenly stopped them. "Uh, one more thing. The king, he gave me a spot in the Royal Guard."

"Aye. We know." Brunhilda raised a hand to stop him. "That man isn't a quiet talker. I'd be surprised if half the arena didn't hear him promise ye that. I got him to allow me to place a shrine on this island, while he was being generous."

Kiru chuckled. "That's great, Brunhilda. Still, if I have to go join the Royal Guard, we'll be separated." Kiru wanted to say more, but he stopped himself from saying anything of his true plans out loud. He truly had no intention of staying in the Kingdom of Blades after he got his father's artifact. He needed to travel the continent.

Still, seeing the degree of power Van Blaine casually displayed earlier and having actually talked with him face-to-face, Kiru's caution had gone up significantly. He wouldn't be shocked if the winged man's senses could pick up every word they were having at this moment. He decided not to talk to them until he was sure they were away from prying ears.

"We'll figure it out, Kiru. If Hlin brought us together, surely she'll find a way to reunite us," Brunhilda said.

He smiled at that, and his friends returned the gesture. They continued their descent through the round archway into the treasure room. Ensconced torches began to light themselves as they approached the magic items, illuminating the friends' pathway. The same thing happened when they entered the treasure room, only on a much grander scale. Multiple torches lit all at once as soon as they crossed the threshold.

The room had to be at least a mile long and a few hundred feet wide. The party's awe distracted them from what was going on behind them. As they entered, the archway's stone door slid closed with a boom, sealing them inside. For a moment, they were concerned, but when nothing else seemed to occur, they proceeded in the pursuit of their prizes, simply presuming their exit would be on the other side of the room.

On Brunhilda's insistence, they all sat down and cycled the pure mana from the regeneration pills through their cores to replenish their lost stores. Kiru *really* wanted to keep going as he was literally at the place he'd worked so hard to get to for years, but he had to agree with the dwarf's cautious instincts. More mana was never a bad thing to have.

They learned that only the first third of the rooms had prizes for the first-year winners. Each prize was set in a case, shelf, or podium, all covered by glass with protective runes around the edges. Under each was a token slot with a label listing the price. After a certain point, the labeled prices increased from one to two tokens, meaning they couldn't choose those.

Just because they could only choose from a third of the prizes didn't mean that their selection wasn't wide-ranging nor spectacular. There were so many valuable things to choose from: a flying sword, a mithril vest, technique manuals, rare pills, uncommon alchemy ingredients, and more! They even saw a tome written by the "Sage of Two Stars." It was hard for Kiru to make out the title, but it did seem like a *really* cool book.

Zhaden decided to purchase an enchanted dagger with his token. "What can I say? I like daggers," he said, and this one was definitely impressive. The Bloodstep Stiletto, once attuned to its owner, would teleport them to the spot where it landed when thrown. That would allow him to cross large distances in an instant, and get up close and personal in any fight—ideal for a rogue. But there was a catch. The Bloodstep Stiletto had to strike a living thing with blood pumping in its veins for it to work, and the blade had to draw blood as well. So if it hit and bounced off someone's plate mail, it would have no effect.

Brunhilda took a sphere made of jade, with concentric rings of gold spread across it. She closed her eyes, and the gold rings glowed. Holy energy coursed from Hlin through the paladin and into the orb. The rings seemed to squeeze the stone orb, forcing its form to change as if it were made of pliable clay. After ten seconds of morphing, the glow faded, and the jade orb had transformed into a statue of Hlin, wielding her two tower shields.

When asked about the item, Brunhilda explained that it was called a Shrine Stone Statue. One attuned it to their deity by allowing it to drain some of their mana while offering the orb up in service to their divine patron. After that, the orb would take on their deity's likeness. Once that was done, a cultivator in service to that godly being could auto-create a shrine just by simply investing some mana into the statue. It would allow for repeated use, so Brunhilda wouldn't need to burden herself with carrying and paying for all the materials for spreading her goddess' worship.

As she planned to journey with Kiru across the Great Alliance, she wouldn't need to worry about getting those rare items. The statue could also construct shrines much quicker than she could herself. It truly was a major benefit for the paladin in service to the minor goddess. To showcase her point, she placed the statue on the ground by a blank section of wall. The purple-haired paladin knelt and prayed by the statue for a good half-minute, siphoning mana from herself into the stone.

The gold rings glowed, and before their eyes, the wall behind the statue changed. It created a round indentation as a smaller replica of the statue on a pedestal formed inside it from the same dark stone as the wall. Around the statue, wax candles grew up from the ground like plants from fertile soil, their wicks coming alight with flame once finished. A small booklet with Hlin's emblem on the cover formed in front of the statue out of holy light, the glow finally dulling once it was all finished. Since she got permission from the king, it was an official shrine, too. The party was seriously impressed. Thirty seconds was much faster than the thirty minutes she'd taken to construct a shrine at The Strongjaw!

Mutt was true to his word to the dwarf about helping her ascend, and for his prize chose a scroll containing a rare life mana technique for her. There was a problem, however. Although Mutt's enhanced senses helped him locate the scroll—from a combination of sensing the life mana brimming off if along with the scent of parchment—he had hastily put his token in the slot without realizing that it was written in an unknown dialect that even Kiru couldn't decipher. Mutt guided them back to where he found it, and the party read its description. It was left there by a traveling paladin who had long passed. Anyone who could obtain the knowledge needed to decipher the scroll would receive his life's work—his most powerful technique.

Despite not being able to read it yet, Brunhilda was still thrilled. She gave the muscular orc a bear hug before jumping up and planting a big kiss on his cheek. Both of them blushed after that.

Meanwhile, even though Kiru was excited for the rare items everyone had acquired, he was having trouble sitting still. He was bouncing off his toes and pacing in anticipation, even when trying to stand in one spot.

The psion could practically feel the sensation of something pulling at him, resonating deeply with his core. That sensation was guiding him, beckoning him closer. Kiru knew on instinct that it was emanating from one of his father's artifacts. When his friends were done, Kiru had to restrain himself from going on a full-on sprint. They went deeper into the prize room, going past the second-level prize section and into the third one. After five minutes of walking further and further in, the psion suddenly stopped. He looked left at a blank wall. The item was behind it.

*"Ooh, I feel the power! It makes me all tingly! We're so close to the artifact, Master,"* William sent.

Kiru concurred with William's assessment. They were *very* close. On instinct, he pressed his hand to the wall. Mental mana flowed from the meridian in his left arm and out of his left hand, and a humming noise filled their ears as lines of blue light appeared in the wall. They connected to form a door.

Kiru looked to his friends in excitement. They all wore expressions of awe and silently nodded for Kiru to go on. He smiled and pressed on the door.

# CHAPTER FIFTY

# Abomination

The thick, stone door was opened with no resistance, aside from its weight, sliding open as if gliding on air, no sound or feel of stone against stone. A rush of stagnant air hit them, opening into another chamber, much smaller than the gargantuan prize room, but just as tall. Ensconced, enchanted torches burst aflame, illuminating the space. There was a rising stairway on the other side of the room that went up and forked into two separate paths leading to raised doors on each side wall.

In the center of the room stood a single stone podium with only one prize upon it. From further off, it was unlike anything they had ever seen before. They had to approach it to confirm that their eyes weren't playing tricks on them. As they got close, it was clear that they hadn't been: it was indeed a floating ball of writhing, swirling liquid mercury metal.

The metal called to Kiru. His mind tuned out everything else, and he raised a hand toward it. No inscription was carved in the podium, no description as to what exactly this orb was, yet Kiru felt it reaching out to him and his core, like it was extending an invisible line that wanted to wrap around and attach itself to him. He felt his mind forming a connection with the thing. The more he focused on it, the stronger the bond. With only a few more seconds of concentrated focus, the item would be his.

He felt the desperate need to touch it. His subconscious was telling him that he needed a physical connection with it to become more whole. Before Kiru could actually do so, however, both the silence and his trance were cut off by the sound of applause. All of Pandemonium snapped their heads up to the top of the stairs. There, right in the middle where the stairs branched off, was Niazen J'sarko.

The powerful cultivator had a smug look on his face as he gazed down upon the students. "Well done! I was wondering how my brother's ragtag group of misfits was able to beat a team of truly skilled cultivators, but it all makes sense now.

He had a psion!" At his words, the door where the party had entered the room slammed shut.

"A psion? Surely you don't actually think—" Kiru tried to refute.

The elf gripped his head as if in pain and scowled. "Enough!" he shouted, interrupting Kiru's words. "Enough of your deceit!" He took a deep breath and continued, "This artifact is a relic once used by the Mad Tyrant. For some reason, it was transported here after he was slain. I was there the day he died. I witnessed his power. He nearly took off my head." He pulled down on his shirt's collar to reveal a large, nasty scar that almost wrapped around his neck entirely and spread toward his shoulders.

"For my service to Van Blaine, I was given the illustrious position of headmaster, but seeing the Tyrant's power, the power that ruled the strongest of all the countries in the Alliance, I wanted more. I wanted *his* power." Niazen gripped his two strange pauldrons and tore them off with a pull. The entire party gasped in horror at what they saw. There, on top of each shoulder, was a head surgically attached by large suture scars.

One was male. The other was female. They were both sickly pale, their eyes rolled back and mouths open wide as if they were stuck screaming.

"By Hlin's holy shields!" Brunhilda spat.

"Impressive, isn't it? I figured if my body couldn't use the Mad Tyrant's powers, I needed to upgrade my physical form. Behold, Psion, what's left of your kin!"

Kiru scowled at that announcement.

"*Oh, what in the Abyss—?! I can understand adorning yourself with your dead enemies. A necklace of the ears of your dead opponents, sure. Eating the heart of a rival you kill, obviously, duh! But stitching their heads onto your body? That's just weird.*" William said inside Kiru's mind.

"I had the school's cleric graft the heads of these expired honor guards who shared the same abilities as the Mad Tyrant to my shoulders, and sure enough . . ." He began to float in the air. "My attempt bore fruition." The elf then gestured toward the also-floating orb. "I found this item by chance and could feel the Mad Tyrant's resonance coming off of it. I sensed an opportunity to gain more power. So, I kept knowledge of its existence to myself, instead of reporting it to my king. I haven't been able to master how to make it bend to my will, but I'm certain once I add your head, Kiru, its power will be mine as well." An evil smile grew on Niazen's face, and before the party could say anything, he flew down toward them.

Niazen J'sarko was a Complete Emerald, leagues beyond what Pandemonium could handle. The elf's fist landed on the stone ground in the middle of the party. At that, the stone shattered, sending his trademark purple-colored faerie fire rippling in all directions.

All four members of Pandemonium were sent flying, but that wasn't the end of it. The two petrified heads turned outward and let out a pair of terrifying moans as Niazen used Telekinesis to draw two of the airborne students toward him. His targets were the paladin and the psion, letting the other two crash into the walls. Two consecutive booms rang out as Mutt and Zhaden slammed into the stone. Kiru desperately wanted to check on them, afraid they'd been seriously injured, but he had to maintain all of his focus on the opponent in front of him.

Acting on instinct, Kiru resisted, halting Niazen's technique with his own. Sure, the elf was multiple ranks higher than Kiru when it came to cultivation level with his normal mana affinity, but his ability and control of mental mana was wild. It was strong, but not concentrated or directed.

The moaning heads let out a choked noise as they met resistance. Both Kiru and Brunhilda's bodies were halted midair, the pull from two different directions keeping them stuck. Niazen chuckled. "As I thought, a psion indeed. Three heads are better than one." The two grafted psion heads restarted their shrieks, intensifying in pitch. Both Kiru and Brunhilda were drawn toward Niazen once again, this time more slowly.

*"Fuck this guy! C'mon, Master, take down this poser. Are you going to let your friends die here?"*

"No," Kiru growled, pressing his feet to the ground and slowing his speed down even further.

*"Are you going to let Flamebringer's sacrifice and your father's death be in vain?"*

"No!"

*"Then prove it! Show him who you are!"*

"I am Kiru Chromebane. I am Kiru the Conqueror!" he shouted. Forcing more mental mana through the meridian around his mind, he planted his feet and stopped once more. He breathed heavily through his nostrils and was gradually able to halt Brunhilda's movement once more, as well.

Niazen gave an amused look as he locked eyes with Kiru. He was surprised . . . but not worried.

Kiru, on the other hand, was doing his best to keep up the fight. A blood vessel in his right eye popped from the effort, and his vision swam with red on that side.

"Chromebane? That explains it!" He laughed. "The bastard actually had a bastard! Well, 'Kiru the Conqueror,'" he mocked, "you were able to stop your friend from getting closer to me, but what's to stop me from getting closer to her, hmm?" He gave a predatory grin and began walking casually towards the prone Brunhilda, exuding an aura of malice.

The paladin strained, but was unable to move, stuck as if restrained by invisible rope.

Kiru's eyes widened as he fully grasped his predicament.

Niazen stuck out his hand as he advanced upon the dwarf, setting it alight with purple flame. He grinned maliciously. He clearly could have gone for Kiru's other likely more injured allies, but he wanted the psion to despair.

If Kiru didn't do something, and fast, Niazen would burn a hole straight through Brunhilda. Desperate, Kiru decided to try and use the elf's own technique against him. The psion let go of the resistance he'd been holding around himself against Niazen's Telekinesis. Now, he zoomed forward as if drawn by a strong magnetic force, readying his Fu Tao and positioning them for a surprise attack.

The elf gave him a look that said, "Gotcha," and transferred the flames around his hand to under his feet, now charged with even more violent force. Niazen, propelled by the flames, went flying towards the incoming psion. He released his control over Brunhilda, sending the dwarf in the opposite direction with the force of his takeoff.

Caught off-guard, Kiru desperately shifted his blades in a defensive position to block the incoming strike. It wasn't enough. The former headmaster shattered one of Kiru's hook swords with his fist, breaking it into multiple pieces. His fist continued and punched Kiru under his left eye. The only reason half his skull wasn't caved in was the boon Hlin had given him. The enchantment in his head-band kicked in, and a helmet composed of life mana manifested, intercepting the punch and taking a majority of the abuse.

The mana helmet still took too much damage, however, and broke. The enchantment had lessened the blow but hadn't been able to stop it completely. Kiru rolled across the ground, his back colliding with a wall.

He groaned as he lifted his head up, his right eye full of blood and his left eye beginning to swell. His vision was getting worse by the second, but he was still able to see Niazen clearly. The dark-haired elf walked toward him, all three heads now locked on him.

Niazen cracked his knuckles and grinned, a stream of blood dribbling from each nostril. "Of course you would try to save your friend. Pitiful! It seems my brother's weak morality has infected you, too." He wiped some blood dripping down his neck, feeling his old scars. He smiled, remembering his past. "I think it's only fitting that it should end this way. Your father tried to take my head off. It's poetic justice that I remove his son's." He picked up Kiru by the collar of his armor. "You should've tried to run. How could you think to defeat me all by yourself?"

Kiru gave a chuckle. "You got it wrong. Just like you, I'm never alone."

"Surprise, motherfucker!" William appeared from his core and wrapped his body around the elf's face, poking him in the right eye with his sharp clawed finger.

"Grah!" Niazen cried out in pain and grabbed William with his free hand. He flung the small demon like a used dishrag, then glared at Kiru.

Taking advantage of the distraction, the psion headbutted the elf. It wouldn't have done much damage if not for the jewel embedded in the center of Kiru's forehead. Niazen took a step back, gripping at his head in pain, a trickle of blood flowing from the new wound in the center of his forehead. He looked down at the blood in his hand, then back to the psion.

Kiru smiled. He'd bought enough time for his friends to rejoin the fight. Mutt, Zhaden, and Brunhilda, all sporting new injuries, ran at Niazen in hopes of saving their friend. The elf, now in pain and disoriented, was unable to fully fight off the trio with complete focus. Zhaden was even able to cut off one of the surgically-attached heads with his dagger. It fell to the ground with a sick plop, and its grimace of pain changed to a slight smile as its eyes closed; it was finally free from its torture.

Seizing the opportunity given to him by his friends, Kiru charged at the former headmaster, dropping the hilt of his broken blade. With not much of his mana remaining, he pressed his palm against Niazen's temple and shouted "Subjugate!"

The elf's focus was in multiple places. With that plus his injuries, Niazen fell easily to Kiru's technique. The elf's eyes went distant, and Kiru sighed in relief as his mana began to wrap around the elf's mind. On the cusp of complete control, the other psion head, still attached to Niazen, turned to Kiru and shrieked.

Kiru's mind was flooded with an oppositional force of mental mana. After the day's constant fighting and being repeatedly drawn to near exhaustion, his endurance was spent. The zombie-like head's mana attacked his mind. Kiru's head snapped back as his thread of mana was broken and the magical energy whiplashed back into his core.

His brain practically bounced inside his skull from the sheer force of the recoil. His mind was in a daze and his body went limp as he was unable to focus to use any techniques.

In contrast, focus returned to Niazen's eyes as a boom erupted from the wall behind him.

# CHAPTER FIFTY-ONE

# Old Soldier

Niazen J'sarko, just coming to his senses, was about to flood the room in a burst of faerie fire, when he suddenly sensed a deadly force coming at him. His eyes widened in surprise as the groundskeeper of all people burst through the wall, revealing a tunnel carved behind him. He was adorned in high-quality cinnabar scalemail and wielded the same type of swords Kiru did. There was a significant difference in quality between the blades, however, the half-orc's being far greater and ornate.

A shiver went up Niazen's spine as he noticed that the edge of each blade was made of razor sharp trollstone. The students he'd been facing had backed away when the psion boy had tried to take over his mind, with the impudent brat now flat on his back in front of him with his eyes rolling. Before he could grab him, however, the groundskeeper closed the distance, swiping his trollstone blades at the former headmaster. Niazen backflipped and fired a beam of faerie fire at Giiyam. The half-orc was ready and intercepted the beam with his blades. The nullifying effect of the trollstone instantly eliminated the technique on contact, destroying the mana.

"I see where the Chromebane bastard received his training! A traitorous devotee to the Mad Tyrant has been hiding under our very noses. If you're still brainwashed after all these years, then his power was indeed worthy of a tyrant. It shall be mine."

"King Ruken Chromebane was no tyrant! He was my lord and friend, and this old soldier will protect his friend's son." He then pointed one of his Fu Tao up at the prideful elf. "As one of Ruken's personal guards, I will reclaim my honor by ending you."

"You may have powerful blades, but I can tell you really are a Defunct. Pray tell, how can you make good on your promise? Ah!" He cried out in sudden panic as the half-orc threw one of his blades at him. Niazen dodged but noticed too late that the orc had some sort of chain attached to the blade. Before Niazen could react, Giiyam tugged down on it, pulling the Fu Tao back down. It grazed the elf's forearm, disrupting his mana and his ability to float.

Niazen landed in a three-point stance. The now-two-headed abomination of an elf then spread both arms out. "Mischievous Flames." Seemingly out of thin air, hundreds of tiny, winged fairies made of purple faerie fire appeared around Niazen in rapid-fire succession. "Die!" both he and the attached head shouted in unison as he shoved his hands forward and sent the conjured fairies flying like arrows.

Giiyam's eyes widened, and then he began deflecting the projectiles of purple flame to the best of his abilities. For the most part, it was working. That still meant *some* came through, however. He grunted as he was struck by more than a few of the fairies. When they made contact, they exploded against him, burning his flesh. Niazen rushed over to grab Kiru, and Giiyam had to throw one of his blades to intercept and stop the former headmaster.

He managed to hold him back, but his body paid the price.

He breathed heavily, glaring at his opponent. His body was sizzling, multiple areas blackened and smoking from third-degree burns. Half of his face was charred. His right eye was spared, but he was barely able to keep it open.

The members of Pandemonium looked at Giiyam in awe. He had somehow not only withstood a Complete Emerald's technique and survived, but he managed to force his opponent to a standstill. Giiyam may have been a Defunct, but it was abundantly clear that he had managed to use mana to improve himself in some unique, incredible way.

Meanwhile, Kiru was still dazed. He was struggling to come to and fully grasp the situation at hand. His focus and senses were overloaded, and he felt like he had to vomit. William ran over to his master while the psion's friends stood beside Giiyam, their weapons at the ready. Brunhilda wanted to heal Kiru, but she was too scared to take her eyes off Niazen.

"Take Kiru and go!" Giiyam barked.

"Are you sure, Teach?" Mutt asked.

Giiyam just grunted in response.

"No! His power will be mine! Do not underestimate me, Defunct!" The furious elf released a reckless, powerful Faerie Fire technique. From his meridians and out through his every pore, his mana was forced out. It quickly coalesced and grew until it was a giant bird made of his purple flames. "Faerie Fire Phoenix!"

"Now!" Giiyam brokered no argument.

Seeing the giant raptor made of living fire, the party didn't question him again.

The phoenix breathed a gout of flame directly at them, but Giiyam intercepted. He threw one blade through the stream of fire, but before it could touch the phoenix, it dodged to the right and shot out more purple flame. Realizing this conjured technique had some form of intelligence, unlike the small fairies from earlier, Giiyam responded purely defensively. He spun one of his blades by the chain like a fan. The speed and diameter of the spin kept the flames from hitting the party.

Right as Mutt threw Kiru and William on his back, Niazen appeared. The elf tried to flank the group once more, using the massive phoenix's direct attack to distract everyone so he could get to the psion.

While still busy intercepting the flame attack with his right blade, however, Giiyam flung his left blade directly at the elf zooming at the young cultivators.

Niazen gritted his teeth in frustration as he was forced to take a step back. He could've used Telekinesis to redirect the blade, if it weren't for the damn troll-stone. He rushed forward again after the blade struck the ground, but Giiyam was able to catch Niazen off-guard by snapping the chain connected to the blade like a whip. The former headmaster was struck in the shoulder, and the last attached psion head was bisected, leaving just two lifeless chunks of flesh attached to him.

He winced as he touched his injured shoulder. Niazen bared his teeth as blood started to flow in thick rivulets from each of his nostrils. The elf let out a savage, desperate scream echoed by his conjured phoenix who had finally stopped its flame breath attack.

"Run through the tunnel, and don't look back!" Giiyam shouted with urgency as he raised both blades again.

Pandemonium readily complied, not even bothering to say goodbye.

"Wait, no!" Kiru groggily said as he reached a hand toward Giiyam.

The half orc's ears twitched. Though he didn't look back, he gave the psion a rare smile.

Kiru moaned in protest, not wanting to leave his mentor, but he still wasn't in full control of his motor functions nor mentally restored enough to put up a real fight.

"Master, the prize!" William called.

"The what?"

"The damn orb of liquid metal! Don't forget the orb!"

A surge of panic gave Kiru sudden clarity. They had entered some tunnel, with the prize room getting further away. He could see the podium and the orb just floating above it, undisturbed by the violence surrounding it. Kiru recalled William in order to aid his power. He still had the mana that had been whiplashed into his core to use.

Still able to see the orb through the swelling and blood, Kiru furrowed his brow and concentrated on it. For some odd reason, he wasn't concerned about getting farther away, as long as he could see it. He focused on the strange orb. It began to ripple, and after a few seconds, the bond was secured. Kiru inhaled in overwhelming relief; it felt like a missing piece of him had just been reclaimed.

Exhausted from all the emotional and mental exertion, Kiru went on autopilot. As his mind began to tumble out of consciousness, he mentally called the object to him. His head slumped as the orb turned into a flying stream of metallic liquid and went inside his storage ring. The last thing he registered was the sound of rumbling stones.

# CHAPTER FIFTY-TWO

# Resolution

A splash of cold water hit Kiru's face, and he awoke. Before he could summon any words, two gauntleted hands cupped his face, and healing light emerged from them. Kiru sighed in relief, Brunhilda's new Healing Hands technique already proving useful. He sat up slowly to view a striking sunset set against a large savannah. He'd never seen tall, brown grass like that before! It was absolutely stunning against the pink backdrop of the sky.

Around him, his friends all gave him warm smiles. They were on a rocky out-cropping overlooking the savannah. He looked over at a few narrow, jagged mountains and the green forests and grasses of the Kingdom of Blades. They were at the border of the kingdom, at the very edge of the Blade Mountains!

"H-How did we get here?" he asked.

"The tunnel Giiyam came out of," Brunhilda answered. "We followed it, and it led us here."

"Where is Giiyam? Is he okay?"

Everyone gazed back at him, somber expressions on their faces.

"Not long after we entered the tunnel, he must've done something to col-lapse it. The room we were fighting in appeared to have been collapsing, too," Zhaden said.

Kiru's eyes watered. "No. No, that can't be!" He turned to try and find what-ever tunnel they came from in order to go back. His heart sank as he saw a hundred-foot pile of thick rubble against the side of one of the cliffs.

He had come so far, but he still wasn't strong enough. He'd resolved to pro-tect those dear to him, but instead of being the realm's protector, he was the one needing protection again.

Kiru lowered his head, and his gaze fell on his one remaining Fu Tao, the unbroken one. It was still with him—a gift from his teacher, and Kiru was glad to still have it. Despite his flaws, despite his weaknesses, Giiyam knew who and what he really was and believed in him.

Kiru could wallow in his own failings, but that would dishonor both Giiyam and his mother's sacrifices. No, he would continue to grow and get stronger, and he would become the man they knew he could be.

"He was a good man," Kiru managed.

The others nodded in agreement.

After a few moments' silence, Kiru asked for more details as to what happened, and the others updated him what had happened after he'd suffered his concussion from his Subjugate backlash.

The reason that the orc was such a deadly fighter finally made sense, along with his reclusiveness: Giiyam had served Kiru's father as one of his personal guards. Ironically, he served Kiru too, in a way. It made the young psion wonder how many other faithful followers of his father were still out there.

Despite being a Defunct and giving off the energy of a Zeta Gold-rank, there was clearly more to Giiyam than met the eye. There always had been, but Kiru hadn't realized to what degree. For the groundskeeper to fight off a Complete Emerald-rank to a standstill, he must've accomplished some truly revolutionary method of cultivation. Kiru hoped he was somehow okay.

At least with the collapse of the tunnel and the prize room, people would hopefully assume them all dead, which might allow them to travel without anyone actively searching for them. It also prevented Kiru from having to come up with some excuse or reason to *not* join Swain's Royal Guard. The psion then noticed that his headband was damp from the water. He took it off to wring it out, and the gold crystal in his forehead glowed as soon as it was exposed. As it had done previously, an image of Ruken projected from the gem.

The others gawked in amazement at the sight. Mutt needed the others to explain to him what was going on. The orc almost tried to attack the hologram after it began speaking, but Brunhilda stopped him.

"You have found Metal Psyslime." A projection of the orb appeared by the king. "It may seem strange, but its utility is unmatched." It then began spinning around Ruken. "Once attuned to you, the slime will take on any form you desire." It stopped and turned into a sword, then a shield, then a key, then a hammer, then a chair. "But it will always maintain metal consistency.

"This slime has been with me since my coronation. It formed the blade of my legendary katana and has felled many foes. Practice with it, treat it well, and the slime will do the same for you." The projection of the dead king then looked up, seeming to lock eyes with his son. "Acquiring this item means you had to go into the belly of the beast. I am proud of you, my son. Take heart. Go forth and manifest your destiny. I know you can do it. You can save the world."

With that, the projection dissipated.

There was a collective "Whoa!" from the rest of Pandemonium as they took in the projection and his words.

"Wow, Boss!" Mutt said with a grin. "I mean, I believed you already, but wow! That was . . . your dad, the Mad—I mean uhh . . . the falsely accused king!"

Brunhilda elbowed the orc in reprimand. "What he means, Kiru, is that actually seeing your dead father's remnant confirming your words is pretty incredible. It be reassuring to see that we succeeded in getting your item, too."

He smiled and nodded in agreement.

"Well?" she asked.

"Well, what?"

"Show us what you can do with it, silly!"

Kiru chuckled and complied. He closed his eyes and reached out with his mind, instantly connecting with the Metal Psyslime slushing in his storage. It was as if it were another limb, completely in sync with Kiru's neural network. It zoomed out and floated beside his head. It was no longer an orb but rather swirled about continuously in a figure eight pattern. Thinking about how it felt like another limb, Kiru held his right arm beside the slime, touched it, and with a flex of his will, made it turn into its exact copy.

The young psion lacked his father's fine control and needed to be in physical contact with the slime to control it, but a simple-looking metallic right arm and hand had formed. One of Brunhilda's shields lay against a nearby rock, and he willed the Psyslime to copy its shape. It looked more like a mushroom cap versus a forged, crafted shield, but he was still able to grab the handle inside and wield it.

"That be a good look on you!" Brunhilda beamed. "You should consider fighting with a shield all the time. I know Hlin would approve."

Kiru shook his head. "I appreciate it, but that's not my style. After all my training, I'm going to stick with my pair of Fu Tao . . ." Kiru trailed off, suddenly reminded of his one shattered blade, leaving him with a single sword. While he could execute his mother's style using a dagger as a substitute, the Cruel Mantis style he knew so well required two actual swords. Specifically, he needed *two* Fu Tao to execute the style's forms appropriately.

Knowing what his master was thinking, William spoke inside his mind. *"Master, you have two swords. Your father used it as a blade. I say you should honor him by using it for one, too. Oh, and you also have to make sure to bathe it in the blood of your enemies. Your father won't really be honored unless you do so."*

The psion chuckled, then sent a mental command to the Psyslime. The shield turned into a Fu Tao in his hand. Unlike his other attempts, this one matched his blade much more precisely. It had the same textured handle to ensure a steady grip, a dual edge to cut opponents from either side, and a wicked hook at the end. Maybe it was the fact that it had been used as a blade in the past, maybe it was

Kiru's fondness and familiarity with the hook blade, but whatever the reason, his control at guiding it into this form was flawless.

Feeling a new sense of confidence and control, he then mentally carved an inscription in the flat of the blade in Japanese. When studying the language, Kiru had learned that their culture had held swords in high regard, and many would inscribed their swords similarly. In memory of his father, he had written the words "The King's Blade" on it in Japanese. Before anyone could ask, he drew out his other blade and went through a few of the forms Giiyam had taught him, smiling fondly as he remembered the menial tasks he'd been required to do to acquire the muscle memory for the forms. The Psyslime blade was a flawless copy of his other, matching it in weight, balance, and speed.

Kiru ended his swings with his blades pointing toward the tall grassland, in a land that was clearly not his home. The circlet had shown Kiru the general locations of every one of his father's artifacts, so he just needed to get his own bearings to gain a better understanding. "This looks like the way we're going to have to go. Which country is this?"

"Oh, that's easy, Boss," Mutt said, then took an exaggerated inhale through his nostrils before sighing contentedly. "Ah! The warm, fresh air and strong winds of my home, Imakandi."

"Imakandi." The psion tasted the word in his mouth. From what his father had shown him, the item Kiru needed to get was southwest, far from the nation's center. He looked back at his friends, summoning William, who appeared on his shoulder.

They all smiled at the psion.

"Well, we'll come back to the Kingdom one day, but it's time we take our journey elsewhere. I think it's time the orc homeland gets a dose of Pandemonium."

# About the Author

Maxwell Farmer is the author of the Ashen Plane, Dr. Druid, and Last Psion series. He spent his youth in Metropolis, Illinois, the home of Superman. There, the seeds of his love for fantasy and science fiction blossomed. Like the caped crusader, Farmer dons an alter ego: During the day, he's known as Dr. Farmer and treats the ailments of all the local cats and dogs. At night, however, he works hard to write captivating stories full of action and adventure with the goal of transporting readers to new and magical worlds. Farmer lives in the Great White North of Wisconsin with his wife, son, and two dogs. To learn more, visit his website at www.maxwellfarmer.com.

# DISCOVER
# *STORIES UNBOUND*

PodiumAudio.com